Infidelity

TARA PALMER-TOMKINSON has been a
household name ever since she first came to the
attention of the media in 1996 as the original 'It' girl.
She is a notorious presenter, a witty interviewee and a
fashion icon. A gifted musician and songwriter, TPT was
the winner of *Comic Relief Does Celebrity Fame Academy*
and won our hearts in the first ever *I'm a Celebrity Get
Me Out of Here!* She has written for a number of
national newspapers and magazines, including
columns in the *Sunday Times* and *Closer*.
Infidelity is her second novel.

Also by Tara Palmer-Tomkinson

Inheritance

TARA
PALMER-TOMKINSON

Infidelity

PAN BOOKS

First published 2012 by Pan Books
an imprint of Pan Macmillan, a division of Macmillan Publishers Limited
Pan Macmillan, 20 New Wharf Road, London N1 9RR
Basingstoke and Oxford
Associated companies throughout the world
www.panmacmillan.com

ISBN 978-0-330-51333-3

A CIP catalogue record for this book is available from
the British Library.

Typeset by Ellipsis Digital Limited, Glasgow
Printed and bound by CPI Group (UK) Ltd, Croydon, CR0 4YY

Visit **www.panmacmillan.com** to read more about all our books
and to buy them. You will also find features, author interviews and
news of any author events, and you can sign up for e-newsletters
so that you're always first to hear about our new releases.

For my father, who taught me that life is all about standards and civilizations
– I'm still learning

'. . . I hereby state my last will and testament . . .'

The door opened, and the Withers junior staffer escorted the late arrivals into the room. They exchanged solemn nods and the odd word with those already present, but there was no conversation. A frosty atmosphere hung over the meeting, and the nervous anxiety of those seated around the highly polished table was palpable.

The executor looked up from the document he was sombrely reading and gazed around the room, its walls lined with old leather-bound copies of Law Reports, the deep windows looking out over the Inns of Court, traditional and historic. Despite the efforts of the ancient radiators, the room was cold and austere, like a headmaster's study, and the executor felt an old, familiar sense of churning anticipation in the pit of his stomach. He tentatively surveyed the sea of faces gazing expectantly back at him. Sometimes the executor really hated his job. A ray of late afternoon sunshine infiltrated the conference room of Withers – solicitors to the great, good and noble (also safe, reliable, discreet) – through the windows, offering no warmth, but instead teasing with the reminder of the fresh, breezy air outside, and highlighting the myriad dust particles between him and his audience. They seemed to the executor to represent his words, hanging heavy in the oppressive air, falling like slow, deliberate drips of water torture onto the cynical ears of the gathering.

Although breeding and good manners prevented them from being anything other than perfectly gracious on the surface, he could feel the hostility emanating from the remaining two generations of the deceased's extended family.

The pain and loss of recent bereavement was still visibly etched across the faces of some. But not all, noted the executor privately – nor, in his opinion, enough of them – and he wondered at the family tensions, the years of feuding and fall-outs, that had wrought their influence amongst these two generations of the family tree.

There was the one trying not to look needy, but who, the executor determined, really did need a healthy share of the prize – the one shaking with hysterical and, he thought, outlandish tears. Another, head to toe in full-length fur, diamonds and Chanel, and dipping frequently into an antique pill box, would not have looked out of place at the State Opening of Parliament. Yet another, apparently struggling to choose the correct 'will reading' facial expression: humble? Grieving, or unmoved by the current situation? Evidently, this person hadn't decided, for each of these expressions and a dozen more passed across their face at regular intervals. One, he noted, was a visible bag of nerves, unable to sit still, nails razed down to the quick. The executor's eyes popped as his glance flicked back to the Chanel-bedecked doyenne, while she nervously wiped imaginary rings from beneath her water glass and slipped another pill down her throat, bestowing a saccharine smile upon the group. He wasn't sure, but he could swear that the little white pill had a smiley face printed on it . . .

And in amongst them, there was one individual who seemed to be a tower of strength: solemn, a scarred cheek twitching slightly, showing discomfort and obvious distaste at these proceedings. Next to him sat a beacon of gracefulness, her beauty and dignity outshining everyone who surrounded her; but still, like the others, seemingly unable to exchange more than the most forced, polite chit-chat with her closest blood relatives.

Along the table from the executor sat senior partner Fawcett-Ryland, immaculate in a three-piece Savile Row suit, flanked by the equally well-groomed Ogilvy, Withers's man on tax, and Jarvis, his colleague who dealt with equity. All were experts in their respective fields and had been formally introduced to the family, and all were present to help deliver this most important of documents. The whole performance reeked of old-school decorum, of a system unchanged for decades, intended to put those in the room at their ease, but which, given the circumstances, only added to the tension.

Wall by wall, the room suddenly seemed to start closing

in on the executor, and the temperature appeared to rise by several degrees. Despite his considerable experience in such situations, beads of sweat appeared on his hairline. There was an impatient cough from the gathering, and the executor hurriedly bowed his head and resumed relating the wishes of the deceased in the carefully measured tones of his trade. Part vicar, part game-show host, his job was to deliver the news with a delicate balance of humility and detachment, warmth and professionalism, condolence and fatalism. He was careful not to convey incredulity, enthusiasm or enjoyment throughout his task. His was the role of facilitator, and, after his initial glance around the room, he thanked the Lord for this, and mentally recoiled from the idea of any further involvement with the characters gathered for the reading.

'. . . I bequeath my mother's engagement ring . . .'

As the smaller items of the deceased's estate were allocated, the executor disguised his surprise at the lack of perceptible reaction from the remaining family. Only a facial twitch here, a stifled sigh of exasperation there, a rustle of a designer dress and twiddle of a gold cufflink betrayed the mounting impatience as the objects of lesser value were divided up.

The executor reached the end of the miscellaneous items, and turned to the last page of the document. The grand finale. Not that anyone realized that yet, he thought; in families as wealthy as this, it was normal to split the estate between siblings, spouses and offspring, and they were all expecting their own generous share. He drew a deep breath, allowing himself a dramatic pause, and nearly choked as his lungs filled with the fusty air. He wasn't sure why, but the prospect of delivering this news to his audience filled him with a deep and unfathomable sense of satisfaction. It was going to rock their very foundations – more so, probably, than the benefactor's death had done.

'And now, as regards the family estate –'

An expectant hush fell over the family and, subconsciously, each shifted almost imperceptibly, stealing sidelong glances at their immediate neighbours, bracing themselves for some news that would benefit them alongside, or even above, the others present? The air now all but crackled with hostility.

'Oh, get on with it, man,' he heard someone mutter irritably from the back of the room. His hackles rose, and he resolved to eke this out for as long as he possibly could.

'I, the deceased, find I have lost faith both in myself and you, my nearest, dearest and blood relations. Once a family of such standing, of high morals, good breeding and impeccable behaviour, I fear our current incarnation offers little in the way of respect to our ancestors. And, although we still have upstanding examples of humanity amongst us, over recent years and months I have found myself in the main looking forward to the youngest generation for new hope and renewed faith in human kind.'

There was neither a sound nor a movement around the table, and even the effect of a cloud covering the sun and casting the whole room into shade didn't inspire the smallest reaction from the family.

The executor cleared his throat and relished another dramatic pause.

'Therefore I, the deceased, bequeath the house and estate to be held in trust for an as yet unborn child. The firstborn of the family's existing third generation will inherit all of Broughton Hall. And until then, no one else is to receive anything . . .'

There was silence, a gasp and a moan as the shock waves rippled through the group and then took hold. Someone groaned as if in physical pain. Someone else wailed. Several thousand pounds' worth of couture was ruined as the wearer slumped on their chair and fainted to the floor. And then there was pandemonium.

The executor sat back and watched with interest as the drama unfolded before him.

Sometimes, he really loved his job.

Six months earlier

One

'Philippe! It's after five p.m. We should be getting down the mountain.'

'Oh, *chérie*. But here we are so snug. Outside it is *cold*.'

Philippe pulled Lyric towards him and nuzzled her neck. She leaned into him, feeling herself melt again at the touch of his soft lips on her skin, the feel of his strong, muscular arms wrapped all around her, and gave herself up once again to the exquisite sensations his kisses sent through her. She felt his hand wander and start to caress her breast under the blanket, and she sighed in delight and turned to roll over on top of him.

As she moved, a strange light cast through the window of the hut and caught her eye, reminding her of their predicament. Reluctantly she extricated herself from Philippe's embrace and, peeling herself away from him and pulling a fur blanket around her, tiptoed across to retrieve her salopettes. The hut was littered with their clothes, cast aside in the heat of passion, and she bit her lip in guilty pleasure. They had only stopped off at the Kreuzweg hut – ostensibly an SOS refuge halfway down her favourite

Klosters ski run, but also a picturesque rustic log cabin complete with log fire, traditional Swiss wood furniture and bubbling spring outside – so she could show Philippe how cute it was. The Charlton family had taken ski holidays in Klosters for as long as she could remember, and this was the first time she'd skied here with Philippe Chappeau, the love of her life and now her fiancé. But it was so romantic, they'd lingered and then . . . That had been over two hours ago – and now, if they didn't get a move on, they were in danger of having to use it for its prime purpose. For their own self-made SOS . . .

'The ski runs shut at five p.m., and the *Dienst* have probably already done their sweep of the mountain,' she reminded him. 'We really need to get a move on.'

'*Oui, chérie*, I know you're right,' said Philippe with a twinkle in his eye. 'But can I remind you, it's your fault we're still here.'

'My fault!' repeated Lyric in mock outrage. 'How do you work that one out?'

'Your fault for being irresistible,' growled Philippe, grabbing hold of her and squeezing her curvaceous bottom, now encased in tight black ski trousers.

'Philippe!' squealed Lyric, though secretly she loved his adoration – and returned it. He gazed at her searchingly and she could see her own big brown eyes reflected in his.

'Just one more kiss,' he bartered, 'and then I'll let you go.' He smiled wickedly, revealing a set of straight white teeth set in his tanned face. She ran her fingers through his curly black hair and kissed him passionately.

'That will have to do you,' said Lyric, finally pulling away and jamming her woolly hat over her long, honey-blonde hair. 'We need to go.'

'I'm not sure you'll need your hat,' remarked Philippe as he opened the door. 'It seems to have warmed up.'

Lyric was filled with a sense of foreboding as she peered out after him. The weather had closed in, and the afternoon sky, slightly overcast earlier, was now suffused with an unusual flat light. A warm, claustrophobic gust of wind blew into the hut, lifting the red checked curtains and making the dying embers of the log fire flicker.

'The föhn,' murmured Lyric in concern. The warm wind that prevails across the Alps every year was notorious amongst locals. It was said that the wind, which came in from the Sahara, could blow sand in your face. It affected people and their emotions, and could make you feel sexy or hormonal, even bringing on menstruation in some women. Folklore had it that a woman had been acquitted from murdering her husband because it had happened during a föhn.

Lyric smiled, worried. Murder was hardly going to be an issue for her and Philippe, but, as far as feeling sexy went, the wind had clearly made its mark on their afternoon already. Their immediate problem was that the föhn was also extremely dangerous to ski in. The flat light it cast made it almost impossible to detect the contours or the pitch of the slope, even for expert skiers.

'We can't ski down in this,' she said decisively. 'We'll end up skiing off a precipice to our deaths. We'll have to call mountain rescue.'

She rummaged in her ski jacket for her mobile phone, pulled it out and stared at it disbelievingly. There was no reception. She held it up to Philippe in defeat.

'I'll try and attract the *Dienst*,' suggested Philippe. The *Dienst* were almost like ski lifeguards, a select team of men who skied the length and breadth of the mountain at the end of the day, clearing it of stragglers and wayward skiers. Lyric nodded in agreement and he disappeared out the door.

'Careful, though, Philippe,' she called. 'Don't stray far from the hut – you'll never find your way back!' Lyric perched on a stool and waited tensely, listening to Philippe's voice falling flat on the foggy air.

After about five minutes, he reappeared. 'I'm getting nowhere,' he said simply. 'The air is too thick with fog. A man could be a foot away from me and not hear me. Or see me, come to that. And anyway, the snow is starting to melt.'

Lyric drew a sharp breath. The föhn was also known as 'the snow eater'. And with quickly melting snow came another risk.

'Avalanches,' she stated simply.

'*Oui*,' said Philippe seriously. '*Chérie*, there is no way I am going to risk your safety by us skiing down. We will have to stay here until the weather lifts.'

Lyric stared at him in horror. 'But that won't be until morning at least!'

Philippe shrugged. 'We have firewood.' He inspected the small pile by the fire. 'At least, we will have when I bring some more in.'

He disappeared outside again and returned within moments, arms full of firewood from the store outside the hut. 'Well, we won't go cold.' He piled up the logs and then unzipped his fleece. 'Not that there's much chance of that in this weather.'

Seeing Lyric's downcast expression, he moved across to her and held her face in his hands.

'Hey, *chérie*, why so worried? It could be much worse. We have a fire, we have water, we have candles. We are safe in here, and you are safe with me.'

Lyric smiled and felt herself relax. He was right. There was no one she trusted more – crisis or no crisis – and there were certainly worse situations in which to be stranded on a mountain.

She looked up at him sheepishly. 'But what will we eat?'

Philippe threw back his head and laughed. 'Trust you, Lyric. Always thinking of your stomach. But, you know what? I have chocolate.'

He produced a half-finished bar of Ritter Sport.

Lyric eyed it dubiously. 'Well, that's seen better days . . .'

Eyes dancing, Philippe looked around the hut for inspiration.

'I know!' He reached out for one of his ski poles,

propped up against the door. Lyric looked at him questioningly for a few seconds before light dawned.

'Your hollow poles!' she cried.

'*Oui*!' said Philippe delightedly. 'My hollow poles – my Christmas present from you! This is one of the first times I've used them, so that means . . .'

'. . . they're still full of cherry brandy!' laughed Lyric.

Philippe pulled her to him in a tight hug. 'So you see, *chérie*, we have everything. Who needs food?' His hands ran down her body. 'And anyway, I'm hungry for something else entirely . . .'

Early May

Two

Concentrate, Lyric!

Lyric screwed up her eyes against the warm spring sunshine and put her hand to her head in an attempt to blank out the quick-fire patter of the race-day compère, and focus her attention on the job in hand – judging the Best Turned Out Horse at the Two Thousand Guineas over the Rowley Mile in Newmarket. It was early May, and the first flat race of the UK season, and she knew De Beers's prestigious award (not to mention the fifty-thousand-pound prize money) – would change the deserving winner's life forever. She *had* to make the right decision!

But the Panadol she'd taken to ease the headache her Philip Treacy hat had given her was wearing off, and the cheeky glass of champagne she'd enjoyed earlier wasn't helping matters. She looked around her, eyes dancing mischievously. She couldn't believe she'd been asked to judge something so *serious*. Was it too late to duck out? The friendly wink from the man with the clipboard told her yes, it was. Having grown up around horses, she was an expert judge of temperament, form and physiology, but, as the grooms paraded the horses around the paddock, she found it hard to tear her eyes away from a Black Beauty lookalike. She'd fallen for the flighty, shiny gelding with a wild look in his eye the moment she'd stepped into the ring; he seemed like a kindred spirit. He reminded her of Doppelganger – aka Thumper – her own beautiful three-year-old bay gelding, a Christmas gift from her racing-mad father that was yet to make his flat-racing debut. This horse eyeballed her on every circuit of the ring, and Lyric had the feeling he was bidding her to leap onto his back and gallop off into the warmth of the May afternoon, to somewhere they could both let loose and not have to worry about grooming, appearance and awarding first and second prizes.

Lyric wiped her now clammy hands down the skirt of her Chanel suit and tried to blot out the sea of interested faces around the ring – a twittering throng of flat racing's glitterati, all decked out in their finery for the first meet of the season. Designer labels, elaborate hairdos and fake tans jostled for position in the members' enclosure, whilst in the ring some of the world's fastest, bravest racehorses stepped out for the glorified beauty contest. At least she could be confident her *own* grooming was up to scratch, thought Lyric with relief. Her honey-blonde hair was swept into a soft chignon under the chic pillbox hat that enhanced her chocolate-brown eyes, and her camel bouclé skirt suit was perfectly tailored to fit her curves and show off her endless legs – even if her Jimmy Choos were ever so slightly sinking into the turf. Clearly *their* best form was not on soft going, she thought wryly.

'This one here, Persistent Offender, has a fine fetlock,' noted De Beers's international director of sales and marketing to her left. Lyric looked around her, trying to work out which horse he was talking about. Following his gaze, she realized it was her 'Black Beauty'.

'So *that's* his name. Well, looks like we have something in common!' she quipped. When she looked at him she could almost feel the wind in her hair and his powerful hooves galloping beneath her. 'Not seriously of course,' she added hurriedly. 'He's stunning. And very well turned out.'

Come on, Lyric, this competition is really important to these people, she reminded herself sternly. *Focus!*

'And so, Miss Charlton, I'm going to have to press you for a decision,' said the grinning compère, striding over to the centre of the ring. 'Which lucky horse is going to be crowned the Best Turned Out of our first race of the season? And which lucky groom is going to have their life transformed by you today?'

Lyric looked around, trying to make out Philippe standing amongst the crowd, silently supporting her, rooting for her as always. She found him, mobile phone raised to his ear, and smiled in relief, her tummy flipping in excitement at the thought of the news she was going to share with him later on – the secret she'd been keeping for the past couple of days, unable to find the right time to tell him. But Philippe didn't return the look and the smile froze on her lips. His eyes weren't on her, but staring right past her. Clearly, his thoughts were elsewhere, with whomever he was talking to. She bit her lip, stung, and stared at the ground, trying to blink away the tears that had suddenly sprung up.

The sales and marketing director leaned over her to speak into the microphone.

'Yes, come on, Lyric, tell us – who's it to be?' he pressed. She looked up wildly. Hundreds of expectant faces gazed back at her – all except Philippe, whose brow was still furrowed, ear to his phone.

'Black Beauty!' she announced.

The compère looked at her quizzically and tried to cover the microphone with his hand.

'I'm . . . sorry?'

'Black Beauty!' repeated Lyric insistently.

Now the sales and marketing director was frowning at her, too. 'Lyric – there is no Black Beauty in the competition . . .'

Realizing her faux pas, Lyric blushed and pointed at the winning horse. 'The gelding!' she said stubbornly.

Light dawned, and the compère and the sales and marketing director seemed to share a sigh of relief.

'Ahh! You mean Persistent Offender!' announced the compère triumphantly.

'Yes!' said Lyric with equal relief.

'And so, ladies and gentlemen, to confirm – the De Beers Best Turned Out of the Meet is Persistent Offender!' The compère turned to her, still smiling, as the ecstatic groom turned the horse into the centre of the circle to collect the prize. 'And so, Lyric, can you tell us exactly why you chose Persistent Offender for this prize?'

Lyric stared at him, her mind suddenly blank again. 'Well, he looks exactly like Black Beauty.'

~

Lyric extricated herself from the gushing thanks of the De Beers team – all of whom, fortunately, seemed to have found Black Beauty-gate endearing rather than disastrous – and elbowed her way through the crowd of overdressed racegoers in a bid to find Philippe.

This isn't his thing, she reminded herself, as an over-enthusiastic bookie flung his arm out and nearly dislodged her hat. Philippe's 'thing' was *their* thing – the simple life they'd chosen to settle into when they'd fallen in love. Philippe Chappeau abhorred the kind of life Lyric had previously led in the limelight – even though he had certainly come a long way from the days of his apprenticeship to his father, tending the grounds at the French finishing school. Now a world-renowned landscape gardener, sexy Philippe had turned horticulture into phwoar-ticulture and made it bona-fide celebrity territory before turning his back on a world he found superficial, disposable and utterly distasteful. He now eschewed publicity as much as possible, and happily avoided the glare of the world's flashbulbs in favour of a quiet life in rural Buckinghamshire, developing the now famous gardens at Broughton Hall, the Charlton family estate. An avid proponent of organic horticulture and farming, he was busy developing ranges of eco-friendly gardening accessories and organically grown seeds and saplings, as well as a line of organic wines and preserves. Philippe dreaded any distraction from his new life; from his dual passions of Lyric and the business. Lyric, for her part, loved the country and, having put her wild party days behind her, was happy to remain ensconced there with him, in their very own little love bubble.

Lyric's ankle turned as her heel got caught again in the soft earth, and she bit back an expletive. She longed for a pair of Hunters and her jeans. Her new life was light years away from her previous incarnation as the UK's favourite It girl – and light years away from today. Today was a favour to please her father – even though part of her was undoubtedly enjoying the buzz. Racing was George Charlton's life, and so Lyric had agreed to this personal appearance. Dear Daddy. He asked so little of her, how could she refuse him when he did?

At last, she spotted Philippe's towering frame just yards in front of her, and felt a wave of love wash over her. He turned to face her, all curly black hair and brooding green eyes – *those eyes!* – and she felt herself melt inside, as she had the first time he fixed them on her. He was the classic strong, silent type, laced with an intensity and a hint of mysterious cavalier that his years on the front line had only enhanced. It was an intoxicating combination. Lyric smiled, a wide, dazzling white smile, and she saw his eyes crinkle at the corners, stretching the scar on his cheek – a war wound from his days in the army (though he would never discuss exactly how he'd got it) – and in return a smile hovered over his mouth as he spotted her.

'Lyric! There you are! Omigod, you were HILARI-OUS!'

'Edward!' Before she'd had a chance to reach Philippe, Lyric spun around joyfully at the sound of her twin brother's voice. 'Where have you been?'

'Watching you, of course – you were fantastic.' Edward beamed back at her, and not for the first time Lyric marvelled at his very existence, let alone the identikit features staring back at her: the big chocolate-brown eyes, with the same wicked twinkle as hers; the honey-blonde hair, now sun-lightened by an Easter skiing break in Klosters, and shorter than the shoulder-length surfy style he'd had when they'd been reunited. Instead, now, he wore the casually cropped shaggy style of the super-rich. How well he'd slotted into their lives. She'd been a very happy only child for so long – thirty years, in fact – but Edward's appearance in her life had filled a gap she was barely even aware existed. He'd not only answered the nagging and unfathomable sense of loneliness she'd often felt, but Edward, with his solid working-class upbringing, had made Lyric, her father, George, and her mother, Constance, look anew at their lives and appreciate even more the privilege they'd all enjoyed since birth. After a blip in her twenties when her party lifestyle had threatened to get out of control, Philippe had changed everything – handed her back her mojo for real life, even. But, whilst Lyric loved the simpler existence they now led together, it was Edward who reminded her how exciting parts of her old life could be.

Lyric smiled at Edward, shaking her head and laughing in embarrassment. 'I was anything but fantastic,' she protested. 'I was all over the place.' There was no hiding his unabashed pride in her, and Lyric suddenly wondered if indeed the judging hadn't gone as badly as she'd feared. 'Really?'

'Yes!' insisted Edward. 'Everyone said so. And hardly anyone notices I'm even there – so they would hardly have been saying it for effect.' Lyric detected a hint of bitterness in Edward's voice. People still forgot who he was, or failed to recognize him, and whilst he'd seemed to have welcomed wholeheartedly the discovery of his new-found family, it still must be so hard for him, having to explain not just his birthright but his very existence to everyone he met. 'And everyone thought you were funny as well as genuine,' continued Edward. 'So much for flaky It girls! My twin sister proves them all wrong yet again!'

Lyric giggled. Maybe she'd imagined it. Overcome with sisterly love, she gave him an impulsive hug, breathing in deeply as she embraced him, as if to inhale him. Over his shoulder, she caught the eye of Philippe standing uncomfortably to one side, and her tummy did its customary somersault again: the wild, curly black hair, the brooding expression born of his Gallic roots, the sexy, rangy frame, the tanned skin from a life spent, on the whole, out-doors. But again, Lyric's smile froze as she registered his expression. Not disapproving exactly, but guarded – and definitely distant. Lyric wavered, became shy and uncertain, and loosened her grip on Edward as she held out her hand to her fiancé.

'Philippe!' She tried to ignore the age-old insecurities that flooded over her. The feeling of never really being quite good enough. Funny enough. Glamorous enough. Was there something wrong with her? Was Philippe going off her? Lyric shook herself. These self-doubts were normal – part and parcel of being a girl! After all, however wealthy you were, however beautiful, everyone was flawed, and no matter how much self-awareness you invested in, there would always be part of you that doubted yourself. And, maybe, doubted the person you loved most in the world, too. It didn't help that the mysterious aura that had first attracted her to Philippe also represented the last ten per cent of him she felt she hadn't totally conquered.

Then maybe he wouldn't be the enigmatic person you know and love, she reminded herself sternly. *And maybe it would be you doing your normal routine of trying to destroy what you've got together. Don't analyse the chemistry, Lyric. Philippe swept you off your feet and is the love of your life. It's too important to question.*

'Are you having fun, *chéri*?' She squeezed Philippe's huge, gnarly hand and his eyes twinkled down at her.

'Oh, you know. Not really my thing,' he said in an

undertone. 'Give me a space like this and I'd rather see it covered in a planting scheme than a load of day-trippers and the thundering hooves of racehorses.' He kissed her lightly on the nose, and Lyric smiled. Philippe was always like a fish out of water in these situations. She hugged herself inwardly at the thought of how much those eyes would twinkle later when she told him her news – *their* news.

'Edward seems to be enjoying it, though.' Philippe nodded over to where her brother was standing, looking around like a child in a candy shop. 'He's certainly embracing his new life, isn't he?'

'Yes, isn't he?' agreed Lyric, eyes shining. 'He's fitted in perfectly. It's as if he was never apart from us at all.'

Philippe gave her a guarded look. 'But he was, Lyric. For thirty years.'

Lyric looked at him quizzically. 'What do you mean? Has Edward said something to upset you?'

'No, not at all. But you're spending so much time with him – investing so much of yourself in him . . . just don't expect too much from him too soon, that's all. I wouldn't want you to get hurt.'

Lyric frowned. 'Don't be silly, Philippe! No one's going to get hurt.' She hugged him reassuringly, but inside her mind was spinning. Why would Edward do anything to hurt her? He was her twin brother! And what could he possibly do, anyway?

She felt a pang of disloyalty at the thought of exactly *how* much time she'd been spending with Edward whilst

Philippe was slaving away at the business, and scuffed the floor with her shoe guiltily. Maybe Philippe was feeling resentful at the time she'd lavished on her brother. She bit her lip. There were a few occasions she'd spent with Edward that she hadn't admitted to Philippe, too. A few trips into town with him that she, for some reason, had felt necessary to pass off as lunches with her close friends Crispin, Laura or Treeva – almost as though she was having an affair or something! It would be so much easier just to admit to Philippe that, after years of not knowing she had a brother, she was over the moon with his sudden appearance in her life. But no, instead, something about Philippe's reserved approach to Edward made her hold back – fib, even.

Just then, she heard Edward give a low whistle through his teeth as he wandered back over to where they were standing. Lyric looked up in the direction of his gaze. The crowd parted, as with Moses and the waves, to make way for one of the most beautiful women she had ever seen. Against the backdrop of ill-fitting suits and garish mutton-dressed-as-lamb outfits that the members' enclosure of every racecourse seemed to inspire, this woman was a vision of graceful elegance in scarlet Lanvin, the pop of colour setting off her pale cocoa skin, long, shiny black hair and cat-like amber eyes. On her hands she wore white gloves, giving her the elegant air of a modern-day Grace Kelly.

As Lyric turned around and gazed impassively at her,

she felt some flicker of recognition from the depths of her memory – she knew this woman, but from where? Some long-forgotten launch party, or *Hello!* spread, she supposed. But, judging by the smile the girl was giving Lyric, she remembered her, too. Although, Lyric reminded herself, her own notorious past meant she was a familiar face to many people outside her immediate set.

The girl paused in front of them with a half smile, and a deliciously musky scent emanated from her. Lyric breathed it in. What was it? Like the girl, she half recognized it, but couldn't absolutely place it. To her left, Edward had clearly noticed it too, and was breathing in deeply. He gave the woman a flirtatious bow, then turned to his sister.

'Lyric, you've let me down. You're my social guide – how am I meant to know who's who if you haven't told me?' Edward's eyes were dancing but his voice was serious, and Lyric's cheeks coloured.

'Well – I'm sorry, I – we've met before, haven't we?' She gave the woman a questioning look.

In return, the woman arched one eyebrow ambiguously and shrugged elegantly. 'I know you're Lyric Charlton,' she said graciously, and held out an elegant gloved hand. 'Amba.'

Lyric nodded in sudden recognition. Amba had made her society debut some months previously, with an enigmatic glamour so unique she needed no surname. Lyric had seen her photograph in diary pages but, embroiled in her romance with Philippe and their new life together, had paid

Amba little heed beyond the excitable titbits fed to her by Crispin, Laura and Treeva. Beautiful and stylish, Amba was curiously without cultural anchor. Her exotic colouring suggested she was from the East, but her accent hinted at Russian roots. Her unlined skin could be that of a twenty-year-old, but she had the grace and maturity of a woman well into her forties. Either way, her immaculate grooming, designer clothes and Cartier jewellery could only belong to a member of the super-rich, and gossip was rife as to how she had come by these millions. Certainly, there was no husband on the scene now, and Amba's impeccable breeding and finishing-school grace suggested she had grown up wealthy. Without evidence as to her extraordinary provenance, she'd provided the gossip-mongers with some of the best raw material they'd had in years, some even swearing that the third finger of her left hand bore the imprint of a long-discarded wedding ring.

Now, though, Lyric gazed at her, mesmerized. What must it feel like to be that stunning? Lyric was hardly un-attractive herself, and many, she knew, considered her to be a natural beauty. But she never really felt that she was – and anyhow, Amba was in a different league altogether. She was a real *woman*. She took Amba's hand – a large hand, she noticed absent mindedly – and shook it. Suddenly, Lyric felt a sharp dig in her ribs and she jumped.

'And this is my brother, Edward Charlton,' she said hurriedly, remembering her purpose, standing to one side to introduce him. Edward gave Amba his most charming smile and kissed her hand with a flourish. Amba smiled in delight, but Lyric saw something else flash across her eyes. A look of what – surprise?

'Your brother?' said Amba, turning back to Lyric. 'But of course . . .'

She turned back to Edward with a dazzling smile, and in a split second Lyric saw her brother fall under Amba's spell, instantly bewitched.

'We're recently reunited,' he said quickly. 'Which will be why you and I have never met before.'

Lyric smiled at him. 'Amba hasn't been on the scene long herself,' she said pleasantly. 'Which is why *we've* never met before.' She gave Amba a warm, sisterly smile, and tried not to feel snubbed when Amba returned it with a cool look. Wow. She might be all woman, but it was all *man's* woman.

'Edward, my boy! Edward, over here. I've got some people I want you to meet.'

Lyric nudged Edward at the sound of their father's voice, and her brother reluctantly dragged his eyes away from Amba. 'Go on, Edward. There'll be another ancient Jockey Club member he wants to introduce you to. He loves having a son to show off.'

She nodded over to where her father, George, dressed in his ancient, faded country clothes, was standing with a bunch of similarly attired men, all with weathered, ruddy complexions, and she smiled indulgently. He was so full of life, so passionate about his hunting, shooting, fishing and

– most importantly – racing, that it was hard to believe he was seventy. Only the weather-beaten skin and early signs of arthritis gave away his advancing years.

'Looks like you're wanted again, Edward,' she said, happy to share her father's love on the basis that no one could steal the special place she occupied in Daddy's heart. 'Anyone would think you were his only child.'

Edward laughed and watched wistfully as Amba nodded farewell and disappeared back into the crowd, retaining that enigmatic air. 'Well,' he murmured, almost to himself. 'I guess – for a few moments at least – I was . . .'

Behind him, his father slapped him on the back. Edward jumped in surprise, and gave him a sidelong glance in case George had heard his last comment. But his father, too, was staring after Amba.

'Walks like a racehorse herself, that one,' said George in admiration. 'Beauty is in movement, my boy, and there is a particular kind of grace that links women to thorough-breds.' He turned to Edward, a serious look behind his twinkling eyes. 'Mind you, that one could probably kick like one, too.'

Edward frowned at the implied slur on Amba's charac-ter. 'What do you mean?' His face suddenly creased in concern as his father shut his eyes and swayed alarmingly. 'Dad? What's the matter?'

George stood up straight again, trying to put a brave face on it. But his skin was ashen and Edward was sure he was shaking.

'Oh, nothing, my boy. Just a little dizzy spell. Get them all the time at my age. Nothing to worry about.'

George turned back to his friends, attempting to brush off the incident entirely. Edward gazed at him thoughtfully.

That wasn't the first dizzy spell his father had complained of lately. It was one of several. And it hadn't looked like nothing to worry about. It had looked like something he should be very worried about indeed.

Three

Where on earth, thought Lyric, looking around her in concern, *is my mother?* She'd been acting very strange all morning. Now she came to think about it, Lyric hadn't seen her since before the prize giving.

'Have you seen Mummy?' she asked Philippe.

He frowned and scratched his head. *'Non, chérie.* Not since we arrived, in fact.'

They shared a 'look'. Her mother, Constance – gracious, stylish and a legendary hostess famed for turning every social occasion into a personal entertaining opportunity – had initially reacted well to the appearance of her long-lost son. She'd been shocked, of course, but mostly delighted. Recently, however, she seemed to be suffering some kind of post-traumatic shock, relying ever more heavily on the pills and shakes that she had long subsisted on, and employing a small army of personal staff to carry out obscure duties.

Lyric smiled fondly as she thought about her eccentric parents and squeezed Philippe's arm. He squeezed back and looked down at her.

'Do you think we'll be as bonkers as my parents when we're their age?' she asked.

'Bonkers?'

She laughed as Philippe looked quizzical at this unfamiliar word. 'Mad. Eccentric. A bit nuts.'

'Ah.' His eyes twinkled teasingly as he grasped the full meaning. 'Well, some might say one of us already is . . .'

She laughed and nudged him playfully. 'Well, then, that makes two of us, *chéri* – so we've got nothing to worry about, have we! Apart from, obviously, where my mother has got to . . .'

'Let's take a look over there,' said Philippe, nodding to where the members' enclosure gave way to the exercise ring and the paddocks beyond.

'What would Mummy be doing over there?' said Lyric, her heels sticking in the soft ground again as they moved off the gravel path and onto the grass. Philippe grabbed Lyric's hand as she swayed, and picked her up, carrying her in a fireman's lift across the practice ring and towards the horseboxes lined up in the paddocks. Lyric shrieked and laughed, kicking her legs helplessly as he ran. 'Philippe!'

'Maybe I just want to get you on your own,' he replied, swinging her around and placing her gently back on the ground with a kiss.

She looked up at him, his eyes full of love, and her heart leapt. She paused. Now was the perfect time . . . 'Well, *chéri*, I did have something to tell you . . .'

'Constance!' Lyric felt Philippe's voice reverberate in his chest as he interrupted, calling out over her head. 'Constance!'

She turned around and gasped as she saw her mother, Lady Constance Charlton, emerging from a horsebox, her elaborate greying coif in disarray, her powdered cheeks flushed and her lipstick smudged. Waiting for her outside the box was a young male groom looking sheepish as he spotted Lyric and Philippe standing stock still amongst the pre-race activity in the field.

Constance, rooting around in her Hermès handbag, finally looked up too. Slipping something into her mouth, then patting her hair back into place, she waved gaily as though she were stepping out of Chanel back into Bond Street. She trotted over to them.

'Woo-hoo! Lyric, how wonderful. I've been looking for you all over. When is your little prize draw, darling?'

Lyric stared at her mother, open-mouthed. 'It's finished, Mother – I've already done it. What on earth have you been doing? *We've* been looking for *you* everywhere.'

Constance looked shocked, as though it were perfectly obvious. 'I've been checking the form, darling – what on earth do you think I've been doing?' She looked at Lyric as though she were mad, and then turned coquettishly to Philippe. 'Philippe, darling, would you give me your arm? I simply must find George before the next race – I expect he's with Angus and I want to put a bet on.'

Philippe looked at her, bemused, and then concerned,

but held out his arm regardless. 'Are you quite all right, Constance?'

Constance stared at him, her eyes bright and darting. 'All right, Philippe? Why, of course I am! What on earth could be the matter with me?' She turned back in the direction of the members' enclosure. 'Well, darlings, what on earth are you waiting for? The Derby won't wait for us, will it?'

'No, Mummy,' said Lyric, ineffectively attempting to straighten her mother's skirt as Constance started to stride out across the turf. 'But it might wait for you to look like you've got dressed properly.'

~

As the three of them re-entered the members' enclosure, Lyric could see her father, still holding court with his old cronies, his arm proudly clutching Edward's shoulders. She smiled to herself as she clocked Edward's expression. He had very little knowledge of racing – never having had any contact with it before he was reunited with his birth family – and, from what she could tell, he had even less interest in it. And, right now, that lack of interest had transformed itself into a study in determined concentration, as Edward tried to feign some kind of connection with the assorted septuagenarian racing buffs surrounding him.

Wanting to erase the feeling of grubbiness her mother's odd behaviour had left her with, Lyric ran over and flung her arms around her father's neck.

'Daddy, you're boring poor Edward to tears. Poor thing – you can't cram six decades' worth of accumulated racing knowledge into six months! Let Edward learn about it gradually and let Angus go so he can tell Mummy where to place her bets!'

Edward shot her a grateful look and then dug his father playfully in the ribs. 'Yeah, Dad, it's hardly as if I've got a horse myself, anyway, is it? Not like Lyric, that is.' He looked enviously at his sister.

'Well, young man, you listen and learn, and you never know, in time your father might deem you deserving of such a fine commodity,' said a warm voice from the other side of his father.

Lyric gave the small, scruffy man a wide smile. Likeable, jovial and shabby, Angus Roach was an old school friend of her father's, and had been a familiar face at Broughton Hall over the years. Lyric associated Angus with Café Crème cigars and humbugs that tasted of soap, on which she had broken more teeth than she would care to remember. Despite his unassuming appearance, Angus owned half of Scotland and had never needed to work – instead, he had spent his life hanging around racecourses, and was now an internationally renowned – if not formally recognized – expert on form. He was simply the only person to seek out for a winning tip, and Constance and Lyric were two of the few people with whom he readily shared his insider knowledge. George often joked that Constance could have bought Broughton Hall twice over with her Angus-advised winnings, if she hadn't always immediately spent them in Yves Saint Laurent.

George hugged her delightedly and guffawed, turning to ruffle his son's head. 'I'm sure Edward would tell me if he wasn't interested, Lyric.'

'I'm sure he wouldn't,' she protested. 'Angus, seriously, Mummy has been like a cat on a hot tin roof, please put her out of her misery.' She looked over to where Constance had let go of Philippe and was flirting with a thirty-something racegoer, swaying mildly as she leaned in to talk to him.

'Righty-ho, my dear,' said Angus jovially, leaving the circle and expertly extricating Constance from her current exchange. 'Come on, my dear, let's go and increase that fortune for you.'

'We were just talking about that Bumper of yours,' said George to Lyric.

'Thumper, Daddy,' corrected Lyric fondly, referring to her own racehorse. Its racing name – Doppelganger – was simply too long for everyday use and, in common with most racehorse owners, she'd given the colt a 'stable name' for private use. 'Remember, I named it after the rabbit I had when I was little. It had the same colour fur as my horse,' she explained to the group, who all chuckled politely.

'It played football, you know,' confided George proudly.

'I thought that was Lyric's first pony?' piped up Philippe in confusion.

'Enough!' laughed Lyric. She turned to her father's

friends again. 'All we really need to know is that this is Thumper's first race, and that we have high hopes for him. He's my first, you know!'

'You say that like you're expecting more,' interjected Edward. 'There's a queue, you know!'

Lyric turned to him in surprise, and looked around to assess everyone else's reaction. But it seemed that no one, not even Philippe, had heard – instead, they were all listening to George describe Thumper's breeding and expected form. She watched as her brother pulled out a packet of Marlboro Lights and searched his pockets for a lighter. Had he meant it as a joke? Or was Edward secretly resentful of a gift her father had given her months before they even realized Edward was still alive?

Her eyes widened as Edward found the lighter in his pocket. It was a vintage silver Zippo, a valuable heirloom that until now had resided in a cabinet at Broughton Hall.

'Edward – isn't that Daddy's lighter?' she asked tentatively.

Edward turned a charming smile on her. 'Yes, well spotted!' He looked so innocent that Lyric instantly chastised herself. Daddy must have given it to him.

'Lucky you!' she said brightly. 'I was after that for all the years I smoked, but Daddy would never cave in and give it to me. It was too precious.'

Edward shrugged. 'Well, I guess what's his is mine – at least it will be one day.' He smiled cheekily. 'And, let's face it, he's always so preoccupied with his horses, his guns and his dogs – if he notices I've got it in the meantime, I'll deal with the fallout then!'

Lyric stared at him, part shocked, but part still adoring that she had someone else who could recognize and poke fun at her father's idiosyncrasies. A tannoy announcement heralding the appearance of the horses taking part in the last race in the warm-up ring – the prestigious Derby, and Thumper's first ever race – interrupted her thoughts.

'Come on then, troops,' boomed George jovially. 'Let's see what Skankton has been doing with our pride and joy, eh, Lyric?'

Lyric cringed at the thought of Roger Skankton, George's racehorse trainer, and, as far as she was concerned, out-and-out rogue. George and Roger had been introduced many years previously, when Angus had spotted Roger Skankton's talent as a young assistant trainer and set him up in business. He had, of course, recommended him to his best friend George, and Roger had trained George's string of horses ever since, a partnership that had worked surprisingly well. Roger Skankton was everything George looked for in a winning yard owner, but nothing he liked in a man – so they had frequent fall-outs over his business ethics, or lack thereof. Not that this had done the Skanktons any harm – Roger was now one of the UK's most successful new trainers – but he was new money through and through, and his resume read like a 'how to' for the nouveau. Mock-Tudor mansion built on its own golf course, a fortune spent on his children's education at Millfield and a holiday villa just the wrong side of Cannes – in the Costa del Sol. So central to Roger's success was George's trust in him, and his constant investment in ever more spirited steeds, that Roger had even moved his family and yard lock, stock and barrel next door to Broughton Hall. The arrangement had benefited everyone and, whilst Roger continued to increase the success of George's stable, it had also enhanced George and Angus's friendship.

But Lyric, even as a girl, had found Roger somewhat repulsive and kept as much distance as she could from their nearest neighbour and closest business partner.

As they approached, Lyric could see Roger towering above everyone, ingratiating smile placed firmly on his perma-tanned face and showcasing his over-white veneers, giving him a strange leer. His rangy frame was encased in the ubiquitous camel overcoat of the racing fraternity, a trilby hat covered his thick wavy hair. Roger's hair was still the same rich shade of brown it had always been, without a hint of grey, and if his perfect hairline was anything to go by it owed more to a packet of Grecian 2000 than to good luck or good genes. With his shiny manicures and box-fresh designer shirts, Roger looked like he was straight out of a tumble drier. Yet despite this, thought Lyric, the overall effect always seemed to be more Del Boy than Del Monte. Roger's once-good looks were now fading, the lines of his chiselled face blurring with age and his waistline thickening in spite of the weekly squash sessions and furious pounding in the gym. Not that that stopped him pawing anything in a skirt, of course. Roger was a notorious philanderer, a serial shagger whose mousey 'bit on the side' secretary Janice filled his diary with appointments to cover up his many illicit liaisons – and, rumour had it, his many dodgy business dealings, too . . . He was the only person Lyric knew whose dental hygienist performed extra-curricular services. Broughton Hall's long-standing cook, Mrs Gunners, had confided this during one of Lyric's many early-morning visits below stairs on her way home during her party heyday. Interesting, Lyric thought now, that he'd never tried his charms on Constance – not in Lyric's presence, anyhow. As outrageous flirts went, her mother and Roger would make a right pair – if they weren't too old for each other, that is . . .

Lyric's eyebrows shot up into her hairline as she caught Roger pinching the ever-present Janice on the bottom. Janice, wearing a too-tight pencil skirt and blazer, skyscraper heels and too much make-up, jumped theatrically and turned to give him a 'Carry On' slap in retaliation. Instinctively, Lyric looked around to see if Roger's long-suffering wife Angie had witnessed the whole debacle, too.

As it transpired, she had. As always, Angie was standing slightly to one side, watching on passively, a pinched expression on her gaunt face, her painstakingly coiffed hair as static as her tense posture. Having perfected the art of turning a blind eye, and with the full-time occupation of ignoring Roger's ostentatious philandering now apparently second nature to her, instead Angie put all her energies into being thin and controlling her children: cosseting 'her Darren' and attempting to further her two twenty-some-thing daughters' social trajectories with eye-watering faux pas. Today, as always, Kimberley and Cheryl were protec-tively glued to her side like a pair of glamorous clams, one in peach and the other in coral, both wearing orange fake tans and Minx manicures, and repelling each other with the static caused by their hair extensions. The angle at which Cheryl was holding her elbow gave away the fact that there was one of her chow chow puppies nestled there. Angie herself wore a Jaeger London shift dress under her mink wrap, both hanging off her tiny frame, her head resembling an elaborate lollipop. How did one live that kind of life, enduring that kind of behaviour, day in, day out? Lyric marvelled. She squeezed Philippe's hand lovingly. He would never even dream of cheating on her, let alone dis-respecting her so publicly.

'So this is the famous Roger Skankton, is it?' Lyric jumped as Edward clapped his hand on her shoulder and peered across at the ring.

'Yes – don't tell me you've never met him?' She looked at her brother in shock.

Edward shrugged nonchalantly. 'Never met any of the Skanktons. Dad keeps threatening to introduce me, but something always gets in the way. Our holidays, their holi-days, you and I up to no good in town . . .' Lyric blushed and looked guiltily up at Philippe, but he was busy frown-ing at his phone and didn't seem to have heard.

She laughed and shook her head. 'Unbelievable, Edward. Have we really all been so busy that you've been home for months and not met our next-door neighbours, and Daddy's business partner, yet?'

Edward stretched and tutted laconically. 'Well, sis, maybe my immersion in your lives isn't quite as complete as you'd like to think it is,' he said mildly. 'And, as Daddy didn't give me a racehorse for Christmas, there's not really been an incentive to leap over the fence and go trotting up to Skankton Manor.'

Lyric laughed uncertainly, unsure if it was irony or bitterness she detected in Edward's voice. 'Well,' she said purposefully, spotting Roger Skankton's son Darren lurking around at the fringe of the crowd. Darren was the same age as her and Edward, a committed party boy and a sometime wing man for the It girl Lyric of old. 'We can remedy that right now. Philippe, we're just going to say hi to Darren.'

He looked up at her from his text. 'OK, *chérie*,' he said in a preoccupied voice. Lyric grabbed Edward's hand and set out across the turf to Darren. She took a deep breath as they walked. Darren had his father's charm and his mother's good looks, which had made him the ideal teenage party escort when one was needed, not to mention a lift home at the end of the night. But, despite his privileged upbringing, Darren Skankton was nothing but an ignorant – and very rich – yob, and theirs had always been a friendship of convenience more than anything else.

As Lyric had left school for finishing school and then London, Darren had remained behind at home, dabbling in his father's business, literally charming the pants off the female population of the Home Counties, and also making half-hearted attempts to become famous (and even richer) on his own terms. Their friendship, such as it was, had first faltered, then disintegrated entirely, until he felt like little more than a distant and vaguely undesirable relative. But he could be fun, and she guessed he was harmless; and he would make a good new buddy for Edward while her brother continued to find his feet socially.

Darren waved back and strolled over to meet them, looking Lyric up and down and giving her a rakish smile. 'All right, Lyric?' he said in gravelly mockney tones. 'Have you seen Mum?'

Lyric turned and pointed out Angie, still standing forlornly in the ring as her husband continued to ignore her. Her heart sank as her own mother tottered giggling into view, arm in arm with her fey assistant Michael on one side and a foppish young man on the other. What on earth was Constance up to now?

As she saw George wave fondly at his wife, Lyric forced herself to relax. After all, if her father saw no reason to treat her mother's odd behaviour any differently than he ever had, why should she? Lyric dragged herself back to the conversation. 'She's over there, Darren. I would have thought that was the first place you'd have looked.' Darren shrugged and turned to Edward.

'So, you must be the prodigal son,' he said with a grin, holding out his hand to shake Edward's. 'I'm Darren, pleased to get acquainted finally. How's life at the manor?'

Edward smiled matily. 'Oh, you know. Has its moments. Could do with getting out and about a bit every now and then, though!'

Darren laughed. 'Well, you've come to the right place. Out and about's what we do best, eh, Lyric?' He winked lewdly at her and she tutted.

'You wish, Darren.'

Darren nudged Edward. 'Lyric's been off the scene too long, mate – we need another Charlton to swell the ranks of the party massive. I know everyone, me – I'll have to do you some introductions!'

Lyric patted Edward's arm, pleased to see him making a new friend so easily, even if it *was* Darren. 'Well, brother, I'm going to leave you in Darren's capable hands – I'm off to find Thumper. Have fun, people!' She walked off excitedly in the direction of the enclosure, where shiny-coated horses with rippling muscles were being led into the ring by proud grooms, followed by wiry, wily jockeys in bright racing colours.

As Thumper was led into the enclosure, she ran up, hugging his neck and rubbing his velvety soft nose. The horse breathed heavily and nudged her back gently. Lyric smiled. She had a natural way with horses, and there had been an instant bond between them. She adored Thumper, and she had the feeling it was mutual.

'How was he with the journey?' she asked Natalie, Thumper's pretty groom.

'Oh, you know – a bit skittish!' Natalie replied, a soft burr of an accent enhancing her fresh, outdoorsy appearance. 'But once we were here, he calmed down OK. There was too much else going on for him to worry about his nerves. Nosey beggar!'

Lyric laughed, and was about to chat to the jockey when she spotted Philippe approaching, and waved excitedly. He jogged over to her, smiling expectantly. 'Look, Philippe – isn't he just gorgeous?' She patted Thumper, her eyes shining.

Philippe smiled back. 'He looks just as spirited and beautiful as his owner,' he said, drawing her in close and breathing in the smell of her hair. 'And just as wild,' he murmured. Lyric felt a wave of passion as his strength enveloped her. At times like this she just wanted to breathe him in until there was no telling where one of them started and the other ended.

Philippe pulled back and held out his hand, palm up. His skin was hard and calloused – a worker's hand. 'Blow into it!' he said.

'What?' said Lyric, looking at him, puzzled.

'Blow into it, *chérie*! For good luck.'

She blew hesitantly, half laughing.

'Harder, *chérie*! Like you mean it!' They were both laughing now, and Lyric blew so hard she made a raspberry noise.

Philippe closed his hand as if around her breath. '*Bonne chance*, Thumper,' he called, and opened his hands above his head as if to release the breath again. At that moment, it seemed to Lyric, a spring breeze stirred as if from nowhere, lifting the sentiment and carrying it away on the air. Thumper raised his head and harrumphed softly as Natalie led him away.

The grooms were leading the final horses towards the starting blocks, where other jockeys were already mounted and calming impatient steeds, and Lyric stepped to one side as they moved past her. She grabbed hold of Philippe's arm and pulled him in the same direction.

'Come on! We need to get prime position!'

They hurried over to the edge of the racetrack, where the Skanktons and her mother and father had already gathered.

Constance, flanked by George and Darren, on whose arm she was coyly leaning, waved girlishly at her daughter. 'Oh, Lyric, darling, I've been looking for you everywhere. Is there nowhere you can get a decent G&T around here?'

Lyric shook her head in bewilderment. 'Mother, I have no idea. And, to be honest, I couldn't care less.' But her voice softened as she looked at Constance. Her eccentricities only seemed to be getting more pronounced with age. 'We'll take a look after the race, if you like,' she offered brightly. 'Although, who knows – we might be wanting champagne if the race goes Thumper's way!'

There was a ripple of appreciative laughter from the two families lined up along the white railings.

George gave her a paternal wink. 'Don't get too carried away, my darling,' he said gruffly. 'I know Thumper has potential, but Roger would need to have been feeding him super-charged oats in order for him to win this!'

There was an uncomfortable silence from Roger along the line, which Lyric interpreted as irritation.

'Well, Roger's training talents have surprised us before – and I'm sure they will again,' she said determinedly.

Lyric caught the eye of King Abu Rhuba, standing with his son, Prince Abu Rhuba, and nodded politely. The king inclined his head slightly, and then, without an attempt to acknowledge her father or the rest of the family, turned back to the race. The frostiness was no surprise. He was her father's main racing rival, which made his playboy son's close friendship with Darren ever so slightly awkward. The king, she knew, had also been interested in buying Thumper, but had been outbid by her father. King Abu Rhuba hated to lose anything and his nose was clearly still severely out of joint.

Putting it to the back of her mind, Lyric turned her attention to the race. Silence fell across the group as the horses went under starter's orders. Even Constance stopped wittering while the commentator indicated the last few seconds before the race.

And then – they were off!

'Come on, Thumper,' Lyric called, as the horse quickly took fourth place.

After another furlong he was a nose away from third place.

'Come on, Thumper,' called George jovially.

Thumper swallowed up the next few furlongs, covering the ground easily, until he had overtaken the third placed runner.

'Come on, Thumper,' Lyric heard Roger mutter from between gritted teeth.

Thumper was now comfortably in second place, his legs almost horizontal as he stretched them out over what remained of the course.

The Charltons and the Skanktons held their collective breath as he closed the gap between him and the leading horse. There were just a couple of furlongs to go—

'Argh!'

They all looked in shock at George who was holding on to Angus, who in turn was struggling to support his much taller and heavier friend.

'George?' shrieked Constance.

'Daddy?' yelled Lyric.

With a visible effort, George pulled away from Angus and stood up unaided, waving them all away with one hand as if they were making a fuss.

'Just a little wobble,' he murmured. 'Too much excitement. Or sun. One or the other.'

'And Doppelganger wins the race!'

They all stared at each other in shock, having missed the last triumphant seconds of the race through concern for George. Lyric looked at the course, then at Philippe, and then at her father. Thumper had WON?!

Suddenly, she and everyone around her burst into action, hugging each other and shrieking. She felt Philippe lift her in the air, over and over, whooping loudly in her ear.

'I put five hundred pounds on it!' she heard Edward yell.

'Good show,' managed George, attempting to stand up straight.

'Get in!' roared Roger in a vulgar fashion, pumping the air with his fist.

'Bloody hell, Angus, why didn't you see that one coming?' grumbled Constance, reapplying her lipstick. 'I could have won a small fortune on those odds.'

'Well, Constance, you can't win them all – and the fact that your horse even finished that race is a bloomin' miracle,' muttered Angus from amongst the celebrations. But Lyric didn't care. Thumper – her darling Thumper – had not only romped home and won the prestigious Derby race, but he had also created the most dramatic climax of the day – one that would in turn create headlines on every racing page in the country the next morning.

Eventually, Philippe put her down and she turned to George to give him a delighted hug.

'Daddy?'

He squeezed her hand reassuringly. 'Good race, darling,

good race. Couldn't have hoped for a better start to his career. I never lose my touch, you know, darling!'

Lyric felt Philippe's arms around her as he hugged her from behind.

'You see? I told you it would all be all right.'

She pulled his arms into herself and thought joyfully of the secret she had yet to share with him. Her secret, soon to be theirs. He was right. It *was* all right. This win could only be a good omen. And this secret would bring them as close together as – if not closer than – when they had first met . . .

Something out of the corner of her eye made her start. She turned sharply, just in time to see her father stumble and fall to the ground.

'Daddy!' she cried. 'Someone! Call an ambulance!'

And as the family rushed over to George's unconscious form, slumped like a dead weight on the ground, she had a feeling that everything was very far from all right. Very far indeed.

Four

Lyric wandered sleepily down Broughton Hall's sweeping main staircase, trying hard to lift the fog of a sleepless night from her head. Her father's illness was preying heavily on her mind, and in the days since his collapse at the races she'd found sleep was eluding her. Despite his protestations that he was well enough to be treated at home rather than in hospital, she couldn't help but worry from the moment his day nurse went home at six p.m. to the moment she returned the next morning at seven a.m., and found herself pacing up and down corridors fretting about his well-being.

Last night had been no different – and it wasn't just worry keeping her awake. Guilt gnawed like a persistent rodent, nipping away at her, crawling into every thought. Having been diagnosed with acute kidney failure, under the doctor's interrogation George had finally admitted to recurring dizzy episodes, light-headedness and unusual tiredness. With hindsight, she remembered her father's recent spells of fatigue, which Philippe had pointed out to her; incidents she'd barely paid any notice to, putting them down to over-exertion, or excitement over the refurbishments to Broughton Hall, or any number of inconsequential things. Why hadn't she, George's daughter, sussed there was something more serious going on?

Lyric had finally retired to bed only a short while before Philippe had got up, heading for the fields, or the garden, or whatever part of Broughton Hall's land he was transforming at the moment. His dedication to the estate's restoration and the organic produce business he'd set up with her father had been fuelled even further by George's convalescence. In fact, what with them seeing so little of one another, and the worry over her father's illness, Lyric's secret had remained unshared and was still hers and hers alone.

Brushing the thought aside, Lyric descended into the hall, running her hand along the banister as it followed the elegant curve of the staircase. It was hard, sometimes, when you were looking at the overall lived-in beauty of Broughton Hall, to pick out individual characteristics and really appreciate them. Although her mother's exquisite taste and penchant for overseas travel were self-evident in the eclectic mix of artefacts dotted around the house, the interior decor was more about comfort than grandeur. Broughton Hall was resolutely old money, and the epitome of shabby chic. Most of the expensive ornaments, broken by children or dogs, had been superglued back together at some point over the years, and, together with the familiar smell of wet dog, year-round log fires and Jo Malone candles, these made up her childhood home.

At least, they *had* made up her home, Lyric reminded herself as she turned left at the bottom of the staircase, continued through the grand yet welcoming hall and strolled towards the drawing room. That was, before Constance's mid-life crisis really took hold and she had given the stately home its recent 'facelift', transforming the grande dame of the Berkshire countryside into a wisteria-covered Grade One facade fronting a glorified Marrakesh nightclub behind. Gradually, she was working her way around the house. Upstairs, one of the elegant bathrooms had been retiled as a Turkish hammam, complete with rainforest shower head and subtle mood lighting in the ceiling. But the *pièce de resistance* was George's former pride and joy: the wine cellars, which had been transformed into a louche after-hours bar, where Constance entertained, at different times, eager young Broughton Hall staffers, her and George's oldest friends, and her WI committee peers.

In short, the whole of Broughton Hall now resembled a cross between the inside of a luxury yacht and an opium den.

It was as though Constance had come off the Valium and replaced it with daily acid tabs.

With one hand on the doorknob, Lyric steeled herself for the assault she knew the refurbished drawing room would have on her senses.

'No, Edward, I won't hear of it.' The sound of her father's voice behind the door, unusually abrupt, made Lyric pause before entering.

'Why?' demanded her brother. He, too, sounded hostile; aggressive, even.

'You're young,' stated George flatly. 'You have your whole life ahead of you. I couldn't live with myself if I took something so precious from you.'

'But Father – you may not be able to live at all if you don't. And this is something I really want to do. You heard the doctor. I'm the only match. I'm the only person who can donate a kidney to you. I'm your son – you gave me life, now it's my turn to give it back. What's the alternative – a lifetime of dialysis? No lifetime at all?' Her brother's voice broke on the last sentence, and a lump formed in Lyric's throat. Her father dying was something she refused to consider.

Lyric held her breath for George's response.

'Well, Father?' prompted Edward.

'There is another option,' said George slowly. 'And I know it's not going to be a popular one . . .'

'Lyric, darling, whatever are you doing?' Lyric jumped as her mother clip-clopped along the corridor towards her, a vision of Berber glamour in jewel-coloured kaftan, harem pants and high-heeled ornate slippers. Since George's collapse, Constance had been even more of a highly strung whirlwind, spinning around Broughton Hall, combining her day-to-day delegations with dispensing loving care to her husband. 'You'll give yourself a chill hanging around in draughty corridors like that.' She brushed past Lyric and opened the door for her, smiling efficiently like the born hostess she was.

'Oh, I, erm – I thought I'd forgotten something in my room,' mumbled Lyric hurriedly, pasting a smile on her face in return, as her mind raced.

In the dim light of the drawing room, George and Edward were facing the door, startled expressions on their faces after the interruption to their exchange. The decor fought bravely to counteract the lack of natural light. The faded grandeur of the antiquated wallpaper had been replaced with vivid shades of 'sunset'. Where once artlessly placed classic paintings had hung from heavy chains on the walls – a Constable here, a Soames hidden there – a circular camel-bone mirror from Essaouira took pride of place, surrounded by exotic silken drapes suspended in Technicolor glory, like in some cavernous student digs. The scuffed oak flooring had been replaced by mosaic tiling, and the old familiar kilim rugs scattered around the room were now covered up by vibrant Moroccan carpets. Huge iron floor lights, mahogany-coloured leather cabinets, hand-painted screens and *moucharabi* chairs completed the hideous transformation.

'Hi, Edward,' she said more brightly than she felt. Edward grimaced at her from across the room, trying to hide his inner turmoil. Lyric could tell he was bristling from the conversation with George.

'Morning, Daddy,' she said. George was sitting upright on a chaise longue, a pillow propping up his back and a copy of the *Telegraph* – which he'd apparently been trying to read by the light of a henna lamp – discarded on a brown-and-white embroidered leather pouf next to him.

George tried to push himself up and failed, instead holding his arms out beseechingly to his daughter, and Lyric bent over, smiling, and kissed the top of his head.

'Not really morning, darling,' he grunted, looking at his watch pointedly. 'Your Philippe's been up for hours. Even managed to get him involved in the lambing this morning. Talented boy, that.'

'I know, Daddy.' Lyric ignored the fact she'd been up worrying about her father and focused instead on her delight at his pride in her fiancé.

'Gets more like "Harem Nights" in here every day, eh, Lyric?' George shook his head in mock exasperation as he abruptly changed the subject. 'The latest of your mother's fads. Let's just hope it's as quickly forgotten as all the rest. Oh, hello, darling.' George's eyes twinkled as he teased Constance, who tutted dismissively as she floated out of the room. George eyed the room's very permanent-looking new decor doubtfully, then turned wistfully to look out of the window. He raised an eyebrow at Michael and a friend walking past and then turned to Lyric, eyes still dancing. 'We've not had so many poufs in the house since the last time Jacob came to stay, eh?'

Lyric laughed at the good-natured reference to her cousin.

'Actually, talking of Jacob . . .' George began, then seemed to think better of it.

'What, Daddy?' pressed Lyric, perching on a mosaic table.

George, still looking out of the window, turned back to her. 'No matter. I'll talk to you about that later. But I also wanted to ask you something else. He's all right, is he, that young man of yours?'

'What do you mean, Daddy?' asked Lyric, confused. It was unlike George to ask indirect questions.

'Well, nothing to worry about, I'm sure,' replied George after a moment's consideration. 'It's just he's been a little distracted. Irritable, even. Not like himself at all.'

Before Lyric could answer, there was a loud crash, and Philippe burst through the door.

'*Impossible*,' he spat in French, glowering at nobody in particular, but nonetheless managing to envelop both her and her father in his bad mood.

He flopped onto a chair, and then sprang straight out of it again as he sat on a stray hookah pipe. '*Merde!*'

Lyric ran across to him with a reassuring smile and gave him a hug and a chaste kiss on the cheek. 'You look like you'd be better off smoking that than sitting on it. Bad day?'

Philippe's expression softened, and he allowed himself a reluctant smile at his fiancée.

'We had an unexpected frost last night, and it has damaged some of the specimen plants for my garden,' he said in a dull monotone. His brow furrowed again. 'The wild cultivation on the hill has survived, but the important ones for my garden – they are completely destroyed.'

Lyric bit her lip. Since Philippe had been invited to enter the Chelsea Flower Show earlier that year, he'd been tirelessly planning his secret design, which as far as Lyric could tell was a seasonal, organic wildflower garden that represented both Broughton Hall and Philippe's signature garden designs. He would be up against royalty and some of the top gardeners in the world. Philippe might not court celebrity, but he guarded his hard-won reputation fiercely, and this opportunity had rekindled all his professional competitiveness. The show was at the end of May, in just a couple of weeks, and she knew this setback would spell certain disaster for his original plans.

The door opened again and Constance wafted back in.

'Oh, there you are, Philippe, darling. Have you run out of herbal tea?'

Philippe looked at her, perplexed. 'I'm sorry, Constance?'

'Herbal tea, darling. That's what those funny little golf carts of yours are run on, aren't they? Only there's one abandoned right outside the tepee, which is spoiling the view from the hookah circle and making Michael extremely upset.'

'The carts are electric, Constance,' said Philippe, mouth twitching in amusement in spite of his bad mood. 'Let me go and move it right away.'

'Well, don't be long,' trilled Constance. 'It's lunchtime. Moroccan lamb tagine and couscous.' Edward screwed up his nose and pulled a face at Lyric. Constance, blissfully unaware, shooed them all into the dining room. '*A table*, everyone!'

~

'Mmmm, that was very exotic and surprisingly delicious, my dear.' George scraped his bowl of vermicelli pudding and eyed the half-eaten bowls around the table. 'No one else going for second helpings?'

Lyric hid a smile. At least George's gargantuan appetite seemed back to normal, even if his usual carver chair had been replaced by a wheelchair. Her father would suffer any number of Constance's new fads as long as they were accompanied by delicious new recipes for him to try. And, despite his fragile health, of the five of them seated around the stately dining table (its French polish still intact and – as yet – uncustomized), it was George who'd made lightest work of the Moroccan-style lunch they'd just been served.

She looked at her parents fondly. Hard to believe they were soon to have been married forty years. Even harder, on the face of it, to know how to celebrate it. But she and Edward had settled on the idea of a surprise party – a party to mark their long union, but also a belated celebration of the reappearance of their long-lost son. The idea had been that it would also give Edward the chance to meet many of the Charltons' far-flung family friends who would be dying to get to know him. Plans were already underway. But would George be fit for it?

Edward pushed his almost untouched bowl away in distaste. 'No thanks, Father. I think I'll opt for a coffee instead,' he said, eyeing the tray being brought in by Jeffries, the Charltons' loyal butler. With one eyebrow sceptically raised, Jeffries began distributing its contents from between forefinger and thumb.

'What's this?' said Edward, picking up a dainty jade-green jewelled glass with no handle. 'Ow!'

'Take care, sir, the contents are hot,' added Jeffries, too late, from across the table as he served George the final one.

'It's mint tea, darling,' said Constance airily, sipping hers delicately. 'It's simply divine.' Pulling a minute pill box towards her, she tipped out a tiny white capsule and knocked it back expertly.

'In a glass?' replied Edward, unconvinced. 'How do you pick it up without burning yourself?'

'With your teeth. Then you down it in one,' teased Philippe, and the tension around the table eased for a moment as they all laughed. 'Oh, sorry, I guess that was last night. Which must be why you're in the state you are this morning . . .'

George cleared his throat ostentatiously.

'Touché,' said Edward, picking up his glass and raising it to his future brother-in-law.

They all laughed again, and Lyric looked at Philippe adoringly. Say what you like about her eccentric family, their company was good fun, and, seeing his smiling face, it was clear the loving, slightly crazy atmosphere had worked its magic on Philippe.

George cleared his throat again.

'So, Philippe, how is that little garden display of yours coming along?' put in Constance tactlessly, and Lyric kicked her hard under the table. Honestly! Why did she have to bring that up now, when Philippe finally seemed to have relaxed? It was at times like these that her mother's airy eccentricities annoyed her more than they amused.

'Might I say a few words?' George burst out, changing the subject abruptly for the second time that day. Her father was rarely impatient; but, now Lyric looked closer at him, seated, as always, at the head of the table, she could see he was preoccupied – flustered, even. 'I've been trying to say something for some time now, I might add.'

There was silence at his outburst, and George took advantage of the moment.

'Recent events have forced me to make a radical decision on matters of my health, and our family' – he paused – 'but I feel it necessary to consult you before acting.'

Lyric, Philippe and Edward exchanged surprised glances, whilst Constance studied an apparently fascinating spot on her kaftan.

'It's fair to say that I have been in better shape. You all know I am in need of a kidney transplant. And while a match has been difficult to find' – he paused as Edward gave a derisive snort from down the table – 'there is, it appears, another possibility we haven't yet explored.'

He paused again, and the family stared back at him breathlessly.

George took a deep breath. 'Quentin, my brother.' He looked at first at Lyric, then Edward. 'Your uncle,' he added unnecessarily. 'It's likely he is a match and could be a suitable donor. We will need to find out in person, so to speak, before we can even discuss the likelihood of his agreeing. But, should he agree, I would have no alternative but to welcome him back into the heart of the family.'

There was another stunned silence. Lyric stared at her father incredulously.

'Uncle Quentin?' she repeated stupidly. 'But isn't he *dead*?'

George shook his head emphatically. 'No, darling, he's not. I have reason to believe your uncle Quentin is alive and well and doing penance in a Buddhist retreat in India.'

'A Buddhist retreat is hardly what I'd imagine Uncle Quentin would head to India for,' scoffed Lyric, thinking of her estranged uncle's greedy ways. 'Are you sure you're not mixing temples up with curry houses?'

George raised a hand to silence her. 'Let me finish, Lyric. Your uncle wrote to me some time ago declaring his remorse for what he'd done, and asking for my forgiveness. Nothing more, mind, but it's been preying on my thoughts ever since. Now, of course, I have a good reason to accept that apology. I'm going to ask him to donate his kidney. To me.'

There was a shocked silence.

Lyric was the first to speak, even though she felt blind-sided.

'How can you be sure his kidney will be any use?'

It was a cheap shot – her uncle had spent most of his life half cut – and George fixed her with a steely gaze. 'Lyric, I expect better than that from you.'

Lyric clamped her mouth shut momentarily, and looked around the table in dismay. The shocked expressions of her nearest and dearest said it all – but when she saw Edward's crushed countenance, she could keep quiet no more.

'This is the uncle that tore our family apart. Who, in a crazy attempt to make his own son rightful heir of Broughton Hall, deprived you of Edward for thirty years, tried to deny that same son his inheritance, and even attempted to kill me?' Philippe had moved from his seat to stand behind her and was now squeezing her shoulders in support. Lyric raised her hand to hold his arm. She knew that, after all they'd been through, he must be as horrified as her. Across the table Edward simply gaped at her father.

George paused as a pained expression passed across his face. 'There is no forgiving his actions, Lyric. But we must forget. And in doing so, we must encourage the police to drop all charges.'

Again, there was silence. The air was thick with astonishment, outrage and unanswered questions, and the jovial atmosphere had now been completely replaced by a *froideur* that Lyric could feel enveloping all of them in its clammy fingers.

Lyric felt Philippe squeeze her shoulder again and she leaned back into his strong, warm body, glad of his strength. Edward said and did nothing. He sat, head bowed, staring numbly at the table in front of him. Lyric tried to make eye contact with him, but still he stared straight ahead, his expression unreadable.

George cleared his throat again. When he spoke, his voice was calm and steady. 'Without a transplant, my condition is serious. This is no time for recriminations. This is a time for forgiveness. And action.'

Edward's body twitched, as if he'd been shot. A blotchy rash had started to creep up his neck.

'But I could give you my kidney, Father,' said Edward suddenly, in a strangled voice. 'You know I would. And the quicker you have the transplant, the better the prognosis. I'm here now. Quentin isn't.'

George shook his head mulishly.

'What if your body rejects the first kidney?' said Lyric, desperately wanting to back her brother up – and make her father see sense.

'Yes, Father,' said Edward, eagerly clutching the new argument. 'It might. Then you could still ask Quentin.'

'You're too young.'

'I'm also your son.'

'You're too young. I won't hear of it.'

'But—' Now Lyric and Edward spoke simultaneously.

There was a scraping noise as Constance pushed her chair back and stood up regally. 'Your father has made up his mind. It's not only what he wants to do, it's the right thing to do. Family is family, no matter what water there is under the bridge. There will be no more discussion on this matter. Now, more mint tea, anyone?'

~

The family filed out of the dining room behind Edward in complete silence. Lyric rushed past her mother and touched Edward's arm. He shook it off angrily. 'Not now, Lyric,' he growled.

She turned to Philippe with a helpless look, and he shrugged. 'Leave him, *chérie*. He needs time. We all need time. Walk with me to the woods instead.'

Lyric took his arm and they walked in silence across the field to the small copse on top of a hill. As they climbed, the scent of the bluebells increased and she breathed in deeply, inhaling the familiar smell and revelling in the fragrant cloud of nostalgia that enveloped her. As they turned a corner into the woods, she let out a cry of delight at the carpet of blue spread out before them. A soft spring breeze blew through the wooded dell, moving the flowers like a gently rippling sea. No wonder people came from around the world to see these bluebells – Lyric herself never tired of the sheer beauty of them.

But though she'd seen this sight in each of the thirty-one years of her life, this year there was something different – and it wasn't just the fact that she was seeing them with Philippe for the first time. Beautiful though it was, the smell wasn't quite as sweet as she remembered. Not quite as evocative. Was this the effect of the events of the past few days, another trick her body was playing on her, or something else?

She looked up at Philippe tentatively. He, too, was breathing in deeply, his gaze set over the bluebells spread out in front of them. But his eyes – his eyes seemed somewhere else. Somewhere a million miles away from Broughton Hall.

She squeezed his hand softly. Now was the time. She had to redress the horrible events they were going through with something good. It wouldn't change the bad stuff, but it would be something they could share . . . Lyric felt a surge of excitement.

He looked down at her, as if willing himself back to the present. '*Oui, chérie?*'

She turned to face him and grabbed his other hand, swinging both back and forth.

'I – erm – I have some news,' she said shyly.

He smiled distractedly. 'Is that right. And what is your news, *chérie?*'

She paused, her heart beating dramatically. 'I'm – we're

– pregnant!' Lyric's heart was in her mouth now as she searched Philippe's face for a reaction. He looked back at her, his face expressionless, his eyes blank. Finally, he tore his eyes away from hers and looked down.

Lyric stared at him in shock. Philippe was a man of few words by nature, but – surely he had something to say about *this*?

The next few seconds felt like an eternity as Philippe stared at the ground, kicking the grass absently with the toes of his desert boots. Was he happy? Shocked? Horrified? Lyric hardly dared breathe as she resisted the urge to shake a reaction out of him, and waited. And waited.

But when, finally, he looked up, Lyric had to bite her lip to stop crying out in joy. Philippe's face was a picture of pure delight, his eyes filled to the brim with unshed tears.

He reached out and pulled her to him, holding her tight with one arm and stroking her hair with the other. 'Oh, *chérie*. We're going to be mama and papa!'

Lyric hugged him back, full of happiness and just the tiniest hint of relief. And there it was. There was always something to feel optimistic about; despite her father's illness, despite the prospect of her wayward uncle returning to the family fold, this – this was the one thing that was going to cement their future, and bring them more joy than she had ever thought humanly possible.

Five

Quentin Charlton repeated his personal mantra for the final five times that morning, and replaced his meditation beads around his neck. Careful not to put his weight on his gammy knee, he struggled up out of the lotus position and clambered down from the meditation plinth, looking out over the spectacular forest-covered slope that gently undulated down to create a valley of the deepest green, framed by towering mountains on the other side. Delicate wisps of cloud were lightly suspended, creating the illusion of some kind of fantastical dreamland. The air hung heavy with the scent of spice and incense, and the only break in the reverential silence was the occasional low chanting thrum of a meditating monk.

Quentin turned before leaving his meditation spot and took a moment to savour the view, inhaling a deep, satisfactory breath. Who would have thought only a few weeks, let alone months ago, that he could be so content in such a medieval backwater as this Buddhist retreat? (In fact, he reminded himself, some might say that, after his brush with death, it was a wonder he was even alive.) But his near-death experience had inspired his first foray into the spiritual world and he'd given himself up totally to the Buddhist experience (not until after he'd tried to score hash off the retreat's security guard, that is). Whilst there, his commitment had led him to be recommended to go for the real deal – the full-on Buddhist experience – and the monks here in Darjeeling had welcomed him with open arms. Unlike his family and friends – and the police, for that matter – back home, they were not interested in his previous misdemeanours. And rightly so – he was, after all, a reformed man. Who needed wheeling and dealing and all the bad karma that his previous life, full of underhand scams, brought with it? It was more trouble than it was worth, all that plotting and planning. And hard work, too. Plus, his exposure as a liar, a blackmailer, a kidnapper and a crazed would-be murderer – followed by a dangerous escape and exile – had proven beyond a doubt that crime really didn't pay.

He'd started off, as so many Buddhist disciples did, seeking out the Dalai Lama in Dharamsala. But, even then, Quentin had surprised himself, finding this most holiest of places rather spoilt and touristy. It seemed to him that the Dalai Lama's palace was surrounded by KFC and McDonald's.

Instead, he'd headed up here, to the mountains, to live in an old tea planter's house, now a beautiful if somewhat rundown hotel, a relic from the heyday of the British empire, and a stone's throw from the monastery; here, where the very air was holy and the monks so spiritually elevated that they could make themselves levitate and even, it was rumoured, invisible (Quentin had asked them to prove it every day for the first week he'd been here, but disappearing on demand was seen as showing off and appealing to their ego – strictly banned under their religious vows); here, where the rag-tag village children reverently called him 'Mister Botham' for the same questionable bowling skills that had earned him only ridicule at school, and tugged persistently at his robes begging him to play yet another game of cricket.

And so here he was, having renounced all his material goods and sold off the rest to Brad Pitt and Angelina Jolie (who were rumoured to be looking to buy in order to adopt a British child) to fund his escape, thousands of miles away from all the trappings of the modern world. He was surrounded by the simplest of villages and the poorest of people, with no Château Lafite, no cigars, no brandies – and he was surviving. What's more, he was content. You might even say he was enjoying it. He nodded at Michael Caine and Shakira as they pottered past. Of course, the company wasn't bad, either.

Quentin wrapped his orange robes tighter around him as he flapped his sandals along the roughly paved path. Thanks to early morning yoga, the three- or four-hour daily hikes through the hills with the monks, visiting different monasteries and temples, bathing in the mountain springs and his newly adopted vegetarian diet (he'd tried to go vegan, but missed his scrambled eggs, not to mention the serving of meat; he now had his tofu, rice and vegetables enhanced every other day 'to keep his strength up'), he was losing weight and his saffron robes hung like a tent canvas around him. He faltered as he caught his red string bracelet on a low-hanging branch, and twisted it anxiously to inspect it for damage. There was none, and he gazed at it proudly before continuing with his stroll. He'd seen one on Madonna once, in a *Hello!* magazine in a dentist's waiting room, and so he'd jumped at the chance of owning one himself. Funny that such a trapping of celebrity had reached this backwater – still, his was not to reason why. It must have some religious significance or something, Quentin thought, and continued, humming, on his way.

'Brother Quentin! Brother Quentin!'

A fellow monk, a wizened, Tibetan ancient, scurried out of a hut as Quentin passed, brandishing a mobile phone.

'I have a call for you! From England!'

Quentin started and turned, smiling a beatific smile at his new colleague. But as he saw the phone his face fell. Fearful of who might be on the other end, he started to back up the path. He'd come so far with his promise to turn his back on crime and purge himself of the evil he'd committed over several decades, and he'd hoped all that was behind him. Divine remission of past sins was his future.

But now, the sight of the phone filled him with fear that his past had managed to catch up with him, even in this isolated backwater. Certainly, in his situation, no news was good news – and whoever had managed to track him down here had a purpose. In Quentin's experience, other people's purposes didn't generally go in his favour.

'No!' he almost shouted, causing several passing monks to turn their bent heads sideways in shock. No one raised their voice on this retreat. 'No! Brother, I have renounced all materialism. I cannot use a mobile telephone – it would be against my principles. It's not Zen. Bad karma. Spiritual disaster. Either way – I don't want to take the call!'

The monk looked at him, dumbfounded, and then looked at the phone. 'But – it's just a phone. And it's your brother, brother!'

Quentin physically relaxed. So George had managed to discover his latest hiding place, had he? Well, he had to hand it to him – persistence was definitely a Charlton trait. When Quentin's previous retreat had contacted him to explain a family member was trying to reach him, he'd guessed it would be George. His older brother was the only one big-hearted – some might say misguided – enough to try, after all. But Quentin had asked them not to tell George where he was. Quentin wasn't ready for forgiveness. Wasn't worthy. Had more self-exploration and repenting to do before he could even contemplate a reunion. And despite his brother's assurances that he'd called off the police search for him, he couldn't be certain Interpol weren't still after him, could he?

The monk screwed up his face. 'He says it's an emergency. A matter of life and death.' His tone of voice was clear. Karma ruled the roost here, and the refusal of such a request would have bad karma stamped all over it.

Relenting, Quentin held out his hand and took the phone from the monk. The size of a small house-brick, the phone must predate the Dalai Lama himself, thought Quentin as he raised the handset to his ear.

'George?'

'Quentin! How the devil are you?'

Although theirs had been a difficult relationship, fraught with the jealousies and competitiveness that huge inheritances inspired within families, Quentin had to admit it was good to hear his brother's voice.

'Well, George, I'm fine, thank you. Though I'm pleased to be keeping the Devil at arm's length – which is exactly where I intend to keep him for the rest of my life.'

'Well, old chap, I'm pleased to hear it. About time, too. Which must mean it's time for you to come back to Broughton Hall.'

'How did you track me down?' wondered Quentin out loud, ignoring the question. 'And, more to the point, why?'

'Well, to persuade you to come home, of course!' said George. Quentin nearly laughed out loud at his brother's perplexed tone. Poor George. He had no idea of the depths of depravity Quentin had gone to before his self-induced rehabilitation, and how his desire to purge his soul was his only purpose in life. Yes, of course he missed things about his old life – his son, Jacob, certainly; and, yes, members of the extended family and Broughton Hall, too. But he had much work to do before he considered himself able to return. If ever.

'George, your call and the depth of your heart are like a balm to my soul. I am truly humbled that you have not only forgiven me, but want me back in your family – the very family I set out to destroy when I deprived you of Edward all those years ago. Truly, brother, I am not worthy of such magnanimity.' He took a breath, and could feel George clicking his tongue in exasperation at the other end. His brother was not one for decorative statements or emotional outbursts, and Quentin could tell he was only just tolerating them. 'But I still need guidance, brother – spiritual guidance – and here there are people who can offer me just that. I don't feel worthy to return to Broughton Hall and sit with you – and your family – at your dinner table, sharing the fruits of your labour and the harvest of your soil.'

At the thought of one of Constance's famous Sunday lunches by the fire, washed down with a bottle of claret, Quentin felt his mouth begin to water, and he fumbled around his neck with his free hand for his meditation beads.

'Brother, I'm slowly getting my life back. I feel such shame for what I've done, and I want to start afresh. Properly, that is. And only when I can actually face myself in the mirror will I be able to sit down opposite you and apologize in person. And only then will I consider returning home to the family fortress.'

There was a silence, and then a cough from George. 'I

have a life-threatening condition, Quentin. I may even be dying. And only you can save me.'

There was another silence.

'I'll be in touch, brother,' said Quentin, handing the phone back to the monk and kissing his beads thoughtfully. 'I'll be in touch.'

Six

Lyric pushed through the throngs of floral tea-dresses and wondered, not for the first time, just what it was about garden parties and flower shows that made women want to compete with the exhibits. For her part, she'd chosen a yellow 1950s-style prom dress and wedges for the occasion, with her hair pulled back into a loose ponytail. The effect made her look younger than ever; and, although she had worried she'd gone a bit too pared-down for such an important day in Philippe's career, now that she was here amongst the sunshine and flowers she was glad she'd chosen something so simple and girlish.

She bit her lip, worried. When she'd left his show garden to nip to the loo, the judges were about to announce the results. What she hadn't reckoned upon were huge queues at the loos and, overwhelmed by the crowds, getting lost on the way back; now she'd been gone over an hour and had missed the announcements altogether. She kicked herself for missing Philippe's big moment. Why did she always have to be so ditsy? Not sure where to find him, she decided that heading back to his exhibit was a good start – someone there would know how he'd done, and where she could find him.

She turned onto a familiar access path and breathed a sigh of relief when she saw his garden up ahead. Inspired by Broughton Hall, the space was a riot of colour and action – a tangle of wild flowers and hedgerow plants that stood out amongst the carefully landscaped modernist structures and painstakingly tended Asian-influenced spaces that surrounded it. Butterflies and bees lazily bobbed in and out of the flora, carefully chosen to attract insects, and, despite the activity around it, a stray blue-tit had even popped in to investigate the nesting materials and spaces provided. A collection of ornate water-filled tubs weren't just lovely to look at – they were a rain management system, designed to irrigate the garden cost-effectively. As she had done every time she looked at it, Lyric thought she would burst with pride. Philippe had somehow managed to turn untamed nature into a work of eco-art. And not only that – the garden itself was recyclable, designed to be transported to an inner-city sink estate after the show.

As Lyric got closer she could see Philippe in the middle of the garden, surrounded by visitors and – was that a journalist? Suddenly, from behind the exhibit, a man appeared carrying a boom mic. Philippe was being interviewed for television! Lyric's heart leapt with excitement. Could this mean he'd won a medal? It was one thing being a celebrity gardener, but Lyric knew that fame meant nothing to

Philippe. Recognition of his talent was far more important to him, and what higher accolade could there be than a Chelsea Flower Show medal? Again, she kicked herself for missing the announcement.

As she got closer, Lyric slowed down, not wishing to disturb his interview. She watched as Philippe animatedly described his garden and his inspirations.

'How can you improve on the beauty of nature?' he was saying. 'All I, as a gardener, can hope to do is enhance it by careful choice of colour and positioning, and under-standing of what works where. Most importantly, I can help preserve it for generations to come and –'

He suddenly caught sight of Lyric watching him and ran across to her, oblivious of the film crew trying to follow him.

'*Chérie*! I got a gold!' he said excitedly, picking her up and swinging her around.

Lyric shrieked in excitement. 'A gold?!'

'I know,' said Philippe, eyes shining. 'My first Chelsea medal is a gold! This is the best possible news we could have for Broughton Hall and your father's dream for the gardens there. Everyone will want to see them now!'

Suddenly remembering the television cameras, he turned back to them proudly.

'And this – this is my inspiration. Ladies and gentlemen, my fiancée – the beautiful Miss Lyric Charlton!'

~

'Morning, *chérie*.' Lyric felt Philippe kiss her softly on the shoulder and she turned to him, his green eyes warm and loving. She screwed up her eyes and opened them again, and he laughed softly.

'What is that for?' He kissed her again, this time on the tip of her nose.

'I was just checking that this – you – is for real.' She giggled and snuggled into his embrace. The distance that circumstances – not to mention George's illness – had foisted upon them had gone. The excitement over Philippe's Chelsea win, their conspiratorial planning for their new arrival, the return of their passionate lovemaking – once again, they weren't just lovers, they were best friends, too.

Philippe smiled again. 'Of course it's for real, *chérie*. And soon there will be someone else to share it with us. Forever.'

Lyric let the joyful reality sink in again.

'There's only one problem,' said Philippe in her ear.

Lyric looked at him, concerned. 'What's that?'

Philippe felt under the duvet, pulled out her left arm and indicated the diamond sparkling on her wedding finger.

'Another important event might have to wait a little while. Unless you want to walk down the aisle heavy with child.' His eyes twinkled at her.

Lyric smiled and cuddled back into him. 'I wouldn't care how I walked down the aisle, as long as you were at the other end,' she mumbled.

'Me neither,' said Philippe, pulling himself away suddenly. '*Chérie*, I have to get on.' Lyric looked at him questioningly. 'The Chelsea win has only increased the focus on Broughton Hall!' explained Philippe. 'With your father out of action, there's even more to do. I am determined to succeed, for his sake if nothing else. And with everything that's going on, let us just say, it's not exactly going smoothly. It needs all the help it can get – and that's not going to happen if I stay here in bed with you much longer.'

'Off you go, then,' said Lyric, snuggling back down into the warmth of the duvet. 'Baby needs some more sleep. So I might just have a little doze, too, before I get up myself.'

From her sleepy daze, she heard him laugh softly as he pulled on his clothes and padded out of the room. Her Philippe. Their baby. Despite everything, life was good . . .

~

Two hours later, after a quick shower and – unable to face the breakfast buffet of Moroccan pastries proudly presided over by her mother in the dining room – a snatched espresso standing with Mrs Gunners in the kitchen, Lyric resisted the urge to stay down below stairs amidst the hustle and bustle of the servants' quarters, and stole back to her room. She'd cut down on her caffeine intake massively over the past few weeks but, she supposed, she should swap even that delicious first coffee of the day for the decaffeinated variety. She closed the door gently behind her and walked over to the ancient wardrobe, pulling open its heavy wooden door carefully as though she would be overheard if it made so much as a creak. From the top shelf, she pulled down a paper shopping bag, the type used by the most upmarket boutiques, and sat on her bed, looking at it longingly. Carefully, she reached inside for its contents – the palest lemon tissue paper covering folds of baby-soft lemon cashmere. She held up the first item – a tiny Babygro – and then the second – a delicate matching cardigan – and stroked her cheeks with the cloud-like wool. She knew it was tempting fate, but as soon as she'd discovered she was pregnant, she hadn't been able to resist just one baby buy. She'd promised Philippe she'd now wait until their first scan before she bought any more – but, until then, at least she had this exquisite little set to drool over.

Lyric folded the clothes back up thoughtfully and, for what already seemed like the hundredth time that day, let her mind roam to how their life might change over the next few months. It was a welcome distraction from everything else, and anyway, there were so many plans to put in place.

Replacing the shopping bag, Lyric heard a noise outside and moved over to the window, from which she saw Constance – elaborately dressed in some kind of exotically coloured sari – leading a trail of what looked like Bedouin shepherds across the drive and towards the path that led through the gardens, over the meadow and out towards the folly. Lyric smiled to herself. What crazy project was her mother working on now?

Sensing a blanket of quiet descend over the house, Lyric slipped down the stairs into the music room and over to the ancient baby grand piano, nestled in a bay window overlooking the formal gardens Philippe had worked so hard to restore. She could see him now, walking slowly with her father in his battered old Barbour jacket, no doubt checking on progress and discussing planting plans for that summer.

Lyric opened the keyboard and ran her finger lightly along the ivory keys. Since she had stopped going out so much and making public appearances, she had started to enjoy music again. She was playing with a quality, a lightness of touch and a depth of feeling she'd never before experienced. Not only that, but she was also writing again – songs that she was never sure would reach the ears of anyone other than her closest family, but songs she loved playing.

Now, Lyric began to play and, as she lost herself in the notes, she thought of how ironic it was that she sometimes still worried about her and Philippe, even when they were about to embark on their happiest time yet. Philippe's occasional aloofness, his air of mystery – particularly regarding his harrowing time in the military, during national service – were part and parcel of the man she'd fallen in love with. She and Philippe didn't own each other, after all. What fun would that be – and since when had Lyric Charlton ever fallen for a complete pushover? In her own way, she was as unreadable and unpredictable as he was. And her worries were probably only what any woman would feel as she embarked on the first vulnerable steps of the most important journey of her life, the product of the jumble of hormones helping create that little bean growing inside her . . .

A twinge in her abdomen made Lyric grimace. Surely not the return of her morning sickness? She stopped playing and waited for the familiar lurch of nausea. But there was nothing. Maybe she should have had some breakfast? Now she had someone else to think about, she should really start looking after herself. From now on, she must make sure she was doing everything she could for the baby.

She stood up, softly closing the lid of the piano, and headed off in search of something to eat. Mrs Gunners would no doubt have something delicious – and non-Moroccan – in the kitchen. Lyric would just have to feign a hangover or something so as not to raise any suspicions. Mrs Gunners always tutted disapprovingly at Lyric's refusal to eat breakfast. The last thing Lyric needed before she made her pregnancy public was Mrs Gunners guessing and giving the game away.

Her stomach twinged again – actually, it was more of a cramp – as she strolled through Broughton Hall's corridors, and Lyric stopped to catch her breath. An uneasy feeling swept over her.

Just then Lyric felt another, more violent pain. It was like the worst kind of menstrual cramp, an all-consuming, evil stabbing. She sank to the floor and leaned over, gasping for breath, and let out a low moan as another pain overtook the last one. Sweat suddenly rushed out of every pore, and her chiffon blouse clung to her like a second skin.

'Lyric! Lyric, are you OK?' She heard Edward's voice calling distantly from somewhere else in the house, and the thundering of feet as he careered downstairs. 'Lyric, where are you?' His voice faded as if he had taken the wrong direction.

Another pain made Lyric cry out this time.

'Lyric! My God – what on earth's the matter?'

As the pain took hold yet again, Lyric grabbed a chair leg and tried to drag herself up. She was like a lame dog, unable to move or answer, and as she looked up in desperation she saw Edward rushing back along the corridor towards her. He was half dressed, pulling his dressing gown around him.

'I sensed something and I knew – Lyric, what's wrong? Can I help?'

Edward held out his arms and Lyric reached out, looking up imploringly into his face, the mirror image of her own, as another excruciating pain overwhelmed her. She opened her mouth to ask for help but no words came out, only another cry – this time a heart-rending wail as she felt a dampness between her legs and the devastating certainty of exactly what was wrong. This time, he couldn't help. No one could.

~

Lyric splashed her face roughly and reached her hand out for the towel Philippe was holding forlornly in his hands. He'd woken her up a few moments ago and for a second – a sweet split second – she'd thought she was still pregnant. But then, not only had the reality hit her like a breeze block, but her dream from last night had also rushed back to haunt her. She'd been losing her baby, again, and she'd been trying, trying so desperately to push it back inside her, but it wouldn't go back. It wouldn't go back. And, of course, it hadn't gone back. That was why she was here, in the Portland Hospital. She closed her eyes as she caught sight of the bunch of lilies by her bedside. Similar bunches, she knew, would be decorating the other plush private rooms along this corridor, bought from the flower shop downstairs by caring friends and family. But, unlike hers, those other flowers would be accompanied by congratulations cards, the contented exhaustion of having given birth, and a sleeping baby in a cot next to the bed.

The reality that she really had lost her baby was as raw as ever, and, try as she might, she couldn't erase the horror.

'I don't need to convalesce, Philippe, I've told you. So I've lost my baby. So do thousands – millions – of women every year. There's no point sitting around moping about it, is there? I'm better placed keeping myself busy – helping children who have managed to get themselves born and—'

Her voice caught on the last words, and Philippe leapt to his feet to embrace her. He hugged her to him, and Lyric felt tears well up. She steadied herself and felt her body go rigid with the effort. After a moment, Philippe released her and led her back to the bed. She clambered back in reluctantly, and he tucked the sheets around her legs, sat down next to her and looked at her compassionately.

'*Chérie*, this is hard for both of us. It's not just you who has lost your baby. *We* have lost *our* baby.'

He stared at her, and she felt herself wobble under his gaze. She steeled herself.

'I know, Philippe. And that is why I have to be strong. For both of us. So we can come to terms with this, and move on from it.'

'But to be strong, you have to rest,' he insisted. 'For me, Lyric. Your charity will wait another few days. Goodness knows you have given enough of yourself to keep them going while you recover from . . .'

'Philippe, I've told you, I'm not ill,' snapped Lyric. 'But right now, I feel like there's six sides of a dice and I've only got five of them. I need to put myself back together, Philippe, and the best way I know to do that is to keep myself busy.'

Philippe sighed and looked away. Something in Lyric yearned to hold out her arms to him, to stop pushing him away and instead to bring him back to her, but something else wouldn't allow her to. First, she needed a little time on her own, to deal with this. But she knew she would need him. So badly . . .

'You know, *chérie*, there are ways of looking at this,'

said Philippe. His voice was a little harder, more detached now, and again Lyric's heart twanged against her ribcage. Still, she kept her distance.

'What do you mean?' she said, her voice sounding strangled even to her own ears.

He cleared his throat carefully. When he spoke, it was slow, deliberate. 'Well, you know, maybe it was meant to be.'

Lyric felt herself go cold. 'What?'

Philippe looked up at her from lowered eyelids. 'Well, Fate takes its hand in unfathomable ways.' He cleared his throat again. 'And, maybe, it was meant to be.'

'Why on earth would Fate wish this on anyone?' asked Lyric. What was he trying to say? That they'd lost their baby because they weren't meant to be? Because the pregnancy wasn't right? *They* weren't right?

'Well, maybe there was something wrong that we didn't know about, and Fate is paving the way for something better. Another pregnancy, this time one that works.'

'One that *works*?' repeated Lyric, wincing at his clumsy use of words. 'And what makes you think we are ever going to do anything that *works*, ever again?'

Philippe looked at her, dumbfounded, shaking his head in confusion, and she stared back, holding back the tears that threatened to tumble down her cheeks – for their lost baby; for their relationship, in which a mile-wide chasm had suddenly appeared; for her.

~

'So I've decided I'm going to whisk you off, to get away from it all – to the Bahamas!' announced Crispin with a flourish. He was half hanging out of the hospital room window, having a surreptitious cigarette. 'Think of it as an impromptu hen night, if you like. It's just what you need.'

Lyric grimaced. 'Yep, it's exactly what I feel like,' she said slowly, setting aside the hospital's mouth-watering menu with a sigh. She couldn't eat. Still couldn't think about anything but her lost baby. She placed the menu card on top of the Agent Provocateur bag Crispin had brought 'to cheer her up'. Dear Crispin. He meant well, but here she was, still in paper knickers, and a Swarovski crystal thong wasn't really high on her list of priorities. 'Except it's Treeva's villa on Harbour Island we're talking about – and you're the hen, right?'

'Well of course, sweedie, what did you think?' said Crispin, genuinely perplexed. 'It's me who's getting married! You should know – you are the best man, remember?'

Sensitivity had never been Crispin's strong point – only he could visit on the pretext of cheering her up and turn it in to an invitation to his own hen night, totally disregarding her own forthcoming wedding.

The door opened to reveal one of the seemingly endless procession of immaculately uniformed, smiling nurses, and Crispin leapt back into the room, flicking his cigarette away and shutting the window with a bang. He gave the nurse a winning smile, and she eyed him with suspicion.

'Has someone been smoking in here?'

Lyric and Crispin shook their heads solemnly.

'Miss Charlton, I suggest you take a stroll later on,' the nurse continued officiously, taking note of the discarded menu. 'After you've had something to eat, that is. You need to get your strength up.' Lyric nodded. This might be one of the UK's most exclusive hospitals and more akin to a five-star hotel, but the approach to care was no-nonsense. The nurse smiled at Lyric encouragingly, and Lyric attempted one back. She had no intention of wandering around the hospital and hearing the tiny cries of babies from all the other rooms. The nurse, however, seemed satisfied with the response and she nodded and disappeared again.

'I thought we'd invite Laura and, obvs, Treeva, too,' continued Crispin smoothly as the door shut behind the nurse. 'Make it a real girlie holiday. We can make plans for the wedding – and get a tan for my other hen nights. It'll be just the ticket to take your mind off all this other horrible stuff.'

He gave a theatrically camp shudder, and again Lyric almost smiled.

'OK, Crisp, you win. Let's go to the Bahamas.' She climbed out of bed and wandered over to the window, wincing as she saw a family go out hugging a bundle of blankets. Leaving by the front door, as it should be; not smuggled in the back door, by the bins, as she'd been when she was admitted – and how she'd be discharged, too, no doubt. There were always so many paps outside the front, and she had no desire to see her very private tragedy splashed all over the papers.

'Fabulous, sweedie!' he exclaimed. 'Now, there are some flights from Gatwick next week . . .'

'Crispin!' exclaimed Lyric. 'Now is not the time to start reciting flight times at me! Why don't you provisionally book whichever you think works best, speak to the others, and we can plan it properly when I'm out of here?'

'Ok, sweedie, keep your hair on,' said Crispin smoothly. 'Leave it with me. Although, I must say, I've never heard of the bride having to book her own hen night.'

'Crisp!' warned Lyric. 'There aren't many brides who get to have several hen nights – including an all-expenses-paid one in the Bahamas!'

'True enough,' agreed Crispin. 'I'll get on the blower as soon as I leave here . . . and then I'll get on the phone to the others.'

'Crispin, you are incorrigible,' said Lyric, and smiled wanly. Maybe he was right. Maybe she did need a complete change of scene. It would certainly give Philippe a break from her moping around – and give her a chance to put everything in perspective.

What she didn't tell Crispin, and what she hadn't told Philippe, was that her miscarriage wasn't the only thing she was dealing with. Although when she lost her baby it had felt to her that she'd lost everything that had ever mattered, something remained.

That inescapable feeling of dread.

Could yet another tragedy be waiting around the corner?

Seven

Climbing over the stile into the Skanktons' oversized front-lawn-turned-eighteen hole private golf course, Lyric took in a deep breath of sweet evening air, heavy with the scent of honeysuckle from the hedgerows that bordered the grounds of Broughton Hall. In stark contrast, the land surrounding the Skanktons' manor house was divided up by white painted fences, behind which fine racing stock grazed lazily. She loved this time of year – everything felt so new and fresh, like it had just been steam cleaned. She wished she felt like that herself. In fact, she wished she could just turn around and run off around the grounds of Broughton Hall, instead of going to the Skanktons' mock-Tudor pile to eat a glorified ready meal with a bunch of jumped-up bullies. But she'd promised her father she'd be there – tomorrow was a big race meeting for Roger's yard – and, knowing how worried frail George was about her since her miscarriage, she wasn't about to give him any more cause for concern. She looked around to ensure there were no late golfers about to knock her out with a stray ball, and carried on across the lawn, up the drive and past the banana-yellow

Lamborghini, the black Hummer with even blacker windows, and the pink Bentley – all showcasing personalized number plates – and up to the imposing double doors that sat behind four bright white marble pillars and two stone lions breathing real fire.

Erratically parked to the right of the pillars was a swiftly abandoned golf buggy, and Lyric had to sidestep a bag of clubs protruding from the back of it. She rang the huge electronic bell, and steeled herself for the rendition of the National Anthem that it usually played. Instead, Cliff Richard's 'Congratulations' pealed out. Lyric looked around in alarm – this was a candid camera moment if ever there was one . . .

Instead, the door swung open to reveal a blast of central heating – even on such a mild evening – and Roger Skankton, dressed in a black-and-white dogstooth blazer, high-waisted jeans and a white shirt, his Hollywood grin clamped around a fat cigar.

'Lyric! My dear. Good to see you. Come in, come in. George said you'd opted for the healthy option of walking. All helps, eh, in getting you back on your feet.' He put his arm around her, pulled her in through the door and clapped her back so hard she was nearly jet-propelled forward through the house. 'Though guess you're used to it now, eh? Getting over things, that is.'

Lyric smiled feebly.

'Hi, Roger.'

Roger looked ostentatiously over her shoulder. 'No

Philippe, eh? Oh, that's a different nationality entirely, eh? Philippe-eh?'

He stared at Lyric manically, willing her to get the poor attempt at a joke, and she gave him a half smile.

'Philippe is busy working,' she said quickly – too quickly – but Roger was too self-obsessed to notice her mistake. The truth was, Philippe loathed visiting the Skanktons even more than she did, and would rather give his eye teeth than spend an evening at their home – or, it seemed at the moment, with her.

'Well, his loss is another man's gain, eh, girl? Come through – we're all in the conservatory.'

Lyric followed him through the shag-pile carpeted rooms, all crammed full of antique furniture, the latest technological gadgets, and the most luxurious of textiles, and tried not to sweat. It was so hot! As always, she made an effort not to marvel at the wealth on display in each of the sumptuous rooms they passed through – everything that money could buy, coupled with bad taste of Olympic proportions. And horseshoes. Everywhere. On the walls, as coasters on tables, hanging on every interior stable-style door.

'Here she is!' announced Roger as they turned a corner and walked through some internal French doors. Lyric tried not to baulk as another wall of heat hit her. The Skanktons' conservatory was a vast glass structure with an Apex roof and comprised a horseshoe-shaped swimming pool, a tiki-themed bar and stools, surrounded by a collection of lounge chairs, sunbeds and plastic garden furniture. Her father, in a wheelchair, and Angie Skankton, perched incongruously on a porcelain temple stool, sat beside what looked like an upturned barrel, sipping psychedelic cocktails that groaned under the weight of fruit garnishes and paper parasols. When her father caught sight of Lyric he put down his drink and turned towards her with outstretched arms.

'Darling, you're finally here!'

'I was only a few moments behind you all,' she said with a sheepish grin. She looked over his shoulder at the rest of the gathered clans.

Edward and Darren were a few feet apart from them, sitting on tall stools at the bar, heads close together over a couple of bottled beers as if plotting something. Lyric waved over at them, pleased to be able to avoid Darren's predictably slimy greeting.

To their left, her mother, resplendent in a 1970s Biba macramé dress – which, thanks to her lifelong regime of pills and shakes and her enviable figure, she was just about getting away with – had reclined a lounge chair to an almost horizontal angle, and was sipping on a two-tone cocktail. 'Hi, darling!' she trilled, moving her head slightly to one side, then returned to her original position without waiting for a reply. Further around the pool, a young woman with long blonde hair extensions lay relaxing in a silver bikini, on two furry cushions, under an orange sunlamp. In the pool, another young woman with matching extensions –

this time brunette – was busy doing breaststroke widths of the pool.

'Hi, Kimberley,' called Lyric. The girl under the lamp turned her head and waved lazily, not even bothering to remove her sun goggles. 'Hi, Cheryl!'

Cheryl, the youngest Skankton, waved cheerily from the pool.

'One more width, then it's dinner,' called Roger amiably. 'Drink, Lyric?'

As if on cue, Angie got up hurriedly and scuttled behind the bar, ready to serve up another concoction.

'Oh, just a Perrier, please,' said Lyric distractedly. Her smart Houlihan jeans, white tee and Chanel bouclé jacket had seemed the perfect look for a casual dinner with friends, but, in the cloying humidity of the Skanktons' conservatory, she was beginning to prickle with sweat.

'Are you sure, Lyric?' said Angie. 'I would have thought you'd be making the most of being able to drink, after . . .'

There was an uncomfortable silence as Lyric bit back her retort. As if any drink would compensate for having lost her baby.

'A Perrier will be fine, Angie, thank you,' she repeated firmly, and then perched on the edge of a sunbed.

Kimberley suddenly rolled expertly out from under the sunlamp and stood up, and Lyric saw that it wasn't in fact the sunlamp that was orange – it was Kimberley herself. She was a tall girl, with a slim figure honed by the gym but which looked primed to bulk up in later years, and with the tiny pot belly that hinted at a junk food diet laced with too much booze. Nevertheless, with her fluorescent tan, long tumbling hair, full-on make-up and perky fake boobs, Kimberley made a strikingly sexy figure in the best tradition of an Essex glamour model.

She stretched languorously, showing off a diamond belly stud, and then bent down to pick up her cerise-pink Juicy Couture tracksuit. Behind her, the two cushions suddenly leapt up, revealing themselves to be two peach-coloured chow chows, black tongues panting, fluffy coats almost visibly wilting in the heat.

'Peachie! Schnappie! Calm down!' chastised Kimberley, as she pulled on her velour tracksuit bottoms and zipped the hooded top up over her bikini. She leaned down and let Peachie lick her face. 'Oooh, kissy wissy! So cutey wutey!'

Lyric recoiled at the thought of getting that close to the notoriously smelly breath of one of the designer dogs. 'Don't you want to give him a Polo first?' she wondered out loud.

There was a splash, and Lyric turned to see Cheryl pulling herself out of the pool, modelling an elaborate cut-away Versace swimsuit. The eighteen months between the Skankton sisters was about all that had separated them throughout their lives. Now aged twenty-five to her sister's twenty-seven, Cheryl sported the same rangy figure as Kimberley, heavy head of hair extensions and identikit boob implants. They might all be in an episode of *The Only Way is Essex*, thought Lyric. These girls must have been breastfed collagen in place of milk. The only real difference between them was their social ambitions. Whilst Kimberley kept a copy of the Premiership Rich List by her bed and hankered after a WAG lifestyle complete with blinging footballer boyfriend or rich racing-mogul husband, after a one-night stand with the party-mad son of a hereditary peer, Cheryl was more of a Debrett's girl and aspired to climb up a social class or two and 'land Prince Harry'.

Now, Cheryl – a few shades paler than Kimberley, and none the less attractive for it – dried herself with a pale pink towel and reached for her own coral-coloured Juicy Couture tracksuit. Little wonder, thought Lyric absently, that together with their brother Darren's penchant for salmon Fred Perry tees and his own Skankton Jr neon glow, the siblings had been christened the 'Three Little Piggies' amongst the horseracing circles they all moved in.

'How's Treeva?' asked Cheryl.

'She's good,' replied Lyric, referring to her oldest school friend, as the girls nodded reverently. The two Skankton girls held Treeva's own particular version of trash-glam in unashamed awe, and had successfully modelled themselves on her distinctive sense of 'style'. 'In fact, we're off to the Bahamas next week.'

'Oooh,' cooed both girls in unison, each absently scratching behind a different dog's ear.

A butler appeared in the room and spoke discreetly into Roger's ear. He stood up and opened his arms magnanimously.

'So, my Lord, Lady and – erm, other ladies.' The group groaned politely as Roger beamed through his regular 'funny'. 'Dinner, I believe, is served.'

'OK – I've just got to go to the toilet,' said Cheryl, and scurried off.

'Leave that,' reprimanded Roger, as the group stood up and Angie fussed around trying to clear away the glasses. 'We have maids for that, remember?' He looked around at the Charltons mockingly. 'Honestly, you'd think she was born in a barn, our Angie, eh? Oh! Silly me! She was! Eh? Eh?' Roger roared with laughter at his own joke, and, giving her father a 'look', Lyric took the handles of his wheelchair and pushed him through to dinner.

~

'Well, you could always try inviting him to a soirée here,' suggested Lyric half-heartedly, trying to give Cheryl advice on ensnaring her latest beau.

'Got you,' nodded Kimberley approvingly. 'A dinner party – told you, Cheryl.'

'You can't beat a dinner party,' trilled Constance from across the table. Her eyes were overly bright and she winked ostentatiously at the waiter clearing away her untouched chocolate dessert. 'My, my, aren't you just the young stud,' she said, nearly causing Lyric to choke on her instant coffee.

Lyric shook her head at an After Eight mint and visualized the regulation standard school dinner she had just endured. 'How about a drinks party?'

'Oooh! What a fabulous idea,' squealed Cheryl. 'A cocktail party!'

Another image, this time of the lurid cocktails that had been served earlier that evening, popped into Lyric's horrified head.

'How about a champagne reception?' she suggested weakly. She looked across the table to where Edward was still deep in conversation with Darren. They were an incongruous pair – Edward with his fair, honey-blond hair and fine-boned features, and Darren with his thick-set face and neck and close-cropped style. She'd hardly spoken to her brother all evening; and, whilst she was glad he was making friends, something about the way they were plotting was making her uneasy. Although, in a way, Darren's love of the high life was his saving grace, Lyric feared that if he were ever sober enough to use his conniving brain to put his get-richer-quicker schemes into action, he might actually end up doing some damage with it.

'More coffee, Lyric?'

She turned with a smile to Angie, who was hovering over her shoulder with a silver tea pot.

'No thanks, Angie. I'm all done here.'

~

'Come on, Edward, it's still early doors. Stay for another couple of jars and a game of pool. I haven't shown you the yard yet!'

'There won't be anything to see now – it's pitch black!'

laughed Edward, aware that his family were all sitting around the table pointedly wanting to go home – in particular Lyric, who had taken charge of the car keys earlier in preparation for a quick getaway.

'Mate, there is ALWAYS something to see in the yard,' winked Darren with a suggestive sneer.

'You stay here and explore, son,' said George approvingly, entirely missing the double entendre. 'About time you got to grips with a racing yard. Would've taken you around it myself earlier if I was up to it.'

Edward smiled nervously and looked back at his family. He was keen to stay, if only to enjoy the company of someone his own age. Much as he loved his new family, and relished the closeness of his relationship with Lyric, he missed the banter of the old mates he'd grown up with.

'Look, if you want to stay, stay – you'll just have to find your way back across the fields,' said Lyric in exasperation. 'But make up your mind one way or the other – I told Philippe we'd be back ages ago.'

Edward smiled sheepishly at his sister. 'All right, if you really don't mind – I will,' he said finally. 'I won't be back late.'

'Byyeeee!' called Lyric, already halfway out of the door. 'Thank you, Angie, we've had a wonderful time, as always.'

Darren stood up, grabbed his beer and downed it. 'Well, mate, let's go. I'll get us another couple of cold ones and let's go check on the fillies!' He gave Edward a lewd wink.

Cheryl offered Edward a dazzling smile and sidled up to him. 'Can I come?'

'No, you can't,' snapped Darren from the drinks trolley. He slung an arm casually around Edward's shoulder and propelled him expertly out of the door. 'When I say fillies, obvs, the girls are, like, totes out of bounds. You got me?' he said, his brotherly protectiveness only a shade short of thuggish.

Edward looked at his new friend out of the corner of his eye. Was Darren *threatening* him?

'They're not really my type,' he laughed. His voice had raised an octave or so with nervousness, and he cleared his throat to lower it again.

Immediately, Darren pulled his arm away and squared up to Edward aggressively. 'Why, what's wrong with them? They're beautiful girls, my sisters.'

Edward stepped back, hands up in mock surrender. 'There's nothing wrong with them!' he protested. 'Quite the opposite. They *are* beautiful. But I'm not going to make a move on them – it's not my style. And anyway, I've kind of got my eye on someone already.'

Darren replaced his arm and pulled Edward to him in a gesture of reinstated comradeship.

'Don't tell me you're a one-woman man, surely?' he teased, holding open a back door and gesturing him through. 'Not in your position, anyhow. Just found out you're the heir of a massive fortune like your Dad's, and you're limiting yourself to one chick? I don't believe a word of it.'

Edward laughed. 'Well, no, not really,' he said, following Darren through the dark of the yard. It was eerie with only the sound of their footsteps, the occasional harrumph of a racehorse, and the clip of a hoof against stable floor.

There was a loud barking from one of stables.

'All right, boy, shush-shush,' called Darren. He turned to Edward with a smile that revealed a flash of gold molar.

'That's my Doberman, Rolex.' He stared at Edward, grinning. ''Cos he's a watchdog. Geddit?'

Edward laughed. 'Nice one.'

'Yep. Here.' Darren fumbled in what seemed like a broom cupboard and, with the flick of a switch, the yard was bathed in light. The two horses looking out of their stables turned away at the sudden brightness, and Edward himself blinked at the assault on his retinas.

The 'yard' was actually two rows of smart wooden stables facing each other, separated by red-brick paving. Most of the top stable doors were open to reveal whitewashed walls inside.

'So just how many of these are my father's?' asked Edward.

Darren turned to him, wide-eyed. 'You seriously don't know?'

Edward stared back at him. What was it about these racing people that made him feel so bloody *stupid*?

'No, I don't,' he said honestly. 'Why would I? I've never

been here before. Never asked my dad. How many race-horses he owns wasn't one of my priorities when I first found him after thirty years in suburban wilderness. Where I was very happy,' he added swiftly, before the look of pity could fully form on Darren's face. And why did they *have* to be so damn patronizing about his upbringing all the time?

'Well, there's one very good reason why you would, in my book,' said Darren decisively, walking over to one of the boxes and peering in expertly.

Edward raised a questioning eyebrow.

Darren turned round with a flourish. 'Because they're all going to be yours one day!' he announced, holding his hands up in triumph. 'So, er, how much do you stand to get, then?'

Edward looked at him, wondering if he'd heard correctly. 'You what?'

Darren sniggered. 'Your inheritance, mate. How much?'

Edward shrugged. 'I dunno. Haven't asked.' Why would he? He'd just found a family, not a goldmine. He shifted uncomfortably from one leg to another, feeling a little stupid in spite of himself.

Darren looked at him incredulously. 'Mate, you've got to sort that out. Mind you, can't see George being that forthcoming with it, can you? Not like my old man. He's got it sorted, has Rog. Laid it all out for me, keeps me posted and lets me dip into it whenever I want. That way, there's never any friction, see? Georgie boy could learn something from him, I reckon.'

Edward nodded vaguely. Darren had a point.

'Probably too worried what the consequences might be,' guffawed Darren. 'Too much at stake, eh?'

Edward stared at him closely. He'd met men like Darren before, of course, all mouth and no trousers. They were there in every walk of life, larging it, paving their way with charm. But with Darren, he got the feeling there was no 'stop' button – he had every means available to indulge his recklessness, and no reason to curb it.

'What do you mean?'

'Well, there has to be a way of getting Georgie boy to part with some millions before he carks it, right? Because he sure as hell ain't giving it up to you spontaneously, is he?' Darren leaned in closer. 'All I'm saying, mate, is I know people. Right?' He laughed loudly and Edward laughed along with him, not quite sure where the joking finished and reality started – but determined that if he ever found out, he wouldn't be on the wrong side of the joke.

'Oh – all right, Nat?' Darren turned again as Thumper's groom appeared out of the tack room at the end of the right-hand row of stables and stopped in surprise at the sight of them. 'What are you still doing here?'

'Thumper was a bit restless. I was worried about him,' she said with a shrug.

'Thumper? That's my sister's horse,' said Edward, unable to make out the young woman's features from where she was standing in the shadows. All he could see was her silhouette, backlit by the light spilling out from the tack room. It was enough to establish she had a curvaceous body, perfectly built for jodhpurs.

'I think he's got all excited thinking he's going to be racing tomorrow,' said the young woman fondly. 'He hasn't got a clue it's not his turn, bless him. You must be the famous Edward, then.' She stepped out of the shadows and looked him directly in the eye. Her look was partly shy, partly challenging. Edward grinned flirtatiously. She reminded him of the girls he'd grown up with on the estate – bashfully playful, trying to cover up their natural shyness by self-consciously attempting to compete with the boys' affected swagger.

'Famous, eh? So what have you heard about me?'

She blushed and looked down. 'Only that you know as much about horses as I do about fine wines,' she half mumbled.

Darren laughed. 'Oh, come on, Natalie, do me a favour. I bet the yard has been rife with gossip over the reappearance of the good-looking young heir to Broughton Hall.'

Edward stared at Darren in surprise. What was it about money that seemed to infect everyone who came into contact with it with an element of bitterness, no matter how well-off they were? He'd done it himself, almost instantly begrudging his own family the years of happiness they'd had before he'd found them again, when those years he'd been apart from them had been happy and fulfilling – certainly giving him no reason to regret them.

Natalie shrugged, and Edward looked at her with

renewed interest. The remark about the wine had piqued his curiosity. Something about her being an ingénue in a world full of jaded experts resonated deep inside him.

'Perhaps less of the "good-looking", Darren,' Edward said. 'Natalie doesn't seem that impressed, anyway,' he teased gently.

She looked up at him defiantly. 'It's not my place to have an opinion either way,' she retorted. 'I'm just here for the horses. So if you ever want to meet them properly, let me know. Right now, though, I've got an appointment with my bed. I'm due out of it again in five hours to get them all ready for the race meeting.'

She walked between Edward and Darren, and they turned to watch her disappear into the darkness.

'Great arse,' said Darren thoughtfully.

Edward turned to him sharply. 'Don't tell me you've . . . ?' Inexplicably, he felt himself tense at the thought of Darren and Natalie together.

Darren sneered. 'What, frigid Natalie? Do me a favour. Thinks she's above it all.' After a moment's thought, Darren laughed and nudged Edward. 'Had the rest of 'em, though!' He folded his arms and stared into space, nodding thoughtfully. 'I tell you what, mate, if you manage to get Natalie in the sack you'll get almost legend status in our shagging stakes.'

Edward laughed nervously. 'What shagging stakes?'

'Exactly that,' sniggered Darren. He looked at Edward, waiting expectantly for a reaction. 'Team Shag.' Still,

Edward didn't react. Darren ploughed onwards. 'It currently only has two members – me and my mate Prince Abu Rhuba. His dad's King Abu Rhuba – you probably met him at the races the other week. Massive racehorse owner. Your father's main rival.'

Edward shrugged noncommittally, unable to recall exactly whom he had or hadn't met.

'Well, he's completely hilarious. His dad's worth millions, but Abu doesn't give a monkey's. He's only in it for the wine, women and song. Or, in his case, sex, drugs and rock 'n' roll.'

'Oh, right,' said Edward, unsure of how he felt about that. Someone had been born into that level of luxury, and chose to blow it on good times? On the other hand, why not? He did sound like a laugh . . .

'Anyhow, we shag out this lovely lifestyle we've been born into – and our father's credit cards, of course. But the main prize is something money can't buy – well, at least, it can, but it doesn't count if you do.'

Edward frowned at him. 'I'm sorry, I don't . . .'

'Women!' leered Darren. 'The main focus of Team Shag is our shagometer. We keep track, mate, compete – week by week, night by night, even hour by hour sometimes. You name it, we score it – and we score *on* it. But the ultimate trophy is a married woman.'

Edward laughed nervously. So *this* was how the other half lived. 'Right. Sounds pretty good to me. So when do I get to meet Abu?'

Darren put his arm around Edward's shoulder for a final time.

'Soon, mate, very soon. I'll make sure of that. Because the prince, mate – don't know how you're going to feel about this one – but he's going for gold.'

He took a self-satisfied swig of beer. His eyes, noticed Edward, had suddenly taken on the red, glazed expression of someone who was very drunk.

'How *I'm* going to feel about it?' repeated Edward, puzzled. 'What have I got to do with it?'

'The ultimate aim of our shagometer, mate – well, we've got someone in mind.' He looked knowingly at Edward. 'It's a woman, a very rich woman. Older, of course. And married. And looking like she puts out. But not only that, she's titled.'

'Oh?' said Edward, suddenly feeling nauseous. 'And who would that be?'

'Lady Constance Charlton,' said Darren proudly. 'Your mother.'

Eight

'. . . and a watermelon juice for madame.'

'Thank you, Frances.' Lyric smiled her thanks at the villa host as she passed the glass on to her friend and tried to ignore the stab of jealousy she felt that it wasn't her who had cause to order non-alcoholic drinks. She raised her own lychee martini to Laura, Crispin and Treeva, who were sitting with her on the terrace.

'To Crispin, and his most fabulous of hen *weeks*.'

'To Crispin!' cheered the other three. Lyric took a sip of her cocktail and looked around from under her floppy Philip Treacy sunhat, trying to relax. How lucky was she to be spending the week with her three best friends in the lap of luxury in a place that could only be described as paradise? If she couldn't get over her loss here – even if Philippe wasn't with her – then she was going to find it hard to get over it anywhere.

It wasn't just this place, she thought as she took in the view from her sun lounger beneath the flower-strewn pergola. The grand residence was set right on the beach, along with the grey slate infinity pool that emerged from within the house, stretching out until it appeared to reach the horizon and become part of the beach itself. Beyond the fine white sand was the shimmering aquamarine sea, turning pink in the setting sun, with a vintage Riva and a cigarette speedboat lazily bobbing up and down. It was more about being with people she loved, and who loved her. Making each other happy.

Of course, staying in five star surroundings helped. And this villa, with its airy colonial neatness, green topiary gardens, Swarovski bathrooms, red Elton John baby grand piano, sea-themed Tatyana Murray fibre-optic light sculptures and pool with underwater speakers, had to be one of the most luxurious in the world. She pushed aside the pang of longing for Philippe. Despite speaking to one another two or three times a day, she was missing him more than she could have imagined. Enforced absence was definitely helping to heal the wounds that her miscarriage had inflicted on their relationship, and she longed for the feel of his arms around her.

'God, I wish we could get married here,' said Crispin, draining his martini and waving for another.

'Well, why don't you?' offered Treeva.

'We'd never get enough guests to fly the distance,' said Crispin. 'I was thinking somewhere nearer to home – more like Klosters.'

'Well, that's lucky,' said Lyric, a telltale twinkle in her eye.

Crispin looked at her quizzically.

'Because one of your wedding presents from me . . . is to organize your wedding!' announced Lyric proudly. 'I know what you're like – you need taking in hand, Crisp. So you wanting to get married in Klosters helps, as I know it so well.'

Crispin clapped his hands together, drew a deep breath and stared at her with undisguised glee. 'A-mazing,' he finally breathed out. 'I'm seeing a real gay extravaganza. Like, Elton and David – one hundred times over!'

Lyric laughed and shook her head. 'Uh-uh. I don't think Gabe would thank me for allowing you to go down that path,' she cautioned, referring to Crispin's TV producer boyfriend. 'He'll want it to be beautiful, and gay in a classy way. Just like I suspect you do, really . . .'

Crispin turned to her reproachfully. 'Ohhhh . . .'

Lyric shook her head again. 'Uh-uh.'

He sighed theatrically and placed a hand on her knee. 'Well, you know, sweetie, I've always secretly wanted to be you – and I always love your style – so if you're paying, and Gabe's saying, I really should do as I'm told, shouldn't I?'

'Yes!' chorused Lyric, Treeva and Laura together.

'So what will it actually mean when you're married, Crisp?' said Treeva casually, adjusting her jewelled Melissa Odabash bikini around the diamond ring in her tummy button.

He stared at her. 'Funnily enough, it will mean we promise to remain exclusive to one another for the rest of our lives and are seen as husband and husband forever,' he said sarcastically. 'What on earth do you think it will mean?' He looked at Lyric, despairingly, and she giggled.

'I just wondered,' said Treeva. 'You know what I mean.'

Again, Crispin stared incredulously at her. 'No, Treeva, I don't.'

'Well, but it would have to be *open*, wouldn't it? You being – you, and all.'

'You mean me being me, or me being gay?' asked Crispin. 'God, sometimes you are so stupid, Treeva.'

'Wow, I'd forgotten how hot it is out here,' interrupted Laura, plucking at her Elizabeth Hurley kaftan fretfully, then lifting her long black hair off her neck and wafting it ineffectually. She looked around at the others – Lyric, cool in cotton pyjamas, Crispin in casual linen and Treeva still dressed in bikini and bling, as she had been all day. 'Isn't anyone else simply *boiling*?'

Treeva stretched noisily. 'It'll be your hormones,' she said airily, nodding at Laura's just-perceptible bump. Ever since she'd given birth to her own baby, a little boy named Fiddy, a couple of months before, Treeva had become the world's expert on pregnancy and childbirth. At first, it had made Lyric reluctant to confide in her about her own loss, not wishing to become another statistic or experience for Treeva to drop into every conversation, but she'd relented, equally not wanting it to become the elephant in the room during their week away. 'Have they made you really horny? I wanted sex for the whole of my first and second trimesters. And third, come to think of it.'

'Chance would be a fine thing,' snorted Laura. 'Robert's only spent about five nights in the same bedroom since I found out I was pregnant.' She looked around at the group and pasted a well-practised public smile on her face. 'He's been working late on his new job,' she added positively.

There was an uncomfortable silence as the group acknowledged the unspoken truth – that Robert was more likely to be working late on his addiction to prostitutes. 'Maybe you should have a dip in the pool,' said Treeva helpfully. 'The baby will love it.'

'Oh God, no, I've only just managed to get the frizz under control,' said Laura in horror, and Lyric looked at her sympathetically. Laura's unruly hair had blighted her childhood – as had her general appearance – and she now relied on weekly blowdries to smooth her jet-black tresses. It can't have been easy growing up with leggy Lyric – her natural metabolism on overdrive, her limbs honed from several months a year spent skiing. Five-foot-nothing Laura had spent her adolescence fighting a losing battle with puppy fat. But during the final year of school, she emerged from her fat-suit like a butterfly from its chrysalis, and ever since then her alabaster skin and dark brown eyes had been set off by the appearance of some striking cheekbones and an hourglass figure that drove men wild. Her looks – not to mention social status (as daughter of banking supremo Tiny Goldstein) soon saw her married to star city hedge-funder

Robert Hoffman. She'd embraced her new role as society wife, running charitable events for ladies who lunched – and liked to bitch. But the discovery of Robert's infidelity with a string of hookers, not to mention the funds he had embezzled to pay off huge gambling debts, had sent Laura's world – and that of their two young children, Max and Kitty – into a tailspin; and, although things were ostensibly back on track between them both, Lyric privately hoped that the new life growing inside her friend was the fruit of a genuinely repaired relationship and not the ubiquitous 'Band-Aid baby' so many people seemed to resort to. 'Anyhow, I'm scared some of the fake tan that's soaked off you will find its way onto my skin – and I'm not sure it's really "me".'

'I don't know what you're talking about,' said Treeva sulkily. 'I'm naturally olive-skinned. I tan easily with almost no sun protection whatsoever.'

The rest of them looked at her Tango-orange limbs and exchanged amused glances. Laura had a point – Treeva had been in and out of the pool so many times that day, it was in danger of turning brown from her frequent applications of fake tan! Lyric never stopped marvelling at how different she, Laura and Treeva all were – and how they'd stayed friends for so long. They even dressed differently, she thought – today, for example, Laura's floaty, casual glamour was offset by Treeva's sunshine glitz: metallic bikini, full make-up, an armful of jangling gold bangles and three heavy Givenchy gold chains around her neck. Even her

Cavalli sunglasses were encrusted in Swarovski crystals. The parts of Treeva that weren't soaking up the sunshine were all busy reflecting it, and she made a dazzling poolside decoration. Lyric, on the other hand, was lazing in the shade wearing her current favourite loungewear – Turnbull & Asser men's pyjamas, no make-up and bare feet.

Crispin had pulled on linen pants and an open-neck shirt for drinks, with white espadrilles to complete the carefully styled look.

'Talking of boiling, Treeva, what on earth are you doing still carrying that hot-water bottle around with you?' He pointed at the pink hot-water bottle that had barely left her side since taking off from the UK. 'It's over thirty degrees out here.'

Treeva looked at the bottle in surprise, as if she'd only just noticed it was there. 'This isn't just any hot-water bottle, Crispin,' she said as if speaking to a particularly truculent child. 'It's MY hot-water bottle, used for medicinal purposes as well as comfort. These days, I don't go anywhere without it.'

She gave him a 'look', as if to remind him about her stint in rehab the previous year.

'Like for what? Lyric didn't have one when she left rehab.' Crispin looked genuinely perplexed.

'Well, Lyric didn't have menstrual cramps, airsickness or chills,' replied Treeva vaguely.

'Not all at the same time, I didn't, no,' agreed Lyric.

Suddenly she was intrigued, too. 'But then, neither do you. Do you want me to take it through to your room?'

Treeva hugged it to her body possessively, nearly upsetting her martini glass. 'No! No need. I'm happier having it with me.'

Lyric reached out. 'Honestly, Tree, I don't mind.' She made as if to take it from Treeva, who snatched it out of her reach. As she did so, Treeva squeezed it so hard the stopper popped out and water flowed out of the top. She made a futile attempt to put the stopper back with one hand and mop up the spilled liquid with the other. Meanwhile, Crispin leaned forward casually, dipped his finger in the liquid and licked it expertly.

'Tree, that's not hot water you've got in there, is it?'

She scowled at him. Lyric's eyebrows shot up towards her hairline. 'Then what is it?'

Crispin tutted and leaned back, enjoying the moment of suspense.

'Crispin,' warned Treeva. 'Remember that late birthday present I promised you when we get back? Well, now's the time to decide if you really want it or not, because if you—'

'Oh, come on, Tree, we're all friends here, aren't we?' teased Crispin. 'After all, what does it matter to Lyric or Laura that you're carrying around a hot-water bottle with VODKA in it?'

'Oh, Tree,' said Laura, the disappointment palpable in her voice. 'I know you never said you were going to quit drinking completely after having Fiddy, but still . . .' Laura had undergone her own battle with alcohol during the previous year, when her life had started unravelling, and the prospect of anyone else showing signs of dependency seemed to make her immeasurably sad.

In an attempt to regain her lost self-esteem in front of the group, Treeva placed the hot-water bottle carefully on the table in front of her. 'I am not an alcoholic, nor do I ever plan to be,' she said carefully. 'But I gave up drink and drugs for the whole of my pregnancy, and now I'm just enjoying the odd indulgence now and again – OK?'

Lyric winced. 'Maybe. But if it's that innocent, why all the secrecy?'

'And if it's that innocent, you won't mind me tweeting about it,' said Crispin triumphantly, pulling his iPhone out of his pocket.

Now it was Lyric's turn to speak warningly. 'Crispin! We agreed, it's No Tweet Week!' She felt like a killjoy, but this week away was a refuge for her – the last thing Lyric wanted was to have it broadcast all across the world. Crispin, an aspiring TV presenter-turned-national treasure after last year's sex scandal involving Lyric's then-politician cousin Jacob, had been given his own chat show a few months before and was forever tweeting to his fan base, to the point of obsession, wanting to share every minute detail with the world. He was also overly precious about controlling his own image, and was so self-obsessed that he saw everyone as a potential stalker. Only that morning, strutting about on the villa's beach – private beach, at that – he'd objected to a woman taking pictures of her children because he thought the lens was pointing in his direction.

'Banned Twitter and everything else fun,' grumbled Treeva. 'Apart from booze, of course.'

'We banned Twitter and drugs, that's all!' protested Lyric, put out. 'And for good reason, too!'

Treeva sighed and rummaged in the fake Hermès bag she'd picked up that morning. 'Which reminds me. I wonder if I brought any Tampax with me?'

'It doesn't stop you getting texts, though,' said Crispin wickedly, not letting the Twitter conversation go.

Lyric shot him a look. 'Crisp . . .'

'Go on, they'll love it,' said Crispin.

She giggled mischievously. 'No. It's not fair.'

'Why?' asked Crispin.

Lyric smiled. 'Because I've had another text since.'

Crispin shot up in his lounger. 'Not true! Why didn't you say?'

Lyric smiled secretly. 'Because it's really embarrassing for him.'

'What text?' asked Laura. 'Why don't I even know about the first one?'

'Lyric's got a stalker,' said Crispin airily. 'She's pretending she hates it, but she loves it really.'

'Who's that, then?' said Treeva, still rummaging in her bag.

Lyric leaned over and nudged Crispin playfully. 'Shush,

you. You're being mean.' She turned to the girls. 'I met Andy Reynolds at a Sunny Street Hospital event.'

Treeva's ears pricked up at the name of the hard-man soap star. 'Oooh, I love him. As a bit of rough.'

'He's actually a very nice guy,' agreed Lyric diplomatically, eyes dancing.

'With stalker tendencies,' added Crispin. 'Go on, tell them. Better still, *show* them.'

'Oh, go on, Lyric,' urged Laura.

Lyric laughed in defeat, reaching for her phone. 'Well, I've told him I'm engaged to Philippe, told him categorically I'm not interested, but he keeps asking me out. And listen, even if I wasn't completely in love, I'd never be interested in him anyway – so *obviously* I keep saying no. But he's got a cameo in a play and, so that he wouldn't think I was a complete bitch, I said I'd go.'

'When will you learn that no means no, Lyric?' sighed Crispin.

'Well, I know that *now*,' she agreed. 'But I told him I was going to take Philippe with me, so I never dreamed . . . Anyhow, I couldn't go because of the – because I was in hospital. Of course, Andy didn't know that and so he tried to persuade me otherwise . . .'

'And sent her a nudey-rudey picture of himself,' finished Crispin quickly, to shrieks from Treeva and Laura. 'Show them, Lyric!'

Lyric flicked through the photos on her phone. 'It's not

the most flattering picture . . .' She found the photo of Andy – a burly ex-bouncer who was currently the heart-throb of the soap mags – naked, with nothing but a flat cap to cover his decency.

'And he thought that would persuade you?' marvelled Laura, laughing hysterically.

'Look – he's even got tan lines!' shrieked Treeva, point-ing at the marks where his T-shirt and shorts had been.

'Isn't it the most God-awful thing you've ever seen?' said Crispin. 'And you wonder why I'm gay. If that's the best straight men can do . . .'

'Don't be mean,' said Lyric, putting her phone away. 'I told you, he's a nice guy. Just not for me.'

'Still, it's the closest to sex we'll get this week,' grumbled Crispin, still clearly intent on reminding Lyric how much she was out to spoil their week.

'Oh, I don't know,' said Treeva, pulling out a Tampax and starting to unravel it. 'You can find sex anywhere in the world. I would have thought you'd have known that.' She gestured over to Frances. 'Could I have a cup of tea, please? Loose leaf, not a tea bag.'

Laura laughed. 'Treeva, even you wouldn't be able to find anyone to have sex with in this deserted oasis. Because you surely wouldn't mess with the villa staff?'

At that moment, a burly blond Swede with blown-up pecs strolled through the villa carrying a tiny mixed-race baby. Not for the first time, Lyric marvelled at the happy twist of fate that meant the baby's father had proven to be a little-known but well-meaning – if distant – LA rapper, rather than the caddish Ralph Conway, who was languishing in jail for his part in a drug-smuggling ring.

'Fiddy!' cooed Treeva, without bothering to get up. She fixed Laura with a knowing look. 'No need, sweedie. With a super-fit "manny" like Johann, you get it as employment benefits. At least, I'm working on it . . . Lyric, could you – I've got my hands full.'

Treeva winked at Laura as Lyric took Fiddy and cooed over him, trying to swallow the lump that appeared in her throat whenever she looked at him and thought how much she would have treasured her own child.

'Anyhow, I'll have you know I've got my eye on someone,' Treeva continued, studying the Tampax intently.

'Sweedie, is there anyone you haven't got your eye on?' shot Crispin tartly. 'Treeva, what in God's name are you doing?'

Treeva looked up at him, the Tampax wrapper now a thin sheet of tissue paper held delicately between her thumb and forefinger. 'Well, a girl's got to make do somehow, hasn't she?' she responded, placing the paper on the table and smoothing it out. She picked out a pinch of tea leaves from the bowl in front of her and spread them out over the paper. 'I'm making a tea spliff! Anyone got a light?'

Lyric shook her head in astonishment, rocking the baby gently on her lap. 'Treeva, you never cease to amaze me.'

There was silence as they all watched her smoke, and then Lyric remembered her friend's most recent revelation. 'So, who's the lucky man, anyhow?'

Treeva eyeballed her over the 'spliff'. 'It's someone you know very well. Very well indeed. Who doesn't live a million miles away from you.'

Laura gasped. 'Not Darren Skankton!'

Lyric stared incredulously. Surely even Treeva wouldn't . . . would she?

Treeva shook her head vehemently and exhaled a series of smoke rings. 'Of course not! Give me some credit.'

'Jacob?' said Crispin, his voice wavering.

'Nope,' said Treeva. 'I don't do gay, sweedie.'

'Oh, I don't know. I'm bored with this game now. Who is it?' whined Crispin.

Treeva looked around at them all triumphantly. 'Edward!' she announced.

Lyric stared at her. 'As in, Edward, my brother?' She wasn't sure why, but this didn't feel like good news.

'So what's your game plan, sweedie?' asked Crispin, suddenly interested. His own engaged status had made him vicariously interested in other singletons' love lives.

'Well, I haven't got one yet,' said Treeva. 'Jump on him at some point, I suppose. What do you reckon?'

'I'd suggest something a little more subtle than that, Tree, sweedie,' deadpanned Crispin. 'You need to engage him cerebrally before you do it physically. You know what

I always say – never sleep with a man until he asks your opinion on something.'

Lyric opened her mouth as she felt an irrational rage well up inside her, then shut it again until she trusted herself to speak. This was her twin brother they were talking about, after all! 'And what about my opinion – doesn't that count for anything?' she snapped. 'I mean, no one's asked me how I feel about this!'

Treeva looked at her in genuine surprise.

'I thought you'd be pleased! Keeping it in the family, so to speak . . .'

'Well, you thought wrong,' said Lyric.

'You know, Lyric, I'm surprised at you,' said Treeva. 'Don't you want me to be happy? We haven't all been lucky enough to find our perfect Mr Right, you know. Some of us are still scrabbling around trying to find our way. I mean, even your parents seem to be having problems on that score!'

Lyric stared at her in shock.

'Come on, Lyric, your mother's high as a kite on script drugs the whole time and is all over everyone. I mean, if even your parents can't seem to find lasting happiness, what hope do the rest of us have?'

Lyric's eyes filled with tears and she sat staring at the stone floor of the terrace, willing herself not to cry. Treeva was right. She was being petty and mean-minded.

And what if Treeva was right on the other score – what if there really was no hope for lasting love with anyone?

She chewed her finger. Suddenly she had never felt further away from home, from the person who meant more to her than anyone else in the world.

Were she and Philippe *really* as indestructible as she'd once thought? Why was she so ready to doubt him?

Nine

Lyric plopped down on the back stairs and bent over to pull off her gumboots. At least she tried to, hampered as she was by Stan, her panting golden Labrador, as he pushed his wet nose into her lap and gazed up at her adoringly.

'Oh, Stan, you old softy, you've got to let me get my boots off!' She laughed and then gave up, rubbing his head fondly instead. She felt exhilarated from their walk around the grounds of Broughton Hall, and here on the stairs, the place where she'd habitually taken refuge since she was a girl, it was hard to believe that anything more serious than a lame pony or broken doll had happened in her world. Overcome with love for Stan and a sudden rush of memories for her cotton-wool-wrapped girlhood, Lyric hugged him tightly as he wagged his tail, excitedly thumping it against the banisters.

'Anyone for a cuppa?'

Lyric's ears pricked up as she heard Mrs Gunners clatter into the kitchen for her coffee break. Along with the rest of the staff, Mrs Gunners had been there almost since the trees were planted, and Lyric looked upon them all as extended family – as they did her. Lyric's lack of airs and graces and natural sense of fun had long made her a favourite with the staff. Though Mrs Gunners and Jeffries, the Charltons' ancient butler, still insisted on calling her *Miss* Lyric.

'Well, I never – so that Quentin is really coming home. Today! Why Lady C is letting him back in this house, the Lord only knows, let alone putting on a luncheon in his honour.'

Lyric had many happy memories of sitting perched on the wooden bench that surrounded the staff dining table, hugging a mug of hot cocoa as she let their chitter-chatter wash over her. It was amazing what you could learn. The staff generally knew more about the family than the family themselves. Lyric leaned back against the wall, cocooned in the comforting glow of nostalgia, and allowed herself to be transported into their world.

'It's a rum old do, that's for sure,' agreed Queenie, the chambermaid, in outrage. 'You know, once when he was staying here I found a bottle of brandy in his bed. In his bed, I tell you!'

'Each to their own, Queenie,' chipped in the deep, pompous voice of Jeffries. 'Everyone is entitled to their preferred nightcap.'

'Well, inviting the black sheep of the family back to Broughton Hall is asking for trouble, make no mistake,' continued Queenie, her voice sounding even shriller as it travelled up the stairwell.

'I've told you before, Queenie, the Charltons and their sort do things differently to us,' said Mrs Gunners authoritatively. 'I've been here long enough to have seen things as would turn your hair grey. You've only got to look at old Mr Jeffries here to realize these people aren't like ordinary folk.'

There was a shriek of laughter and some clattering about, and Lyric strained to hear what had tickled them.

'You look like whatsisname,' hooted Queenie. 'Him off me mum's telly – Henry Cooper.'

'You mean Tommy Cooper, Queenie,' corrected Mrs Gunners. 'Honestly, Jeffries, the very state of you. I'd have refused to wear it, I would.'

'If Lady C is of a mind to change my uniform, it's only right I should show the courtesy of indulging her,' said Jeffries stiffly. 'And fez hats are apparently very in keeping with her new vision for Broughton Hall. So, during work hours, I shall abide by her wishes and wear one at all times.'

'Yes, but not with pyjamas and carpet slippers!' They collapsed with renewed laughter.

'That's another thing,' continued Queenie, clearly warming to her theme. 'Why would you want to turn a beautiful house like this into a *ride*?'

'A *riad*,' corrected Mrs Gunners. 'Mr Gunners says it's what they call big houses in Africa, or Morocco, or whatever place it is that has caught Lady C's fancy.' Mr Gunners, Broughton Hall's head groundsman for the best part of a century, was, according to his wife, an expert on anything you cared to mention. She lowered her voice. 'It's the pills, you know. Sending her funny.'

'Well, it's not making me laugh,' replied Queenie tartly. Lyric could almost imagine her adjusting her ample bosom in disapproval as she spoke. 'All these candles and incense burners everywhere. It's a fire hazard and they make my eyes water,' she added for good measure.

'Well, it's like I say. They're different. Different lives, different rules. She's always been a one, Lady C. Eccentric, I s'pose you'd say. It's all normal to the likes of them. And the likes of us, well, we've just got to put up with it. Put up or shut up, I always say. Now, are you all going to get back to work or am I going to have to come after you with my rolling pin?'

Lyric hid a smile as she silently motioned to Stan to get up and follow her up the stairs. She hadn't meant to eavesdrop and she'd hate to be discovered, but in a world as ever-changing as her own, it was comforting to know that some things would always stay the same.

~

'I'm not sure if I've walked into Broughton Hall or La Mamounia,' roared Quentin as he strolled confidently into the drawing room, dodging what appeared to be a Bedouin carrying a hawk on his wrist. 'Have I got the right address?' He slapped Jeffries on the back. 'Or have I interrupted a fancy dress party?'

'It's a fez hat, sir,' deadpanned Jeffries, giving a slight

bow with as much dignity as he could muster. 'Part of my new uniform.'

'Oh, Quentin, you old fox,' teased Constance flirtatiously as she floated around the room in yet another exotic kaftan, smoking a Gauloise from a cigarette holder and distributing mojitos, with Michael trailing behind, appearing to help. 'Stop teasing Jeffries. I've got one, too – they're designer, you know. I had darling Philip Treacy run me up quite a few.'

Quentin took a deep breath, closed his eyes and folded his hands together in a pious act of worship. 'Ahhhh. Constance, that scent takes me right back to India.'

Once he'd inhaled fully, he let out his breath noisily, and then clapped an arm around the shoulder of Jacob, his sometime estranged son, who squirmed awkwardly at the unfamiliar physical contact. Or, wondered Edward, leaning against the door frame, it could have something to do with Quentin's obvious lack of hygiene – perhaps the facilities in Darjeeling left something to be desired – and he resolved to give his 'uncle' a wide berth.

Edward watched them through narrowed eyes. Quentin may claim he'd changed – and, indeed, everything about his appearance, from the suntan to the weight loss to the saffron robes and sandals, was the exact opposite of the photographs Edward had seen of him. But, even though he'd never known his uncle, Edward didn't trust first impressions. Anyone could disappear to India and claim to have found enlightenment, right? Quentin's current bluster was hardly that of a religious convert. Could none of them see that he could well be duping them?

His father, his mother – they all seemed quite happy to receive him back into the family. Constance looked like some mad hippy trapped in a Sixties time warp. Never mind that his uncle was quite clearly one buckle short of a sandal – the fact that he wasn't all there only seemed to make him more endearing to her. It was like 'welcome to the fucked-up club', or something.

He turned and sought out Lyric, who was sitting quietly in a high-backed chair by the bay window. She'd certainly dressed for the occasion, in a smart jumper dress and pair of Chanel gun shoes given to her by her friend Treeva. She seemed withdrawn – uneasy, even – yet she, too, had accepted her father's rationale and her uncle's return practically without a whimper.

As Edward gazed at Lyric, he noticed Quentin turn his attention to her.

'So, Lyric,' said Quentin, his voice uncharacteristically gentle. 'You're looking well, as always.'

Lyric looked up at him, her face expressionless, her eyes clear and cold. 'Well, I came prepared for you this time, Uncle Quentin,' she deadpanned, indicating the gun-shaped heels of her shoes.

There was a momentary silence across the room when you could have heard a pin drop. Edward felt himself holding his breath along with the rest of the family, all wondering what would happen next.

Suddenly, Quentin threw back his head and laughed. 'That's my girl, Lyric. I see you haven't lost your sense of humour!'

Lyric smiled – a smile, Edward noted, that didn't reach her eyes.

'Now, what about a drink, Quentin?' asked Constance coquettishly.

'Bet the last person you thought would come and steal your thunder was my dad, eh?' said Jacob under his breath, with a sympathetic look at Edward. 'I know it must seem weird, but that's just my father for you. He tried to disown me when he found out I was gay, you know.'

'Oh, well, that's all right, then,' said Edward sarcastically. 'And they say blood is thicker than water.'

They were interrupted by the clanging of metal on glass. 'If I might say a few words,' said George, tapping his cocktail glass with a letter opener. The gathering fell silent, and they turned towards him. His face was flushed – whether with pride, mojito or embarrassment, Edward couldn't tell – and he looked as uncomfortable as he always did when making a public speech, even to family.

'I think a few words are called for on this most unusual – some might say extraordinary – of occasions,' he said with no hint of irony. The faces stared back expectantly, waiting to hear what he might say. 'The Charltons have become, throughout our long and salubrious history, no strangers to scandal, and upset, and controversy,' he continued. 'Each of which might have threatened a weaker unit.' His voice rose and became stronger with resolve. 'But time and time again, the Charltons have proved that we are not like anyone else. Not like any other family. That our belief in blood ties is stronger than anything. And that it will continue to be the case. So now, today, gathered together here in Broughton Hall—'

'Broughton Riad,' corrected Constance from behind her cigarette holder, blowing delicate smoke rings out like Puff the Magic Dragon.

'So now,' continued George, unabashed, 'as we celebrate the resolution of a rift that threatened to destroy us for ever, I ask you to raise your glasses to the Charltons, to us – and to family.'

'To family,' echoed the rest of the gathering – some tentative, some gung-ho, but none so sincerely passionate as George.

Edward, however, was silent. Speechless, in fact. Even if he'd had the ability to speak, he certainly had no desire to do so.

Suddenly, he felt all his anger channel towards his father. He couldn't blame his uncle for coming back. Who wouldn't have done, after all? His mother seemed incapable of rational thought about anything. No – the person who'd engineered this whole sorry scenario was his father. And, now he came to think about it, his rejection of Edward's offer to donate a kidney was actually more selfish than selfless – based on some misguided and egotistical desire to reunite the family.

'And now, I ask you to join me in the dining room for a Charlton first – a meal with every single one of us around the table together. That is, with both my son, and my brother.'

George looked round for Edward, who snarled in contempt.

'You must be joking – you're mad. I'm off to the Skanktons'. They might not be blood, but at least they're not mental.'

As he left, he kicked the door shut in fury, stubbing his toe, and bit his lip as he felt the pain stop him in his tracks. Just who did his family think they were, bringing his uncle back? Whether he'd atoned for his sins or not, Quentin deserved to rot in hell for the injustice he'd brought on all of them. Edward stood up slowly as the initial stab of pain receded, and found himself face to face with his image in the imposing hallway mirror, now surrounded by wall-mounted oil burners full of Constance's favourite incense.

His reflection stared back at him, but Edward had the curious sensation of not recognizing himself. Suddenly, he saw a mishmash of all the faces he'd left in the dining room. George, Constance, Lyric – even his uncle, Quentin. How life had changed for him in the past few months. And, he felt sure, it was destined to change even more.

He rubbed his eyes and looked back, hoping to see the face he knew so well instead of those from which he wanted to escape.

But he was disappointed. He was stuck with this face, just as he was stuck with this family. And, however hard he tried to escape it, he never could.

Ten

'This way, *chérie*.' Philippe touched the small of her back gently and Lyric allowed him to propel her into the bustling, adrenaline-fuelled frenzy of the restaurant. As they walked through the doors of Scott's, they were hit by the wall of noise coming from inside as London's busiest – and buzziest – crowd high-spiritedly competed for air space. It was a welcoming atmosphere, but Lyric shrank back into her coat – this was the first time she'd been out in public since she'd lost their baby and, despite her fierce Nicholas Kirkwood heels, purple Halston jumpsuit and Burberry trench, she felt intimidated by the sheer confidence of the people inside. Vulnerable, even.

Not that Philippe had noticed, she thought, as she reluctantly shrugged off her coat and handed it to the cloakroom attendant. Over the past couple of weeks, despite the excitement of winning a gold at the Chelsea Flower Show, Philippe had returned to his previously preoccupied self and seemed impervious to anything Lyric said or did. She smoothed down her jumpsuit. Even tonight, when she was feeling like an all-round failure as a woman, when she'd made such an effort for their dinner *à deux*, he had made no comment about her appearance.

'I feel a bit overdressed,' murmured Lyric as Philippe removed his battered leather jacket, noting his cable-knit jumper and casual jeans.

'You look fine,' he said distractedly.

Lyric felt stung. *Fine?* When had 'fine' ever been an adequate assessment of the love of your life?

'Mademoiselle Lyric! *Bonsoir, bonsoir, comment ça va?*'

She smiled patiently as the maître d'hôtel bustled over excitedly.

'But this is weeks, months, even, since we have seen you here! It is so good to see you, *ma chère* – and looking so beautiful, too!' He looked at Philippe admiringly. '*Mon dieu*, Monsieur Chappeau, she is looking radiant, *n'est-ce pas?*'

Philippe grunted the affirmative. 'Always, Jean-Luc. Always.'

There was an uncomfortable moment's silence before the maître d'hôtel held out his arm graciously.

'*Alors*, follow me. As always, we have the best table for you both.'

Lyric stalled and gave Philippe a worried look. The best table in the house was, as befitted one of London's glossiest and most scene-y restaurants, right in the middle of the action, perfectly positioned to see and be seen.

Philippe caught Jean-Luc's sleeve and cleared his throat.

He leaned in and spoke rapidly and quietly in French to him, and the maître d'hôtel nodded discreetly.

'*Pas de problème.*' He held out his arm once again, this time indicating a booth at the back, in a quieter corner of the restaurant.

As they walked through the room, Lyric looked down, trying not to catch any of the admiring glances and looks of recognition sent her way. She knew these strangers didn't mean to be hostile, but their interest felt intrusive, and she was beginning to question the wisdom of coming somewhere like this. It was like being on stage when you hadn't learned your lines. Like every kind of naked-in-public nightmare come to life.

Lyric, following behind Philippe, could see the table they were targeting over his shoulder, and focused on that as her safe haven. Only a few more steps – just a couple . . . but, just before they reached it, Philippe suddenly veered off to a table to their right.

Lyric watched in dismay as he embraced a wealthy-looking woman sitting with another couple. The woman's dinner companions were of a certain age, but she looked to be mid-to-late thirties – a very well-preserved beauty who was now touching Philippe's shoulder in a proprietorial fashion and regarding Lyric with what could only be described as a combative look.

'So this must be the wonderful Lyric Charlton?' She smiled archly. 'I've heard so much about you. Well, we all have, of course!' Her laugh was dangerously tinkly, and she looked Lyric up and down as though what she'd heard wasn't anything to write home about, and what she saw before her didn't even match up to that.

Lyric opened her mouth, willing one of her trademark one-liners to come out, but there was nothing. She shut it again, feeling even more foolish. She looked at Philippe for assistance, and saw a crinkly smile and a warmth in his eyes that hadn't been there for days – except they were directed at the woman, not at her. The woman shook her jet-black hair over her shoulders and Lyric instinctively smoothed her own. She was suddenly acutely aware of how attractive the woman was. The curvaceous figure, the hair, the ice-blue eyes. She looked down at the woman's legs, currently curled around her chair. Yes, they were long and shapely, too.

'*Chérie*, this is Pamela Shepherdson. Pamela, yes, this is indeed Lyric. Lyric, you remember I told you I worked on landscaping the gardens in Pamela's home in Wiltshire? Pamela and I met up recently to discuss developing a formal garden on her new Gloucestershire estate.'

'Divorced now, darling,' laughed Pamela, waving a naked ring finger around to amused glances from her dinner companions. 'Such a shame, but does mean one gets to do all these fun things all over again. Isn't that right, Philippe?'

He laughed and put his arm around Lyric. 'Well, we must eat,' he said, nodding at the two others around the table and winking at Pamela. '*Bon appétit*!'

'*Bon app*!' trilled Pamela.

They continued on their way to their table, Lyric now following Jean-Luc with Philippe behind her. As the maître d'hôtel pulled out her chair she was dismayed to find Pamela directly in her eyeline. The other woman waved prettily and Lyric tried to smile back. She felt unaccountably shaken.

She turned to Philippe as he studied his menu. 'I'm sure you've never mentioned Pamela to me before,' she said, wincing as her words sounded, even to her ears, whingy and petulant.

He looked at her, genuinely surprised. 'I must have done – it was a huge job, just before we met,' he said, and then shrugged. 'Ah well. I have now!' He returned to his menu, and Lyric followed suit. She found it hard to concentrate, though, her eyes drawn again to the woman just a few tables away, and then to the other diners around them. So many people, having such a good time. The atmosphere seemed to compound Lyric's inner misery, and she bit her lip. That used to be her, once upon a time. In fact, not so long ago. She'd had so much fun. She looked at Philippe, who was studying his menu with a frown. *They'd* had so much fun. Would they ever do so again?

'What are you having?' she asked Philippe. He looked up at her, distracted, and returned immediately to the menu.

'I'm not sure,' he mumbled. 'I can't find a single thing I want to eat.'

'But you can always find something to eat in Scott's!'

Lyric closed her menu decisively, determined to change the atmosphere of the evening. 'I'm having sea bass,' she said helpfully. Philippe looked up at her with a raised eyebrow. 'I know!' she said, giggling. 'It's what I always have. But I thought it might give you a lead.'

He smiled and placed the menu down on the table. 'Then I, too, will have sea bass.'

There was a silence. 'But – you don't like sea bass,' said Lyric in a small voice. Was he so emotionally removed from the evening that he couldn't even care less what he ate?

They looked at each other, suddenly awkward in each other's company.

'So—' they both said in unison. Lyric laughed nervously as Philippe smiled.

'Go on—' Again, together.

'No, you go first—' There was a silence and they looked at each other, complicit for the first time that evening in their uncertainty.

Philippe looked around at the hubbub surrounding them and Lyric toyed with her cutlery.

'Monsieur, madame – are you ready to order?'

The waiter took their orders, then the sommelier arrived for the wine order. Yet another waiter arrived to pour water and then another with bread. Then their Sancerre arrived, to be tasted before it was served. Finally, they were alone again.

After a few moments, Philippe spoke softly. 'So . . . he's back.'

For a moment, Lyric was confused as to who he meant. Then, recognizing the hard look in Philippe's eyes that had only ever been reserved for one person, she realized he was talking about Uncle Quentin.

She paused, uncertain about where this was heading, before answering guardedly, 'Yes. I can't quite believe it.'

Philippe stared into his wine glass. 'Neither can I.'

Again, there was silence. But not their customary comfortable quiet – the prickly kind that had recently permeated their times alone together.

Suddenly, he looked directly into her eyes. 'How do you feel?'

She opened her mouth to speak, trying to collect her thoughts. 'How do I feel?' How *did* she feel? She felt lonely, she felt isolated, she felt – desperate. And she felt sorry. Sorry for spoiling their happy time. Sorry for being a failure. Sorry for losing their baby.

'I mean, how do you really feel?' he persisted. He hit his chest where his heart was. 'Here, inside. It cannot be as easy as you make out, surely, to accept him back?'

'Oh! You mean about *Uncle Quentin*?' Lyric stuttered.

A waiter appeared at her right elbow. 'The sea bass, madam?'

She turned to him, unseeing. 'Thank you.'

Philippe leaned back to allow the waiter to serve his fish, but his eyes never left Lyric's. Now, they were full of compassion. But Lyric only saw pity.

'Yes . . . about your uncle.'

She stared at the plate in front of her, feeling oddly deflated by his response. 'Well, I guess, whatever makes Daddy happy.'

He stared back, a veil falling over his eyes. 'Yes. I guess so. That, after all, is the Charlton way.

She looked up sharply at him. 'And what do you mean by that?'

He shrugged apologetically. 'I mean, you always get your way. Your father, even your uncle.'

Now it was Lyric's turn to shrug. 'Of course. I mean, when it's right for the family.'

Philippe took a mouthful of fish and chewed deliberately. 'And do you think you'll always get your way, Lyric?'

Lyric was stunned. How could he say that to her now, after everything that had happened? She hesitated. 'I think we know that that's not always so,' she said slowly.

Philippe shook his head gently and toyed with his food. Finally he looked up. 'All that worry, Lyric. All that drama. For . . . for what?'

Lyric felt her head start to spin. What on earth was he trying to say? Surely, he couldn't be saying that their desire for a family wasn't worth the pain of the miscarriage? 'Well, most people would think it was worth it. It's all part of life's rich tapestry, surely? How else can you cope with the bad times if you are not always looking to the good?'

Philippe avoided her gaze and said nothing.

Lyric leaned forward, her voice breaking. 'Are you saying we shouldn't have tried for a baby in the first place? Shouldn't ever try again?'

The sommelier arrived at the table to refill their glasses. Lyric put her hand over her glass to indicate no more. Philippe raised an eyebrow.

Lyric felt the dam of emotions inside her burst. 'Just because I'm not pregnant any more, doesn't mean I have to get plastered every time I'm out,' she cried desperately. She looked around and lowered her voice. 'Please, don't make me feel any more like a social leper than I already do.'

Philippe looked at her. His eyes seemed to be pleading with her about something, but she couldn't tell what. Why was everything so difficult to fathom all of a sudden?

'*Chérie*.' Now it was Philippe's voice that caught. 'Don't.'

Lyric took a deep breath and chastised herself inwardly. No point taking things out on Philippe. And this was hardly the time or the place for an emotional exchange. Maybe she should change the subject.

She took another great lungful of air. 'So, clearly you don't approve of my father's forgiving Quentin,' she stated, and immediately kicked herself. It had sounded sharp, and more confrontational than she'd intended. Why bring this up again? She changed tack, her tone more measured. 'You think one misdemeanour means people should be cast out for eternity?'

Philippe's forehead creased in another frown. 'Of course

not. And I know he has saved your father's life. But not making your uncle atone officially for what he did seems to me a huge miscarriage of justice.'

Lyric felt a lump appear in her throat at the 'm' word. She looked down, unable to speak. Was Philippe trying to make her feel as bad as possible?

'Oh – *chérie*, I didn't mean –' he stumbled, as though genuinely in pain. He gazed at her imploringly, but Lyric, still staring at the table, didn't see. He held out his hand gently but she shook her head, silent, not trusting herself to speak, and kept her hands folded together.

'Don't worry. It's fine.'

But she knew in her heart that it wasn't. Things were anything but fine.

Every mouthful of her fish seemed to stick in her throat, tasting of cardboard, but Lyric carried on eating, desperate to fill the empty silence with something – even if it was more silence. Eating, luckily, was a necessary activity in a restaurant, and it helped create some semblance of normality – even if out of the corner of her eyes she could feel Pamela Shepherdson's inquisitive gaze boring into her, and was aware of Philippe's introspective glower.

She closed her lips and chewed slowly. *What now?* she wondered, swallowing the last mouthful.

All of a sudden, she felt the fish lodge in her throat and choked violently. She felt her face go bright red and the tables around her fell quiet as she struggled to dislodge it.

'*Chérie!*' Philippe leapt to his feet and rushed around to her aid, clapping her briskly on the back with one hand and encircling her protectively with the other.

Still Lyric choked, her face growing even hotter with embarrassment. Suddenly, a piece of bone flew out and pinged off her wine glass. She reached for the water and tried to regain her composure as Philippe hugged her in concern. A man on the table next to them broke into a round of applause and Lyric looked up at Philippe, eyes twinkling through the tears. They both giggled spontaneously, which turned into infectious laughter as the absurdity of the situation hit them.

Philippe leaned down and gave her a soft kiss on the lips, to a murmured 'bravo' from the gentleman next door, and then returned to his seat.

'Oops,' said Lyric and Philippe winked at her.

'I almost forgot how you can turn any situation into the Lyric Charlton show,' he teased, and Lyric sat back, happier now. Suddenly, it seemed, equilibrium had been restored by the most bizarre of incidents, and their previous awkwardness had totally disappeared. Even Pamela and her dinner companions had left, leaving Lyric feeling entirely more relaxed.

As the waiter cleared their plates, Philippe leaned forward. 'So can I trust you with dessert?' he said, eyes twinkling from across the table. 'Or might the chocolate fondant prove as challenging as the sea bass?'

Philippe wiped his mouth and placed the napkin on the table. 'And so, *chérie*, if you will excuse me, I must go to the loo.'

Lyric smiled at his curious formality and watched him walk through the restaurant. What a rollercoaster they were currently on. Small wonder, given everything that was happening in their world. But they would get through it – their love was too strong for any other outcome. She just had to keep a hold on her hormones and stop reading too much into every single thing he said or did.

There was a beeping from the middle of the table where Philippe had thrown his mobile when they'd first sat down. Lyric looked around her in embarrassment. She detested people using their phones in restaurants, and hoped no one had heard. There was another beep, and Lyric tried to muffle the sound with her napkin while she fumbled with the cursor, trying to silence it altogether. As she did so, she accidentally flicked onto the list of texts received and the most recent appeared on the screen.

Enchantée de te voir de nouveau, mon cher. J'avais oublié la force de tes bras . . . En attente de la prochaine fois. Gros, gros bisous x x x x

Lyric felt panic grow inside her. She translated the message in her head. *Wonderful to see you again, my dear. I had forgotten how strong those arms of yours are . . . Looking forward to the next time. Big kisses x x x x*

Calm down, Lyric, she told herself. *Do not let your*

hormones get the better of you. There is a simple explanation for this.

But then she saw the name of the sender: Pammie.

Lyric felt the bile rise in her throat and she clutched her stomach as though she were going to be sick.

Pamela Shepherdson. *Pammie?*

Maybe there was more to this than her hormones, after all . . .

Eleven

'And this is my friend Kara. With a K,' finished Cheryl proudly, the sleeve from her floaty apricot dress with plunging neckline wafting dangerously close to Kara's lit cigarette.

'Nice to meet you,' said Edward, subtly removing the proprietorial hand Cheryl had placed on his arm and looking surreptitiously over at Darren. Ever since that first night at the Skanktons', when Darren had warned him off his sisters, Edward had been careful to maintain a discreet distance from them, deftly deflecting their blatant overtures with the practised charm of his years as a good-looking bartender and ski instructor, whilst still managing to keep them on friendly terms. It was only mildly irritating. Not only were neither of them particularly his type, but he had no wish to fall out with his new partner in crime when they'd only just met.

Especially not when there was so much to fall out with his immediate family about. He felt a now-familiar twinge of annoyance over Quentin's reappearance. He knew he should be pleased that Quentin's selfless donation of a kidney had saved his father's life. The doctors had wanted the transplant to take place before George needed dialysis – it was meant to improve the longevity of the transplanted organ – and so the operation had taken place within days of Quentin's arrival from India. George, fit from years of hunting, fishing, shooting and gardening, had astounded doctors with his speedy recovery and, after just a few weeks, was already feeling well enough to attend his first post-operative race meeting – albeit in a wheelchair. But Edward was still stinging from the rebuff of his own offer of a kidney, and his joy over the success of the operation was tainted by his hurt pride.

Not that he was going to let it spoil today. The whole family had turned out to support George and tentatively celebrate his recovery. Of course, there was still a chance his body might reject Quentin's kidney – that could still happen up to two months after the operation – but the signs were looking positive so far.

The problem was, Edward surmised, looking around at the bevy of glamorous babes surrounding him, that the public fuss over his father's illness had only fuelled interest in himself – the hottest and most eligible new bachelor on the racing circuit – and, with no progress being made by either Cheryl or her sister Kimberley, they had assumed the role of his new best friends, basking in the reflected glory of his acquaintance as they introduced him to their interested posse of well-connected, well-heeled, but, as far as Edward was concerned, equally unattractive friends.

It wasn't that the raw material was all that bad, he thought, surveying the gaggle of girls parading in front of him. It was what went on top of it. He found the piles of make-up, elaborately coiffed hair and shiny, revealing dresses really off-putting. And, in their lurid summer palette, he thought they resembled a chirruping group of canaries – hardly how he imagined his next girlfriend to be. He preferred something a little less . . . *done*.

He caught sight of Lyric wandering past and felt a wave of pride. Why couldn't other girls be as classy as his sister? Her honey-blonde hair was caught up in a simple ponytail, and she was wearing a vintage Chanel suit that she'd had re-tailored to fit her curves – their mother's going-away outfit, in fact, she'd confided to him as she drove them to Epsom that morning, but pre-Morocco-gate, of course . . . Lyric wasn't only stylish, she was clever and, combined with her beauty, the overall effect was intoxicating. At least, it would be, if she wasn't his sister. She epitomized the kind of girl who attracted him – like Amba, the elusive beauty he'd first set eyes on at the Newmarket race meeting. The problem was, Amba had slipped out of his life as maddeningly quickly as she'd entered it. And, try as he might, he couldn't get her out of his mind. He shook his head in frustration. He was never going to meet someone like that when he was constantly being introduced to the racing world's answer to *Footballers' Wives*.

Not that these girls weren't beguiling company, he

admitted, as Kimberley trotted over and threw her hands around his neck. They just weren't for him.

'Do you need rescuing, Eddie?' she asked flirtatiously, coming dangerously close to falling out of her strapless mango-coloured dress and leaning her head on his shoulder. Edward looked into her laughing eyes and couldn't help but notice a stray smear of false-lash glue in the corner of her eye. Over her head, Edward spied Darren glowering at him threateningly, and he extricated himself from her grip.

'Oh, I'm fine, Kimberley,' he said, smiling, trying not to wince as she transferred ochre fake-tan streaks onto his pristine shirt collar. 'I was just getting acquainted with Kara here. That's Kara with a K,' he added, eyes smiling.

In an effort to appease Darren, Edward placed his arm very deliberately around Kara's shoulder and she almost whinnied in delight. He glanced up to ensure Darren was no longer mentally planning his demise, and found himself looking straight into a pair of beautiful, almond-shaped eyes. His heart did a somersault. Amba!

He stared at her, open-mouthed, in amazement. Amba, expensive-looking raven hair bouncing behind her, was immaculately dressed in what looked, even to Edward's untrained eye, to be couture. Delicious, sorbet-coloured Dior. With her tiny pillbox hat, barely-there make-up, Cartier diamonds and tiny white gloves, she was Grace Kelly-cool with the fiery exotic looks of Bianca Jagger. Again, the tantalizing musky scent he'd noticed before hung lightly on the spring air.

He watched, aching, as her eyes passed over him without recognition, and she approached a group. An old man turned delightedly to embrace her. She responded with the lightest of air-kisses and Edward burned with jealousy. Suddenly, he would have swapped his youth and position to be the old man. He wanted it so badly it hurt. He wanted to feel those lips not just on his cheek, but on his neck, his lips, his—

'I said, Edward, did you plan on betting at all today?' sang Kara.

He turned, and when he looked back, Amba was gone. He shook Kara off in frustration. Now what was he going to do?

'Edward?'

'I'm sorry, I – I need the toilet. The loo,' he corrected himself, remembering Constance's horror when the social faux pas of saying 'toilet' had first passed his lips in front of her.

In a daze, he pushed his way through the crowds, unaware as he knocked one lady into her husband and upset another's drink. All the while he searched the blur of faces for a glimpse of Amba – the sherbet-coloured outfit, that beautiful, finely boned face, that hair – but she was gone.

As he reached the Gents, he pushed open the door violently and stood at the urinals, cursing his bad luck. How had he let her slip through his fingers again? As he relieved himself, he stared at his face in the mirror. He would find her, he promised himself. All was not lost. She would be at the race meeting for the rest of the day – and he would comb the racecourse until he had found her, introduced himself to her and eventually made her feel about him the same way that he already did about her.

There was a click from the cubicle behind him and he glanced instinctively in the mirror.

'It's Edward, isn't it?'

Making a choking sound, Edward did his zipper up hurriedly, almost catching himself in his flies. Amba!

'Um – yes! Fancy seeing you here.'

He kicked himself. Suave, Edward. Just when he really needed his natural charm it deserted him. Typical.

Amba laughed, a low, confident, but soft laugh. 'Sorry. Bad habit of mine. The Gents, I mean.'

'So you come here often?' Edward breathed a sigh of relief, then cringed at his corny line. *You never lose it, Eddie.*

Amba smiled, acknowledging the joke. 'I just can't abide queuing,' she said unapologetically. 'Such a British pastime, isn't it? Even in the most unappealing of places.'

Edward shrugged. 'Most ladies would find that about the Gents. Unappealing, that is.'

Amba gave him an amused glance. 'Well, maybe I'm not such a lady.' Her eyes held a promise that made Edward crumble inside. That look certainly had seemed all woman to him.

He watched as Amba sashayed over to the basin and

turned on the tap, washing her hands energetically. Remembering his manners, he took his hands from his pockets, where he'd only just placed them, and also began to wash.

He caught her looking at him in the mirror and stared back at her, once again tongue-tied.

'I thought you hadn't . . . I thought you didn't . . .'

Her forehead creased in a frown. 'Wash my hands? I might not be British, but I do follow the basic rules of hygiene, you know.'

Now it was his turn to laugh. 'No. I mean, I thought you hadn't recognized me.'

She raised a questioning eyebrow as she held her hands under the drier.

Now he felt stupid again. 'When we saw each other. Earlier.'

Amba gave no response, merely straightened her dress and made as if to walk out. Edward felt gauche and silly again. She was in the doorway now, smiling graciously as a besuited gentleman made way for her with undisguised admiration lighting up his face. Edward ran out after her, feeling like a lovesick puppy, but unable to stop himself.

'I like your necklace.'

She turned back to him and fingered the tiny pearl-sized piece of bone strung artlessly around her neck. Alongside her otherwise priceless gems, the ethnic piece seemed slightly incongruous, but oddly fitting.

'Well, I know you're not supposed to wear ivory any more, but I just love elephants.'

'Right.' Edward, marvelling at her candour, could think of no other response. 'So, umm, what do you do?'

He kicked himself again for his less-than-original chat-up line. But Amba appeared unperturbed. Instead, a smile played around her lips. 'Oh, what I do covers a multitude of sins,' she purred.

Suddenly, she stepped towards him, leaned in close – too close – and touched his face. He felt his heart racing. '*Chutzi*,' she said, almost under her breath. Edward stared, drinking in the very closeness of her.

It was, he decided, as if she had no cultural anchor at all. As if she were the amazing combination of the most intoxicating elements of the entire world. It was certainly as baffling as trying to work out the bloodlines of a racehorse. And how apt, when she was like a finely bred racehorse herself – expensive-looking, flighty, but class through and through.

She looked down at him, and Edward felt a suffocating surge of longing. Slowly, with the long, perfectly manicured Rouge Noir talons at the end of her extraordinarily long fingers, she traced the line of buttons down his shirt until they rested mid-lapel. Deliberately, she picked a tiny piece of lint from his jacket and then brushed his shirt collar delicately with her fingertips, looking up at him all the while.

'You should be more careful about the company you keep,' she murmured.

'The company chose me,' said Edward quickly.

Amba pulled back from him with a secret smile. Edward's heart sank. The spell was broken. But she was still very close to him, perhaps just a little too close for socially acceptable comfort. As if he cared. He wanted her closer still – hell, he wanted to *wear* this woman – who gave a stuff about the boundaries of personal space?

A tannoy announcement heralded the start of the first race and Amba looked around her restlessly. Edward racked his brains for a way to keep her there.

'Do you bet?'

She turned to him in amusement. 'Do I *bet*? What a question to ask a lady.'

Edward frowned. 'But you said you weren't a lady . . .'

'That depends what we're talking about.' Amba allowed a half smile to play around her lips. 'A lady is always happy to have bets laid on her behalf.'

Edward's heart leapt. She was as good as inviting him! He grabbed her gloved hand. 'Come on, then,' he urged, suddenly more excited about racing than at any previous point in his short spectating career. 'Let's go check out the odds.'

He led her proudly across the members' enclosure and over to where the bookies were competing for attention – some standing on stepladders, some interacting on a level with racegoers, others underneath traditional coloured umbrellas.

Amidst the frenetic chaos of shouting bookies, jostling racegoers and tannoy announcements, Edward stared at the names of the horses in the first race, trying to make sense of it all. He had no idea what any of it meant. He gave Amba a sidelong glance. This was the second time he'd seen her at a racetrack. He was desperate to impress her, yet she must know more than him about racing. How was he going to get through this without making a complete fool of himself?

Amba seemed to be watching the horses warm up with interest, but hardly scrutinizing them. Maybe he was safe – maybe she *was* just a casual spectator after all.

Looking around, he spotted a familiar form bumbling through the crowds, shabbily dressed in crumpled Turnbull & Asser. Angus! Of course.

'Angus!' he called, beckoning the old man over. 'Over here!'

Amba looked around with interest as Angus bustled over.

'Well, well, Master Edward. And how are things with you today?'

'All good, Angus – let me introduce a friend of mine, Amba. Amba, this is Angus Roach, an old friend of the Charlton family.'

'Delighted,' said Amba, smiling politely but coolly. Edward turned back to Angus and lowered his voice.

'So, Angus, who've you got your money on for the next race?' He folded his arms and rocked back on his heels, awaiting Angus's response. Angus was hardly ever wrong. He was Edward's sure-fire ticket to racing recognition with Amba.

'Well, hum, I never usually – well, as it's you . . .' hedged Angus, always loath to reveal his tips to anyone other than the closest of family friends. He looked furtively up at the board, as though it, rather than he, held the answers Edward sought.

After more humming and ahhing, Angus cleared his throat. 'Well, young man, I've got a few shillings on Roman Legend each way,' he said quickly out of the corner of his mouth.

Edward raised his eyebrows in mock surprise. 'What a coincidence! That's the one I was going to back,' he said. 'What are the odds?'

Angus looked behind him at the boards. 'It's currently on at five to one. Oh – oh, you're joking. Yes, yes, very good. Well, fingers crossed, what?'

'Fingers crossed,' beamed Edward. 'And I guess the same for Thumper, too, eh?' he added, referring to Lyric's horse, which was due to race later on.

Angus shook his head. 'Regretfully, I shan't be backing young Thumper this afternoon,' he said. 'Not his day today. But it will come again! Just not today.'

He toddled off, leaving Edward to rifle hurriedly through his wallet for some cash. He pulled out a crisp fifty-pound note, one of many that came courtesy of the generous allowance George was paying him while he 'got on his feet'.

'Fifty on Roman Legend,' he said confidently to the closest bookie.

'To win?' asked the man from the depths of his heavy overcoat.

'To win,' repeatedly Edward firmly. 'Now, Amba, your choice.'

He turned to his companion, who was gazing disinterestedly at the list of runners.

'Oh, I don't know,' she said lightly. 'I'm no judge of form. Why bet on a horse because of numbers? I prefer to go for the prettiest names. Like – look, there's Catwalk Prince. I like that. I bet he's a handsome devil. Sometimes in life it's good to leave things up to Fate, don't you think?'

Edward tore his eyes away from her mesmerizing face and glanced at the board. Catwalk Prince was running at 30–1. There wasn't a cat's chance in hell it would win, but money on Amba's horse was money well spent, whether or not it won for her . . . Still, it pained him to throw good money after bad. Reluctantly, he peeled off another fifty-pound note from his wallet.

'And we'll put fifty on Catwalk Prince.' The bookie raised his eyebrows, and Edward nodded affirmation, his confident manner belying the turmoil beneath. He couldn't bear the thought of looking like a fool in front of Amba. Was she convinced by his swagger, or was he about to be exposed as the fraud he was?

He turned to her. 'Well, it's your call. If you win, it's all yours. But I don't hold out much hope . . .'

Suddenly animated, Amba touched his arm, eyes shining. 'Edward, you shouldn't have . . .' Her voice, decided

Edward, was like soothing tiger balm for the soul. If he closed his eyes he could listen to her talk for the rest of his life. 'But you should ALWAYS believe in Fate. Now, let's go and watch the race!'

~

Not all eyes were on the race. One pair in particular was seeking out Angus as he pottered off, away from Edward and Amba.

Quentin smiled in satisfaction as he caught a glimpse of Angus's diminutive form, and folded his arms over his stomach. In fact, with his newly trim waistline, this habit of his had almost ceased to exist, but – after only a short while back on his feet following the transplant operation – much to his chagrin, his impressive paunch seemed to be re-appearing. How so, he really couldn't say – after all, he'd only had the odd (very modest) glass of Château Lafite that Constance had practically forced upon him. And he'd been reluctant to get back into the habit of a brandy before bedtime – if it wasn't so darned rude to decline the offer of a drink when he was at the mercy of other people's hospitality, he would still be practically teetotal, he was sure of it.

Come to think of it, once he'd tapped Angus for a tip or two, he might head off in the direction of a *tipple* or two. After all, it was practically sacrilege to place a bet without a Pimm's in one's hand. He fingered the red string around his wrist and promised himself he'd drop Madonna a text later on if the lure of a second drink got too much. After all, she was no stranger to temptation herself. He chuckled to himself. No, there was no chance he'd be lured into having more than a polite welcome drink. He was a different person now. He needed different things – cash, for a start, and a lot of it.

Living the frugal life of the monks in India had lulled him into a false sense of security and almost made him forget how expensive real life could be. No surviving on a wing, a prayer and a chickpea balti back here. Not only were his living expenses eye-watering, but he was also completely and utterly broke. George had been characteristically generous, of course, and, in a rush of brotherly love and gratitude for the enormous debt he now felt he owed his brother, financially he couldn't do enough for Quentin – but Quentin was having none of it. He would show George he was well and truly rehabilitated – a new man – and that included standing on his own two feet. For the short term, anyhow. He was sure that once he was fully recovered George would see fit to change his will, so that he and Jacob would stand to inherit significantly more than they were currently in line to do. After Lyric had discovered that her brother was still alive and solved the mystery of where he'd been all her life, Edward's reappearance on the scene last year had meant he was not just George's son, but his heir apparent, too, a position that Jacob, until then the firstborn son to the Charlton brothers – by decree of an ancient family covenant – had previously occupied.

Although this had hardly crossed Quentin's mind since his spiritual conversion in India – his focus being on entirely more cerebral matters – he was quietly confident that George would eventually see fit to swing things in his favour.

Quentin no longer bore any grudges. He answered to a higher power than greed these days. He scratched his bare left big toe with the underside of his right flip-flop and stretched his arms out purposefully. A close bystander ducked out of the way with a grimace. Something else Quentin hadn't updated since he returned was his personal hygiene. Bathing in a mountain stream may have cut it with the earthy ways of the Buddhists, but since returning to the UK he still hadn't had any of his clothes laundered, and he exuded the smell of a man who'd slept in them for a year. He was in need of soap, and a lot of it.

'Angus Roach? Well, I'll be . . . Fancy seeing you here!'

Angus gave Quentin a bemused look. 'I've spent most of my life at a racecourse,' he said mildly. 'I would have thought it was exactly where you'd expect to see me. Particularly,' he added pointedly, 'close to the bookies.'

Quentin pressed his hands together prayer-fashion and gave a little bow. He'd seen the monks use it in India, and it seemed the perfect gentlemanly way to acknowledge that Angus had taken the upper hand in the conversation.

'I'm a new man now, Angus,' said Quentin proudly. 'I've been through hell, recognized my sins, atoned for them and come out the other side.'

Now it was Angus's turn to acknowledge Quentin with a bow. 'Well, I would certainly agree that everyone deserves a second chance,' he muttered. 'And what you have done for George and all those who care for him is truly wonderful.'

There was an awkward pause as Quentin, uncomfortable with the unaccustomed praise, pondered how to respond. 'So, how have you been keeping?' he finally blustered. 'Business good? I hear you had a little – erm – fall at the first, shall we say, with one of George's new steeds?'

Angus nodded thoughtfully. 'Yes, it would be true to say that I underestimated Lyric's new horse's first outing,' he agreed. 'Damned strange business, though – everything was stacked against it, yet it still came through.' He frowned up at Quentin, clearly still rattled by his mistake, but trying to move on from it. 'Still, I have retained my otherwise unblemished record and, since you ask, business is indeed good.'

'Excellent, excellent,' enthused Quentin, patting Angus on the back. 'Don't suppose you've got a little tip you could throw my way, have you? Since I've been home I've rekindled my love of racing, but I'm a little rusty on the old mechanics.'

'Humph,' muttered Angus. Quentin had never shared George's instinctive passion for racing, and over the years had only been seen at races when there was a decent VIP welcome. Even then, he would only have left the hospitality area to visit the Gents' or to leave. 'I'm not in the habit of giving away my hunches. Because that's all they are, you know. As demonstrated by that darned business with Lyric's horse,' he added.

Quentin smiled again humourlessly, trying not to show his irritation. Gambling was hardly the prescribed recreation for a Buddhist, but as an income stream it was, at least, legal – which, of course, none of his previous occupations had been. It was a step in the right direction and, more importantly, it was currently his only option. The last thing he needed now was Angus playing hard to get.

'Oh, come on, old man – it's just one tip, to get me started and back on the horse, so to speak. What's that old Christian commandment – love thy neighbour?' pondered Quentin craftily. 'I thought we were practically family.'

'And I thought you were a Buddhist,' countered Angus, squinting into the spring sunshine. He turned to Quentin, suddenly razor-sharp racing pundit rather than dithery old man. 'I'll give you one tip – for what you've done for your brother. But this is the first and last, so use it wisely. Now, which race were you wanting to bet on?'

Quentin's eyes bulged excitedly. 'Well, the first race, my good chap. It might be the start of a winning streak!'

Angus nodded sagely. 'Well, I've just parted with a tip to your young nephew over there, so it's an open secret now that I'm backing Roman Legend each way. And as I *am* a betting man . . .'

He chuckled at his own joke and Quentin stared at him, totally uncomprehending, then roared with false laughter and patted Angus on the back. 'Good one, Angus, good one. And thanks for the tip. Brandies on me if it romps home – which I'm sure it will!'

He chuckled again happily and strolled off towards the bookies, his laughter trailing off as he tried not to be irked at Angus's open adoration for George. All Quentin's life, it seemed, he'd been battling a universal love for his brother. Could no one see that George wasn't the noble saint that everyone thought he was? That if he had half a brain on his shoulders he would have fought the unfairness of the Charlton inheritance covenant once and for all and overturned it, righting the wrongs that had been done to second-, third- and even fourth-born Charltons over the centuries?

Quentin checked himself. He was over this now.

He was so deep in thought that he didn't see the towering form of Roger Skankton until he had physically bumped into him. He reeled back, rubbing his forehead where it had bashed into Roger's chest. Good Lord! The man was built like the proverbial brick—

'Quentin, old man! Good to see you again after all this time. And good work with all that kidney business. How are you finding it back in civilization, eh? Good to be reunited with a flushing toilet and all mod cons?'

Roger, resplendent in mustard trousers and dark green blazer that gave his tan an even more pronounced orange hue, laughed heartily at his own joke. He looked over Quentin's shoulder and around him to check who'd overheard it, ready to bask in the adoration of the racing fans that surrounded them. There was none.

'Sometimes, Roger, there are more important things than home comforts,' said Quentin piously. 'Like inner peace and sanctity. You should try it some time.'

'Eh, Quentin, you old dog – takes one to know one, eh?'

Quentin stood back, happy to take the higher ground over this poorly educated shyster. He'd never had much time for Roger, secretly feeling he was somehow eclipsed by the younger man's overt glamour and wide-boy approach – and right now was no different. Roger was standing between him and the start of his new fortune.

'I'm not sure what you mean by that, old boy. And if you don't mind, I'm just on my way to place a bet.'

Roger's eyes shone. 'Going to support your neighbours, Quentin? I've got a runner in the next race. Catwalk Prince. Lively little fella. *Entre nous*, could be a good bet . . .' He leaned forward and tapped the side of his nose confidentially.

Quentin chuckled without humour. 'Thanks, Roger, but I've been tipped off by a more reliable source than you. And it wasn't for Catwalk Prince.'

Roger gave a self-satisfied nod. 'Well, it wouldn't be. Catwalk Prince is a rank outsider and the odds are stacked against it. Which would make it a good choice. But, if your source is a trusted one, far be it for me to get in the way . . .'

'My source is Angus Roach,' said Quentin brusquely,

irritated by Roger's complacence, and intrigued in spite of himself. 'And, if you don't mind me saying, he has a more reliable track record than yourself.'

Roger shook his head in amusement. 'Every dog has its day. And Angus Roach has long had his. He's out of date, Quentin, yesterday's news. He was tipping another horse at Newmarket and Lyric's new colt romped home instead. He's getting on, Quentin. He's lost it. Time for the new guard.'

Something in Skankton's voice made Quentin look at him searchingly. What was he getting at?

Immediately, Quentin felt his insides churn, as good wrangled with evil – what he should do, and what he shouldn't. Roger was up to something, that was certain, and all Quentin's instincts told him to find out more. But something else – a new-found integrity – prevented him. It was an unfamiliar feeling – previously, he'd never been held back by conscience – and he didn't like it.

'Well, that's as may be,' said Quentin. 'But as a member of the old guard myself, I'll stick with what I know. Nice seeing you again, Roger.'

He nodded courteously. After all, no point antagonizing the fellow, was there? Now Quentin was back at Broughton Hall, he'd no doubt be bumping into the Skanktons more often. Doffing his hat, he wandered off whistling, fingering the change in the pocket of his linen trousers. And while he was at it, he might just have a little flutter on Roger's horse. No point putting all his eggs in one basket, now, was there?

~

Later, much later, Edward pulled out his final fifty. He was at once defeated and delirious. On the one hand, his horses had, without exception, failed to come in. Even Roman Legend, his tip from Angus. How was Edward to know that a bet each way – which was Angus's tip – meant he was expecting it to come in second? Angus would have been quids in on that one, whereas Edward had been left with nothing. Instead, Catwalk Prince had romped home an unexpected winner, leaving Amba to collect the winnings. It was a pattern that had been repeated throughout the afternoon. He would try to interpret the form and choose one based on merit, whereas Amba would seemingly pick one from thin air based on its name, or its racing colours, or some other apparently random characteristic. His would fail miserably – sometimes even to finish – whereas Amba's had all won.

But what an afternoon. Edward would have paid the same money over again to spend the time with an exotic creature such as Amba. Now, accepting defeat on his racing prowess, he was trying to think of a way to ask her out on a date. A proper date. Where there would be just him and her . . .

Edward shivered, unable to think about getting closer

to Amba without succumbing to a powerful wave of desire.

'So,' he said, brandishing the note. 'Out of loyalty to my sister, I insist this last bet is a joint bet – on Thumper. Even though,' he added hurriedly, still careful not to let the appearance of being a racing expert slip despite his dismal performance throughout the afternoon, 'form-wise, he doesn't have a hope.'

Amba shrugged and smiled. 'Family loyalty is the most important. And I can hardly complain this afternoon, can I?' She hugged his arm and Edward felt a lightning bolt move through him. Buoyed, he handed the money over to the bookie and they moved to the fence to join his family watching the race.

'Edward, there you are!' shrieked Lyric, jumping around in excitement between her father and Philippe. 'I've been looking for you all afternoon! Have you put a bet on Thumper?'

'Of course!' he said, grinning, chest puffing out with pride as his family looked at Amba with undisguised inter-est.

George put his arm around Lyric and hugged her to him. 'Now, now, Lyric, remember not to be too disap-pointed if Thumper doesn't shine today. Last time was a one-off – he's entered in this race for the experience, not for the win. Isn't that right, Angus?'

Angus shrugged noncommittally. 'Well, I wouldn't tip him on this one. Better on hard going. Too soft today.

Plenty of time for another victory yet, Miss Lyric, don't you worry.'

'Well, there's a lot to be said for putting your money where your heart is,' said Edward, looking at Amba shrewdly out of the corner of his eye. She gave him a secret smile and his heart soared.

'And they're off!' As one, they moved to the fence as the commentator announced the start of the race. Thumper or, in his racing guise, Doppelganger, seemed to start well, and was soon in third place. As his pounding legs galloped up the furlongs, he nudged into second place. Every one of the Charltons watched, open-mouthed, as he took on the leader.

'And out of the blue, it's Doppelganger coming up fast,' gabbled the commentator. 'And it's Doppelganger taking the lead, and as they reach the final furlong, it's Doppelganger in front – and Doppelganger wins by a leg! Doppelganger has done it again! Doppelganger wins the race!'

For a split second, the Charltons stood stock still, staring at one another in disbelief. Then they erupted into cheers, hugging one another. Philippe picked up Constance and swung her around, whilst Lyric bent down to her father, still in a wheelchair, and embraced him joyously. Edward turned to Amba and threw his arms around her impulsively. At last! Finally he was a winner in her eyes. She seemed stiff in his arms and he pulled away, trying to recover his cool, suddenly embarrassed. Had he overstepped the mark?

Amba righted her hat and brushed herself down. 'Congratulations,' she said in that same low, sexy voice. Outwardly, he smiled as if this kind of thing happened all the time. Inside, he burned with unrequited passion.

'We've got ourselves a winner!' shouted George, shaking Angus's hand vehemently.

'What you've got is a bloomin' miracle,' muttered Angus, shaking his head. 'The going was all wrong. Out of character. Totally against the odds. Simply impossible.'

'These things happen in racing!' roared Roger Skankton in disagreement as he appeared from behind them all. 'George – what a victory!'

'Humph,' said Angus, still shaking his head as he wandered off in shock. Only Quentin seemed to notice, and stared after him, his head cocked at an inquisitive angle, fingers softly stroking his chin. As Angus bumbled out of sight, Quentin turned to consider Roger, who was celebrating the win with unadulterated joy, if not surprise. A light seemed to come on in Quentin's eyes and a knowing smirk crossed his face.

'Well, on that note, it's time for me to disappear,' whispered Amba in Edward's ear. He turned to her in dismay.

'No! I mean, of course. I mean – could I see you again? Take you for dinner, maybe?'

Amba studied him levelly, the hint of a smile playing around the corner of her mouth.

'Oh, I don't think so,' she said.

Edward stared at her, crushed. 'Oh,' he said. 'I mean, why?' He kicked himself. He was sounding more like a plaintive schoolboy by the second. Time to move on. Retain what scraps of dignity he had left. He watched as Amba removed the glove from her left hand and opened her tiny clutch bag to retrieve a phone. Her hand, though uncommonly large, was like the rest of her – soft, sensuous, with long fingers that moved slowly and sexily. A piano player's hand, his adopted mother would have said. But was that – was that the ghost of a ring on her third finger?

There wasn't time for a second look before the face cracked with a smile, this time a playful, teasing one. Amba leaned in conspiratorially. 'Oh, Edward, *chutzi*, here you are, after an afternoon with me, still confused about the definition of a lady. Don't you know, if the lady says no, she means perhaps? If the lady says perhaps, she means yes, and if the lady says yes, then she's not a lady?' She held his gaze, eyes dancing. He stared back, enthralled. God, she was cool. Not just beautiful, but *cool*. The hardest thing for him would be to captivate her the way she'd captivated him – but he was determined he was going to do it. And – had she just thrown him a lifeline?

Edward opened his mouth, but no sound came out. That was it. This was the woman he'd been searching for all his life. And he was going to let absolutely nothing stand in his way.

~

Quentin stood slightly to one side, concealing his delight at his own win and watching Angus hurry to join the celebrations. So, the old man was fallible after all. And not once, but *twice* in a matter of hours. Beaten both times by an outside runner, both times from Roger Skankton's stable. Quentin gazed thoughtfully as Roger grabbed a bottle of champagne and popped the cork theatrically.

Something was amiss here. Quentin felt the familiar feeling of anticipation as he began to sniff out someone up to no good. Angus was legendary for his failsafe tips. To fall once was unlucky, but three times – twice in the same day – was unheard of. Quentin had sought Angus out as the solution to his financial woes. But, looking at Roger now, it suddenly occurred to Quentin that he had (to coin a phrase) backed the wrong horse . . .

Quentin tutted. He forgot himself. Inwardly, he chastised himself and remonstrated with the devil on his shoulder. He was a new man. He had turned his back on underhand tactics and embraced life as a pillar of society. He tried to ignore the temptation.

Whatever Roger's secret was, it didn't concern him. And wouldn't.

~

Lyric turned to Philippe, eyes shining. 'I still can't believe it! Thumper is such a little star! He won again! What a way to celebrate Daddy's first day back at the races!'

They were strolling along towards the members' bar,

where George was busy ordering more champagne to celebrate his horse's win.

'It's amazing,' agreed Philippe. 'Angus didn't seem too impressed, though, did he?'

Lyric shrugged. 'You know Angus. He is always spot on with his predictions. To get something so wrong – well, I'm sure he was just feeling a bit put out.'

'Hmm – I think there was more to it than that,' pondered Philippe.

'Oh well, you can ask him yourself,' said Lyric, tucking her arm into his and hugging it to her. 'Angus never misses out on a party – and Daddy suggested we all go on afterwards to celebrate properly.'

'*Non, chérie*, I cannot. I have to get back,' said Philippe abruptly.

Lyric pulled away from him and looked at him in shock. 'What? You're not coming on with us? I know it isn't usually your scene, but . . .'

Philippe shook his head stubbornly. '*Non*. Sorry, *chérie*, I'm leaving now. I cannot come to the celebration at all. Something has come up. But you have your brother, your family, here, *n'est-ce pas*? They can bring you back to Broughton Hall.'

Lyric stared at him. 'What on earth can have come up that's more important than this?'

Philippe turned to face her, his eyes flashing dangerously. 'Lyric, there are other things in life than self-congratulation. I have been here all day, as your prop.

That's what I'm here for, right? To prop you up . . . But now something else requires my support, and I must go.'

He turned away and started to walk across the grass. Lyric stared after him, uncertain as to whether she should be feeling outraged or upset.

'Philippe!' she called. It fell flat in the air and, to her ears, sounded weak – pathetic, even.

Philippe lifted his hand in acknowledgement – but didn't turn round again. Lyric stood alone, crushed, watching him walk away.

What was the something that could be so important as to take him away from her like this? She felt a sick feeling in the pit of her stomach. And was it something, or some-*one*?

Twelve

Funny how the familiar soon became unfamiliar, thought Lyric, as she looked at the exaggerated revelry going on around the plush members' club. Once upon a time she'd have felt more at home in the VIP area of a place like this than anywhere else – surrounded by her It girl partners in crime, of course – but tonight she felt like a square peg in a round hole. Glamorous women flirted with suave men, as waiters served them expensive cocktails – all against a back-drop of the very latest in chrome-and-leather interior design. In a booth at the back of the room, a DJ pumped out sexually charged R&B. It was the picture of controlled hedonistic fun, and she should be enjoying it like everyone else – especially considering what she was here to celebrate. But for some reason she was feeling unaccountably edgy.

She tried not to dwell on Philippe's absence and his abrupt departure earlier that day from the racetrack. Better to wait until they were back together and could talk about it face-to-face instead of letting it get out of proportion on her own . . .

Not only that, she felt underdressed in the simple

Chanel suit she'd been wearing all day. She hadn't planned ahead for a night out and, alongside Cheryl and Kimberley's sexy chiffon Cavalli creations, she was feeling like a bit of a wallflower.

'What's that?' shouted Kimberley across the table as Cheryl approached brandishing a huge cocktail glass with a sparkler in it.

'It's a Racey Race Day cocktail!' shouted back Cheryl proudly. 'Want one, Lyric?'

Lyric smiled and shook her head. 'Last time I had something that looked like that, someone had spiked it,' she said, shuddering inwardly at the memory. 'I think I'll give it a miss.' She raised her champagne glass cheerfully at Kimberley.

'Lyric! Honestly. Who's gonna spike a drink in a place like this?' marvelled Cheryl, and turned her back on the group, jigging along to the music.

'Way-ey!' Darren appeared with a glamorous poppet on either arm and winked at Edward, sitting along from Lyric on the banquette. 'One for me, one for you! Haw haw.'

Edward laughed as Darren released the two girls and they stood to one side, chatting self-consciously.

'Not really my type, mate.'

'Nor mine,' agreed Darren, perching on the arm of the banquette and winking at Edward in a Team Shag conspiracy. 'I've got my eye on some bird at the bar, anyway. Real posh totty. Gonna see if I can get a bit of aristo skirt tonight!'

Lyric winced. 'Lucky girl,' she said, deadpan. 'Does she know what delights you have in store for her yet?'

'Nah, that would spoil the surprise, wouldn't it? That's the weapon of the skilled hunter, Lyric. Anyway, I've got my own ways and means, thank you very much.' Darren winked again at Edward and slid off the banquette, swaggering back to the bar.

'I can't believe how packed it is!' said Cheryl, turning back breathlessly. 'Everyone who's anyone is in here!'

Lyric looked around her interestedly. It was true that everyone seemed to come to Chester these days. It felt like there was more of London's social scene here tonight than there was in the capital itself.

'Look – isn't that Tara Palmer-Tomkinson over there?' asked Kimberley, leaning over and pointing. 'There, in that Prada dress?'

Lyric peered in the direction of her finger. 'Is she *still* on the circuit?' she said wonderingly.

'Lyric Charlton! I don't believe it! Is it really you?'

Lyric turned and her heart sank at the sight of the handsome, kookily dressed girl with retro make-up and carefully coiffed hair standing in front of her. 'Oh. Hello, Pippa. Long time no see.'

'*Long time?*' shrieked the girl. 'It's years! Budge up, will you?' Obediently, Edward and Cheryl moved up to make space for her on the banquette. 'Omigod, I just don't believe my eyes. What brings you to these parts?'

Lyric opened her mouth to reply, but Pippa didn't wait

for her response. 'Of course. Must be the racing. Forgot your dad is really into all that. So who's this, then?'

She looked at Edward with keen interest.

'This is my brother, Edward.'

'Your *brother*?' shrieked Pippa again. Her eyes widened and she looked closer at Edward as if he were an exhibit in a zoo. 'Oooh yes, I remember reading about it. I always thought you were an only child, you dark horse.'

'So did I,' said Lyric mildly. The irony was lost on Pippa, however, as she looked Edward up and down. 'Edward, this is Pippa Pankhurst.'

'Hi, Pippa,' said Edward flirtatiously. 'So, how do you two know each other?'

There was an uncomfortable silence as Lyric and Pippa looked at each other, both clearly reluctant to speak first.

Eventually Lyric spoke. 'We were partners in crime for a while,' she said slowly, not taking her eyes off Pippa's.

'Party girls united!' followed Pippa, holding Lyric's gaze. There was another silence. 'So no man in tow?' Pippa ventured. 'I thought you'd got engaged – I'd love to meet him.'

Lyric shook her head. 'He, erm, couldn't be here tonight.' She held out her finger for Pippa to admire the ring, but her heart felt heavy. She was engaged to be married to the man of her dreams – so why did it feel like she might as well be single?

Noticing his sister's discomfort, Edward interrupted. 'You still haven't told me how you know each other,' he probed. 'And why we haven't met before, Pippa? I thought I knew all of Lyric's friends.'

Pippa sighed theatrically. 'Well, since you ask, we were both It girls together back in the day. Practically inseparable. We even did the Gumball Rally together – do you remember that, Lyric?'

Lyric smiled guardedly. 'How could I forget?'

Pippa nudged her impatiently. 'Oh, come on, Lyric, it was a right laugh. It was a right laugh,' she repeated at Edward. 'We were in this super-sexy Lamborghini. We did the whole rally in bikinis and high heels. Whether it rained or snowed, we just didn't put the roof up. I don't think we *could* put the roof up with about three hundred pairs of shoes in the back. We even got arrested!'

'Pippa . . .' warned Lyric.

Edward leaned forward eagerly. 'No, go on, Pippa – tell me more. Lyric and I still have so much to tell each other, and I just love hearing stories about what she used to get up to in her hellraising days.' He gave Lyric a wicked look, and she raised her eyes skywards, but her body language relented. She just couldn't seem to refuse her brother anything.

'Oooh, scrummy, a long-lost brother – how romantic,' gushed Pippa, sitting back and taking a swig of her champagne. 'So back to the rally. We had an amazing playlist,' she gabbled. 'And we had a Calvin Klein Rastafarian model in the back of the car – do you remember, Lyric? I don't know where we found him – by a lamppost I think. He did the whole rally with us. We literally picked him up. We were like Thelma and Louise. I have never felt so high on freedom in my life.'

Pippa stopped, ostensibly to take a breath, but also to take a long tug through her straw before continuing at an ever-increasing pace. 'And how did we get arrested? Well, it was in Paris – and I guess it was really because Lyric didn't have a driving licence and we had heaps of shoes in the car and I think they thought we'd stolen them all.'

Lyric allowed herself a smile at the memory. 'I think the fact that we were driving on the wrong side of the road might have been the reason we got pulled over in the first place.' She shot an apologetic glance at Edward. Not having known her before rehab, he must find it hard to believe what she was like in her wilder days.

Pippa laughed. 'They said, how can you do a rally without a driving licence, and Lyric said – in French, of course – I don't know, but I'm doing it. The shoes were honestly for us to wear, because we'd crashed the original car in Milan, we were in a car that you couldn't legally take out of Italy.'

Edward's eyes were now practically on stalks. 'Wha-at?'

Lyric nodded sheepishly. 'In Milan I went too fast around a square and went straight into a tree.' She smiled at the look of horror that crossed Edward's face at the thought of her crashing a supercar. 'I know. It sounds dreadful, but we just didn't think about calling a garage. We just went straight in and got a new car. In those days, the rally had a VIP list – if you were lucky enough to be on it, and unlucky enough to crash, within an hour they'd replace your car with one of the same calibre. But the one they sent us was burgundy, and we didn't like the colour . . .'

'. . . So we asked the garage to let us test drive a gold one and put all the shoes in the back. They told us we weren't allowed to take it out of Milan, so we sneaked it over the border. With the Rasta model in the boot by now – because he didn't have a passport!' hooted Pippa.

Lyric shook her head, remembering. 'Nothing was going to stop us winning.'

'Not even missing the ferry!' shrieked Pippa again, her voice getting shriller with every sentence. 'We were due to get the ferry from Hamburg to England. And we were so late, they said, you're not going to make it, and I'm not joking, it was pulling away. Lyric said to me, what do you want to do? I can floor it or I can stop. And the ramp was going up and all the cars were just there and I said stop – which she took to mean go – and the car took off in the air and came down on the other side, thump-thump-thump, and – bingo! Just two more passengers.' Pippa laughed hysterically, and Lyric along with her. Edward was staring at them both with a mixture of horror, disbelief and humour.

Pippa suddenly waved vociferously. 'Oh dammit, there's my cue.' She stood up and kissed Lyric lightly on both cheeks. 'Well, lovely seeing you again. We simply must meet up.'

Pippa turned around to Edward. 'And you too, you *fox*. Toodle-oo!'

She tippy-toed off, and Lyric sank back in relief.

Edward looked at her searchingly. 'So then what happened between you two closer-than-close party girls?'

Lyric shook her head. 'Nothing much. We went our separate ways,' she said, dodging eye contact. But Edward wasn't going to be fobbed off.

'Oh, come on, Lyric! That's hardly like you,' Edward persisted. 'And if Pippa isn't still off her face all the time, why not hook up with her every now and again? She certainly seems harmless enough.'

'Yes, unless you're a tabloid journalist wielding a fat chequebook,' snapped Lyric.

Edward looked at her in shock. 'She sold you out?'

Lyric nodded numbly. She hadn't intended telling Edward any of this, but she was damned if her brother was going to think she was being unfriendly for no reason. 'With really embarrassing detail. Silly things about what I used to get up to and with whom, not to mention really personal details that you wouldn't want known about yourself. Which is apparently key to making a story marketable, but is also – unfortunately, for the people who sell stories – key to identifying them as well.'

Edward looked puzzled. 'But if other people had sold their stories too, how did you know it was her?'

'Put it this way. The papers may have run their stories

on me, but I was always popular with them. I always tried to be pleasant and polite. So they helped me confirm my worst suspicions.' She took a deep breath.

'So why speak to her now?' wondered Edward out loud. 'If she's such a bad friend?'

'I've only spoken to her once since I found out, when I confronted her about it,' said Lyric miserably. 'She said she'd been in debt. And because she had the honesty to admit it – and, I guess, because her thirty-thousand-pound fee would have been like a drop in the ocean when it came to what she owed – I decided to forgive her. Forgive, not forget, you understand.'

Edward looked nonplussed. 'Until I knew all that about her, I thought she was all right,' he protested. 'Good fun, even.'

'Yes, and the rest,' said Lyric grimly. 'Didn't you see her coming on to you as soon as she found out who you were?'

Edward stared at her, an inscrutable look on his face, and Lyric shifted uncomfortably in her seat. She wasn't used to not being able to read his expression, and it unnerved her.

'Is that what you think? That she was only interested in me because I'm now a Charlton?'

'Edward, there are no two ways about it, that girl is always on the make.'

Edward glared at her. 'Well, there are no two ways

about it – people did like me before I became a Charlton. And, for your information, she was looking pretty interested before you had to start banging on about old times.'

He picked up his drink and stormed off. Lyric stared after him as he sought out Darren from the crowd. What was it about her that had all her favourite men deserting her today?

~

Seething, Edward approached Darren, who stood holding court at the bar. He took a deep breath and gritted his teeth. Bloody Charltons! They really did think the world revolved around them. And whilst he loved them dearly, he really couldn't stomach this assumption that everyone wanted a piece of them simply because of who they were.

'All right, mate – how's it going?'

Darren turned round and grinned at him. 'Not bad.' He nodded towards a beautiful girl a couple of people along from him. 'Just waiting for Fenella Fanny Adams over there to fall into my arms.'

Edward sniggered. 'Hadn't you better go work some of that famous Skankton charm on her, then? You're not going to get very far from here.'

'Oh, come on. Just you watch me. If I want her, money's no object. I can get her.' Darren grabbed Edward in a matey headlock. 'Anyway, what's going on with you? Haven't seen you sniffing out any action this evening – had your head turned by that bit you were mooning over all day at the racetrack, have you?'

Edward laughed. He'd never been friends with anyone quite as laddish as Darren before, but he missed the familiar comradeship of the friends from his previous life – he never seemed to have time to see them any more – and he liked the way Darren had unquestioningly accepted him into his inner circle. Forget hanging on the coat-tails of his ex-It girl sister. Forget organizing some lame fortieth wedding anniversary party for a bunch of OAPs. Darren and his mate, Prince whoever-he-was – a prince! – were much more up his street.

'What are you talking about? She was all right, but she's not here tonight, is she?' Edward looked around, for the first time assessing the talent surrounding him. True, none of them quite had the same effect on him as Amba – but there certainly were some good-looking girls in here. 'I reckon I can catch you up in a couple of minutes. Especially considering current progress.' He nodded back towards the girl Darren was eyeing up.

Darren's smile grew wider and oilier. 'Mate, you've got no chance. I mean, I'm waiting for her to LITERALLY fall into my arms. She's plastered, mate. And if that doesn't work, I'll slip her a bit of Rohypnol. It's a little favourite of Team Shag, you know . . .'

Edward stared at him, appalled, made a mental note to keep an eye on what his friend was doing and leaned over the bar. 'I'll have a beer, please – Darren, what are you drinking?'

'I'll have a beer – and get yourself a tequila chaser, my son. I've got a bottle behind the bar. We're celebrating, aren't we? That's if there's any left, of course!'

Edward eyed the half-empty bottle of tequila, feeling impressed in spite of himself. Had Darren drunk all of that on his own?

'On second thoughts, better not,' put in Darren. 'Tequila makes me aggressive!' He laughed. 'Talking of which, look at that bunch of tit-heads over there.'

Edward followed his gaze to where a blinging entourage had arrived. It was Fabien Figouré, a French rap star currently making it big in the UK. The star himself was only about five feet tall, but, surrounded by a collection of burly bodyguards and sexy, scantily clad women, he seemed seven feet and counting.

'Well, if you've got it, flaunt it . . .' murmured Edward, part of him still agog at the social power that enormous wealth could command. As he watched a red mist descend over Darren's face, he realized – too late – that he might as well have waved a red rag at a bull.

'Well, I've got it – and I'm gonna flaunt it,' said Darren, pushing his way past Edward and staggering over to where Fabien was starting to make shapes on the dance floor.

'Mate –' cautioned Edward as he walked past him, but it fell on deaf ears. He watched helplessly as Darren did everything he could to antagonize the group – mimicking Fabien, touching up the girls dancing around him and mocking the bodyguards. Edward's sinking feeling grew steadily as Darren became more and more disrespectful, batting off the bodyguards' initial warnings and continuing in his drunken harassment of Figouré. Finally, the main bodyguard had clearly had enough, and lifted Darren up off the dance floor and clear of the group. It was the final straw for Darren. Trying to pull himself free, he swung a punch at the bodyguard. It was as effective as punching a brick wall, and Darren was physically stunned by the bodyguard's solid bulk. The effect on those surrounding him, however, was something else. His punch was the touchpaper that lit the kindling of the drunken testosterone filling the club, and the dance floor erupted in one almighty, ugly fistfight.

~

From the relative safety of the VIP area, Lyric looked on in dismay as Darren was dragged out by two of the club's bouncers, and she stood up, searching the moil for signs of Edward. He'd been with Darren, hadn't he? Where on earth was he now?

She surveyed the scene with a sinking feeling in the pit of her stomach. Tonight she should be feeling so happy – her father was on the road to recovery and she was out celebrating with her brother. But instead she wished with all her heart that she was at home with Philippe.

She tried to ignore the little voice in her head. Even if she had been at home with him, would she be feeling any better? Or would the uncertainty she felt at the moment be even greater if they were physically close?

Thirteen

Lyric tried to relax as she indicated left and pulled off the motorway onto the country roads that led to Broughton Hall. Broughton Hall wasn't just the family home; it was her fortress, a haven away from the madness of her whirlwind existence, and the only place she had always felt comfortable being herself. She should be happy to be arriving back – especially as Philippe would be here, waiting for her – but instead, today, she felt on edge, her stomach churning and her eye twitching insistently.

How much she'd changed since she first left Broughton Hall for her tiny Kensington mews house. Back then, this journey would have been a frenetic dash after a well-placed morning wake-up call from Constance. Her mother always phoned to make sure she was up after whatever party she'd been at the night before, and Lyric would dash off in a car full of overflowing ashtrays, unopened post and apple cores littering the passenger seat. Every journey was spent drinking takeaway coffee, doing her make-up at traffic lights and trying to clear her head of the ubiquitous hangover. Now, she generally enjoyed the drive and the head space it gave her.

But today her head was full of problems, including the plans for her parents' ruby wedding party, which were being somewhat held up by Edward's new-found reluctance to help organize it. He'd seemed so excited by the idea of the party when she'd first suggested it – but now, she detected a thinly concealed negativity.

And then there was Philippe. So many times, she'd plucked up the courage to confront him about the text message – courage which then always deserted her at the last minute. It wasn't just fear of how he would react. What if he confirmed her worst fears? What then? And so the anxiety remained – but it was also starting to irritate her. She and Philippe had been the perfect couple; now their relationship was giving her more grief than pleasure. If they couldn't work through it, they should call time on it. There was no point making themselves miserable indefinitely.

But even as she was steeling herself against the possibility of a split, Lyric was dreading it. 'What ifs' kept taunting her at every turn. *What if* she hadn't lost the baby, and they were both still expectant parents? *What if* she had followed the pregnancy advice to the letter, and not had coffee or the odd glass of fizz? *What if* she hadn't worked so hard, been there more for Philippe as he built his new business at Broughton Hall? *What if* she hadn't spent so much time with Edward since his arrival on the scene?

And worse still: *What if* Philippe had indeed been

unfaithful, with Pamela, or someone else? *What if* he was having an affair? She bit her lip uncertainly. Was she perhaps not sophisticated enough for Philippe? Not beautiful enough? Good enough in bed? Had she been too snappy, too self-obsessed, too family-focused, to the detriment of their relationship? Her head was spinning.

Pull yourself together, Lyric, she scolded herself as she turned up the long drive to Broughton Hall.

Lyric drove past an oak sapling, the first tree that Philippe had planted at Broughton Hall, and smiled. He'd named it after her, and they'd marvelled at how they'd watch it grow together, and when they were old and grey the tree itself would be standing tall and proud, in its prime. The thought gave her renewed hope, and banished the 'what ifs' from her mind – at least for now.

As she turned the final corner through the aged copse and the spectacular facade of Broughton Hall finally came into view, Lyric gasped in shock. The old, familiar, shabby gravel drive, punctuated by the odd flowering weed, had been fully tarmacked. It was now a smooth strip of grey – a scar along the front of the dignified old building – and the only weeds visible now were in 'the Constance Project', her mother's new bed of tropical plants and ornamental ganja bushes that stood along the edge of the kitchen garden wall, to the right of the house.

As Lyric drew up, Constance floated into sight, gesticulating wildly.

Lyric opened the car door and leapt out to greet her.

'Coo-ee! Lyric, darling, how wonderful to see you. But you can't park here, darling – this is now a landing strip.'

Lyric stared at her, aghast. 'A landing strip?' The only plane ever to grace Broughton Hall had been her father's old Piper Arrow IV crop plane that he'd taken them for joy rides in when they were little. Hardly the epitome of glamour, but, as her father was always keen to point out, it could get him to Leicestershire in well under an hour. At the time, every take-off had her mother reaching for one decanter or another, and as Lyric and George made the ascent, her father would turn to her with a conspiratorial grin and say, 'Hold tight, darling, we've got to clear the telephone cable.' Now, Lyric looked up dubiously. The cable had long since gone, of course, but she couldn't imagine even a glider making the flight landing successfully.

'Yes, darling, a landing strip. To celebrate your father's recovery. You're quite simply nobody unless you have good transport links to the rest of the world, and with Broughton Hall now fully on the tourist map, I felt we needed to bring ourselves into the twenty-first century somehow. I'm going to call it the George Charlton Runway. I tell you, we're going to be the talk of the season. And if the world thinks St Barts is the worst landing strip in the world – wait till they try the approach to Broughton Hall!'

'OK, Mummy, I'll put the car around the back,' Lyric said compliantly. The last thing she needed now was a contretemps with Constance – no doubt she'd get the back-story from Daddy and Philippe later. She opened the car door, and was about to clamber back in when Constance turned back to her.

'Oh, Lyric, darling, do let me know when you and Philippe set a date, won't you?'

Puzzled, Lyric blinked stupidly at her in the spring sunshine. 'A date for what?'

'Why, for the wedding, of course!' trilled Constance. 'I'm running out of excuses why you and Philippe haven't got one yet, darling, and really, long engagements are sooo last decade. A marriage could be just what we need to really catapult Broughton Hall into the next century!'

Lyric shook her head. 'No, Mummy, we've kind of had other things on our minds recently,' she said pointedly. 'But far be it from me to let personal tragedy get in the way of progress – so, as soon as we have a date I'll be sure to let all the newspaper diary editors know.'

'There's no need to use that tone with me, Lyric, dear,' said Constance mildly. 'You don't want Philippe to be snapped up by anyone else, do you?'

Lyric narrowed her eyes. 'What's that supposed to mean?'

'Well, darling, you're not getting any younger – and with a dearth of eligible young men on the horizon you wouldn't want some leggy twenty-something to come along and snaffle him from right under your nose, would you?'

Lyric gaped, and then shut her mouth hurriedly. She had a strange sense of foreboding about where this conversation might be going.

'Why would you say that, Mummy?'

Constance looked down, suddenly transfixed by an area of tarmac. 'I'm not entirely sure this surface is smooth enough for lighter planes,' she said thoughtfully, then looked up abruptly. 'Only that Julia Merton mentioned she was at Asprey's the other day, and saw Philippe walk past with a young lady. I mean, a *very* young lady. With shopping bags. Of course, I'm sure you knew about it, but just the same – people do talk, darling.'

Lyric frowned, heart racing. What would Philippe have been doing shopping in Bond Street? He hated shopping. And who – who – was the young girl?

'Well, I'll be sure to congratulate Philippe on keeping the rumour mill grinding,' muttered Lyric grimly, unsure of how else to react. 'In the meantime, I'd better move the car before it's hit by low-flying aircraft.'

~

Moments later, Lyric let Stan out of the back door and followed him as he bounded across the gardens. Philippe was working, and she resolved to find him and ask him about the young girl in Bond Street. And the text . . . There was bound to be a logical explanation – and leaving the doubts to fester in her mind even longer would do neither of them any good. Meanwhile, the fresh air and exercise would clear her head and hopefully give her new perspective.

As she passed a couple of gardeners, Lyric felt her phone buzz in her pocket and pulled it out, screening the call before answering. She was pleased to see Laura's number displayed on the LED screen. Laura was her most optimistic of friends – just the person to put her in the right frame of mind.

'Hi, Laura. How was Sardinia?'

'It was a wonderful break. I feel like a new woman! And that restaurant you recommended was great. Superb sunsets!'

'Good! I loved it and I thought you would.' Lyric smiled at the memory of the waterside taverna she'd been to a few years previously.

'Talking of new women . . .' Laura suddenly started to choke violently on the other end of the phone.

'Laura – are you OK?'

Recovering quickly, she came back onto the line.

'Yes, sorry – er, frog in my throat. What was I saying?'

'Something about new women,' said Lyric, amused.

'Oh, really? No, surely not – don't know what I was going on about. How's Philippe?'

'He's fine,' said Lyric, suddenly suspicious. 'Laura, is everything OK?'

'Yes, of course,' said Laura innocently. 'Why wouldn't it be?'

Now Lyric was certain something was up. She knew that fake tone of old. Laura always played the 'glad game', putting a positive spin on everything – especially when there was nothing positive to be spun. If someone lost their mother, Laura would say, 'Well, at least it wasn't her father as well!' And now, Lyric was certain she was covering something up.

'Because I've spent too long agonizing over a text some predatory divorcee sent Philippe. And yes, before you ask, I did read his texts.' Lyric could feel all the hurt and worry threatening to erupt, and she took a deep breath to calm herself. 'And now – now, I've just had a weird conversation with my mother, and suddenly you're acting funny, too,' replied Lyric. 'Are you going to tell me what's up?'

'Honestly, Lyric, I don't know what you're on about.'

'OK, well let me put this in context. Mummy has just been quizzing me about a date for the wedding because she's got this idea he's been playing away with some twenty-something temptress. And now you call up acting secretive and pretending nothing's wrong and I find I suddenly don't know what to believe. Is my mother on morphine or is she actually telling the truth? Has Philippe had a personality transplant? And is he being unfaithful to me?'

There was a stunned silence on the other end of the phone. But when Laura spoke, she was confident and re-assuring.

'Honestly, Lyric, I don't know anything. I just know you, and I could tell something was troubling you while we were away, but I never got the chance to ask you about it. I thought it was the miscarriage, but from what you've just said, it seems to be Philippe. On that score I can put your mind at rest. He won't ever change. I'm sure it's all innocent. He's one of the good guys. If ever there was a couple born to be together, it's you two. And if ever there was a man without a disloyal bone in his body, it's Philippe. I should know about unfaithful men, after all!' She laughed bitterly. 'So instead of fretting about what's *not* going wrong, why don't you put it out of your mind and concentrate on setting that wedding date – and put your mother out of her misery?'

After she'd hung up, Lyric replaced the phone in her pocket and continued with more of a spring in her step. Laura might be overly positive all the time, but she was right. Lyric climbed over a stile and jogged over the hill to where Philippe was working, suddenly keen to see him, kiss him and feel his embrace.

She could see him now, pulling up some roots, one heel stuck in the earth and the other behind him for balance. As she approached she could make out the exertion etched on his face, and she smiled to herself. He saw her and put one hand up to wave. All of a sudden, the roots gave way, and he fell backwards. Lyric laughed out loud, and ran to help pull him to his feet.

'*Merde!*' Philippe spat as he got up, waving her away and brushing himself down irritably. He inspected the palm of his hand. 'Stinging nettles!'

'I'll get you some dock leaves!' said Lyric. 'Daddy always used to rub those on our stings – and there are always some growing near nettles . . .' She searched the ground around him. 'Here!' She pulled up some of the leaves, still wet from the morning dew, and tried to take his hand.

'Don't be pathetic, Lyric!' he snapped. 'I'm a man, for God's sake, not a child – what do I need with dock leaves?'

He sucked at the sting instead, turning away from Lyric, and she stared at his back, crushed.

Laura was wrong. Philippe *had* changed. The question was, did that make her mother right? Was there more to the text after all? And had Philippe been unfaithful? Even worse, was he having an affair?

Fourteen

'So, are we going racing?'

'Erm – well, I guess you might say more rac-y than rac-ing – but there will be horses involved, in a manner of speaking.'

Next to Edward, Prince Abu Rhuba leaned back, stretched his arms out along the back of the chauffeur-driven Mercedes's cream leather upholstery, raised his monobrow and gave a smug smile. In his Tom Ford suit, Cartier watch and expensive cologne, Rhuba was every bit the super-rich 'son of'. Edward smiled back uncertainly, and looked out of the window as the lights of night-time London flashed past.

The evening had gone by in a similar blur. The glitzy club where he and Darren had met Prince Abu Rhuba already seemed to be hours in the past, even though they'd only left minutes ago: the VIP lounge, the bottles of Grey Goose vodka and Cristal champagne at hundreds of pounds a pop casually sitting around in ice buckets on their table, the identikit glamour girls clamouring around them. Then the casino, where Darren and Rhuba had flashed their cash around ostentatiously, buying chips and placing bets with gay abandon, in the process attracting awed attention from all the other guests – at least, so it seemed to Edward. They were all from a parallel universe.

It had been exhilarating, and kind of fun – but more than that. It was addictive. For the first time, Edward felt he had membership of an ultra-exclusive club at his finger-tips yet frustratingly just beyond his reach; and, whether or not he approved of what that club stood for, he liked being an outsider even less, and was determined to soak it all up so that in future, he wouldn't be the gauche country cousin standing on the sidelines, but a bona-fide member able to choose whether or not he accepted the rules of member-ship.

For now, though, he was acutely aware of being in the middle of some kind of initiation, and so when Rhuba had announced a change of scene – exact destination un-announced – he'd willingly gone along with them, even though part of him longed simply to go home to the safety of his bed at Broughton Hall. When Darren had told Edward to bring his passport earlier that evening, he'd assumed naively that he meant for ID to get into the clubs. But now, as they pulled into City Airport, he had the sneaking suspicion it was going to take him much further afield – and so his questions had begun to refer to the next day, rather than the next few hours. He fingered his shirt uncomfortably, hoping it wasn't somewhere too distant – or, if it was, that someone had packed for him. He only had the clothes he was standing in, and he wasn't in the business of wearing underpants more than two days running, at the most.

'Don't worry, mate – we'll be more than happy to call Mummy and tell her where you are!' leered Darren from his seat, facing Edward, giving Rhuba a knowing look. Remembering Team Shag's main aim – to bed Constance – Edward shuddered inwardly.

'Don't be ridiculous, mate. I've got a date tomorrow, that's all,' he fibbed. 'Just wondering whether to cancel or not.'

'That would be advisable,' said Rhuba smoothly as they pulled up alongside a large private jet. 'You may be gone some time.'

Edward's eyes nearly popped out of his head as he realized the jet was their next destination.

'We're going in that?' he marvelled, totally blowing the cool exterior he had been cultivating throughout the rest of the evening.

Again, Rhuba and Darren shared a conspiratorial look and Edward, trying not to be intrigued but fighting a losing battle, felt another pang of longing to be in the gang rather than outside it – however absurdly repellent part of him found it.

'Let's just call it my EasyPeasyJet,' smirked Rhuba, sitting forward but waiting for the driver to open the door for him. Darren sniggered and Rhuba turned to Edward with a self-satisfied smile.

'Why's that?' Edward's cool blown, he decided there was no point trying to retrieve it. He was way out of his comfort zone here – might as well admit it.

Rhuba turned to him and his smile widened ominously. 'You'll see.'

~

'So, come on then, where are we *really* going?' probed Edward from the depths of a soft leather banquette, as he battled with a PS3 control set and a game of *Red Dead Redemption*. To one side of him there was a platter of mouth-watering snacks, and to the other a minibar stacked full of spirits, mixers and ice-cold beers.

The jet was ostentatiously luxurious, with wall-to-wall deep shag-pile carpet and leather upholstery. A team of beautiful flight attendants were hovering, fluffing up cushions and seeing to their every comfort. There were massage chairs, flat beds, a Bang & Olufsen surround-sound stereo system and a 52-inch plasma TV screen. On the lower deck there was even a stable where one of the Rhuba horses lay sedated ready for the journey, and a cabin for the horses' companion to stay in – this time, apparently, they weren't just making do with a groom, but taking a vet with them as well. He'd seemed all right – a bit shifty, but then didn't everyone when presented with such opulence? Only the master suite next door remained unexplored, presumably, thought Edward, because it was Rhuba's private quarters. As far as Edward was concerned, this was heaven, and he would have been quite happy just sitting here on the tarmac for the next forty-eight hours if he had to.

Rhuba, lounging on another couch and idly watching the game, smirked again.

'Whaddaya reckon, Daz, shall we tell him?'

Darren, flicking through a porn site on an iPad, looked up. 'I reckon so, Rhuba. Why not?'

'Well, Edward, my new friend, Team Shag is going to Dubai!' He lifted up his arm lazily and Darren leaned over and high-fived him.

'Dubai!'

Edward frowned. Something wasn't adding up. 'I thought July was too hot to race in Dubai?'

'It is,' grinned Rhuba. 'But it doesn't stop us taking GM for a little holiday, does it?' He looked over at Darren, who gave his trademark leer.

'What – General. Manager?' he articulated carefully and deliberately. The comment was aimed at Rhuba, but he was looking at Edward as he spoke.

'Yes, that's right – General. Manager,' repeated Rhuba, also looking at Edward. 'He's the kind of horse that makes horseshoes lucky.' His eyes glittered in a lively fashion, but seemed to have no warmth, and Edward smiled and nodded weakly. He had no idea what either of them was going on about, but he wasn't about to admit it and make himself look any more stupid.

The plane fired up its engines in preparation for take-off, and Edward felt a surge of adrenaline. Was this for real?

He thought his life had changed when he'd first found his blood family – but the Charltons were resolutely old money in upbringing and attitude. Darren's new-money 'flash Harry' approach had been enough to convince Edward of the power that money could hold – this world of the super-super-super-rich was something else indeed.

'And, as we are treating the horse, I thought we should treat ourselves, too,' said Rhuba, holding up a remote control as the plane commenced its ascent.

Edward looked up from his game as Rhuba pointed it at the door to the master suite, which began to open.

'I thought this might make the flight more entertaining.'

As the doors opened fully, five of the most beautiful girls Edward had ever seen walked out in formation. There was a blonde, a brunette, a redhead, an Asian girl and a black girl, all with bodies to die for and faces that would tame the devil himself. Two were in body-con Herve Leger, another was in Myla underwear and a satin dressing gown, another in Agent Provocateur hot pants and feathered bra, another in Rigby and Peller corset and stockings and the last in skimpy La Perla cami and French knickers. One carried a magnum of Cristal, the next a black silken scarf, another a long horsewhip. The smell of Dior's Poison hung heavy in the air. Behind them, a massive super-king-size bed was covered in satin sheets and strewn with petals, and a Jacuzzi sat bubbling away. The girls looked like a selection of the most exotic, delicious sweets ever made –

and Edward instantly recognized that they were there for his delectation. His and the other boys' . . .

So that's why the master suite had been out of bounds beforehand, thought Edward – it was all part of the 'surprise'.

'I'd always thought tracksuits and sloppy joes were more de rigueur on aeroplanes,' he deadpanned.

'Ha ha ha – and the boy can joke, too,' said Rhuba patronizingly.

'Never mind all that – who's for a Darren Dares?' said Darren, brandishing a cocktail shaker. 'It's Dynamite. It's Dangerous. But, most of all, it's Delicious – if you Dare . . .' He sidled up to the nearest girl – the blonde – and licked her ear. She giggled coquettishly as the other girls gave tinkly laughs.

Not for the first time, Edward marvelled at how his new friend could turn on the charm. Yes, he was a good-looking bloke, and obviously loaded – but Lyric for one reckoned he was seriously slimy, too. Yet whenever Edward had seen him in action, he'd had girls eating out of his hand, not showing him the hand.

Clearly Edward had a few lessons to learn from him.

'Well, mate, choose your landing strip,' said Rhuba lewdly as he patted his knee and gestured for the Asian girl to join him. 'These are top-class girls. And you'll be flying high for the rest of this trip!'

'Just watch the boobs don't blow up when we reach altitude,' joked Darren.

Edward sat, dumbstruck, willing himself to make a move, any move. Eventually he turned to the redhead, who was draped along the back of his sofa. 'Can I get you a drink?'

'Edward,' said Rhuba, leaning over to whisper in Edward's ear as his companion got up to pour herself a drink. 'These girls might be top-class, but you don't have to worry about the niceties. They don't need chatting up. They know why they're here – and they'll do anything. Isn't that right, Darren?'

Darren sent the blonde packing with a smart slap on the bottom, and turned around and winked knowingly at Edward.

Rhuba laughed. 'This is the world of the super-super-rich, Edward. It's not just sitting there in your private jet, reading *Hello!* and drinking champagne, you know. This is a whole world beyond that – a world without boundaries. Welcome to the club, mate.'

As he shook hands with Rhuba, Edward stared around him in disbelief. At last he was a real part of it. Part of the Team. This was just fantastically cool. This really was the life. Wasn't it?

~

As the plane landed, Edward looked around him, suddenly with the fresh eyes of a stranger on board. The eyes, in fact, of the people who would have to clear up after them. He wrinkled his nose at the scene of squalid devastation they were leaving behind. The girls – all now wearing in-flight tracksuits – were still beautiful, but tarred with the seedy brush of their trade and smeared with evening make-up in the unforgiving Middle Eastern daylight.

It was a scene of a bunch of debauched thugs with more money than manners. And whilst Edward couldn't help feeling a guilty thrill at the memory of last night, he still felt uneasy and uncomfortable. Again, he seemed torn between two very different worlds.

He felt another stab of resentment towards his father. Damn George and his spineless acceptance of Edward's 'death' all those years ago. Why hadn't he tried harder to determine what had happened to his son? Why hadn't he smelled a rat when offered only the most superficial of medical explanations for his newborn son's 'demise'? Edward tightened his fists by his side in anger and frustration. And what kind of legacy was this anyway, destined to spend the rest of his life feeling like a stranger, both in his old life and his new?

Fifteen

Lyric lay in bed, wide awake as she had been for hours, listening to the familiar sounds of Philippe getting dressed, creeping around so as not to wake her. It was the same routine every morning and, half asleep, she usually found it comforting. Today, however, the lack of contact – and the fact that he seemed unaware that she was wide awake – seemed to accentuate the gulf between them.

Fully dressed, he crept out of the room and was almost through the door when Lyric found she could stand it no longer.

'So you're not even going to say goodbye?' Lyric shot up from her pillow and stared at Philippe's retreating form accusingly.

He turned back in surprise. 'Lyric! I didn't realize you were awake.' He hesitated before retracing his steps back to the bedside. It was a millisecond pause – but to Lyric it seemed to sum up everything that was wrong between them.

'That shouldn't stop you wanting to kiss me goodbye!'

'It didn't stop me *wanting* to kiss you,' he said, with a

hint of a smile around his lips but more than a hint of bemusement in his eyes. 'It just stopped me doing it.' He leaned forward to kiss her, but she pulled back.

He frowned and clicked his tongue in irritation.

'Lyric, what is going on?'

Still sitting in bed, Lyric pulled a pillow in front of her and hugged it tightly.

'I could ask you the same thing,' she said in a small voice.

'I beg your pardon?'

She looked up at him and spoke louder, her voice shaking. 'I said, I could ask you the same thing.'

Again, that look of innocent bemusement. But rather than pacifying Lyric, it seemed to fuel her anger.

'First a text from a flirtatious, beautiful older woman. And now people seeing you with a flirtatious, beautiful younger girl.'

Philippe stared at her. 'What are you talking about?'

'The text from Pammie?' Lyric almost spat the woman's name.

Philippe shook his head dismissively.

'Or the girl half of London has seen you walking around town with? Am I not enough for you, Philippe? Are you finding me lacking in some way? Some way that makes you seek to supplement me elsewhere?'

Philippe's frown now turned into a scowl. It seemed to deepen the scar on his cheek, giving him a brooding air. 'You don't lack anything,' he said simply. 'I thought you knew how I feel about you.'

'So did I!' Lyric thought she would burst with the unfairness of it all. Why couldn't he understand how this was making her feel? 'But all these other people. They're making out you're having an affair. Having *affairs*, even.'

'Other people – pah,' spat Philippe. 'What do they matter to us? All that should concern you and I is just that – you and I.'

'Well, that's not so easy when other people concern themselves with us. Or, more accurately, *you*.' She was crying now, as the weeks of pent-up frustration and suspicion began to overflow. Tell me – just tell me. Are you having an affair?'

Philippe's scowl got deeper. His eyes didn't leave her face – but he said nothing.

'Are you having an *affair*?' Lyric was almost shouting now. 'Just. Tell. Me!'

'Lyric, I thought we were better than this. I do not have the time or the energy for this kind of stupidity,' he said flatly. 'And I am surprised that you do. I suggest you get up, and get dressed, and get on with your day. Maybe at some point you will realize how silly you're being.'

He left, banging the door behind him. Lyric hugged the pillow to her and stared after him, numb from the exchange. So much for the adult conversation she'd planned. It had turned into a petty argument, leaving Philippe angry and her feeling deficient.

Only then did she realize. He hadn't actually answered

her questions. In the heat of the moment, she'd let him leave without telling her any more than she already knew.

She was none the wiser. Just exactly what *was* going on?

~

The smell of the soft leather upholstery seemed to envelop Lyric in a hug as she sat back and watched London flashing past her. It was a while since she'd had the luxury of a chauffeur-driven car, and she was glad that PP, her once regular driver, had been free to drive her today – especially after this morning's argument with Philippe. He'd even remembered to bring the duvet that she used to snuggle up in on the way home, watching dawn break after a wild night out. Now she pulled it around her, as much for the comfort as the warmth, and tried to relax ahead of her long day.

It was the Sunny Street Hospital AGM, and Lyric had felt unaccountably nervous and unprepared, so she'd booked the car in order to give herself more time to gen up on her speech and on the paediatric cancer hospital's highlights of the previous year. However, after giving it a quick read through, she'd found it hard to study it more. Anyway, she was bound to stray from the script, as she always did when speaking on a topic she was so passionate about; the important thing was knowing your facts, and Sunny Street was something Lyric was an expert on. When she'd been asked to become patron of the charity, she'd pledged to take the role extremely seriously – no turning up with a smile and a sound bite and leaving straight away – she'd put in hours of under-the-radar hospital walkabouts and fundraising, and there was very little she didn't know or understand about the daily running of the place. In fact, it could almost have been her *Mastermind* specialist subject . . .

Which was just as well, after this morning. As her mind wandered to Philippe again, Lyric clicked her tongue in annoyance. She hated this person she was turning into – suspicious, paranoid, even – but she couldn't seem to shake it off. The more she told herself it was ludicrous that anything could be seriously wrong between her and Philippe, the more he seemed distant, moody, and the less confident she felt broaching the subject with him. And after their conversation this morning – she simply didn't know what to think.

She leaned forward. 'Can we pull over at the next garage, please, PP?'

'No problem, ma'am,' he beamed in the rear-view mirror, his fleshy face and wide, toothy smile filling the whole of it. 'There's one coming up just now.' He indicated left and pulled off into a petrol station.

Lyric scrabbled in her bag for her purse. 'And do you want anything, PP?'

PP shifted his bulk slightly in his seat and smiled at her again, adjusting the headpiece he always wore, which was, Lyric had always suspected, connected to nothing. 'Just a pork pie, please, boss.'

Lyric leapt out of the car, sprinting across the forecourt and into the shop. Dear PP. His love of a Melton Mowbray had inspired his nickname – Pork Pie – until Lyric had shortened it. He was ex-Met Police, although, from the size of him these days, you'd never believe it. Years spent in a sedentary job – and countless pork pies – had made him more fat than cuddly, and she wasn't sure he'd be able to run if you paid him.

Pork pie and chewing gum purchased, Lyric clambered back into the car and settled herself back in the seat. Chewing often seemed to help her think, especially when she was nervous, and although she hated seeing people doing it in public, in the comfort of her own car she found the regular rhythm of chewing calmed her.

'You're very quiet today, boss,' observed PP shrewdly. 'Normally you're rabbiting nineteen to the dozen, especially when we haven't seen each other for a while.'

Lyric caught his eye in the mirror and smiled to herself. 'I guess so,' she agreed. 'I've got a lot on my mind.'

'Surely nothing to trouble you,' remonstrated PP. He'd always been peculiarly perceptive where Lyric was concerned – and, over the years, he'd become something of a confidante to her. Drivers could be like that – they saw their clients through every part of their lives, from the highs to the very vulnerable lows – and, God knows, there had been enough of those in Lyric's life. But, as with the staff at Broughton Hall, Lyric's non-hierarchical way of treating people meant they often took her – and the lost soul she'd once been – to their hearts. PP was just one. But PP knew her better than most – not much had happened in Lyric's adult life that PP didn't know about, and he was clearly happy to resume his quasi-paternal role now. 'A lovely girl like you should be full of the joys of life, not carrying the woes of the world on her shoulders. I thought all your troubles were behind you these days?'

At the unexpected kindness, to Lyric's horror she suddenly felt her eyes fill with tears. 'Oh, PP,' she wailed. 'So did I!'

And suddenly, it all came out. How much she loved Philippe. How she'd thought he loved her – until recently when, rather than being the slightly reserved but strong person she'd fallen in love with, he'd become distant and secretive.

'And so now – now, PP – I know it's not my imagination. It's been going on too long, and we've had too many missed opportunities to fix it. The only thing I can think is that he's found someone else – that Philippe is being unfaithful!'

There was a heavy silence and Lyric began to sob quietly. There. She'd said it. And it felt good to get it off her chest. Even if it did sound even more unbelievable than the thought had seemed. Philippe, unfaithful. Was it really what they had come to?

PP cleared his throat and glanced in the rear-view mirror as he changed lane, sneaking a glance at Lyric. She noticed, of course, and felt reassured by his concern. Sensing she needed more time to compose herself, he concentrated on the road and waited for her to recover.

'So what on earth am I going to do, PP?'

'Well, boss, seems like there's only one thing you can do.' He paused.

Lyric stared at him impatiently. She'd forgotten how worldly-wise her driver could be. He seemed to know not only everything, but everyone, too. What was he going to suggest?

'You've asked him. And you're none the wiser. But, boss, you've got to find out what's going on once and for all.' He sighed and paused for effect. She nodded in agreement, willing him to get the preamble over and hurry up with his solution.

'Seems to me talking hasn't solved it. And, for whatever reason, that young man of yours there doesn't seem willing to tell you.'

Again, another pause. It was all Lyric could do to stop herself shouting out in frustration.

'So, if I was you, I'd find out myself. By other means.'

'Other means?' repeated Lyric, cottoning on to what he meant but wanting to be absolutely certain.

'That's right, boss. You've got to get a private investigator on him. And fast.'

~

Three quarters of an hour later, they arrived at Sunny Street Hospital. Lyric felt cheered by the sight of the familiar

Victorian building. Of course, as a children's hospital, Sunny Street had its tragedies, but most of all she saw it as a positive place, somewhere full of hope. She looked forward to every visit with excited anticipation, and cherished her time here.

Suddenly jolted from the deep deliberation in which she'd spent the rest of the journey, and remembering the purpose of the day ahead, Lyric leaned forward in her seat. 'PP, pull in here, will you?' she said quietly, indicating a lay-by up ahead. He did as he was asked, and she quickly pulled a tissue and a compact mirror from her bag, wanting to check her face after her earlier outburst. Lucky she didn't wear much make-up – her face was devoid of the black streaks you'd expect to see after sobbing for twenty minutes. Her eyes were still a little puffy, but clear, and with a slick of lip gloss she'd look fine . . . At least she had dressed for the occasion. She preferred to keep her visits low-key, and so she usually pitched up in jeans and trainers, not wishing to draw attention to herself but also to put the children at ease.

As she checked her appearance, she thought about her decision. It wasn't ideal. If Philippe did the same to her, she would be horrified. But then, she wasn't leading him on the same dance that he was her. She'd tried the more conventional means. This way, she'd be left in no doubt – and he might never have to know.

PP got out of the car and went to open the door for her, but not before making a big deal out of checking this way and that for the paparazzi, stalkers and any other hazards that might lie in wait for Lyric. There was no one, of course – the paps had long since left her alone on Sunny Street business – and she would normally find PP's officiousness embarrassing. Today, however, she found the familiar ritual strangely comforting.

Lyric tried to brush aside her doubts about the momentous decision she'd made in the car. *What about trust? What about transparency? What about having no secrets between you?* A conscience was all very well, but, frankly, it didn't help one sleep at night.

She'd have to find someone new, of course – the one she'd used before, to great effect, had met Philippe. That, of course, would be taken care of by PP and his army of underground contacts. But, despite all her reservations, she knew PP was right. There was only one way to settle this.

She was going to hire a private investigator to follow Philippe. And to find out once and for all.

Was it her he really loved?

Sixteen

As Edward's car navigated the sunny Chelsea streets of early-evening London, he felt his heart race with nervous anticipation and his Armani trousers tighten at the thought of the evening ahead.

His courtship with Amba had so far been short. And, to be honest, virtual. But, despite the lack of physical contact, the texts had become more and more frequent, and increasingly sexy, to the point that he could barely think about them without crying out in as yet unrequited passion.

But now . . . now all that was about to be resolved. At least, the physical encounter part of it was. What else might happen, he had hardly dared wonder.

Her texts were just like her – unpredictable, sexy, enigmatic and vague. His repeated requests for a date had been ignored since they had met at Chester, until – oh, glorious day! – just forty-eight hours ago she'd invited him for dinner at her house. A very special dinner, no less.

Edward felt his whole body shiver with the delicious prospect, and he looked out of the Bentley window impatiently. How much longer was this going to take? He looked at his watch. She'd told him on no account to be late. And whatever that meant, he was determined he wasn't going to risk spoiling her plans for this evening. Still unused to London traffic, he'd asked the driver to collect him at Broughton Hall at a ludicrously early hour, and yet the minutes were ticking away at an alarming rate.

He'd be arriving in style, that was for certain. When he'd tentatively asked Rhuba if he could lend him a car for the night to impress a girl, he'd never expected his new friend to hand him a Bentley and driver for a month, with instructions to pretend they were his own!

Edward watched the people hurrying past with pity. Wherever they were heading – home after a day's work, the theatre or simply to Kensington Gardens to bask in the last of the day's sunshine – they weren't going to have the evening that he was. Tonight, he felt utterly blessed, the only person on God's earth to be in this privileged position.

They drew up in front of a smart stucco-fronted townhouse. 'Here you go, sir,' said the driver, clambering out and opening the door for him. Suddenly, Edward's confidence deserted him. He stared at the man, rooted to the seat in panic.

'Sir?' questioned the driver politely but insistently.

Pull yourself together. Edward chastised himself. *What are you playing at?*

He stood on the pavement and took a deep breath. *Well, it's now or never, sunshine.*

He rang the bell and, hugging the large bunch of flowers

he'd bought, took in his surroundings. Two neatly clipped bay trees stood either side of the wide, bright scarlet door, and the front garden had been gravelled over to provide off-street parking – although there were no cars parked here now.

His thoughts were interrupted by the door opening. He drew in a sharp breath of anticipation, then let it out in disappointment as he realized it was the maid.

'Good evening. Mr Charlton?'

He nodded and she opened the door wider for him to enter. 'Miss Amba is expecting you,' she said softly with a little curtsey, and indicated that he should follow her.

Edward, momentarily overwhelmed, began to remove his shoes, but, feeling somewhat bourgeois, straightened up sharply and tried to recover his aplomb.

The house, like Amba, smelt wonderfully erotic. And though it was classically decorated, there were occasional touches of flamboyance – an elaborate hookah pipe here, a Chinese opium bed there. Beautiful music was playing softly in every room they walked through. It seemed to Edward like his own private Aladdin's cave, and he felt his senses heighten as the anticipation grew to unbearable levels. He could smell Amba everywhere. The total effect on him was a powerful aphrodisiac.

At last, they reached a closed door. The maid curtsied again. 'Miss Amba is waiting for you in here, sir,' she said, and scurried off.

Edward took another deep breath and placed his hand on the door knob. Other, even more erotic scents were drifting out from under the door. What on earth was he going to find on the other side?

It didn't take long to find out.

'What on earth is keeping you?' He heard Amba's low, husky voice from beyond the door. 'Come in.'

Slowly, excruciatingly, Edward opened it. Inside, the lights were dim. At first he couldn't see her. He could smell her – Amba's scent was even stronger here – but he couldn't make her out. Instead, the room was more or less filled by a huge glass dining table, surrounded by high-backed velvet chairs.

Candles flickered everywhere – from niches in the walls, from the floor, and all around the table – and it was only when his eyes grew used to the light that he saw her. There, on the table, a beautiful composition of creamy skin, lithe limbs and never-ending curves, lay Amba. Totally naked, save for strategically placed pieces of sushi. This was it – his very special dinner. The feast wasn't just *with* Amba. It *was* Amba.

She spread her legs erotically and beckoned him with a long forefinger.

'Edward!' she said, in that low, sensuous voice. 'You must be starving. Come over here, *chutzi*, I'm absolutely stuffed full of caviar.'

~

Later, much later, Edward lay wrapped in silken sheets in Amba's bedroom. He was sated by hours of the most expert lovemaking he had ever experienced, and exhausted from previously unchartered levels of passion. He had, quite frankly, never known ecstasy like it – and he knew he never would again. He leaned over to where she was lying, propped up in a huge cloud of pillows, considering a crystal flute of champagne. Edward shivered at the thought of what they'd done with that same champagne only moments earlier, and planted a lingering kiss on her perfect breast. He must never let this woman go. He wanted to inhale her – know everything about her, and her body, and her story.

'So tell me about you,' he said. 'I want to know everything.'

She smiled knowingly. 'There is nothing to know,' she said mysteriously. 'Everything you need to know is here, and now.'

His head spun with the intoxicating spell she was casting over him.

'Amba, darling, I fear I am . . .'

'Shhhh!' she warned gently, placing a forefinger on his lips to silence him. 'Speak only words you mean in this room, Edward. It is the law of the house.'

Edward laughed at her seriousness. 'I was about to tell you how wonderfully, gloriously in love with you I am,' he whispered. 'And it's the truth. Is that allowed?'

She considered him, running her long scarlet fingernails through his tousled blond hair.

'Oh, Edward, *chutzi*, how sweet you are.'

He grabbed her hand and attempted to pull it to him, intending to kiss it, but she whipped it away sharply and wagged her forefinger as if scolding a naughty boy.

He sat up, furious that his attentions were not only being spurned – but mocked, too.

'I'm not sweet, Amba. I'm in love. And I intend to prove it to you.'

Amba gave a tinkling laugh, and pulled a sheet up over her breast before taking a delicate sip of champagne. 'Oh, *chutzi*, you don't need to prove anything to me. And anyhow, what on earth could you do that we haven't just done tonight?'

She gave him a wicked look that made his loins stir again, and he shook his head in irritation.

'It's not just about – that,' he said haltingly. 'About sex. It's about everything. It's about you – you're in my head, my heart – my everything. I – I . . .' He stopped, momentarily stumped.

'You what?' Amba said, still teasing.

'I want you to be my wife.'

There was a pause, and she looked at him, her face at first registering shock and then amusement.

'I'm afraid you'll have to repeat that for me, *chutzi*. I thought I heard you say you want me to be your wife.'

'I do!' exclaimed Edward, sitting bolt upright in bed and grabbing her hand passionately. 'Amba, will you marry me?'

Again, she looked at him, her face serious now, her eyes searching.

'I mean – I'm a good bet,' said Edward. He gestured to indicate the obvious wealth in the rooms around him. 'All this – I know I don't have a place of my own or any of this now, but that will change. I'm my father's *heir apparent* – when he dies . . .' He stopped, aware of how it sounded. 'One day, Amba, Broughton Hall and the Charlton estate will be mine. Ours. And in the meantime, I mean, my father will realize I have to keep you in a certain manner . . .'

Amba stared at him blankly.

'But we've hardly been together any time at all, my darling *chutzi*.'

'I know, but . . .' Sensing he was getting somewhere, and hardly able to believe his luck, Edward scrabbled around for a solution. 'We don't have to tell anyone!' he yelled. She looked at him disparagingly.

'At least – we don't have to tell anyone, *yet* . . .' he continued. 'We could keep it secret until we've been together long enough to make it more acceptable. Until it seems more . . . normal.'

And until I've got more than the few beans my new-found family throw me as salary and presents, he added to himself. Now was the time to flex his financial muscle and claim what was rightfully his. He was the Charlton heir, and he had found the love of his life. He was going to make her his – but to do that, he needed some serious cash. And he would get it.

Suddenly, Amba laughed again, a tinkling, musical laugh that he thought he could listen to over and over. She stroked his cheek lovingly. 'But, *chutzi*, you have no ring. How can we be engaged?'

The ring! Edward cursed his impetuousness. He should be doing this properly – a woman like Amba would be used to nothing but the best. He looked around him for inspiration.

Amba laughed again. 'Look in the oysters, *chutzi*! There might be a pearl,' she said, reaching across to a platter by the bed and dropping an oyster seductively into her mouth.

Edward watched her, and slowly reached across for one himself. He picked up the oyster and gasped. There, nestled inside the shell, was a tiny round pearl.

He looked back up at Amba and her eyes were once again dancing. Was she mocking him? Or was this some pure, genius, stroke of luck – or hand of Fate, if you followed Amba's beliefs – to indicate he'd been right to propose? And that – he hardly dared think the words, let alone say them – she might accept?

He picked it out and held it up between thumb and forefinger.

'A pearl!'

'Ah, but, *chutzi*, is it a *real* pearl?'

He looked at it, confused. It looked like one to him. But then, he had to admit, he hadn't come into contact with many pearls in his lifetime. How the hell could you tell?

Amba reached across, plucked the pearl from his fingers,

opened her mouth and rubbed it across her teeth. She took it out and gazed at it thoughtfully.

'Well, *chutzi*, a real pearl feels gritty, whereas a faux pearl would have felt smooth. It's real! You have won yourself a very good real pearl,' she said, handing it back to him. 'And, you have won yourself a fiancée, too.'

He gazed at her in rapture, hardly able to believe his ears.

'Oh, Amba,' he breathed, leaning over and giving her a long, deep kiss. He sat back and gazed at the pearl. 'I'll have it set in a ring,' he said decisively. 'A beautiful ring, worthy of you.'

She smiled and patted his hand. 'Oh, *chutzi*, how sweet. And then we can choose a diamond one.'

Seventeen

'There he is! That's the one I was telling you about! Coo-ee!'

Glad of some distraction from the hoopla going on around her, Lyric grabbed hold of her hat to stop it falling off and allowed Treeva to take her hand and pull her across the Ascot members' enclosure in hot pursuit of Treeva's latest beau. Or beau-to-be. Lyric couldn't exactly remember.

Lyric stumbled as her Yves Saint Laurent wedges wobbled on the uneven ground, hard-baked after weeks of hot July sunshine. 'Treeva, we need to find this guy before we both injure ourselves.'

'Mike! Hi!' said Treeva, ignoring Lyric and stopping abruptly in front of a short, wiry man. Treeva's breathing was laboured after the unaccustomed exercise, and she was panting noticeably. The man wore small glasses and a striped shirt, and looked bookish and earnest – although not unattractive, Lyric had to admit. Hardly Treeva's type, however . . .

'Oh, hi, Treeva,' he said easily. 'Great to see you.' He looked at Lyric questioningly.

'This is my friend, Lyric,' said Treeva in an offhand manner. 'She's engaged to be married.'

Lyric smiled despite the curt dismissal. That was so like Treeva. She'd always been competitive, especially where men were concerned. Never mind that Mike was hardly Lyric's type. He wasn't Treeva's either, on paper – but that wouldn't stop Treeva from staking her claim on him, Lyric knew only too well. Still, Treeva had dragged her halfway across the enclosure to meet him – surely that was worth more than a spurious introduction?

Of course, really, Lyric knew full well that the reason Treeva had insisted she come with her was to save face if Mike had failed to acknowledge her, or walked away, or any one of 101 other possible scenarios. 'So, how do you two know each other?'

'Oh, we met last time I came racing with you,' said Treeva breezily. 'Didn't I mention it? Mike gave me something to help get rid of that nasty infection I had "down there". Worked a treat.' She turned to Mike as Lyric's jaw hit the floor. 'So I'm all clear now!'

'That's great, Treeva,' smiled Mike. He seemed genuinely delighted.

'Mmmm,' murmured Treeva seductively, hooking her arm through his and steering him off in the direction of the bar. 'So what great strapping beast are you tending to today?'

Lyric looked around her, wondering what to do until she could go and see Thumper ahead of his appearance in the Queen Elizabeth Stakes. She was using today's meeting to put some space between herself and Philippe – and tried not to think that it might also be an opportunity for him to provide the private investigator with some material. Or not, of course.

She knew it was wrong, but she'd felt much happier since she'd employed the PI and put him on Philippe's trail. It had made her feel stronger, more in control and more empowered – much more like the Lyric who'd first fallen for Philippe – and enabled her to focus on the here and the now, rather than the possible consequences of the PI's investigation. As a result, she and Philippe were getting on much better again, and *Do you really want to know?* was a question she didn't dare ask herself.

'Lyric! All right, darling?'

She groaned as she felt someone pinch her bottom, and turned around to see a leering Darren with a teenage racing groupie on each arm.

'Hi, Darren. What are you up to? Where's Edward?'

She could smell the booze on his breath from several feet away, and it was quite obvious what he was up to, but frankly she couldn't think of anything else to say.

'Oh, he's mooning around over some bird,' Darren moaned. 'I've had to focus my attentions elsewhere.' He kissed one of the girls full on the mouth.

Finally, Darren came up for air. 'Well, no rest for the wicked, Lyric – there's a pint with my name on it not too far from here. Come on, girls!' He slapped both of them playfully on the bottom and they squealed obediently as he dragged them off in search of a drink.

'Lyric!' This time, it was a much more welcome voice calling her name, and Lyric turned into the sunshine, shielding her eyes from its bright rays, as Edward approached with Amba on his arm. As ever, she looked intoxicatingly beautiful, resplendent in vintage Missoni and with *Charlie's Angels* hair.

'Hi, Amba,' Lyric said warmly, kissing her on both cheeks. She smiled back widely, but Lyric couldn't tell whether it was genuine or not because of Amba's oversized sunglasses.

'We're just going to find Mum and Dad,' said Edward. 'Amba hasn't met them yet. Are you coming?'

'No need.' Lyric pointed over his shoulder. 'Here they are now.'

She smiled as her parents approached, George leaning heavily on his stick and Constance visibly veering between concern for her husband and frustration at his slow progress. Lyric watched in amusement as Constance waved at them and then clocked Amba, her expression turning from one of maternal delight to unadulterated intrigue.

'Edward, darling! So this is the young – erm – lady you've been talking about!' Constance held out a hand delicately to Amba, all the while looking her up and down like a farmer at a cattle auction. 'Of course, we've seen you in the social columns. I can't believe we haven't met before! Where did you say you were from?'

Edward stood forward to stop Constance peering any closer at Amba's face. 'Mother, Father – meet Amba.'

George held out his hand. 'How do you do, my dear.'

Amba removed her glasses and smiled graciously, dropping into a barely discernible curtsey. Lyric saw her mother note it with interest. 'It's wonderful to meet you both. Edward has told you so much about me.'

'You mean, told you so much about us?' began Constance, but she was interrupted by George's mobile phone. 'Honestly, George, you never have that blessed thing on and when you do you can guarantee it will ring at the most inopportune moments,' she grumbled.

'Apologies, everyone,' said George cheerfully as he pulled the phone from his inside jacket pocket and stared at the number. 'If you'll excuse me . . .'

He half turned away, and Constance returned to admiring Amba's outfit as Lyric gazed idly at her father. She still couldn't believe they had nearly lost him. How lucky they were he'd made such a fast recovery.

A change in his tone of voice brought her back to the present.

'Yes, I'm with them now,' he was saying. He paused and looked over at Edward and Amba chatting to Constance. 'Is that right. Well, I never. Of course. Of course, you can rely on me. I'll keep you posted.'

He hung up, and paused for a moment with a thoughtful expression on his face. Seeing Lyric staring at him, he smiled brightly and turned back to the rest of his family.

'Well, now, you all seem to be getting on famously! Edward, why don't you take your mother and Lyric to find a drink while I take a little stroll with Amba here?' He held out his arm to her. 'There's so much about you I don't know!'

Lyric spotted Laura in the crowd and waved. 'You know what, I'll catch up with you later,' she said. 'I want to see Laura first.'

She hurried over to where Laura had been watching a race with her toddler daughter Kitty bouncing on her hip. 'Hi, Lyric!' beamed Laura. 'Perfect timing. Kitty wanted to pat Thumper for good luck before his race. What do you reckon?'

Lyric kissed Kitty's baby-soft cheek and stroked it gently. 'I think that sounds like the best idea I've heard all day,' she said, smiling.

Laura nodded cheerfully over at Lyric's family retreating into the distance. 'That must be Edward's new girlfriend. She seems to be getting on famously with you all!'

Lyric looked after them and nodded in satisfaction. 'Yes, isn't she? Thank the Lord. It can take Daddy a while to warm to people – but he seems to have taken to her straight away.' She turned to Kitty. 'Anyway, enough of boring grown-up stuff. I've got some Polos. Maybe Thumper would like one of those before he races. Let's go!'

~

Quentin watched Lyric from across the paddock, and frowned. George may have completely forgiven him, but he had a hunch the same couldn't be said for Lyric – or that French bloody fiancé of hers, for that matter. Oh, they were polite, make no mistake – when they saw him at breakfast or in the corridors of Broughton Hall they were civil enough – but there was a coldness behind the eyes that seemed no closer to thawing now than it had weeks ago when he'd first reappeared.

He sighed. *Dissatisfaction and suffering exist and are universally experienced*, he reminded himself. That was the Dalai Lama's First Noble Truth of Buddhism. The third, of course, was that *there is an end to dissatisfaction and suffering*, he reminded himself. So, what will be, will be, he thought. Was that the DL too, or was Quentin mixing up his maxims?

Either way, there was betting to be done – and fast. His big win on Catwalk Prince had spurred him on to bet again, and he'd had extraordinary luck following Skankton's horses. The racing papers were full of what a great season George's trainer was having – and his owners, too – and Quentin had stopped wondering why and decided to focus on the 'why not'. But his passion for the sport was swiftly turning into an addiction, and so he'd promised himself that he would stop after this race – or rather, turn it into a more reliable income stream.

'Charlton! Wait up, old man!' Quentin turned irritably at the use of 'old', and his brow furrowed further when he saw who was calling him. Skankton! What on earth could he want with him?

'Oh hello, Roger,' he said pleasantly. 'What's up?'

'Oh nothing, old man, just wondered how business was.'

Quentin frowned. 'Business is booming, thanks,' he said defensively. 'So, I see, is yours.'

'Yes,' said Roger, patting him forcefully on the back. Quentin winced – he still had the occasional twinge from his operation scar. 'And for those who support us. Still laying those bets, are you? Thought so,' he added, not waiting for a reply. 'Anyhow, your brother seemed to think you could do with a helping hand.'

Quentin drew himself up. 'Quentin Charlton has never been a charity case – nor has he built his life on the basis that he will simply inherit a fortune,' he added pointedly. 'George has no right to discuss my affairs in such a manner. Although, as I said, business is good, thank you very much.'

Skankton shrugged. 'Oh well, never mind. I thought you might be interested in coming in on a little venture I'm undertaking. If things change, let me know.' He looked from left to right shiftily and then back to Quentin. 'Although, either way, probably best not to mention it to anyone. Including George.'

'Oh? And why is that?' questioned Quentin, his interest suddenly piqued.

Roger winked at him theatrically. 'Never pays to spread

your business too thinly – but nor does it to reveal all your cards to all players,' he stated flatly. 'I'm sure that's a rule you've played by in your time.'

'Well, now you come to mention it,' said Quentin, flattered at the implication that he was a player. Then, remembering his new position in life, he changed tack. 'Of course, now I find transparency is the best policy at all times.'

'So do I, old man, so do I,' said Roger. 'I guess that just depends on your interpretation of transparent. It's in the eye of the beholder, surely?' He smiled smarmily. 'See you at the track!'

'Humph,' said Quentin in reply, more to himself than anyone else. He headed off towards the bookies. In the face of Skankton's wide-boy glamour, his life on the straight and narrow was suddenly seeming – well, a bit straight, and a bit narrow . . .

~

'Oh, Lyric, there you are. I was wondering when you'd turn up.' Natalie, Thumper's groom, looked up at Lyric over Thumper's haunches as she brushed his gleaming coat to an even higher shine. 'He's looking great, isn't he?'

Lyric breathed in the warm, fusty smell of horse and smiled at the groom as she nuzzled Thumper's nose with the palm of her hand. She liked Natalie and had got on well with her ever since Thumper had been assigned to her care. 'Fabulous,' she agreed. 'He's got a couple of other visitors, in fact – do you think he's up to them?' Lyric was always careful not to impose huge crowds on her highly strung horse before a race. 'It's my friend, Laura, and her daughter, Kitty.' She jumped as Thumper suddenly flinched and danced on the spot flightily. He rolled his eyes and looked at her out of the corner of his nearest eye with more than a hint of the wild streak that she loved in him.

'Oh, right, that's fine,' said Natalie in relief. 'I thought you meant Treeva. She's a bit loud, you know . . . Although I've just seen her disappearing into a Land Rover with Mike Halford, the vet, so . . .' She trailed off and gave Lyric a sheepish look. Lyric peered through a slat in the stable wall and saw a battered old Land Rover visibly swaying from side to side.

'Oh, well, you know the saying, "Don't come a-knocking if the van it is a-rocking." Shame "Land Rover" doesn't scan quite so well!' They both shared a conspiratorial smile.

'Just don't let Kitty get too close – he's been a bit jumpy today,' advised Natalie with concern. 'A bit keyed-up. Very out of character. Maybe because he knows now what to expect from a race . . . I can't really make it out.'

'Hmmm,' said Lyric, her nose screwing up in concern. 'Maybe it's best if Kitty and Laura keep their distance, then. I'd hate to upset him any more. Let me just give him a lucky Polo and I'll get out of your way, too.'

'Well – Mr Skankton said no treats,' said Natalie doubtfully. 'But I suppose it's only a mint . . .'

'It's a Polo!' exclaimed Lyric, fishing in her Lanvin clutch. 'And he loves them. Don't you, Thumper?'

The horse responded by enthusiastically crunching the sweets and breathing out a sigh tinged with horse feed and mint. He followed up by pawing the ground excitedly.

'See you in the winner's enclosure!' Lyric said with a wink to Natalie. 'Break a leg, Thumper!'

~

Lyric watched carefully as the jockey tried to mount Thumper. Natalie was right. He was being much more flighty than usual, foaming at the mouth and rolling his eyes until the whites showed. But then, his overall performance had definitely improved and this could just be another part of his development. This season, he had gone from a just-below-top-class colt to one of the top three in his class. More than likely he was simply exhibiting his true spirit.

'He's beautiful, Aunt Lyric, isn't he?' lisped Kitty, peering through the fence by her left-hand side. She pronounced 'Lyric' as 'Lywic', and it made Lyric think of Kitty's brother at the same age. He'd done just the same thing, and she smiled at the memory.

'Yes, he is, Kitty,' she said with a smile.

'Did you know, Kitty, that horseshoes bring good luck?' asked Laura, bending down so she was head to head with her daughter.

'Really, Mummy?' Kitty looked up at her in awe, and

Lyric felt a pang. How wonderful to have a child to share that kind of bond with.

'That's right,' said Laura with a smile, standing up again and stroking her daughter's head fondly. 'And if you're lucky, and your Aunt Lyric asks Mr Skankton nicely, she might just get you one for you to keep.'

Lyric pulled a face at Laura, who smiled sweetly in return as Kitty jumped up and down in excitement. 'Really, Mummy? Oh really, Auntie Lyric? Please can you? Purlease?'

Lyric laughed and held her hands up in mock defeat. 'Oh, all right then! I'll ask Mr Skankton for you.' She leaned across and spoke so only Laura could hear. 'Even if it will stick in my craw to do so.'

They both laughed and, each taking one of Kitty's hands, one-two-three swung her across to where a handful of Charltons and Skanktons were gathered at the side of the racetrack, just in time to see the horses go under starter's orders.

As the starting gun went off, binoculars all around the course were raised up as one. Lyric stood on tiptoes as the horses thundered past and followed the track around the bend. She strained to see as they galloped further out of sight, and tried to make out the names from the commentator's quick-fire commentary. Thumper was second and then – in the lead! She was aware of Kitty tapping her leg excitedly, of Laura jumping up and down beside her, and of her father's quick look at her over his shoulder. Skankton passed her on his way to the front of the crowd, squeezing her shoulder in anticipated triumph. They were going so fast! It was all happening in a blur but there – yes, definitely, there was Thumper, pulling out from the crowd and leading by a leg. By two!

Lyric held her breath as she watched her darling horse approach the final furlong. He was going to win again! His legs seemed to be mechanic pistons moving at the speed of light as they carried him closer to them. Eating up the ground he passed right in front of her, pumping in and out, in and out, in and—

And then, he fell.

There was an audible gasp from the crowd as they watched the majestic animal tumble, and roll, and finally lie, his head moving up and down, trying to lift himself up. The jockey rolled out from under him and then stood up, safely away from the other thundering hooves. Then he crawled back to Thumper as the horse lay, panting and distressed, on the track.

It seemed to Lyric that things suddenly went from moving at the speed of light to slow motion. People, faces, voices – they were all blurred, as if in a dream. All that mattered to Lyric was her Thumper, lying out there, in pain and distress, in the middle of the racetrack.

'Get the bloody vet out there!' screamed Skankton into his mobile phone. 'That's a million quid's worth of racehorse, for goodness' sake!'

Lyric tried to run onto the course but someone held her

back. She watched, numb, as other figures ran out, as helpless gestures were made to her and her family, as Skankton shrugged apologetically at her father, as George enveloped her in a hug as the inevitable was decided.

The screens went up and the gunshot, when it came, seemed to come from another world. But it was over. Thumper was dead.

~

'Mummy! Mummy, look, there's a horseshoe!' From their position at the side of the racetrack, where the group stood frozen in horror, Laura tried in vain to shush her daughter as Kitty tugged insistently at her sleeve. Kitty had no idea of the significance of what was happening, of course – Laura had no desire to expose her to the horror of Thumper's demise and had told her he was simply having a rest. No one seemed to be taking any notice of Kitty, but Laura pulled her away from the group and bent down to speak quietly to her.

'Shush, darling, just wait a little while and then we can go home.'

Kitty was insistent. 'But Mummy, Mummy, you told me they were good luck, and look! Thumper's taken one off and sent it to me!'

Laura looked her daughter in the eyes.

'Kitty, listen to me. Thumper hasn't sent anything to you. He's having a little rest and so I need you to be a good girl and stay quiet until it's time to go home. It won't be long now.' She looked anxiously over at Lyric, who had her face buried in her father's chest.

'But Mummy, Mummy, it is Thumper's shoe! I saw it fly off when he stopped running. Please, Mummy.' Kitty wormed her way out of Laura's grip and ran onto the track to pick up the shoe. She held it up proudly from the middle of the course.

'Look, Mummy!'

Horrified, Laura ran out to drag her daughter back.

'Kitty!' she hissed. 'Stop waving that shoe around and do as you're told!'

Kitty hugged the shoe to her and hid it under her cardigan. 'But Mummy, Thumper meant me to have that shoe,' she lisped. 'It's going to bring good luck.'

~

Quentin watched closely as the drama unfolded. But his focus wasn't George, or Lyric, or even Natalie, the pretty groom who'd caught his eye on many occasions and who was now sitting weeping behind the screen as the vet made arrangements for Thumper's body to be removed.

It was Skankton.

His reaction had been the predictable shock of a trainer – panic about the horse's welfare followed by steely resolution as the inevitable dawned. But then, intriguingly, a new, darker concern. Quentin narrowed his eyes as he saw Roger appear from behind the screen, gesticulating wildly to Natalie. He was pointing at the foot of the dead horse.

It seemed that Thumper had lost a shoe. And it seemed that this was a cause of great upset to Skankton.

As Skankton pulled his phone from his jacket pocket and scanned his contacts, Quentin shuffled over into earshot.

'Never mind the horse, get the shoe, man,' he heard the trainer hiss into his phone.

There was a pause.

'Listen to me. It can only be on this racetrack. And you need to find it. Because if you don't there will be serious consequences.'

Another pause.

'Did you hear me? Whoever's got the shoe is going to fucking die.'

Eighteen

'I still think one of us should keep our outfit secret – you know, do the big reveal, like most brides do,' fretted Gabe, Crispin's TV producer fiancé, as they left the Tom Ford boutique and navigated the tiny Zurich cobbled street. 'Not in a dress as such, but giving the ceremony that element of surprise. Of drama.'

Lyric smiled, thinking back to their initial conversations when Gabe had wanted classy and Crispin had been all for an uber-camp celebration. Since then, wedding fever had struck and Gabe had turned into a veritable groom- (or bride-) zilla. Now, it wasn't just Crispin's flamboyant plans Lyric was in charge of reining in. She squeezed the arms of both men from her position walking in between them. 'I think we'll have enough drama and theatre to keep everyone happy, Gabe. All within the realms of good taste, of course,' she added. Keeping tabs on Crispin and Gabe's natural sense of opulence was almost a full-time job – but she knew the Crispin of old and, much as he might seem to be hankering after an OTT glitz-fest, she knew that when push came to shove he always preferred to be seen as tasteful and classy. Which was where she came in. She did classy – and knew him well enough to add the perfect twist.

'Babes, isn't it enough that we wear our sexuality with pride – we don't want to over-egg it with a groom in drag,' put in Crispin tartly.

'Yes, but matching Tom Ford tuxedos at four grand a pop – we could have had Elie Saab sequins for that,' mused Gabe.

'Well, one of us could,' retorted Crispin across Lyric's head. 'But if we did that, what would you end up wearing then, sweedie – non-iron M&S?'

'I don't think M&S do non-iron suits in white,' added Lyric playfully. 'Anyway, you two, I'm beginning to feel like piggy in the middle. Quit with the jibes, can you?'

Gabe suddenly stopped dead, striking a pose and thrusting his hand in his jeans pockets. With his tight white T-shirt, aviator sunglasses and buff, sculpted body set against the sunny, picturesque street, the lake glittering in the background, he could be starring in a high-fashion ad campaign, thought Lyric. No wonder Crispin had declared love at first sight when he'd been introduced to Gabe – he was gorgeous. 'Hang on a minute – what do you mean, what would I end up wearing? Who says you get to wear the sequins?'

'We're not having sequins,' reminded Lyric.

'Because I'm the bride, and you're the groom, sweedie,' said Crispin, ignoring Lyric, adopting a similarly defensive stance to Gabe and effecting a stand-off. 'We discussed it.'

Gabe wagged his finger at him and shook his head, laughing humourlessly. 'Uh-huh. We have never discussed who would be the bride. In fact, we agreed NOT to discuss it on the basis that we would never agree. We are groom and groom.'

'Does it really matter?' pondered Lyric, staring at them in wonder. Honestly, these two could row over just about anything.

Suddenly, both men rounded on her.

'Does it matter?' they repeated in horrified unison.

'The bride is the one who gets most attention!' exclaimed Crispin, hands over mouth in distress.

'How can it NOT matter who is the one who gets the most attention on the most important day of our lives?' shrieked Gabe, massaging his temple with his fingers to relieve the onset of imaginary stress.

'Lyric, this has thrown a totally new light on your attitude to our wedding and given me serious concerns about how you view our day,' said Crispin as though he were delivering a life sentence. 'You are not only, erm, *organizing* the wedding . . .'

Lyric hid a smile. For 'organizing', also read 'paying'.

'. . . but you are best man. Best woman. We need you to be totally at one with our vision.'

'And I am,' she said, calmly gathering up one on each arm and continuing on their way to the restaurant for lunch. 'Which is why I am confident that BOTH of you will be the centre of attention on what will be a very special day for everyone. Now hurry up, I'm starving.'

~

'Oooh, well, that's enough for me. Need to leave room for the famous *Apfelkuchen*!' Crispin pushed aside the remains of his fish, straight out of Lake Zurich that morning, drained the rest of his white wine, patted his six-pack and leaned back in satisfaction.

The sunshine outside was pouring in through the windows, creating a summery haze across the wood-panelled room of the brasserie in the Kronenhalle, Zurich's buzziest lunchtime restaurant. Gilt-framed pictures covered the walls, and with the red upholstered chairs the whole effect might have been dark and oppressive had it not been for the bright white starched linen tablecloths, polished glassware and chrome booth partition.

Lyric, halfway through a veal *Zurichois*, put her fork down.

'That's a good point. What am *I* going to wear?'

'A dress?' said Crispin, wrinkling his nose.

'Not if you or I aren't allowed one,' grinned Gabe through his wiener schnitzel.

'What about a YSL tux?' suggested Lyric. 'Nothing as elaborate as yours – no tails or anything. But in white, of course. Kind of complementary.'

'Another suit?' protested Gabe. This time it was his turn to wrinkle his nose. 'Are we having a trousers-only dress code, or something? I understand why you've vetoed Crispin's pink flamingos and Disney place settings, but *really*. Where's the glamour, darling?'

'The guests have to reflect the glamour of *us*,' confirmed Crispin. He turned to Lyric. 'In fact, while I'm thinking about it, put that Amba down on the guest list.' He winked at Gabe. 'She's simply divine, sweedie, you'll love her. She *has* to come.'

'OK,' said Lyric. 'But, Crisp, me in a suit *will* be glamorous. Just very low-key glamour. Understated chic. Maybe with trainers. I don't know – I was kind of thinking a Bianca Jagger vibe. But with trousers, not a skirt.'

'Bianca Jagger . . .' echoed Crispin, almost cooing at the thought. '*I like* . . .'

'Anyhow, you were telling us about that awful business with your horse,' said Gabe, suddenly bored of wedding chat. On the strength of his limited attention span for the wedding, if Lyric had to pick a groom from between them right now, it would definitely be Gabe. 'What's the deal with it all?' He pushed his plate away, pulled a Marlboro Light from a packet on the table and lit it, sitting back in his chair. She allowed him one deep puff before reminding him that Swiss restaurants were smoke-free zones.

Lyric sighed heavily. Even after a couple of weeks of non-stop talking and going over it, she still couldn't mention Thumper without getting a lump in her throat.

'Well, Daddy seems to think something doesn't add up about his death. Of course, racehorses fall all the time, but he'd been acting very out of character that day and for a few days leading up to the race. It could have been some kind of illness, of course, or a hidden heart defect or something that we didn't know about – or even that Polo I gave him . . . Who knows? But the autopsy hasn't revealed anything. To cut a long story short, he wants to call the police in.'

'How can he call the police in if there's no evidence of foul play?' questioned Gabe. Ever since he had worked on a series of *Criminal Minds* a year or so earlier, he fancied himself as something of a DCI.

'Oh, I don't know,' said Lyric dismissively. Frankly, the whole business made her feel so depressed she couldn't bear to dwell on it.

There was a momentary silence as a waiter arrived to take their plates and they ordered apple cake and espressos. He scowled at Lyric as her phone rang loudly. She picked it up self-consciously, intending to reject the call until later, when she noticed the number. The PI.

'I should just take this,' she said apologetically.

She looked at Crispin and Gabe, nervous. Of course, she hadn't told either of them that she was having Philippe tailed. She couldn't be sure they would understand – but, secretly, she was also worried either one of them might inadvertently let the cat out of the bag. She was going to have to fib her way through this. She swallowed hard. That wasn't the only cause of the butterflies that had suddenly appeared. She answered the phone, heart beating loudly in her chest. What could this mean for her and Philippe?

'Hello?' Her voice was tentative, and she cleared her throat, trying to assume more confidence. It must be OK, she tried to reassure herself. He wouldn't deliver bad news over the phone, surely?

As she listened, the colour drained from her face, and she grabbed the table to steady herself. Crispin and Gabe looked on in concern. When she spoke, her voice was strained and forced.

'Find out who she is. And, more importantly, *what* she is. I'll need to meet you to see the evidence. Please don't send it to me at home.'

Slowly, she hung up – and even more slowly replaced the phone on the table.

'Sweedie? Who was that – and what's the matter?' Crispin's face was etched with concern.

Lyric looked up at him, ashen.

'Just some news. Some not very good news, actually.' She laughed a hard, brittle laugh. 'Well, not for me, anyway. It's Philippe. He's been photographed. With another woman. Well, a girl, by the sounds of it. A very beautiful girl.'

Crispin opened his mouth as if to offer a potential explanation, but Lyric raised a hand to silence him.

'They were holding hands. And they kissed.'

~

Back in London, Lyric opened the door to the house with trepidation. She already felt uneasy, even in the place she'd once thought of as home. The rooms felt unloved and unlived in – a bit like she did, she thought. But it was central, neutral and Philippe-free – and the obvious place to meet the PI.

Behind the front door stood an average-looking man, of average height, in average-looking jeans and jumper, and average-looking trainers.

'Hello,' he said, in an average-sounding voice.

'Hi,' said Lyric miserably. She led him through to the sitting room and sat while he produced a stiff envelope. Inside, she knew, was certain heartbreak. She tried to steel herself for what she was about to see.

She tried in vain. The pictures were grainy and over-blown black-and-white images, but what they depicted was clear.

Philippe, in jeans and leather jacket – the jacket she'd bought him! – WITH another girl. And what a girl. Lustrous honey-blonde hair, big brown eyes, bee-stung lips and a curvaceous body with long, long legs. It could have been Lyric. Except it wasn't. And the girl was a good ten years younger. Numb to everything but the evidence in front of her, Lyric flicked mechanically through the pictures. Philippe and the girl were walking along a London street with his arm casually slung around her. Then they were stopping, looking at one another, laughing. Then they were embracing and then – oh! – they were even closer, with Philippe, it seemed, nuzzling the girl's neck. Lyric felt like she might pass out. Her throat felt tight, and she was struggling to breathe . . .

'Lyric? Lyric?' Hand over her mouth, she looked at the PI blindly.

'I know how it looks. But this may not be as it seems,' he counselled. 'I have many years of experience in this job and there is something about this that doesn't quite add up. I—'

'It seems crystal clear to me,' said Lyric robotically. 'Philippe is having an affair.'

And with that, her heart broke into a thousand tiny pieces.

Nineteen

Lyric smoothed the lines of her nude-coloured Lanvin cocktail dress and regarded her mother. Constance looked like the smaller, prettier younger sister of Penelope Keith in a vivid floaty Missoni maxi dress and matching ochre turban teamed with sparkly Turkish slippers with a clattery kitten heel. How did her mother manage to pull off such a hideous outfit and not just look presentable, but enviably chic?

She crooked her arm and held it out to Constance. 'Shall we go?'

'Yes, darling, but let's just wait for your father. What on earth has happened to him?'

Lyric laughed. This familiar ritual had been repeated every time her mother and father had gone out together, ever since she could remember. George would mooch around, moaning about how Constance was taking forever to get ready and then, finally, when she was ready, he would disappear somewhere.

'Well, he can't have gone far, bearing in mind that he's banned from downstairs,' she reasoned calmly. 'Look, here he comes now.'

She gazed fondly at her father as he strolled slowly down the long corridor of Broughton Hall's west wing, leaning heavily on his stick. Every day that passed meant her father's body was less likely to reject Quentin's kidney. He finally seemed to have recovered from a recent bout of sickness and diarrhoea, the only thing that appeared to have hampered his recovery in any way. It was frustrating, really – in all other ways he'd made such great progress, but this persistent little bug really seemed to have knocked him for six. Ironically, over the past couple of weeks he'd been suffering from it, the one thing that had buoyed him were his regular holistic sessions with Amba. On the day they'd met at the races, she'd offered to treat his arthritis with her 'special blend' of massage, and he seemed to want to spend as much time as he could with her. At first he'd been sceptical about how much it would help, of course – George always was when it came to anything but proven science – but, whatever Amba's secret mix of Ayurvedic and Swedish massage was, it worked. Now, dressed in his ancient dinner jacket, with his handsome weather-beaten face and twinkly eyes, George could pass for twenty years younger than he was. Apart from his hair, which had grown visibly greyer since the kidney transplant, and which, he claimed, was thinning at an alarming rate, she felt confident that he would soon be abandoning his stick for anything other than his beloved hill walking.

Lyric shook the thought from her mind, but then another, equally unpleasant one entered it. She'd assumed she and Philippe would still be together when they reached their sixties and beyond. But now, after the detective's findings, would they even see out the week? She shut her eyes to try and stop thinking about the pictures. The girl was dressed casually in the uniform of the twenty-somethings: skinny black jeans, ballet pumps and a baggy vest. And as the secret photographer had captured them walking hand in hand, laughing, hugging each other – even kissing, in one – Philippe had looked relaxed, amused, caring. Happy.

Lyric swallowed hard as she felt the now-familiar stab of hurt at the memory of the pictures.

She shook her head. Not wanting to rock the boat before the party, she hadn't confronted Philippe yet, and so the issue of the photographs still remained unresolved. She didn't allow herself to consider the fact that, in pushing it to one side, she was denying the fact that it was happening at all . . . How could that be, when she spent every waking moment torturing herself with the thought of them, and the ever-present spectre of 'what if'?

Following the example her mother had always set her, she took a deep breath and smiled brightly. 'Come on, Daddy, we've been waiting for you!'

George raised his eyebrows in mock surprise – again, a practised response in this oft-played-out tableau – and Lyric giggled.

'*You've* been waiting for *me*, have you?' he asked mischievously as he reached them and stood in front of them, feigning outrage. 'A man could die of thirst waiting for you two. Although, my dears, it would be worth it for the spectacle of beauty that I see before me.'

Constance tutted and pretended to be nonplussed as George kissed her cheek and hugged her to him, but Lyric could tell she was secretly pleased.

'Honestly, George, you're like a teenager on heat,' she said crossly, righting her turban where his embrace had sent it slightly skew-whiff.

'Well, it's our special night,' he reasoned, squeezing in between the two of them and taking an arm each. 'I'm allowed to.'

'We're too old for that kind of nonsense,' continued Constance. 'I mean, of course we're still married, darling – but can you imagine either of us having the energy to try anything new?'

Lyric bit back a retort. It was just her way, she reminded herself. She looked at George, but he just smiled and shrugged. He was used to Constance by now – if it didn't bother him, it shouldn't bother Lyric.

So instead of snapping at her mother, Lyric again smiled brightly. 'I don't know what you're talking about, Mummy. People in your position get divorced like other people get parking tickets! The fact that you and Daddy are still together is not only admirable, it smacks of true love – whatever you might say to the contrary.'

'Well, if you insist,' grumbled Constance. 'I've worn my diamonds specially, you notice.'

Lyric and George stared at her.

'Well, it is our diamond wedding anniversary, isn't it?'

'Ruby, Mother,' said Lyric. 'Forty years is your *ruby* anniversary.' There was a brief pause. 'But you look fabulous. Now do come on, we don't want to keep the others waiting.'

If she were to be honest, Lyric was surprised George and Constance hadn't rumbled her party plans by now. Ruby weddings weren't, generally speaking, a big event in society, but her parents and their friends had a tendency to celebrate anything, and the Charltons – and Constance in particular – were renowned for their great parties. Factoring in the number of invitations Lyric had sent out, and the fact that on her more lucid days her mother was able to smell a rat from fifty paces, the odds had been stacked against her. But her parents both seemed to have swallowed her story that she had planned a special intimate family dinner. In actual fact, she had invited closer to two hundred friends and family to celebrate with them. Those guests would be silently gathered now in the ballroom, shepherded by Edward and Philippe after having been transported to Broughton Hall via a fleet of minibuses parked around the back of the east wing where her parents – squirrelled away in their quarters in the west wing – would have had no way of detecting them.

'All this fuss over a dinner,' continued Constance as she stepped regally onto the sweeping staircase, holding her turbaned head high. 'Anyone would think it was a state occasion.'

~

A state occasion, thought Lyric as she surveyed the heaving mass of evening-dress-bedecked bodies crammed into the cavernous ballroom, *would have had nothing on this other than more pomp and ceremony and a lot less atmosphere.*

Ruby-red roses covered every surface – outlandishly extravagant bouquets flanked doorways and filled the empty fireplaces, pretty garlands were laid along mantel-pieces and chic single roses in long, slim vases alternated proudly with candles on occasional tables. Waiters in ruby-red velvet YSL jackets and smart black trousers poured Château Lafite into heavy red Venetian glass goblets. The candles seemed to mirror the twinkling light thrown out by the ballroom's huge crystal-tiered chandeliers, and every-one present appeared to be bathed in the softly flattering glow of immense wealth and happiness.

Everyone who was anyone was here, and there couldn't be an invitation she had sent out that hadn't been taken up tonight – and there were probably a few people that she *hadn't* sent them to, she thought as she eyed an inebriated couple she was certain weren't on the original list. Not that it mattered, of course.

She felt, rather than heard, Philippe walk up behind her and stand awkwardly next to her.

'What do you think?'

'I think you look very nice,' he said stiffly. She felt a pang of longing rise up in her at his closeness, mixed with a stab of hurt at his curt response.

'I meant the party,' she retorted. 'Not bad for a one-man effort, eh?'

She was referring to Edward's distinct lack of enthusiasm over recent weeks, but as Philippe pulled back and a familiar veil shrouded his eyes, she realized he'd taken it personally.

'Philippe – I didn't mean . . .'

But it was too late and, as Lyric trailed off, they stood in silence, each looking around them for a diversion.

Finally, after a few long moments, Lyric spoke. 'Is everything ready for Edward's speech later?' she said, attempting to break the ice. The plan was for Edward to welcome the guests formally, congratulate his mother and father and present them with a yew tree to plant in the new Broughton Hall gardens to mark their anniversary. Philippe had selected the young plant, and had also overcome his disdain for Edward's new friendship with Darren Skankton to give Edward some much-needed help with his nerves – Philippe was not a natural public speaker either, but still had to address crowds on the odd occasion. Edward, for his part, was struggling with the enormity of this important official public appearance as the Charlton son and heir.

'Oh, I didn't think he was speaking now?' said Philippe lightly, not meeting Lyric's eye. She turned to him in slight panic.

'What do you mean?'

'Well, I thought tonight was strictly a one-man effort,' he said with more than a hint of sarcasm.

'Philippe!' Lyric nudged him, and managed a reluctant smile. 'Leave the irony to the British.' For a moment, at least, the tension lifted. The feeling of dread, however, refused to budge. Lyric cursed him inwardly. This should all feel natural and right, still – why did Philippe have to have ruined it all for them?

'I still don't understand why a yew tree, though,' mused Philippe. 'I mean, it starts with a Y, *n'est-ce pas?*'

Lyric smiled weakly. Although he became more fluent by the day, Philippe sometimes struggled with English – especially when the liberties she often took with it didn't fit his own pedantic sense of semantics. She'd taken each of the letters in 'Ruby' to spell out various elements of the night, but he was taking it very literally.

'R is for royalty, which my mother thinks she is,' she explained patiently. 'U is for yew, because it's one of my father's favourites.' She rushed quickly on, seeing Philippe was about to interrupt. 'B is for beluga caviar, because it's the ultimate in extravagant canapés – and Mummy and Daddy are worth it. And Y,' she said triumphantly, 'Y cannot be for yew because I've saved it for "Y not stay married another forty years, you're such a great mother and father." You'll see – knowing Mummy and Daddy, when I spell it out to the guests, they'll roar with laughter.'

'Hmmm,' said Philippe, still not convinced but trying not to show it. 'Well, you've certainly drummed up enough people to create a roar,' he observed, looking around him. 'But don't you feel like there is an odd atmosphere tonight? Something a little – *sinistre*?'

Lyric frowned, loath to let anything undermine the success of the night. 'No. At least, only between you and me!'

Philippe shook his head sadly. 'Here's Edward.' He moved to one side slightly as Lyric's brother approached.

'Lyric! You look ravishing,' Edward said, kissing her on the cheek with relish. 'And Mother seems to be enjoying herself.' They contemplated Constance talking flirtatiously with Prince Abu Rhuba, then flitting off around the party, smiling charmingly and elegantly holding a Gauloise in a cigarette holder.

'She doesn't look like someone who's been married forty years,' observed Edward drily.

Lyric nodded in agreement. 'I'm not sure Mummy or Daddy even remembered they were married until tonight . . .'

'Well, they could have done worse than each other,' chuckled Edward. 'In many ways, they're a harmonious couple.'

'Well, yes, if you ever get them in the same room,' said Lyric. 'The only time I've heard them argue is if Daddy hasn't pressed the record button for *EastEnders* or something.' She smiled, thinking of her parents' old Betamax in the sitting room. No Sky+ for them – their video machine was so old it must qualify for listed status, she thought. 'In fact, the same goes for all of us, really.'

'Apart from when Quentin crops up,' said Edward, glowering as Quentin bumbled past, cheeks as ruby red as the party theme, sloshing wine over the rim of the glass as he brushed past them. He still refused to call him 'uncle'.

'Yes, but only briefly,' said Lyric. 'Everyone's pretty cool now, aren't they?'

'Humph,' said Philippe, unconvinced. 'I'm not so sure about that.'

Lyric stared at him, and something inside her suddenly seemed to snap. How dare he be so judgemental, when he was the one who was cheating, ruining things not just for the two of them but ultimately for the whole family?

'Well, I don't know what gives you the right to say that,' she snapped.

Philippe jumped as though he had been shot. *Guilt,* thought Lyric miserably. *He's just realized he's been caught out.*

'What's that supposed to mean?' he said, looking genuinely affronted.

'People in glass houses, Philippe, shouldn't throw stones. Do you know that saying?'

Philippe's brow furrowed and he looked totally bemused. '*Non.*' Then suddenly light seemed to dawn, before his face clouded over again. 'Is this something to do with that text again?'

Lyric stared at him with a mixture of hurt, love, hate and

total, total injustice. But she couldn't let rip now. Not here. Not on such an important night, in front of all these people.

'No, Philippe, it's not. It's about something else. And maybe, just maybe, if you didn't have so many secrets you'd know exactly what I was talking about. So either go and work it out, or go to hell – either way, I couldn't care less!'

He looked at her sadly, shaking his head, and then turned and disappeared into the crowd. Lyric stared after him, a hundred emotions racing through her heart, and on her lips, but still none of them spoken.

~

'Well, well, well, I might have known you'd be keeping a low profile,' growled Quentin as he slipped behind a heavy velvet curtain, through the open French doors and onto one of the garden terraces.

He eyed Angus, predictably scruffy in an ancient, mis-shapen smoking jacket and mismatched trousers, both of which looked older than the curtain, with distaste. Old rivalries ran deep with Quentin, and he still hadn't forgiven him for the failure of his tip-off, and this was the first opportunity he'd had to confront the pompous old goat about it.

'Not much fun being on the losing team, is it, Angus?'

Angus looked him up and down archly and humphed into his red wine. Refusing to be drawn, he resumed his position looking at the party from the outside in.

'You look like a relic from a bygone age,' continued Quentin in what he hoped was a neutral, observant tone. He slipped a whisky miniature from his pocket and topped up his glass. He'd decided to indulge in a little drink tonight – it was a party, after all – and from experience he knew that glasses were never topped up quite as frequently as he would like. So, to be on the safe side, he'd brought his own to keep him going.

Angus, becoming increasingly flustered at the encounter, looked at Quentin incredulously. 'Takes one to know one.'

Now it was Quentin's turn to consider his own outfit. He'd thought his velvet dinner jacket – a vintage item now, from his playboy days in the 1970s – and matching bow tie had been a witty attempt to show willing and blend in with the theme. Not just the colour, but the era, too – and weren't the 1970s back in fashion? Until this moment, he'd been proud of his effort, and carried it off with what he thought was an air of cosmopolitan panache. Suddenly, he felt like one of the waiters. The thought made a lifetime's feelings of worthlessness come rushing back to the surface, and he was suddenly filled with spite and vitriol – at this loser Angus for pointing it out to him, at himself, for not turning things around until it was too late, but mostly at his brother, George, for putting him in the hopeless position in which he'd spent most of his life.

'Well, Angus, looks can be deceiving,' he retorted, pulling himself up to his full height and backing away. 'In most cases. In yours, I think what you see is exactly what you get. I'll leave you to show yourself out. Oh! You already are.' Quentin took hold of both doors and pulled them shut behind him, taking a deep breath before turning back to face the party in the ballroom.

'I say, old fellow?' Quentin turned around at the question with a practised smile (he liked to think it was intriguing, most people would say ingratiating). He spied a long-forgotten school chum of George's, who was peering at him jovially. But not with recognition. With purpose.

'I've been looking for one of you waiters for bloody ages. Could you get me a refill? There's a good chap.'

~

Smarting from being mistaken for the hired help, Quentin stormed around the room, pushing past people until he found a waiter willing to top up his glass. To the very top. Downing the lot, he held out his arm for some more, and, with the hint of a raised eyebrow, the waiter acquiesced.

Bringing it to his lips again, Quentin made as if to down the second when he felt a slap on his back that nearly caused him to choke. Good job his red velvet wouldn't show up the wine, he thought, brushing away some stray drops with irritation.

'Now, there's a man on a mission!' roared Roger Skankton. In his white dinner jacket, he looked like a poor man's James Bond, a cross between Robert Wagner and Hulk

Hogan. 'Anyone would think you were trying to drown in it, man!'

Quentin grimaced. 'I'd prefer to bath in it – unfortunately I was born at the wrong moment to be able to afford to.'

Roger slapped him on the back again. 'You and me both, old sport, you and me both. Wasted on Georgie boy, all this, eh?' He nodded at the splendour surrounding them and Quentin bristled with annoyance at the reminder that it wasn't his.

'Well, each to their own,' he managed. He was damned if he was going to share his inner demons with this chancer. Far better to make a quick exit and compose himself elsewhere.

Roger leaned forward confidentially. 'Well, if it's any consolation, I wish it was you in his place,' he said under his breath. 'I've always said, the only thing between me and an even huger fortune is George's morality. If you were him, I'm sure it would be much easier. Still, I'm not letting that stop me. Where there's brass there's opportunity, as I always say.' He tapped the side of his nose knowingly and pulled back. Quentin looked at him. This was the second time Roger had waved the prospect of an easy buck under his nose. How many more chances would he get to take him up on it?

Roger leaned in closer. 'In fact, I've got a little business deal you might be interested in.' He held up a cautionary hand as Quentin opened his mouth to protest. 'Totally legit, this one. Small matter of some property I lost at Ascot. Nothing much. A horseshoe, if you will. But it's the sentimental value, you know . . .' He trailed off, eyeing Quentin appraisingly.

'What makes you think I can help you with a horseshoe?' said Quentin, interest piqued by another mention of the elusive object.

'Because there were only Charltons there when I lost it. And because someone picked it up. And, because two and two most often equals five, I've decided it's a Charlton who's got it.'

There was a pause.

'Ri-ight,' said Quentin cautiously, his mind whirring overtime. Roger had said he was prepared to kill for this shoe – he wanted it that badly – but Quentin needed to tread carefully.

'And you're prepared to pay for its safe return?'

'Handsomely,' confirmed Roger.

'Oh, there you are, Roger!' squeaked a high-pitched voice. 'I've been looking for you. I've been trying to shake Angie for the last half hour or so!'

Roger and Quentin turned to see his petite PA bursting out of a Designers at Debenhams fuchsia cocktail dress. In spite of himself, Quentin felt his loins stir at the sight of all that female flesh.

With one eye searching the room for his wife, Roger put his arm around his PA and fondled her bottom. 'Well, we'd better make the most of it, hadn't we?' he leered. 'I'm sure we can find a cosy corner somewhere, eh? Little cracker, isn't she, Charlton?'

Quentin looked lustily at the woman and then peered around the room.

'Not really my type, Skankton. I'm more about young fillies like that,' he said, eyeing up a curvaceous, suntanned young girl in a flirty tangerine mini-dress, not recognizing her momentarily.

Suddenly, Roger's face was squared up to his again – this time more threatening than the first.

'Less of the young filly, Charlton,' he warned. 'That's my daughter.'

~

'Ugh, that old uncle of Lyric's gives me the creeps,' shuddered Cheryl, shivering prettily as she cosied up to the latest 'son of' she was trying her luck with. The boy, a good-looking but braying Hooray, looked around him with interest.

'I thought he was dead?'

'Nah, he turned up again a few months ago,' replied Kimberley in a bored tone, pouting glossily, playing with one of the spaghetti straps on her coral Lipsy dress, and looking around in waning hope for a stray footballer or jockey. 'Like a bad penny, so my mum said.'

'I'm sure there's a few in here you could say that about,' said the boy.

'Yes, but we all know everyone's only here to try and

suss out what happens when Georgie boy carks it, aren't they?' said Cheryl, parrot-fashion. 'So three guesses why he's suddenly back on the scene now . . .'

'Cheryl . . .' warned Kimberley with a sharp look at her sister.

'Well, it's true,' said Cheryl mulishly, not wanting to lose face in front of her new beau.

'What, did your mum tell you that as well?' teased the boy.

'No, it was . . .'

'Cheryl!'

'It was Treeva!'

The boy was fast losing interest in this conversational thread.

'Treeva? Who's that?'

At that moment, a vision in fluorescent Versace tottered past pulling an astonishingly good-looking man along beside her.

'That's Treeva,' cooed the girls in unison. 'She's, like, *amazing* . . .'

~

'Erm, so where did you say you'd left Fiddy?' asked the man, worried.

'Oh, he's back there asleep in his car seat,' said Treeva dismissively, sniffing loudly and wiping her nose with the back of her hand. How could she have been distracted from how *hot* her manny, Johann, was? All that time schlepping after the vet from racecourse to racecourse getting cold and wet and muddy, and this exceptional hunk of manhood had been right under her nose all the time! She returned to the subject of her baby. 'It's fine, honestly – he's in the cloak-room. All those coats will muffle his cries.'

Johann looked at her disbelievingly. 'Look, I don't feel comfortable about this – I'd really rather go and check on him and make sure he's . . .'

He trailed off as Jacob Charlton walked past with a friendly wave, and Treeva, interpreting his pause as latent desire, twirled a strand of hair around her finger coquettishly and stroked her cosmetically enhanced cleavage with it.

'Oh, I'm sure there's no rush, is there? He's a baby – all he does is sleep! We're doing him a favour, sweedie,' she cajoled.

Johann decided it was time for drastic measures. 'Sorry, Treeva, I've got my eye on someone else.'

She pulled back, stunned.

'Someone else? But who?'

He nodded over in Jacob's direction.

'Him.'

~

Jacob took a thoughtful sip of his wine and turned back to watch the interaction between Treeva and tonight's consort. Who'd have thought Uncle George's fortieth anniversary bash would have proved such a breeding ground for hot-ties? First that hot waiter, and now this vision of cuteness.

Jacob laughed to himself at the irony of the situation. Before he'd been outed by the *News of the World* last year, when he'd been caught having a clandestine affair with Crispin, he'd loathed these events. In a bid to cover up his sexuality, he'd always gone out with sturdy girls from good families – exactly the sort of woman he should have ended up marrying – who'd been sweet, but trying, company. The only good thing about parties like this had been the opportunity to canvass the older, moneyed generation to help with his political career.

But now, with his new Lib Dem career direction buoyed with support from young, successful liberals, and his sexuality well and truly in the public domain, he'd thought there would be little to recommend a night like this. But things seemed to be looking up.

The question was, how was he going to prise the vision of cuteness away from Treeva's clutches? As Jacob watched, the pair seemed to bicker about something and Treeva stormed off. Well, maybe there was the answer. Jacob drew himself up in preparation for approaching the man. All he needed to do now was avoid the smug nearly-marrieds, Crispin and his Robocop fiancé, and he might actually end up enjoying himself.

'Jacob! I wondered when we'd bump into you.'

He turned with a sinking feeling. 'Hi, Crispin. Hello, erm – Gaynor?'

'Gabe,' replied Gabe frostily, nodding shortly and then turning his head away with a pirouette-style flick.

'You're looking good,' said Crispin, looking Jacob up and down appraisingly.

Jacob felt a *frisson* between them and smirked at his ex-lover. Crispin might be getting married, but the chemistry between them had always been electric – and, what's more, the abrupt end to their fledgling relationship meant they were definitely Unfinished Business.

'Oh well, you know. Been down at the gym a bit.'

'Oh really?' said Crispin, feeling Jacob's right bicep. 'Oooh, yes, I can tell. You're all hard!'

'Well, you know what they say – in the gay world you're either a top or a bottom,' quipped Jacob. 'And I definitely like to stay on top.'

'C'mon, Crisp, let's go find Lyric,' whined Gabe, sensing something out of his control going on.

Crispin hesitated, clearly happy to stay and flirt a while. Jacob looked over Crispin's shoulder to see the vision of cuteness move further into the crowd, and eventually – dammit! – get swallowed up by other revellers. Well, that had torn that . . .

'Why don't you go off and find Lyric, and Crispin and I can catch up – we're old friends, you know,' said Jacob wickedly. Crispin looked at him with a glint in his eye and Gabe, unsure of what was going on, looked from one to the other as if they were a particularly fast game of table tennis.

Just then, Jacob found his face nestled in Gabe's armpit as he was sent flying across the room. He turned around in outrage, only to find Laura crying hysterically in Crispin's arms.

'Laura – what on earth is the matter, sweedie?' said Crispin in concern.

'Oh, Crispin – it's Robert. I just found him in the library with the cloakroom attendant. Naked!'

~

Darren whistled and turned back to the lady of a certain age he was chatting up. After Darren had played a blinder and convinced Lyric that she should put racing rivalries aside for one night and invite Prince Abu Rhuba, Rhuba had upped the stakes for tonight in celebration, and they were both set on the *prix d'excellence* – an older married woman. Rhuba was going for gold, of course, by chatting up Constance, but Darren had decided to play it a little safer with the wife of a nearby pig farmer and member of the landed gentry who, rumour had it, dabbled in a little swinging now and then.

Like most of the older women here, she was blonde with Kensington highlights and a voluminous blow-dry, well preserved, well dressed and just a little squiffy. She was proving good company – if a little harder work than Darren had anticipated.

He decided on a more forthright approach.

'You see, darlin', everyone's at it,' he said smoothly.

'What on earth are you talking about,' she giggled, with an inquisitive look across at Laura.

'You know perfectly well what I'm talking about,' whispered Darren in her ear. 'It. Shagging. Robert Hoffman's up to no good – even the hostess is.'

He paused for effect and the woman looked at him with a scandalized expression.

'*Constance?*'

Darren nodded authoritatively. 'Uh-huh.' He looked around to make sure Constance wasn't in eyesight to blow his story. 'Or about to be. I know, because she's with my mate.'

'What, Edward?' said the woman in confusion, looking across to where Edward was hovering attentively over Amba.

'No, the other one. The prince. *He's* the key to my love life. He –' Darren cocked his head over at Edward who, sensing their gaze, glanced up at them, smiled and winked. '*He's* the key to my share of the Charlton millions when George snuffs it – you wait and see.'

~

'He's a wonderful man, your father,' said Amba with a seductive smile at Edward. 'How fortuitous for you that father and son finally found each other again before . . .'

'Before what?' said Edward distractedly. In black satin Dior, Amba looked like an exotic panther, and he was finding it hard to concentrate on anything other than getting her alone, away from all these people, and undressed.

'Well, *chutzi*, he's an old man. You must cherish your

new bond and every day you have with him,' she purred, stroking his face with a huge hand. 'Just like you do with me.'

'Well, not quite like with you,' he growled, every nerve on super-sensory alert. Although, he had to admit, he was glad that Amba had hit it off with George and Constance. Constance, of course, had barely registered anything other than Amba's enviable figure and her even more enviable diamonds, but George had seemed to be smitten with Amba within seconds. Her insistence on trying to help his crippling arthritis holistically, using alternative medicine and massage, had only cemented his delight with her. And as Edward and Amba had quickly become practically joined at the hip, there had been plenty of time for her to administer treatment. Watching her, day after day, sit elegantly at his father's feet in the drawing room massaging cream into his legs, chatting and laughing with him, had been one of the many factors helping turn Edward's overpowering passion into a deep obsession. And it seemed to Edward that she was having a similar effect on his father – if in a different way.

But then, Edward thought now, looking at his secret fiancée with undisguised lust, what man could fail to be anything but captivated by her?

Just as well, really. For if the well-laid plans for his and Amba's future were to be realized – financially, anyway – then on side was exactly where he needed his father to be.

Now, how long before he had to deliver this dreaded speech?

~

Lyric politely extricated herself from a conversation with an old charity lunch friend of Constance and touched Philippe lightly on the elbow. Her heart raced at the physical contact, and she swallowed back the rush of unspoken anger and emotions and tried to assume an air of numb detachment. When she spoke, it felt foreign, like her voice came from someone else.

'I'm just going to find Mummy and Daddy – it's about time we did the speeches. Could you tee Edward up?'

Philippe nodded curtly as Lyric made her way through the crowd, smiling graciously at the guests but expertly avoiding being drawn into conversation with any of them. It seemed like hours since she'd seen either her mother or her father, and it was high time they addressed the guests.

Outside the ballroom, she found Jeffries standing on ceremony, ready to direct guests who were lost, drunk or both, to the cloakroom, bathroom or car park.

'Jeffries, have you seen Mummy or Daddy lately?'

Jeffries nodded stiffly and cleared his throat. 'I saw Lady Charlton heading for the gun room, Miss Lyric, only ten minutes ago.'

Lyric stared at him. 'The gun room?'

He nodded solemnly. 'Yes, Miss Lyric, the gun room.'

'But why would she go to the gun room during a party?'

Jeffries cleared his throat again, the model of discretion. 'I heard Lady Charlton tell the Prince Abu Rhuba she was going to show him her collection.' Jeffries cleared his throat again. 'With a big bang.'

'The prince?' repeated Lyric. Suddenly full of a foreboding she couldn't explain, Lyric ran along the corridor and down the stairs towards the gun room. As she approached she slowed, her heart beating loudly in her chest.

Outside the door, forefinger poised and ready to knock, something stopped her. She put her ear to the door, listening to see if her mother was still inside.

'Well, I say, young man, you're a good shot!' she heard Constance gush. 'Talk about explosive – there's no half cocks where you're coming from, is there?'

Horrified, Lyric burst in. As the door opened, Constance tumbled out, dress crumpled and turban askew. Behind her, Prince Abu Rhuba's face was a picture of gloating success.

Constance stood up and straightened her clothes.

'Darling! Fancy seeing you here. Have you seen your brother?'

'Lyric!' Still in shock, she turned at the sound of Edward's voice, which was unnaturally shrill. She saw him appear at the end of the corridor, face pale and panic-stricken.

'Lyric. It's Father. You need to come quickly. He's collapsed. He's unconscious.'

Twenty

The peace and quiet of the library had been restored after the day's fierce exertions. The fading sunlight bathed the room in the soft yellow glow of an August evening, and dust particles danced on the sleepy sunbeams. In fact it seemed to Lyric that the dust, so much a part of the library's very existence, had resettled immediately after the previous hours' disturbance.

As the day had passed, so had The Bed been rehoused and painstakingly rebuilt, piece by piece. No expense had been spared in its careful relocation – all at George's request. Napoleon's campaign bed – a family heirloom, and donated to the British Museum by George after his father's death – had returned to Broughton Hall. Now, complete in its imperial finery, with its dark green frame, gilt four posters and red-and-gold brocade canopy, it brought an air of nineteenth-century chivalry to the house, and a curious grandeur to the library. The crisp Frette sheets, made of one hundred per cent Egyptian cotton and with the highest thread count in existence, were immaculately laundered and tucked in tight around her father, just as he liked them.

The last person to lie in this had been his father, and Lyric's grandfather, when he was near death, and Lyric was refusing to dwell on what it meant for her naturally un-assuming father to demand a move on this scale.

That the museum had insisted on working around the clock to transport and rebuild it immediately, at no charge, said a lot about what they thought of her father, she felt. His gentle nature clearly had an impact way beyond that of more forceful personalities, and inspired people to move mountains on his behalf and make offers of help even where none had been requested.

Rebuilding the historic old bed in the centre of this majestic room had transformed the solemn library from a restful place to a place of . . . Lyric could hardly bear to say the words, even in her head. But place of rest was exactly how this felt now.

George himself, in a macabre joke, had looked at the new configuration of the room and suggested it be repainted and renamed The Death Bed. Now, having been carried in by Philippe and Edward, and having taken another of his pills, George lay asleep, his slumbering shrunken form a barely visible bump under the bedclothes. He had always been so tall, so strong, so indestructible. Lyric shivered. Then it was she who had been the weak and vulnerable one. Now, their roles had reversed.

His nurse moved silently around the room, tidying and

straightening with a practised hand. Next to George on the beside table sat a decanter containing his favourite cognac, a snifter of which he had always insisted on before bed. A vase of roses from the party – George couldn't abide mixed bunches – shared the rest of the space with a humidifier and a bottle of pills. His reading glasses sat forlornly on top of the first-edition copy of *Squirrel Nutkin* – a boyhood favourite – that Lyric had, at his request, planned to read aloud to him. That could wait – right now, rest was the priority.

There was a thump, and Lyric looked down at the floor to see, next to a discarded copy of the *Racing Post*, the smiling face of Stan, their ever-loyal Labrador. She smiled back at him and softly pulled the door open. Even Lyric's presence couldn't tempt him from George's side right now. She knew exactly how he felt . . .

~

'Rum old do if you ask me. Can't find what's wrong with him, can't find out how to treat him – I mean, what's a man to do? Lie in state for the rest of his living days?' Queenie placed the pile of laundry she was carrying on the kitchen table, then picked it up again quickly as Mrs Gunners came at her with a rolling pin.

'It's not for us to gossip, Queenie,' remonstrated Mrs Gunners. 'But, were I one for pondering these things – which I'm not, of course – I'd say it doesn't bode well. For anyone,' she added darkly.

'If you ask me, he should be in a hospital,' continued Queenie. 'I mean, what good's going to come to him here, in this draughty old place? I even found a pair of gloves in Master Edward's bed the other morning. Shows what them that's not used to it make of these cold old places.'

'Well, if someone was asking you – which they're not,' replied Mrs Gunners pointedly, 'I'd say that's the master, he's always very particular about what he wants. When he was discovered collapsed by Master Edward in the middle of the party like that, his first words was "I want to stay at home." All white and drawn and semi-conscious he was, poor man. And to think, one minute he was right as rain, the next – wham – down, he was! Just like that. No warning, nothing. And even though he was at death's door, even though he was critical, like, that's what he insisted on. Mr Gunners has always said Sir George is the finest man you could ever hope to work for. And I, for one, am going to work my bleeding socks off to make sure he's as comfortable as ever he could be, hospitals be damned. Even if we have got all the rest of the extended family under one roof as well. We all pull together for the likes of the master, Queenie, and don't you forget it.' Making the sign of the cross, Mrs Gunners picked up the lump of dough she was kneading and began to put her considerable weight behind rolling it out.

'Still, lot of work, eh, Mr Jeffries? Moving his room downstairs and all.'

Jeffries looked up from his cup of tea and opened his mouth, but Mrs Gunners spoke before he managed to.

'Well, he doesn't mind, of course, Queenie – it means less walking up and down those stairs for him!' snorted Mrs Gunners. 'Now, out of my way – I need to make the master a boiled egg and soldiers for when he wakes up.'

'How many of them egg and soldiers have you made for him, Mrs Gunners?'

'What, since he was taken ill or since he were a boy?' asked the cook with a faraway look in her eye. 'Always wanted an egg and soldiers, he did. I remember even though I was barely out of my teens myself!'

She wiped away the hint of a tear with the back of her hand, popped two eggs in the pan and returned to her rolling. 'Now take that laundry up to the library quick smart. I don't want the master thinking we've left him to rot in dirty linen!'

~

Quentin wiped his brow and tried not to think about his longing for a nice glass of Château Lafite and a cigarette. This confounded search for the horseshoe was proving more difficult than he had anticipated. Five hours he'd been searching today, and he was still no closer to finding it. He'd looked in all the obvious places – not that, now he came to think about it, there was such a thing as an obvious place to find a horseshoe – and all the non-obvious places. With everyone preoccupied about George, he'd gained easy access to all rooms but Edward's (his always seemed to be occupied by him or his foxy girlfriend), and, once he'd eliminated all the communal rooms and the garden sheds, he'd had a quick rummage through the family's personal effects, too. But there was nothing. He'd thought this was an easy assignment, but with every hour that passed and no horseshoe, the task became more and more insurmountable in his head. He had placed unrivalled importance on the whereabouts of this shoe, and he tried not to think of Skankton's reaction if it couldn't be found. But now, short of bribing that busybody chambermaid to have a look in his nephew's room, he really couldn't think where else it could be . . .

~

As Lyric disappeared off down the corridor, Edward emerged from the shadows and took her place at the door. Swigging from a half bottle of whisky, he peered through.

As he leaned, he lost his balance, and the door swung open with a crash.

Immediately, the nurse appeared from her chair in the corner of George's room and put a cool hand on Edward's arm to steady him.

'Mr Charlton, I must ask you to keep quiet,' the nurse said in a low, urgent tone. 'It's imperative your father gets his rest.'

With a flash of anger, Edward pushed past her. 'I'm his son! His son and heir! We were separated for thirty years, goddammit! And you're telling me he won't want to see me?' He stormed into the room and looked down at George's sleeping form. At the noise, George stirred and opened his eyes sleepily, smiled when he saw Edward, then closed them again.

The sight of his father so weak and helpless unleashed a multitude of emotions in Edward. There was sorrow – of course there was. But there was also anger. And betrayal. And – most unfathomable – self-pity. That smile had said it all. For George, the reappearance of his son had filled a huge chasm in his life. Over time, the wounds caused by thirty years of grief had healed and now George felt only joy at the presence of his son. But what had his new family meant for Edward? Confusion, certainly, not to mention the loss of his previous identity and a sense of worthlessness as he tried to adapt to his new one; but, most importantly, a searing sense of hurt at the injustice dealt to him all those years ago. Suddenly, this cauldron of simmering emotions surged up and threatened to boil over.

'Oh, you sleep easy, father,' he spat bitterly. 'You sleep like the baby I was when I was torn away from you. The baby you failed to protect in its most vulnerable moment. The little boy you didn't search quite hard enough for. And the man you didn't realize even existed!'

George's eyes opened again now and he lifted his head. Seeing his son, he tried to sit up.

The nurse rushed to his aid and scowled at Edward as he raised the bottle of whisky to his lips.

'Mr Charlton, I don't want to ask you again. I must insist you remain calm or leave this room immediately!'

'No.'

They both turned in surprise to George, who was now sitting propped up on one elbow. His voice was unsteady and low, but it was firm.

'No. I want to hear what he has to say.'

Edward stared at him, suddenly lost for words. He took another swig of whisky for good measure. The truth was, he didn't know what he wanted to say. This jumble of emotions was exactly that – a jumble. Whereas on the one hand, of course, he was joyful about his new-found family, it wasn't quite as easy for him as for the rest of them. They had always known he was missing from their lives. But he – he hadn't been unhappy before he'd been found. He hadn't felt particularly lacking in any way. Along with all the joy he felt about his new life, he also felt despair. And now, before he had time to resolve any of it, George lay on his death bed? It was too much. Too much.

But he had no idea how to articulate any of this through his alcohol-befuddled brain.

'I think you're weak,' was all he managed. 'And I despise you.'

George stared at him, stunned. 'But Edward, my boy, I –'

Suddenly, he stopped, a look of abject fear on his face, and his throat began to emit an alarming gurgling noise.

From the floor, Stan whined and slunk under the bed, looking up with a worried frown.

The nurse rushed to George's side, laying him back down on the bed and turning to Edward angrily.

'Mr Charlton, I must insist that you leave this room immediately!'

'What's going on?'

Philippe stood at the door, his face etched with concern. Behind him, Constance appeared in a day coat, crystal tumbler in hand.

'What's all the noise about, dear? Is George creating a fuss again?'

'He's not creating a fuss, Mummy dearest, he appears to be struggling to breathe,' said Edward sarcastically, still full of angry bluster but his face pale behind its whisky flush.

'Sir George is very poorly indeed,' said the nurse from his bedside. 'And I must insist that you all leave me to tend to him now.' She turned to Constance and Philippe. 'Mr Charlton is very agitated and has upset Sir George. The best thing for everyone is if he leaves now.'

As one, Philippe and Constance rushed to George's bedside and Lyric appeared at the door, panic-stricken.

'What's going on?'

'That's what we're trying to establish,' said Philippe grimly. He turned to Edward. 'What were you thinking of, man?'

'Edward, what on earth have you done?' said Constance.

Edward peered at her through eyes that refused to focus. 'Oh, well, it would have to be my fault, wouldn't it? The OUTSIDER. And why would you care anyway, Mother?'

Constance put her hand to her chest as if mortally wounded. 'You're drunk!'

Edward laughed callously. 'So are you!'

Constance grabbed hold of Philippe's arm for support. 'Oh! How dare you! Of course I'm not.' She waved her glass around erratically. 'I'll have you know this is water!'

'Water, my arse!' slurred Edward coarsely. 'That's like Caprice saying she's never had surgery. Everyone knows you've been drowning your sorrows, Mum – you can smell it on your breath!'

'Oh!' Constance put her glass down on the bedside table and gestured for Lyric to support her other arm. Lyric, still shocked at the scene, dutifully moved to her side.

Edward looked at the three of them and sneered. 'Yes, you are, Mother. It's your latest prop, isn't it? Aren't the pills numbing this pain enough for you? Had to turn to the bottle of booze as well as the bottle of mother's little helpers, have you?'

There was a grunt from the bed and they all turned to George, who was sweating and breathing heavily.

'He's losing consciousness,' said the nurse grimly. 'Please, I must insist . . .'

'This is real life, Mother!' Edward gestured at George.

'Your husband. Your daughter. Your SON. Not your little faggoty toy-boys, or your pill-induced perfect life, or your pretend Moroccan castle in the air for that matter! We can all see it, but no one will admit it! You might once have been the lady of the manor, the most feted hostess in the county, but right now you're nothing but a desperate old woman!'

'Oh!' Constance swooned and Philippe caught her just in time as she fell. He looked at Edward sternly. '*Ça suffit*, Edward.'

Edward rounded on him. 'Yes, you're right, it's quite enough. Enough of "Where's Lady Charlton – away with the fairies" jokes. Enough of pretending. I've only been in this family a few months and already I've had more than enough of it!"

~

Constance came around and leaned on Philippe, burrowing her face in his shoulder and sobbing theatrically.

'Oh, Philippe! What am I going to do! George on his death bed and my own son abusing me! Lyric, help me!'

Lyric stroked her mother's shoulder and looked at Philippe helplessly. He shrugged and turned to Edward.

A gurgling sound came from the bed and Lyric turned in concern. The nurse, on the other side of the bed, gestured for water. Lyric passed her a glass from the bedside table and the nurse gently gave George a sip from it.

'Mummy, I think you need to have a lie down,' said

Lyric gently. She turned to Edward, now pacing up and down the room. 'And you certainly do,' she added coldly.

He rounded on her, eyes flashing. 'My own twin sister, refusing to see what's going on in front of her very eyes. God, this family!'

He stormed out and Philippe gently led Constance, still sobbing, out of the room.

Lyric leaned over her father, now sleeping more peacefully, and kissed him on the head.

What had her family come to?

~

In the muffled quiet of the drawing room, the ancient grandfather clock struck midnight. Lyric was startled from her half slumber by Philippe strolling in. For his part, he jumped when he saw her.

'Don't worry, I'm going to look in on father before bed,' said Lyric, immediately pulling herself up from the chaise longue she'd been curled up on. Philippe looked at her with a pained expression, then lowered his eyes.

'OK.'

Lyric bit her lip. A subdued air had fallen over the house after Edward's outburst earlier that afternoon, and she – along with the rest of the household, and the very walls of Broughton Hall, too, it seemed – was numb from shock. She was spent of all energy. It was neither the time nor the place to explore things between her and Philippe further. Again.

She padded along the corridor to the library. It seemed

to her that there had been a constant flow of people tread-ing this path all afternoon as George had slipped in and out of consciousness. The doctor, the nurse, an electrician to fit a panic button linked to the local hospital, even George's solicitor, for some unfathomable reason. Numb to every-thing other than her father's well-being, Lyric had trodden it herself every hour or so, as if her physical presence could will George back to health.

She peered in through the door, as she had done so many times that day, ensuring everything was as it should be. And had been, all day. George's body rose and fell with each laboured breath, and next to the bed the nurse was taking a cat nap.

Lyric resisted the urge to tiptoe in and kiss her father for fear it would disturb him, and instead left the room, closing the door behind her.

All of a sudden, there was a low, animal-like groan from the bed and the nurse jolted out of her sleep and jumped up, grabbing George's wrist and simultaneously pressing the panic button.

Alarmed, Lyric pushed open the door and ran to his bedside. George's face was waxy and his breathing was low and shallow.

'What's wrong?' she asked the nurse, staring with wild eyes. 'What's wrong?'

The nurse looked at her compassionately.

'His pulse is very weak,' she said gently. 'Miss Lyric, it might be time to call a priest.'

Lyric stared at her numbly.

All around the house, it was as though time stood still.

In the kitchen, Mrs Gunners, preparing a chicken soup for the master the following day, stopped stirring the pot and let the broth boil untended.

In the scullery, Queenie stood stock still, holding the latest batch of sheets ready for the master's early morning bed change.

In the office, Jeffries placed a teaspoon carefully alongside the teacup on the tray, ready for Sir George's early morning tea.

In the guest wing, Quentin, pulling on his pyjamas and taking a medicinal nightcap, spattered his bed socks with whisky as it poured unchecked from his hip flask.

In the office, Roger Skankton – who had been a regular fixture at Broughton Hall since George had been found ill – looked up from the paperwork he was reading under the table lamp and frowned.

In his bedroom, Edward, rousing from his drunken stupor with a parched mouth, moved to kiss Amba's sleeping shoulder but stopped midway as he sat up and reached for a glass of water.

In the drawing room, Philippe folded up his paper and held his head in his hands.

In her dressing room, Constance, taking her latest handful of prescription drugs and applying cold cream in front of her dressing table, stared unseeingly into the mirror in front of her.

And in George's room, Stan gave a lengthy whine and stopped wagging his tail for the first time anyone could remember.

A blue LED light lit up the room and Lyric looked out of the window with a heavy heart. The ambulance had its lights flashing, but no siren. It was as if it already knew it was no longer an emergency.

Her father was dead.

Twenty-one

The night of George's death passed like a particularly bad dream. Lyric sat numbly at her father's side, stroking his thinning hair and holding his still-warm hand as it got colder and colder.

She was only half aware of the people coming in and out of the room: Philippe, checking on her constantly, softly kissing her head each time before leaving to direct the household staff and start preparing the mountain of paperwork that would need dealing with urgently in the morning; Edward, shell-shocked and already hungover; Constance, wafting around in a prescription drug-induced stupor, fussing about dogs, and glasses of water, and where she'd left her reading glasses.

In fact, everyone seemed to be fussing about one thing or another in George's room: Edward, sheepish now, with a deeply furrowed brow and clenched jaw, looked around with darting eyes every time he came in; Quentin, full of bluster and visibly upset by the sight of his brother, was obsessed with a Bible he felt should be used during George's funeral; Roger, who had entered once, and left as quickly as he'd arrived, was muttering about some missing paperwork; and even Amba, who regally arrived to pay her respects, had seemed, through the haze of Lyric's grief, to hover overly long around the tray of medication placed on a nearby table.

Lyric, moved by some deep-rooted instinct, was guarding George's effects fiercely, insisting the room be left just as it was. Somehow it seemed imperative that things should remain as George had seen them in his last living hours – as though changing even the setting on the humidifier would somehow place his death further into the past, making it more real.

But finally, it was daybreak, and Philippe knocked gently for the umpteenth time and entered the room.

'Lyric, you should get some sleep,' he said gently. 'Please. Leave me to stay with your father. You need rest.'

Lyric looked at him blankly. Her neck creaked as she turned and acknowledged the truth in his words.

Reluctantly, she prised her hand from her father's and handed it to Philippe.

'Look after him,' she said with a wan smile.

Slowly, she walked the length of the corridor and up the stairs to her room. Her bed looked cold and foreign, and she passed it without getting under the sheets. Instead, she undressed and took a scalding hot shower, letting the water warm her stiff, creaky bones and revive her senses.

After a good ten minutes, she stepped out, dried herself and put on a fresh set of clothes. She blow-dried her hair carefully, something she rarely did, and applied make-up – another rare occurrence. The black mascara seemed harsh and spiky, and the rouge incongruous on her pale face, but she knew instinctively it was what she should do. It was how she'd been brought up. All her life, she could remember Constance facing anything out of the ordinary – shock, misfortune or even tragedy – with a fully made-up face and a rigid smile, and now Lyric found an odd kind of comfort in the well-practised routine.

She put on a pair of diamond earrings her father had given her for her eighteenth birthday, and wandered along the corridor to her mother's room. She knocked and, hearing no answer, opened the door unbidden.

Constance was sitting motionless on the day bed, looking out of the bay window over Broughton Hall's gardens. She was backlit by a halo of early morning sunshine, and a half-drunk tumbler of water rested in her hand.

'Mother?' ventured Lyric. 'Mummy, can I get you anything?'

Constance turned, her eyes glassy and vacant.

'No, darling, George has got me everything I need, thank you.'

Lyric frowned. 'Mummy, are you sure—'

'He's still here, you know, Lyric. I can feel it.'

Lyric took a few tentative steps towards her mother, until Constance held up her hand sharply for Lyric to stop. As she did, she let go of the glass and it fell to the floor with a tinkling crash, breaking into smithereens.

'I don't need anything, darling. George has it all covered. But do make sure Mrs Gunners serves the correct
tea at breakfast time. Yesterday it was Darjeeling, and you
know George drinks only Earl Grey.'

'OK, Mummy,' said Lyric, backing slowly out of the
room. 'Make sure you don't cut yourself on that glass. I'll
be back shortly . . .'

She stood for a moment outside the door, then retraced
her steps downstairs.

Before returning to the library, she ran quickly to the
kitchen. Inside, the normal early morning hive of activity
was under way – only today it was conducted in total
silence.

Through in the scullery, she could see that the dog's
bowls remained untouched.

'The dogs have no appetite for their food this morning,'
said Mrs Gunners. 'They must be feeling the same as the
rest of us.' Wiping a tear away, she moved forward as if to
envelop Lyric in a hug. Lips tightly pursed, Lyric shook her
head vehemently. Any random acts of kindness would
surely send her over the edge today, and she owed it to her
father to keep it together.

'Mother asked me to ensure that we have Earl Grey tea
this morning,' she said efficiently.

Mrs Gunners nodded, used to this approach and, so her
businesslike reaction suggested, reassured by it. 'Very well,
Miss Lyric. Breakfast will be served at the normal time.'

'Thank you.'

Buoyed by some kind of action, however insignificant, Lyric walked purposefully back to George's room. She swallowed the feeling of dread as she opened the door, and the huge lump that appeared in her throat as she saw her father, still lying in bed.

Philippe looked startled by her appearance.

'Lyric – what are you doing here? You should be—'

'I should be here, Philippe,' she cut in. 'I couldn't sleep if you paid me. Things need attending to. It's business as usual – that's how we do things.'

'But—' he protested.

'It's called the stiff upper lip,' she said flatly. 'We Brits have a lot to thank it for. Get back on the horse when you fall off, that's what my father used to say. And so that's what we must do. For everyone's sake.'

Philippe shook his head, as if bamboozled not for the first time by the crazy English ways.

There was a knock at the door, and Jeffries cleared his throat discreetly.

'Miss Lyric, the doctor is here,' he said. 'He has another gentleman with him. He says they are both here to see you.'

'Fine,' said Lyric without emotion. 'Show them into the drawing room, Jeffries, I'll be there shortly.'

Jeffries cleared his throat and hesitated. 'Miss Lyric, I believe they are also here to see Sir George.'

Philippe stood up and placed an arm around Lyric's shoulders. She railed against it and shrugged him off.

'Thank you, Jeffries,' said Philippe levelly, showing no reaction to Lyric's rebuff. 'We'll see them now.'

The butler disappeared, and they heard his footsteps fading down the corridor and then returning, their steady rhythm interspersed now with those of the two visitors.

There was a pause as they stood outside the door.

'Come in,' said Lyric impatiently, not waiting for the knock.

The doctor – a short, bespectacled man wearing the same brown cord jacket Lyric could always remember him wearing – entered the room. Behind him was a much taller, distinguished-looking man in a smart, light-grey summer suit and a raincoat. He had a well-groomed moustache and weary hooded eyes.

'Lyric, my dear, I'm so sorry about George – your father,' said the doctor respectfully. 'He was a king among men and will be sorely missed.'

'Thank you,' she said with a slight nod. 'What do you need to do first?' She stood to one side as if to grant him access to her father, but he didn't move.

'Actually, Lyric, I want to talk to you first. Maybe you should sit down?' He nodded towards the chair by George's bedside, but Lyric shook her head, perplexed.

'I'm fine, thank you. What could be worse than finding out my father is dead?' She blanched at the words but smiled brittlely through the pain.

'Well, Lyric, allow me to introduce the detective investigating your father's death.'

Lyric looked at the other man in confusion. She looked at Philippe questioningly and he shrugged in response.

The plain-clothes officer stepped forward. 'Miss Charlton, we need to speak to you about moving your father elsewhere. And about the, ahem, traffic through this room since your father was first taken ill.'

Lyric looked wildly from the doctor to the detective.

'I'm – I'm not sure I understand?'

'Lyric, I also need your mother's permission to conduct a toxicology report on your father,' said the doctor. 'Just to eliminate anything untoward, you understand. Only, I took a blood test a couple of days ago. The results came back in this morning – and I'm not entirely comfortable with the manner of your father's death. I have notified the police of this – and they feel they should investigate further.'

Lyric stared at them, her mind whirring.

'You mean – you mean you think he was *killed*?' They gazed back at her. Lyric put her hands to her mouth as the full weight of his meaning struck her. 'Oh my God. You think that my father was *murdered* . . .'

Twenty-two

'Ashes to ashes, dust to dust . . .'

Constance let out a huge wail at the words, and Lyric looked at her with sadness, biting her lip against the rush of pain that consumed her every cell. She mustn't break down. Mustn't break down. She needed to be strong – strong for her mother, for her brother, strong for all of them. Her father, the quiet rock that held the family together, had gone. Her mother was having some kind of breakdown. And Edward, too, seemed to be struggling with the enormity of his loss. Lyric herself could no longer rely on Philippe, so she was having to bear the full brunt of the family grief.

She looked at the close friends and family gathered around the graveside: Mother, of course, dressed head-to-toe in black Chanel with a Philip Treacy feathered headdress, was performing amateur dramatics at every turn and clutching a lace handkerchief. Philippe, her prop of choice, stood rock still, straight-backed and almost unbearably handsome in his sombre black suit. Ashen-faced Edward had his arm around Amba, who herself looked stunning, if in a black widow kind of way, in a black-lace Prada cap-sleeve dress. Uncle Quentin was clearly coping with the loss of his brother by returning to his previous drinking habits – if the red nose, broken veins and bad breath weren't give-away enough, then the hipflask-shaped bulge in his pocket was proof. The Skanktons, dressed as if for a wedding, were a ragbag group at the foot of the grave, looking uncomfort-able at the solemnity of the occasion. Behind them, Broughton Hall's staff had congregated in their Sunday best to pay their respects to the master. Angus stood to one side, dressed in an ill-fitting suit Lyric had never seen before, pre-sumably because it was only ever wheeled out on special occasions. It was everyone her father had held dear. Further back stood Darren with Prince Abu Rhuba, who had requested that he, too, be able to pay his respects to George along with his friend. Lyric, too numb to protest, had acqui-esced with the simple request that he keep a low profile and give the relatives space. And whilst he had respected that wish, the full gold-brocade military regalia he was wearing in respect of the occasion was hardly low-key.

Lyric turned her attention back to the service. George had picked this spot under the cedar tree at the top of the garden, many years ago, in which to bury his first old faith-ful Labrador, Reg. Since then, other loyal friends had joined him, and George had often remarked that he'd be happier buried here than in some 'damp old cemetery surrounded by people I probably never liked anyway'. So they'd taken him at his word and had the ground officially consecrated.

His body had been dressed in his customary old, faded country clothes, with their faint whiff of cigars and Scotch. On his lifeless body, they looked as much in keeping with Broughton Hall as the ancient beams in the ceiling and the missing roof tiles. Beside him in his coffin they had carefully placed a copy of the *Racing Post*, Stan's old lead and a very worn edition of *Squirrel Nutkin*.

As the coffin was lowered into the grave, Constance let out yet another anguished wail. Lyric felt consumed with sadness for her, as well as for her father. Grief had restored all her mother's natural poise and elegance, and replaced the pill-induced vagueness in her eyes with something much more real.

A lone tear fell down her cheek at the realization that, though she finally had Constance back, it was too late for her mother to be restored to her father. And vice versa: none of them would ever see his kindly smile again. A sob rose in her throat and, as she threw a single white rose onto the coffin, she turned and led the small group back across the grounds to Broughton Hall.

~

'Edward, mate. Wait up!'

Edward turned around and saw Darren and Prince Abu Rhuba jogging up towards him.

'You walk on ahead,' he said to Amba, who, despite her lightweight lace dress, had been complaining about the heat. 'I'll catch you up.'

She tossed her head petulantly, gathered her dress around her and sashayed off across the grass. Reluctantly, Edward tore his eyes away from her retreating curves and back to his two partners in crime.

'So you're still getting your end away, are you?' said Prince Abu Rhuba with a subtle nudge. 'She must be good to keep your interest for so long. I would have tired of the same girl weeks ago.'

'She looks filthy!' leered Darren. 'Anyhow, mate, just wanted to give you my condolences. You know, about your old man.'

'Thanks,' said Edward, falling into step beside them with an outward ease that belied his inner discomfort. Suddenly he felt like an outsider with them both again.

'Terribly tragic,' echoed the prince.

'Yes. Yes, it is,' he agreed.

'Still, mate, your work is done now. And once all this is over don't forget what I said, right?' said Darren, leaning across to him. 'You know, about all my little business ideas?' He tapped the side of his nose as if to indicate a secret that Edward couldn't remember ever having shared with him.

Edward stopped and ran his hand through his hair. He gave Darren a puzzled look 'What do you mean?'

'Well, you know,' prompted Darren, grinning inanely. 'George falling ill "unexpectedly". You falling out with him on his death bed. After our little chat, you don't need to be a genius to work all that out.'

'I beg your pardon,' snapped Edward, stunned, and suddenly full of a forthright courage he'd never found in front of Darren before. 'How dare you suggest I've got anything to do with my father's death?'

'Oh, come on, friend,' said the prince easily, patting Edward on the back and gently pushing him along again. 'You know Darren isn't suggesting anything of the sort. He's just excited about what the future may hold for the pair of you with George out of the way.'

Edward shook off his hand. 'There is no future for us, as far as I'm concerned. And I'll thank you to remember that you're both here to pay your respects to the man you seem to think is so dispensable.' He turned on his heel and stomped back to the house, inwardly boiling with rage.

'Not dispensable – disposable!' called Darren after him as he and the prince followed slowly. 'Disposable income, that is. Think about it!'

~

'Well, isn't this jolly?' Constance, ever the hostess, was putting on a brave face as she balanced a dish of crudités and a glass of white Burgundy and flitted around the room working her magic. 'Wouldn't George have loved it – all his favourite people getting together over some simply delicious drinks and canapés.'

Across the room, Philippe caught Lyric's eye and gave her a caring smile, but she shrugged it off defensively. Since her father's death, he had been trying to act as though nothing had gone wrong, but in her mind the gulf between them had become so wide she almost couldn't remember how it had ever been any different.

Having circumnavigated the room thanking everyone for coming and the staff for all their help, Lyric now felt a strange sense of anti-climax. She wandered across the room to the window and gazed out, looking at the gardens admiringly. Since the lab where George's samples had been sent had confirmed there'd been a mix-up, and that George's sample hadn't been contaminated at all – thus rendering the police investigation defunct – they had at last all been free to grieve. But she still felt numb – almost so overwhelmed that she didn't know where to start. She inhaled deeply, as though trying to breathe in her father's scent. She should be thankful that his last view had been of the gardens, his favourite place in the world in full bloom and looking as wonderful as she could ever remember it. And all thanks to Philippe . . .

'Oh, my dear, I'm so sorry that all this has happened. First your horse, now your father . . .'

Lyric looked at Uncle Quentin in surprise. Not only was he the last person she'd expect commiserations from, she found this one curiously inappropriate.

'Well, I must say this has all rather put Thumper's death into context,' she said quietly.

'Still, it doesn't help,' persisted Quentin. 'But I suppose you have plenty of keepsakes of him? The horse, I mean,' he added hurriedly.

'Photographs and my memories are all I have,' said Lyric quietly.

It was a surprise even to herself, but, reeling from his sudden death, it hadn't occurred to her to keep anything to remind her of Thumper. But then a thought struck her. 'Still, Laura said Kitty has a horseshoe of his, of course . . .'

Quentin went a strange shade of puce and began to stammer unintelligibly. Lyric smiled sympathetically and wandered through to the study. As she did so, she heard a rustle as a figure in black-silk crêpe dashed past the doorway. Something about it intrigued her, and she popped her head around the door. There she saw her mother's unmistakable Philip Treacy headdress disappear around the corner, and the flash of something else catch the sunlight. Lyric frowned. He mother wasn't wearing anything bright. Unless . . .

Lyric felt sick. Unless it had been one of the bright gold buttons of the prince's military jacket . . .

She had a sudden flashback of her mother with him at the party. What on earth was going on? Consumed by a sudden desperate need to find out, Lyric stumbled blindly down the corridor after them.

At the end of the passage, Lyric paused. Where would they have gone from here? She looked to her left, through the garden doors that led onto the terrace. They would still be swinging open if they had left that way. They must have gone down the stairs into the wine cellar – George's wine cellar, that he had taken such pride in over many years, cherishing his collection of some of the world's finest vintages.

Almost falling over her own feet to follow them as quickly as possible, Lyric ran down the stairs. She could tell she was on the right track from the scent of her mother's signature Fracas perfume hanging in the air.

Lyric heard what sounded like a hiccup come from beyond the heavy wooden doors, and rage gave her a rush of strength. She pushed them open as though they were MDF, not ancient hand-crafted oak.

Inside, she stopped in shock. In front of her, as she had feared, was her mother in the prince's embrace. But they weren't *in flagrante*. Instead, the prince stood patting her back awkwardly, looking as though he would rather be anywhere else but there. Constance was crying hysterically; huge, heaving sobs that racked every bone in her body with each rasping gulp of air.

'Mother? Mummy, what the hell are you doing in here – and what's wrong?'

'Oh, Lyric! What is to become of me? Of us?'

Forgetting all her anger at the sight of her mother in such distress, Lyric took a half step forward.

'What do you mean?'

'I've lost everything. *We've* lost everything. George was the most wonderful man in the world. The most wonderful! I mean, everyone loved him. I loved him. And he loved everybody. He forgave his brother, for God's sake, after everything! Over and over . . .' She looked up at Lyric through rivulets of mascara. Lyric marvelled at how small her mother now looked. Shrunken, almost. 'Oh, Lyric, how will we ever go on without him?'

Lyric stepped forward properly now, and took Constance in her arms. As her mother cried, Lyric's own tears started to fall, and then it was her mother cradling her, and she was crying and Constance was hugging her, too, and suddenly something was all right again. Somehow, some way, Lyric had her mother back. She could stop trying so hard. She could cry.

And so she cried. She cried for her father, for her mother, for Philippe, for herself. But most of all she cried for the wasteland of lost love.

Twenty-three

The executor looked across his desk in concern whilst the Charltons rushed as one to rescue Constance from the dusty floor. In the end Philippe prevailed, and she stood up gingerly as he gave her his arm, brushing herself down ineffectually and trying to put on a brave face. She dabbed under her eyes gently with a lace handkerchief.

'Oh, dear me. I'm so sorry, everyone. And it's not what you think. I'm not . . . That is, this is so like George, bless him – trying to right the wrongs of the world even from the grave. But – we've only just pulled through some terrible times as a family and this threatens to tear us apart once more . . . Oh, dear me!'

She reached in her handbag for her pill box and, out of habit, Lyric blanched, despite knowing it was now filled with peppermints, not happy pills. Constance necked several in one go, and then smiled brightly around the group.

'Now, then. We're not going to let this affect us. Are we?'

Lyric stood up, hugged her mother and shook her head vehemently. 'No, Mummy, of course we're not.' Her words sounded more confident than she felt, however, and, brushing aside her own surprise for a moment – what had she done to so disappoint her father? – she snuck a sidelong glance at Edward. How would he react to this? After all, this was not the first but the second time he'd been deprived of his birthright. He'd found and lost his father in the same year; and now, to find out that George was secretly disappointed in him for some reason must have been a tough blow to take. Factor in that he seemed to be getting very serious about Amba, and this was hardly the news he'd be wanting to hear as far as their future was concerned.

'Oh good, darling. Because I imagine you're light years away from having children, which means I'm going to be remaining at Broughton Hall for years to come, and I want to make it perfectly clear that you all have a home there for as long as you want. That includes your lovely Amba, Edward, and of course you, Quentin.'

'Right,' said Edward vaguely.

'Thank you, Mummy,' said Lyric, more enthusiastically than she felt. She looked over at Philippe. She'd spent so long putting off the inevitable confrontation that she'd never considered what a split between them would mean for him. George had bequeathed their business to Philippe. But Broughton Hall was currently his home, too. How would it affect him if he and Lyric were to part company?

The thought gave her a panicky sense of hurt – the first real pang she'd felt since her father's death – and she

swallowed hard. Why was it never the time nor the place –
or was she deliberately avoiding the inevitable?

'Thank you? THANK YOU? That's your problem,
Lyric, you've always been too bloody accommodating!'
Everyone turned in surprise to where Quentin was stand-
ing to one side with Jacob.

'Oh, Quentin!' said Constance soothingly. 'Please, darling, there's no need to get all agitated.'

'Agitated? AGITATED? My brother makes the effort
to invite me back from the dead – and for what? To deprive
me of my rightful inheritance all over again?'

Constance tutted. 'Well, darling, who's to say Jacob
won't be the first to bear fruit for the cause? I mean, there's
never been a problem with firing blanks in the Charlton
lineage as far as I'm aware. As a blood relative Jacob would
be eligible, wouldn't he?' She looked around for confirma-
tion from the executor, who suddenly found something
very interesting on the far wall to look at.

'Well, Mummy, let's not get too hasty about this,' put in
Lyric hurriedly, still with one eye on Edward but suddenly
feeling proprietorial about Broughton Hall herself. It was
her home, too, after all . . .

'Oh, so suddenly Saint Lyric isn't so charitable when
it might get in the way of her own gain, eh?' stormed
Quentin. He rounded on Constance. 'And what bloody
good is this will to me, when I've got a son who, firing
blanks or not, is firing them up the wrong bloody alley?'

Edward looked up from his phone, on which he had been texting furiously.

'I guess whoever gets there first will have to be a bit more careful with their firstborn than George was, eh, Mother? And, *Uncle* Quentin what about that karma you love to preach about – always comes back to bite you on the arse, doesn't it?' He glanced back at his phone as a text came in. 'Anyhow, much as I'd love to spend all afternoon having this out with you, my girlfriend is patiently waiting for me in the car and I'd really like to get back to her.'

'Oh dear. Why don't we all head to the Wolseley for lunch?' suggested Constance, overly cheerful. 'We can chat about it there . . .'

There was a silence as the rest of them looked at one another dubiously. Constance couldn't have made a less popular suggestion, thought Lyric. She herself couldn't wait to be away from them all – or, more accurately, Philippe – and, now that they could finally move on from her father's death, decide exactly what she was going to do about her dysfunctional relationship. Once the news had sunk in, Edward would no doubt be ready to combust. And, frankly, a restaurant environment was hardly the ideal place for her mother to be just one month into her rehabilitation . . .

'I'll see if Amba fancies it,' said Edward doubtfully, texting furiously.

'Oh, well, why not?' blustered Quentin. 'Sitting down around a table in public with the family that loves nothing more than to shaft me sounds like the ideal way to spend an afternoon. Count me in, Constance!' There was a pause as he pulled his hip flask from his jacket and went to take a swig. Beside him, Jacob squirmed as Quentin turned it upside down and shook it. It was empty. Quentin peered into it in dismay and then looked up at Constance sheepishly. 'Erm, unless – I assume you're paying?'

Edward looked up from his phone. 'Count us out,' he said distractedly. 'I've just had another text from Amba. She's got an appointment in Portland Street in an hour. And she's not drinking, anyway, so it would be a rather dull lunch for her.'

There was another silence as the rest of the group absorbed this information.

'Why isn't she drinking, darling?' asked Constance innocently.

Before Edward could reply, the door opened. Behind it stood the detective who'd investigated the suspect blood test.

Every one of the six pairs of eyes stared disbelievingly.

'Good day,' he said in a polite, no-nonsense manner. 'I was told I would find you all here. New evidence has come to light and we are reopening the case into Sir George Charlton's death.'

There was a gasp from Constance and Lyric felt her legs wobble underneath her. She grabbed hold of the table in front of her for support.

'What do you mean?' Lyric's voice wavered and sounded pitifully small.

'I must ask you to remain here while I speak to each of you individually. I have a few questions about the night of Sir George Charlton's death.'

There was a silence.

'But you said there was nothing sinister about his death!' wailed Constance. 'You allowed me to bury my husband! And now, now you tell me this was all a mistake? How can this be allowed to happen?'

The detective cleared his throat delicately.

'A lab technician has come forward and confessed to exchanging the blood test samples. They were paid to do so in order, we can only at this stage assume, to conceal the fact that George's blood test was contaminated. And so in order to establish whom they were paid by, and why, I am reopening the investigation into his death. That includes a thorough examination of you, his closest relatives.'

'Bloody brilliant,' spat Quentin. 'One minute a man's deprived of his rightful inheritance, the next he's under the microscope for killing his brother. Because that's what you're suggesting, isn't it?'

There was another silence and the detective coughed again.

'There are other people I will want to speak to, as well as family,' he said carefully. 'Anyone who was at the party, for a start.'

'But you're focusing on us first.' The tone of Quentin's

voice was stating a fact, not asking a question. 'I knew it,' he thundered, attempting to find some comfort in his hip flask for a second, equally futile time. 'Now we're all bloody murder suspects.'

Twenty-four

'Well, of course, it's no surprise to me,' said Queenie, folding towels purposefully with alarming conviction. 'A man doesn't just keel over and die like that. Not someone as lively as the master, anyhows. He was right as rain come five o'clock that night. And then, a few hours later – bosh! – he's dead? Doesn't add up. It's a rum old do, and no mistake.'

Mrs Gunners picked up the dough she was kneading and slapped it over forcefully. 'You don't know what you're talking about, Queenie. The master wasn't in full health, you know that. What with his arthritis and stomach upsets and all. And you told me yourself his pillow was always covered in hair those last weeks from where it was falling out. If that's not a sign of summat seriously wrong, I don't know what is. What say you, Mr Jeffries?'

Jeffries folded down his newspaper and took a long sip of his tea. He picked the paper up again and returned to his previous position, obliterating his face from view.

'Well, I'm sure you'll be top of their list when they start asking questions, eh, Mr Jeffries?' said Queenie loudly with a knowing wink at Mrs Gunners. 'What the butler saw, and all that?'

The paper moved slightly but Jeffries still made no comment.

'Anyways, if you ask me, that brother of his has got summat to do with it,' continued Queenie, picking up a huge pile of towels and moving them to the dumbwaiter for easy transportation. 'Sure as eggs is eggs, he is Trouble with a capital T. Did I tell you I once found an empty bottle of brandy in his bed? An empty bottle, I tell you!'

'You did. Many times. And now, listen here, Queenie, you can't go around saying things like that,' remonstrated Mrs Gunners sharply. 'The master would be turning in his grave if he was to hear you implicate his own flesh and blood that way.'

'You said yourself he's the black sheep of the family,' replied Queenie sulkily.

'I think you'll find that *you* said that,' corrected Mrs Gunners. 'I make it my business never to get involved in idle gossip about them that put the food on my table and the pillow beneath my head.' There was an outraged silence from Queenie, who pursed her lips so tightly they went white. 'But, if I were one for speculating, like, you know I wouldn't have a clue where to start. The master was a saint in my eyes, you know that' – Mrs Gunners paused to make the sign of the cross on her chest – 'but strike me down, there's enough of them in this household who'd think they'd have as good a reason as any to do away with him,

God rest his soul.' She made another sign with a floury hand and shook her head sadly before resuming her kneading. 'Even Mr Gunners says, they've all got queerness in them, from the master's nephew to that there Master Edward, I'm sure they could all twist things to come up with a motive if you was to give them half a chance.'

'Mmm,' agreed Queenie, slightly mollified. 'It's a rum old do, all right.'

~

'So tell me again, just so I have it straight in my mind,' said Amba, lightly fixing her earrings and looking at her face in the mirror closely as she applied lipstick. 'Just so I can be sure of the details.'

Edward sighed in frustration. He'd already explained the sequence of events at the will reading over and over to Amba and had no desire to rake over the painful truth again. The fact that he would not be able, as he'd hoped, to offer Amba the world on a plate before their marriage was difficult enough to accept, without having to spell it out to her time and time again. He knocked back a tumbler of whisky and reached for the decanter to pour more.

'Really, Amba, darling, there's nothing more to tell,' he said resolutely. 'It's not all going to the firstborn. Of course. I've got my allowance still. And there are some stocks and shares – what hasn't been bequeathed to the Jockey Club, that is. We can all still live at the house. Apparently there is a fund in trust that will see to the upkeep of Broughton Hall while we're all busy trying to procreate. That's if there's anything left once my mother has spent it all on antiques, trying to restore it back to its former Grade One beauty,' he added sharply. 'A riad never went up, nor came down, quite so quick.' He took a deep breath and another slug of whisky.

'But the main thing is that my father has made damn sure none of us is going to inherit until we provide him – posthumously – with a third-generation heir. End of. There's nothing we can do about it.' He looked at her through the red mist of his anger, her long, silky-skinned leg emerging from her evening dress, wrapped around the leg of the dressing-table stool, and felt his loins stir. He moved over to her and traced a finger along her bare arm and up her shoulder. 'Of course, there is one thing we could do to help the baby-making process along . . .'

Amba smiled at him coolly and removed his hand from where it was now tracing a line down her décolletage.

'Not now, *chutzi*, we are about to eat.'

Edward frowned. Their initial levels of non-stop love-making had plummeted since George's death. Sex, although always as mind-blowing as the first time, wasn't quite as frequent. Either Amba had a headache or, he had to concede, he was too drunk. He knocked back another tumbler of whisky and placed the glass back on the table. He wasn't entirely sure when he'd first started drinking so heavily. In fact, he'd hardly even noticed he was, until the hideous day of the will reading, when he'd made overtures to Amba –

but hadn't been able to seal the deal. He felt himself die a little inside again as he remembered the shame, and felt a now familiar rush of anger towards George. Even from beyond the grave, it seemed, he managed to mess up people's lives through his own bloody-mindedness. Just how had Edward managed to disappoint his father so radically in the few months he'd known him? And how was Edward meant to love the woman who pleased him if he had no means of supporting her?

He rubbed his temples. Freudian slip. He meant *please* the woman who *loved* him, surely?

The stress over Edward's lack of significant inheritance had led him to drink too much that lunchtime, which had turned into a binge-drinking afternoon and evening. At least, that was the conclusion he'd come to. Ironic, really, when having sex was exactly what they should be doing in their current predicament. He and Amba had no chance of reproducing if they hardly ever made love any more . . .

Made love. Did that really describe their insatiable passion? It was sex, for sure. Raw, carnal sex. But love – did that really come into it?

Not for the first time, Edward's head felt like a pressure cooker about to explode. Again, he rubbed his temples in an attempt to calm himself, but it only served to fire him up more. He had never felt quite so helpless. For most of his life, he'd never had any money, but he'd always had options. Now, when money was the answer to the one option he really wanted, and which had seemed well within his grasp, it had been cruelly and publicly whipped away from him.

Amba stood up, smiling, and turned towards him, stroking his face tenderly. 'Don't be sad, *chutzi*,' she said softly, and, irritation momentarily defused, Edward's body instinctively reacted to the spark of sexual chemistry between them: he could have almost purred with contentment. 'I know what you're thinking. And, who knows? We could already have you a little heir, just waiting to turn us into our own wonderful family . . .'

Edward stared at her open-mouthed. A maelstrom of emotions tumbled around his head. Shock, surprise, disbelief. He searched desperately for joy. He found none. 'You mean . . . ?'

Amba placed a finger over his lips to silence him. 'Hush, *chutzi*. There is time for all that. Now, we must eat.'

~

'Man, he's stitched you up like a bleeding kipper, hasn't he?' Darren laughed derisively and took a long swig of his beer, watching Edward with mocking eyes. 'What a prick. How can he leave you without a single bean in the world?'

Edward kicked out at the nearest wall angrily. Amba had – once again – retired to bed early and, finding himself at a loose end, Edward had headed over to the Skanktons' for a game of darts with Darren. Rather than use the family board in the plush games room, the pair had headed out to the yard mess room so that Darren could smoke.

'I dunno,' said Edward. Truthfully, he really didn't understand it. He hardly dared consider it – the whirl of emotions that his father's rejection seemed to have created was too monumental to explore.

'So what are you going to do now?'

Just then, the door opened and Natalie, the yard groom, wandered in. She looked at Darren in surprise. 'Oh – I'm sorry, I didn't realize anyone was in here.'

'That's all right, darlin' – we're always happy to have some female company,' leered Darren.

Natalie looked around to where Edward was standing, half hidden by the open door.

'Oh! Edward. You're here, too.' Inexplicably, she blushed, and then tried to hide it behind her hair. Edward smiled at the bashful gesture.

'Just having a beer,' he said unnecessarily, raising his bottle to her as if he was showing her proof.

She smiled and looked down, and there was a moment's silence. Suddenly, she looked up again.

'I was so sorry to hear about your father,' she said sincerely. 'What a tragic loss. And so out of the blue, too.'

Edward stared at her, stunned. He felt his anger dissolve, to be replaced by a deep and unbearable sadness. It was the first time since his father had died he'd actually thought of it in terms of an emotional loss, rather than a financial one. He felt a wave of great shame wash over him. What kind of person was he turning into?

'Thanks,' he said, his voice thick with unshed tears.

Natalie smiled shyly. 'I lost my father, too. Two years ago. You never get over it. But it does get easier to bear.'

Edward nodded, too ashamed to speak, and there was another silence.

'Well, isn't this a cheerful old evening,' cut in Darren, handing Edward another beer. 'Anyone for a game of strip darts?'

Natalie gave him a withering look. 'Not for me,' she said. 'But don't worry, I won't be coming back – so if you want to play your strip darts in private . . .'

'Oh, very clever,' snarled Darren as he pulled out the darts ready for the next game. Under his breath he added, 'Frigid bitch.'

Natalie raised her eyebrows at Edward and he gave her a half smile as she left the room.

'You don't want all her sentimental crap to make you feel any worse than you already do,' counselled Darren as he lined up his next shot. 'Your old man has not only stitched you up, he's made you look a right dickhead in front of your bird, hasn't he? I mean, how's a sort like Amba going to take you seriously without a pot to piss in?'

Edward shook his head as the familiar anger welled up in him. 'I know,' he said miserably. 'I'll just have to get her pregnant, I guess.'

Darren laughed mid-swig, and spat a stream of beer all over the floor. 'Amba? Pregnant? Do me a favour, mate.'

Edward felt immediately riled by his friend's reaction. 'What's so wrong with that?'

'A class act like Amba is not going to let herself get pregnant without a wedding ring firmly on her finger and her position well and truly secured,' scoffed Darren. 'Seriously, mate. I've seen her sort before. She's no pushover. Even if it is for a prize like Broughton Hall.'

'Well, it's not just Broughton Hall, is it?' retorted Edward hotly. 'There is the small matter of how she feels about me as well. It's called love, Darren.'

The words sounded hollow, even to his own ears.

Darren laughed and shook his head in disbelief. 'Love doesn't come into it, mate.'

Edward shook his head angrily in response. This was one challenge he wasn't going to lose. He was going to show them all.

'Well, it may just have done already,' said Edward, almost blind with rage. 'She could be pregnant already, for all you know.'

'She could be, yes,' said Darren mockingly. 'And I could be next in line to inherit Broughton Hall myself.'

Incensed, Edward downed his beer and threw his bottle across the room. It caught the corner of the wall and bounced off, hitting the opposite wall and then falling to the floor with a loud clang. It didn't, however, break. Jesus! He couldn't even smash a bottle properly.

'Nope, seems to me there's only one thing you can do now, mate,' counselled Darren, tightening the fly on a dart thoughtfully.

Edward, fists clenched at his side, eyes blurred with rage, stared at him intensely.

'What's that?' he said from between gritted teeth.

'Contest the will,' said a cocksure Darren. 'It's the only way, mate. Contest the will, get it overthrown, revert back to that ancient old covenant they've lived their lives by for centuries, claim your inheritance, then claim your bird. If you still want her by then, that is.'

Edward stared at him, a glimmer of hope finding its way onto the sea of bleakness in which he found himself.

Contest the will. Darren was right. It might not be the only way, but it was very definitely the *best* way.

Twenty-five

Edward refilled his glass of Burgundy and looked down the long dining-room table at the Charltons and the significant others who were gathered there. They were all currently intent on finishing their cheese soufflé, heavy silver cutlery scraping delicately on the finest Wedgwood china.

Next to him Amba, effortlessly stunning as ever, resplendent in biscuit-coloured Missoni and exuding her own sensuous scent, elegantly dabbed at her mouth with a linen monogrammed napkin. Edward felt the familiar rush of lust at the sight of her, followed by a stab of frustration. Amba's ardour had most definitely cooled in recent weeks. Whether it was the cloud of grief and shock that had lain over Broughton Hall since George's death, or the blanket of suspicion that now covered them all, he wasn't sure – but something had definitely changed. Edward took another gulp of his wine. It was as if he hardly knew the woman he was planning to spend the rest of his life with. He still couldn't get her to open up about her past, and without that, without passion, there seemed very little left.

He hardly dared consider the other option – that it was he who had caused this downturn in Amba's feelings – but one thing was certain. He intended to reverse this, and get things back to their previous passionate best, and then build on that. He would conquer her, whatever it took.

He turned his attention to the rest of the table. As far from Edward as he could be, Quentin sat playing with a grubby string around his wrist with one hand and draining a heavy crystal glass full of wine with the other, all the while eyeing the rest of the bottle with intent. On the opposite side of the table, Lyric and Philippe sat in near silence, both absorbed in their food. Philippe was drinking more than he usually did, Edward noted – maybe there was a side to his future brother-in-law that he'd never seen before, he pondered idly. Or maybe, just maybe, the seemingly interminable friction between him and Lyric was starting to get under his Superman exterior after all. At the other end was his mother, Constance, dressed more conservatively now than in the months leading up to George's death, looking the epitome of the lady of the house. Loss – or maybe the few prescription pills she was now allowing herself – had carved into her already thin face, and gaunt had replaced controlled emaciation as her look *du jour*. The shadow of grief hung around her eyes and under her cheekbones, and Edward felt the first twinge of compassion towards her that he could remember. She'd looked down this table at his father's face for forty years – how must it feel to have it replaced with the face of the son she hardly knew?

Not wishing to dwell on this can of worms again right now, Edward turned his attentions back to the present evening. It was the first time he had seen the table from this point of view and he had mixed feelings about it.

Ever since George's death, his seat at the head of the long, polished mahogany table had remained empty. Dinners had been conducted in reverential silence, with the late head of the family taking on the role of the proverbial elephant in the room. But tonight, Edward had decided that enough was enough. George's funeral was over, the will had been read, and he was still the *heir apparent*, despite the not inconsiderable spectre of the murder investigation hanging over their heads.

Edward, bereft of the kudos a hefty inheritance would have given him in Amba's eyes, needed to establish something else to keep her interest. And if he didn't have the money right now, he did at least have the position – head of the Charlton family, and unrivalled master of the house. Soon he would be able to offer Amba his mother's seat at this table, and her place in society – and until then, he would do all he could to establish this position as a desirable one in her eyes.

He felt a twinge of irritation at the effort he was having to make to secure his future with her. Surely it shouldn't be such hard work? Then, his thoughts turned to the surprise he had in store – that would guarantee his place in her life, and everyone else's, too – and he felt himself calm at the prospect. He leaned across under the table and squeezed her knee. She looked at him coolly, and he felt the frustration of spurned passion burn inside him, followed by the seed of self-doubt. Was this the right thing, after all? For him, as much as for her? Then, all of a sudden those amber eyes burned hotly and she gave him that secret smile. Looking at him intensely, she drew the tip of her tongue around her lips and smiled again. Edward thought he would burst with longing. To anyone else's eyes, Amba would simply have been licking her lips, but he knew better. He knew what that mouth was capable of – and what she was hinting at.

Desire filled him with purpose, and, taking another huge gulp of wine, he tapped on the side of his water glass. The five faces around the table looked up at him in surprise, and he cleared his throat importantly.

'Dear family – friends.' He nodded at Philippe, who returned his look levelly. Edward tried to ignore the hint of hostility in those eyes. His initial fraternal relationship with Philippe had, over the months, deteriorated somewhat. Philippe was always so entrenched in his work, there had been little chance to nurture the bonhomie that had marked the early days of their friendship and, as Edward had become tighter with Darren and Prince Abu Rhuba, so he had become more distant from Philippe, until indifference and, he might almost say, dislike, seemed to radiate from his brother-in-law to be.

Edward switched his focus from Philippe to Lyric, who was looking at him with sisterly amusement. He had never spoken up like this before, and she was no doubt wondering what on earth he was going to say.

'I'm acutely aware of how distressing the past few weeks have been for us,' he began boldly, eyeballing each of the diners in turn as Philippe had counselled him before his aborted speech at the wedding anniversary party. 'And how rocked we have been not only by my father's death, but by the circumstances in which we now find ourselves grieving.' Edward faltered suddenly, surprised by how articulate he was. Buoyed by this realization, he grabbed Amba's hand passionately, not noticing that she drew it away again almost immediately.

'And so I feel it is the right time to make an announcement of an event that I hope will give us new hope for the future, and a positive point of focus in the coming months.'

There was an expectant silence from around the table. Philippe stopped with his glass halfway to his lips, Constance paused in the middle of sorting her pills on her bread plate, even Quentin, gesturing at Jeffries for more wine, stopped and gazed interestedly at Edward.

'I'm thrilled and delighted to tell you all that Amba – my beautiful, wonderful Amba – has agreed to be my wife.'

The hush around the table now became a shocked silence. Four jaws dropped open. One, however, was set hard in anger.

Edward looked around at his family, awaiting a response. When none came, he prompted them.

'That is, we are going to get married!' he said. It, too, fell flat.

Lyric was the first to speak. 'Edward! Amba! That's wonderful news. If a little – sudden . . .' she stood up, and moved as though to walk around the table and embrace them both.

Amba held up a perfectly manicured hand. 'Wait.' Her eyes flashed, her voice shook with rage, and her hand seemed bigger than ever as she held it aloft in anger.

She turned to Edward. 'How dare you announce such a thing without consulting me first?'

There was an uncomfortable silence around the table as Edward stared at her angrily. He was dimly aware of another twinge of irritation. Shouldn't this make him feel even a little bit hurt, rather than furious? Lyric put her hands on the back of her chair and hovered, unsure what else to do.

'You treat me like some kind of glorified breeding machine, and then you play with my very future like this, without so much as a word?'

'But, Amba – *chutzi* – I thought you were . . . You suggested that . . .'

'Pah!' Amba tossed her head, dismissing Edward's use of her pet name for him. 'I am nothing but an incubator for you, Edward. You ask me to marry you – I say yes! But since then, it is all babies this, babies that – what kind of family is it where you cannot inherit for love, or, for that matter, even marry for love?'

She stood up 'I fell in love with you, Edward. Not this.' She gestured around the room. 'Not with the prospect of becoming your brood mare. You think this,' she drew herself up to her full height and indicated her curvaceous body, the body he felt was made for sin, 'this was made for babies? It was made for love. Love, adoration and total *respect*. And so now . . .' She picked up her wine glass and casually threw the contents down her dress. 'Oh dear. Look what you made me do, you snivelling idiot. Now, I must retire. And leave you to your' – she paused and gave a sneering look down the table – 'your cosy family dinner. Goodbye, *chutzi*.'

Amba stalked out of the dining room, leaving an embarrassed silence in her wake. Edward sat, stunned, mouth gaping open.

Lyric, still hovering behind her chair, moved over and placed a reassuring hand on his shoulder.

'Honey, Amba did know that was coming, didn't she?'

There was another silence, followed by the scraping of Philippe's chair as he stood up and stormed out. Lyric stared after him in confusion.

'Oh dear,' said Constance, looking sympathetically down the table at Edward. Her voice was overly cheerful as she tried to make light of it. 'Well, darling, I guess that's what happens when you punch above your weight . . .'

~

'So what's the latest, then?' hissed Queenie as she rushed into the scullery carrying a pile of sheets. 'I just went to turn down Master Edward's bed and the door's locked and bolted – with Miss Amba inside and no sign of him! Oooh, it's a rum old do, this one.'

'There'd be no need to whisper, if you weren't saying something you shouldn't be,' remonstrated Mrs Gunners, putting the finishing touches to a plate of petits fours. 'And I don't know what you're asking me for. All I know is I sent up six main courses and six desserts as was ordered by Lady C. this afternoon, and blow me if five mains and five desserts didn't come back down untouched. Of course, no three guesses who managed to polish off their food despite all the goings on.'

'Who?' asked Queenie stupidly. 'Not Master Edward, surely?'

Mrs Gunners tutted. 'No, Queenie. How would he have finished his dinner, when by all accounts he dashed off after Miss Amba, and then out of the house? No, it was that good-for-nothing brother of the master's, of course.' She shook her head and stood back from the plate of chocolates admiringly. 'I don't know why I'm bothering. There's no one left to eat these, I'll be bound. Eh, Mr Jeffries?'

The butler, meticulously polishing glasses on the other side of the kitchen, raised his eyebrows but said nothing.

'Maybe Mr Gunners will like one with his evening cocoa.' Mrs Gunners looked over at Queenie. 'Of course, I'm not surprised. I told Mr Gunners, that one's trouble, she is. That Amba. Turning up here, all airs and graces, like. Nothing but trouble from the start.'

'Well, I did find that notebook in her room, written in all weird language, like. Hidden in her case, it was. Not a word of English in it. I mean, who does she think she is, coming over here and trying to marry into our family with not so much as a by your leave?' mused Queenie in agreement. 'That's not right, is it now?'

'You want to watch your tongue, madam,' said Mrs Gunners warningly. 'You can get locked up for talk like that these days. Not to mention for snooping around her things.'

'Wasn't snooping,' grumbled Queenie. 'I was tidying. Anyhows, I've turned down Miss Lyric's bed, too. In the nursery,' she added pointedly. 'And that's the third night on the trot.'

Mrs Gunners sighed and shook her head. 'Sleeping alone, well, I'll be damned if I didn't think her and master Philippe were made for each other, even if he is French. What's gone wrong there, I can't imagine.'

'Can't trust those French, either,' said Queenie knowingly.

'Queenie!' said Mrs Gunners, grabbing a tea towel and

flicking it at the chambermaid. 'Now get back up them stairs and turn down the rest of them beds. And don't come down until you've done them all!'

'Or got more gossip!' grinned Queenie, skipping out of the way of the tea towel and up the stairs.

She couldn't be totally sure, but she thought she saw a flicker of a smile across Jeffries's face as he inspected the final glass.

~

Edward pulled his coat around him against the November chill as he wandered along the drive of the Skanktons' mansion. Now he'd stopped running, he was suddenly acutely aware of the cold night air. He looked up at the facade helplessly. He had no desire to see the girls or Darren's parents, and so knocking at the front door was out of the question. But there was no light on in Darren's room, and Edward hadn't thought to pick up his mobile before he'd fled Broughton Hall, so now he was slightly at a loss.

He wasn't sure what was worse – the humiliation of Amba's stinging rebuff, or the realization that she had meant every word. As he had followed her out of the room and up the stairs, she had made it perfectly plain that they were over. However Edward had upset her, whatever he had done to offend her, it clearly ran deep, for before she slammed the bedroom door – *his* bedroom door – in his face, she'd spelt it out emphatically.

'We are finished, Edward Charlton,' she had spat.

'*Finito*. No one treats me like a baby machine. Least of all a dog like you.'

And so, like the 'dog' he was, Edward had whimpered and retreated down the stairs and out of the door. Because it seemed to him there was no comfort in the crumbling walls of Broughton Hall. No comfort in the thought of confiding in his mother, or Philippe, or even Lyric. Nope – Edward was slightly surprised to discover, despite his fall-out with Darren, that in his hour of need the place he most wanted to be was the Skanktons'.

Odd, he had thought through the smarting tears of shame as he ran across the fields. It wasn't as if Darren had been a confidante. Or even a friend, really. But, for some as yet unexplained reason, the Skanktons' residence held the warm allure of home.

Now, as he followed the gravel path around the garden and out to the yard, Edward kicked out at a casually aban- doned golf cart and cursed as it turned out to be harder than it looked. He sat down on its springy black faux- leather seat and rubbed his foot, wondering which hurt most, his toe or his wounded pride.

Another weird thing, that word pride, thought Edward. Not his wounded *heart*. His *ego*. He sat up in surprise, and tried to picture Amba. His beloved. His betrothed. The most beautiful girl he had ever seen. But, to his surprise, all he could conjure up was her twisted, snarling face as she lashed out at him. Amba the temptress seemed to have –

even if momentarily – left the building. Amba the aggressor was the only one left in residence.

Edward stood up and strolled on towards the yard. One thing he knew about himself was that he didn't fall in love lightly. He wasn't used to giving his heart over to someone. And giving his heart was exactly what he thought he'd done to Amba. So why now, in the searing pain of rejection, was he finding it didn't hurt quite as much as he'd expected? Far from looking for a roof to jump off, he was feeling calm, almost . . . free. He nearly laughed. Was this nature's way of shielding him from the pain? Would he wake up tomorrow to the heavy burden of love lost? Or would he return to life at Broughton Hall as if Amba had never existed?

Remembering the awkward faces of his family as they looked on, witnessing Amba fly at him, Edward felt a dark cloud descend over him again and he punched the air in anger. No. He could never pretend that. For, whatever mark she might or might not have made on his heart, his pride was practically destroyed. It would take more than a good night's sleep to restore it.

Suddenly feeling desperate for a beer, Edward turned but, instead of walking back into the Skanktons' landscaped gardens, he headed straight into the yard. One of the lads was certain to be around – if they didn't know where Darren was, they would be up for a distracting game of darts and a drink instead.

The mess room, however, was dark and deserted, and Edward banged the door shut in a fit of temper. Not even this was going right for him tonight! Then, seeing a chink of light under the tack room door, he strolled across the brick yard.

'You'll wake all the horses up banging about like that.' The soft burr of Natalie's accent made him jump, and he saw her, in the corner, sitting in the glaring light of a bare bulb cleaning a saddle. The harsh light contrasted with the gentle glow of her soft English-rose skin, the kind that had rarely worn make-up and had been fed fresh green vegetables all its life. The light threw shadows over the contours of her curves – tightly encased in her jodhpurs and button-down shirt – and lit up the warm lights in her blonde hair, casually tied up in a knot with a pencil through it. The waxy smell of saddle soap hung in the air, and everything about her exuded warmth. And comfort. And . . . something else.

'You look like you could do with a drink,' she said with a twinkly smile, holding up a bottle of cheap red wine.

'I was – erm – looking for Darren,' Edward stuttered.

'Oh, well, you won't find him here,' she said cheerfully. 'He's gone out with Prince Shagalot. I've only got a tea mug, I'm afraid?' She waved a chipped mug that had once held a Smarties Easter egg.

'It's Team Shag, actually,' said Edward distractedly. He looked around him, unsure of where to sit.

'Oh, whatever,' said Natalie, unconcerned. 'He's a wanker, whatever he calls himself. Come on, sit down. I could do with the company.'

Edward laughed and sat down on the bench next to her, suddenly feeling a lot happier. He took a swig of the wine. It was far inferior to the fine vintage he'd been drinking at dinner, but to him wine had never tasted sweeter.

Natalie turned to him, eyes suddenly full of concern. 'So what brings you here, really?'

Edward stared into his mug, unable to decide where to start.

'Don't mind me,' said Natalie, cheerfully waving another bottle. 'I've got enough to keep us going into the early hours. What's wrong?'

Edward looked up and gazed deep into her eyes. 'Everything,' he said simply. 'Everything's gone wrong.'

There was a silence as they stared at one another. It felt like the heaviest, most meaningful silence Edward had ever known.

'Well,' said Natalie, 'I think you could do with a hug.'

She held out her arms to him, and he felt himself enveloped in her warmth, in her delicious softness, in her kindness and inner beauty. And he thought he had never felt an embrace like it. It felt like coming home.

And, later, as he lay sated amongst the saddles and horse blankets, with Natalie lying curled up in his arms, he finally felt like he *was* home. Not the Skanktons' mansion. Not Broughton Hall. But here, with Natalie.

Could this be where home was?

Twenty-six

Lyric lay motionless in her single bed in the nursery, toes touching the end, face staring straight up. If she really strained her eyes, she could see the faint outline of some ancient glow-in-the-dark moons and stars stuck on the ceiling. She couldn't remember a time when they hadn't been there, couldn't even remember her father sticking them up. But knowing they were there – especially now that he wasn't – gave her a strange sense of comfort, a link to him, wherever he was.

Like the bed. And the toys on the shelves. Retreating to her nursery had made Lyric feel stronger, if not any happier. But tonight, there seemed to be no comfort to be drawn from anywhere. As if the row between Edward and Amba had not been unsettling enough, Philippe had then stormed off. She hadn't heard him come up to bed, even though she'd been lying wide awake.

As she strained her ears for any sign of life coming from downstairs, Lyric thought she heard a 'thwack'. Yes, there it was again. She sat up in bed, wondering what on earth it was. And again. Thwack!

Pulling her dressing gown around her and her slippers onto her feet, Lyric padded out of the bedroom, along the corridor and down the stairs, following the noise all the way. Thwack!

At the bottom of the stairs she turned right, in the direction of the games room. The noise was getting louder. Thwack!

As she turned into the corridor, Lyric saw a chink of light from underneath the games room door. The noise had grown louder now, and was more of a 'smash' than a 'thwack'. She frowned and paused for a nanosecond before carrying on. Who would be in the games room at this time of night – surely not Philippe?

The door had been left ajar, and she pushed it open gingerly. There was just one light on in the room – the low ceiling lamp that hung over the pool table. It cast shadows behind everything that strayed into its glow – the balls, the cue, the snooker player: Philippe.

Lyric felt the familiar lurch as she watched him slamming balls across the table. His jaw was clenched and set tight, and she could see it almost twitch from the pressure it was under. A shadow fell across his scar, making it seem deeper and angrier than ever. Her heart went out to him involuntarily, before hardening again instantly as she remembered the pain he was putting her through. He only had himself to blame.

He picked up a tumbler full of a clear liquid and drank deeply. Lyric guessed from the gesture that this wasn't just water. It was so unlike him to drink like this. Philippe slammed the glass back down on the table and Lyric jumped, inadvertently letting out a small cry as she did so.

Philippe turned sharply and glowered at her. Turning back to the table, he took a violent shot, totally missing the ball and instead ripping up the baize in a long, angry white scar. '*Merde*!' Eyes blazing, he glared at her again.

Lyric felt the white heat of anger rip through her. Suddenly, all of her composure, the carefully created facade of compliance and understanding, deserted her completely. She slammed the door shut behind her and it closed with a muffled 'boom'. 'For God's sake, Philippe, what the hell is wrong with you?'

Ignoring the rip, Philippe lined up another shot. As he was about to take it, he looked up at her over his cue. 'Shouldn't that be, what's wrong with your whole family?'

Lyric stared at him in disbelief. He wasn't only being unfair, he was now being downright nasty. 'MY family?' she repeated in astonishment. Wasn't it her parents who had taken Philippe into their hearts – their home, even – from the start? Given him a new career as well as a new future? And how had he repaid them? By cheating on his fiancée – their daughter – when he was living under their very roof.

'I'm not sure I understand,' she said, voice shaking with anger. 'But clearly, loyalty to this family is not your strong point.'

There was a silence, punctuated only by Philippe taking

another couple of shots. Lyric felt herself yearn to scream out loud. Why was he being so goddamn *difficult*?

Philippe eyed her coldly. 'You talk to me about loyalty? You, with the uncle who deprives his own brother of his firstborn son for thirty years – and then tries to kill you when you discover the truth? You, with the mother who has lived her life through a haze of prescription pills? And you, with the brother who has no idea at all of what family means, and who is at this very moment trying to contest the will of the father he denounced on his deathbed? You, Lyric, you can have no idea of loyalty.'

Lyric gasped. Edward, contesting her father's will? 'You lie!' she shouted. 'You lie! Just like you lie about everything. About where you are. About who you're with. About how you feel about me!'

Philippe looked at her, and for a moment Lyric was sure she saw a shadow of confusion cross his face. But then his eyes hardened again and he stared at her coldly.

'And when have I ever lied about that?'

'Now! Today! Yesterday!' screamed Lyric, incensed with injustice. 'Every day that you've been juggling our relationship with your – with your – with HER!'

Philippe stared at her without expression.

'With whom?'

Lyric was mad with anger now, and she hit out at the wall in rage. 'Do I need to go over it all again, Philippe? With HER! The other woman you've been seeing! The beautiful young girl you've been slipping off to see whenever my back is turned. Your BIT ON THE SIDE!'

Philippe shook his head slowly and calmly.

'You're mad,' he said flatly. '*Tu es folle, Lyric. Je te jure.*'

I swear to you. The profession of honesty made Lyric feel like she was, indeed, mad. How *dare* he? He, who had been blatantly lying to her for months. She had the urge to hurl a thousand insults at Philippe, to attack, to make him feel as hurt as he was making her feel. She formulated them in her mind – could almost taste them – until she remembered the most valuable lesson she'd learned in rehab: in an argument, never abuse the other person to make them feel small, or to better yourself. Instead, simply state your case for how the perceived injustice has made you feel. She bit her lip and took a deep breath.

'Well, I'm afraid, Philippe, that I not only don't believe you, I have evidence to the contrary,' she said quietly. 'And it has made me feel more wretched than anything I can remember in my life.' All of a sudden, she felt deflated, weary and very, very old. She rang the little bell that sat in every room ready to call Jeffries at a moment's notice. Lyric hadn't rung it for years, but right now she felt she couldn't leave Philippe even for a second, in case it broke the spell and they failed to get to the bottom of this once and for all.

Philippe looked at her questioningly, then turned back to the pool table with a toss of his head. Lyric leaned against the door frame and gazed at him, astonished again that their perfect relationship could have self-destructed quite so spectacularly.

Within moments, Jeffries arrived, clearly having dressed on the way.

'Miss Lyric?'

Lyric tried to ignore the look of concern he gave her and smiled brightly at him. 'Jeffries, would you bring my port-folio for me? The brown leather one that I keep in my room? That is,' she corrected herself, 'the nursery?'

'Very good, Miss Lyric,' said Jeffries with his customary bow, and hurried out. Had Lyric been in a different mood, she would have been moved by the sight of his nightshirt sticking out from underneath his coat.

The second wait seemed interminable. Lyric wanted to scream at each thwack of the balls. But, eventually, Jeffries reappeared, carrying her battered old Smythson portfolio.

She felt a wave of nausea as she thought about its contents. Philippe, she noticed, seemed remarkably uncon-cerned for a man whose infidelity was about to be revealed.

Clumsily, she fumbled with the clasp. Why would her fingers not do what she wanted them to? Philippe had stopped playing now, and was leaning on the pool table, looking over at her with mild interest. She cursed his arro-gance. He must know what she was going to uncover. Did he not realize how much this had destroyed her?

Finally, she released the catch and pulled out the pic-tures – still pristine. She had only been able to bear looking at them the once. She glanced at the top one – a rear shot of Philippe and the girl walking along hand in hand, gazing at each other happily, their body language hinting at what the eyes could be giving away. *Were* giving away, she reminded herself – Lyric had seen the rest and was in no doubt as to what they signified.

'There,' she snapped, thrusting them at Philippe. He jumped forward to prevent them falling all over the floor and took them slowly, his face grim.

The silence seemed interminable as Philippe flicked through the pictures, stopping and considering each one deliberately for a few seconds, then on to the next. He gave nothing away – only a twitch in the side of his jaw indicated that he was not simply looking casually through some holiday snaps.

Eventually, he looked up. His gaze was steady, and his voice low and level.

'So I wondered where all this – this madness had come from. You had me followed.'

'I –' Lyric started to respond, but found she had no words to continue. Suddenly, even in the face of his betrayal, she found her own actions totally unjustifiable.

'I thought you were different,' he said sadly. 'Different from other people. Different from the rest of your family, even.'

'I am,' said Lyric desperately, shaking with a combination of fear and anger. 'You know I am. So why look for something else with someone else?'

He ignored her, and continued looking at her with those same sad eyes.

'But, in fact, you're all just as screwed up as each other.'

He placed the pictures face up on the pool table, and turned and walked past Lyric. The picture of him holding hands with the girl was on the top and, as she stared numbly at it, it seemed to mock Lyric as her fiancé left the room.

After a few seconds, Lyric found the use of her limbs and turned and went after him. She found herself in a half-run, trying to make up ground following his long stride. He walked quickly down the corridor, across the entrance hall and into the cloakroom. There she stood and stared miserably as he picked up his motorbike helmet and his leather jacket.

As he went to put on the helmet, she spoke. 'Who is she?' Her voice caught on the words, and she kicked herself for sounding so desperate.

'You don't deserve to know,' said Philippe, and his head disappeared inside the helmet.

Lyric stared, stung by his response, mouth gaping open.

Almost as an afterthought, he lifted the helmet again.

'Don't follow me again! Ever.' He replaced it, pulling the visor down over his eyes, and stalked out of the house.

Lyric watched from inside, pulling her dressing gown tightly around her as she watched him sit on his bike and fire up the ignition. As he revved up, she suddenly sprang into action again, and rushed out of the door.

'Who is she, Philippe?' screamed Lyric. 'Who. Is. She?'

In answer, he revved the bike up again and screeched off, leaving behind a cloud of dust and the smell of burnt rubber hanging in the black night air.

Lyric stared forlornly at the skid marks on the drive, and sank down onto the front doorstep. Even the sensation of Stan, nudging her elbow with his wet nose and trying to creep under her arm to lick her face, couldn't console her. Her father had died. Now the person she loved most in the world had left her. And she had no fight left. She placed her head wearily in her hands, and found that she couldn't even cry. She was all out of tears.

Twenty-seven

Quentin looked around at the hullabaloo that surrounded him. Shooting galleries, fete stalls, carousels . . . It was like one big, outlandish fairground. He'd never seen anything like it – not at a racecourse, anyhow. It was as exciting as a carnival, as colourful as Ladies' Day, and as noisy as hell. Everyone, it seemed, was here to see and be seen, and everyone was shouting – at each other, above the crowd – goddammit, even the commentator was shouting down the microphone. No one did sport or parties like the Aussies, of course, and he'd been told the Melbourne Gold Cup – held, as always, on this first Tuesday in November – was the highlight of the Australian sporting season. What he hadn't been told was that the whole country came to a standstill for it. It was worse than Boxing Day for nothing working at all. In fact, if it hadn't been for a charitable pair of fellow guests who happened to be driving from his smart hotel in the city centre to the racecourse, he might even have ended up watching it on the television in his hotel room.

Of course, he thought, as another stocky half-cut girl in

her mid-twenties bulldozed past him, threatening to cover him in yet more XXXX lager, he could think of worse things than sitting in air-conditioned comfort right now. He fanned himself with his racing programme and peeled his cotton shirt away from his damp armpit. The only time he'd ever been able to handle the heat was when he'd been in India, and he thought longingly of the cool mountain breezes and the capacious robes he'd worn during his stay there. However, he thought as another, more comely young woman walked past, more sensuously this time, there were other benefits to being back in the civilized world – so it was about time he started to take advantage of them. Like a cooling drink, for a start, and then maybe a little flutter on the first race.

Quentin patted the bulging wallet in his coat pocket and headed over to the beer tent. He still wasn't altogether sure why he'd been invited here on this all-expenses-paid trip, but he certainly wasn't complaining about the style in which he'd been transported – or accommodated, come to that. Business-class flights to the other side of the world didn't come cheap. Nor did all-inclusive stays at five-star hotels, and his suite at the Hilton on the Park was bigger than the apartment he was currently occupying at Broughton Hall. Anything was better than being back at home at the moment, with reminders around every corner of life's constant injustices. And to think that all he had to do to earn his keep here was to watch a few races!

'George was a popular man on the international scene, not just the British one,' Skankton had explained to Quentin when he'd popped over to Broughton Hall to invite him. 'And the industry is mourning his death. With one of his horses racing in the Cup, they are keen to have his family represented, maybe even to present a prize. Of course, I can't ask Lyric or Constance, or even Edward – far too distressing for them – but maybe you'd like to come . . .'

There had been no further mention of the horseshoe, and Quentin was beginning to relax about it. Maybe that weird business, too, had been built up in his own mind. Death, and the aftershock, had a funny way of making people behave oddly, and if he ignored it, maybe it would just disappear. Which was a shame where cash was concerned, but he really had no desire to get involved in something that might endanger the little girl. Something that might endanger the Charltons and their own smug existences, however, was far more welcome, and the space of several thousand miles would certainly give him time to plot the perfect revenge . . .

Quentin ordered a beer and took a long, cold swig, mopping away the sweat that was building up under his fedora hat with his handkerchief. Maybe he had been a little too hasty in his damning assessment of Roger Skankton. Maybe he wasn't such a bad man after all – George had liked him, hadn't he? And George, as everyone kept reminding him, had been so dearly loved. In fact, Quentin's personal radar for trouble might have gone severely off-message during his exile in India, and Roger might just be the decent chap George had always said he was. Roger might even, for all Quentin knew, need that darned horse-shoe back for something other than the as yet unnamed evil purpose Quentin suspected.

Quentin ignored the instinct that told him his initial reaction to Roger had been right, took another long glug of beer and relished the buzz of the alcohol coursing around his body, followed by the warm, fuzzy feeling it gave him. Not willing to brave the crowds around the bookies, Quentin wandered along the grass to the shady verandas of the members' colonial-style clubhouse and strolled through into the airy sitting room. Bamboo furniture was dotted over the bare floorboards and the walls were covered in racing memorabilia. He stopped under a huge ceiling fan, enjoying the breeze, and idly began to read a history of the Melbourne Cup on the wall opposite.

'Quite impressive, eh, old man?'

Quentin turned to see Roger standing, pristine and fresh in a smart short-sleeved shirt and chinos. He took off his hat and wiped his forehead again in a futile attempt to match Roger's 'straight-from-the-fridge' cool.

'Oh, hello, Roger.'

Roger raised himself up on his tiptoes and back down again. 'Fancy seeing you here, eh, Charlton?'

'Hmmm,' responded Quentin at Roger's characteristically unfunny joke. Roger's smile had sinister overtones, and it was making him a little uneasy. And making him sweat even more.

'I see you're reading the history of the Gold Cup,' said Roger, nodding at the wall.

'Yes, yes, very interesting,' muttered Quentin.

'Great race, this, Charlton. Fit for a great country. And particularly apt this year, after George's death, God rest his soul.' There was a second's respectful silence before Roger continued his monologue.

'The first Melbourne Gold Cup was run under the cloud of mourning, you see. After the death of two of the country's major pioneers. Brave, righteous men, not unlike George in his day. So it is a great thing that you should be here to represent him, Charlton.'

'Right,' said Quentin uncertainly. He had not exchanged more than the odd sentence with Skankton before the events of this summer, and this lengthy spiel was making him uncomfortable.

'It is a race built on dreams, on hard luck and on triumph,' continued Roger passionately. 'A race made famous by some of the greatest racehorses ever. Carbine, Poseidon, Phar Lap – they were all winners here. Doppelganger would have won here, you know – if I'd had my way.'

Quentin laughed in spite of himself. 'I think there's a bit more to it than that, Skankton,' he crowed. 'Like the luck you just mentioned, for a start.'

Roger shook his head smugly. 'Not if you're clever, Charlton. Not if you help nature along a little. You need to harness luck and make it go your way – not just wait and see what the gods have in store. Get my drift? But I don't intend to let that happen again. Not with anything.'

Quentin frowned. It was hard to ignore the sudden menace in the air and, despite the heat, Quentin felt a chill run down his spine as he remembered Roger's anger over the missing shoe at Ascot. So it seemed Roger was indeed somehow responsible for Thumper's death – and the shoe might be a significant part of it. This was not good news for Quentin. Not good news at all. Quentin looked closely at Roger. Beyond the perma-tan and chiselled cheekbones, there was an unhinged air about him. A madness behind the eyes. Really, he had no idea what this nutcase was on about – and Quentin's instinct for trouble was suddenly on red alert. Clearly Roger was delusional at best, mad at worst, but either way, he was hell-bent on making Quentin part of it – and, in doing so, making him stray from the straight and narrow. However, despite his sudden fear, despite his anger at his brother, despite the bad luck life persistently threw at him, Quentin was surprised to find he was determined to get his revenge without reverting to his previous evil ways.

'The Gold Cup given here today wasn't always a cup,' Roger continued. 'Once upon a time, old man, it was a shoe. A golden shoe. Imagine that, eh?'

Quentin turned to him. 'Imagine,' he said carefully.

Roger cleared his throat. 'I rather thought you'd have something for me here, Charlton.'

Quentin stared at him and then started to stutter as realization dawned. Surely, the shoe Skankton wanted wasn't made entirely of gold? Why, that would make it worth a fortune. And surely he, Quentin, hadn't been meant to smuggle it out here on Roger's behalf? Quentin's mind started racing as light began to dawn. Skankton clearly hadn't forgotten about the shoe as Quentin had hoped. He had anything but forgotten about it, in fact. 'The – the shoe? Well, I had no idea, I mean – all the way across the world, I simply never imagined . . .'

Roger stepped in closer to Quentin, so close that Quentin could feel him breathing down his neck.

'Did I not make it clear, Charlton? That shoe is mine – and someone in that family of yours has it. I need it.' He dug Quentin in the ribs with something hard, and Quentin drew in a deep breath. A gun.

'I – I know where the shoe is,' he gasped before he could stop himself. 'I just didn't bring it. I didn't – realize . . .'

But Roger didn't budge. He simply dug the gun in harder. 'So now you know what it is, eh, Charlton? And you know where it is? Then why don't you have it for me? I spend all this money giving you the perfect opportunity to deliver it to me, and you disappoint me. You let me down. Do you understand, Charlton, that those who don't let me down are rewarded, but those who do are punished?'

He dug Quentin for a third time with the gun and Quentin felt sweat break out in places he didn't even know it could.

'Yes. Yes, I do.'

'Good,' finished Roger, finally standing back from Quentin. 'So we understand one another. There is no reason why you cannot get me that shoe. I expect it at the very earliest opportunity. Enjoy your stay down under.'

~

Later, Quentin sat, wallet empty, stomach full of alcohol, watching the sun go down over his umpteenth beer of the day. Often in life he had felt low, or edgy, or bereft of good fortune, but rarely had he felt so numb. He had nowhere to go with this. All day his lows had been tangibly comparable to Roger's highs, as his horses had romped in one after the other. Quentin had watched from afar with a leaden heart as Roger – his aggressor – revelled in the glory and the sympathy of the crowd and the Australian media.

Across the racecourse, backlit by the orange sunset, he could make out Roger, striding out alongside his latest winner, surrounded by a crowd of sycophantic well-wishers. Quentin growled softly to himself. And here was he, as always, cast out on the sidelines, with only his latest dose of misfortune for company. What was he going to do about the shoe? He took another swig from his plastic pint cup and pondered the situation.

Maybe Quentin had read it wrong. Maybe Roger was simply succeeding through good training and some amazing luck, and his horses were winning through talent. And maybe the shoe was simply of sentimental value and, since George's death, Roger was getting carried away.

Or maybe, just maybe, Angus wasn't losing the plot. Through a lager haze, a light started to dawn in Quentin's mind. Maybe there was something suspicious about Roger's recent run of wins. Exactly what, Quentin wasn't expert enough to guess. But he'd met Roger's type before. If there was an underhand way to go about something, they'd find it. He was up to something illegal. Indeed, hadn't Roger himself bragged that he'd been somehow culpable for Thumper's death? How else would this misfortune have come about, other than some kind of illegal performance drug – or worse?

The glimmer of opportunity began to lift Quentin's spirits, and he sat up in his deckchair. Perhaps for once Quentin wasn't on the losing team. Perhaps, this time, he was in the driving seat. After all, he was the only one who understood the potential value of the horseshoe and knew where it was. If the shoe was indeed filled with gold, it would at the very least be enough to enable him to contest George's will and give him the future – and, indeed the present – he deserved.

Quentin reached in his pocket for his new iPhone and caressed it thoughtfully. In India, he'd renounced the material trappings of modern life. Now, it could hold the key to his whole future.

He keyed in his password, Googled Australian emergency services and spoke quickly and urgently. When he'd finished, he sat back in satisfaction, and watched, and waited.

It didn't take long. In just a matter of minutes, he heard a siren in the distance. Quentin felt the crowd tense as they looked at one another in confusion. He followed their gaze as the siren got closer, and closer, until a police van appeared across the racecourse. A couple of burly policemen ran out, and Quentin felt a hiccup of excitement rise in his throat.

The crowd let out a surprised collective 'Oooh' as the men ran across to Roger, handcuffed him and bundled him, protesting, into the back of the van. The doors slammed and the car sped off, sirens wailing once again.

Quentin felt himself puff up with pride. So maybe he had achieved something today after all. He stood up unsteadily, ready to try and wend his way back to the hotel. Just as well there would be no taxis for this public holiday – he'd blown all his money on booze and bets. But the thought didn't depress him as it might have done an hour earlier. This would be the last time he was penniless. He was certain of it.

Roger's violent threats had been sorted. Now for the small matter of Quentin's dead brother. Quentin was full of resolve. He would find that shoe, and use it himself, to contest George's will and – lawfully, this time – claim what was rightfully his.

Twenty-eight

'Get out! Get out! You have no right to ask me to leave. You invited me here! It is you who betrayed my trust, not the other way around. Even your own mother said I should stay here as long as I wished. I shall leave in my own good time, *chutzi!*'

Edward closed the bedroom door behind him and rubbed his forehead wearily. Only a short while ago that pet name had elicited nothing but positive vibes from him – but now, Amba was using it as a form of attack, a weapon in their rapidly deteriorating relationship.

Funny to think it had only been a couple of weeks since the disastrous dinner when he'd ruined their relationship – for good, it now appeared. The days had dragged so much since then, it seemed to him that weeks or even months had passed by and the rest of their courtship had been a mere blink of an eyelid.

He still didn't quite understand what had happened. Granted, with hindsight he could see that his impetuousness had been out of line – at worst, insensitive, at best, over-enthusiastic. But were either of those a reason to break off a love affair of such intenstiy? Amba had, after all, agreed to be his wife. Love him for the rest of her life. Why would his announcing this to his nearest and dearest, wanting to share it with everyone else, mean the end of everything?

On the other hand, part of him wondered if it had been a lucky escape. Since the dinner, Amba's behaviour had turned so ugly that he almost couldn't reconcile her with the woman he'd fallen for. Whenever she allowed him near her – which wasn't often – she was like a spiteful alley cat, all nails and bared teeth and foul language. She had even physically grappled with him on one occasion when he'd tried to gain access to their room, flying at him and pushing him out of the door. Instinct had, for a second, made him fight back, but he'd recoiled when he realized how strong she was. Anger – at what, he couldn't tell – had made her fight like a man.

To begin with, he'd demanded that she leave as a way of making her speak to him, reasoning – in the face of her embittered vitriol – that any talk had to be better than no talk. But it hadn't worked out that way, and now with every heated exchange his desire for her to leave Broughton Hall, and his life, forever, was growing.

But that wasn't the only desire that was on the increase. Whilst he was mourning the loss of the love of his life, it was a bittersweet pill – and the advent of Natalie in his affections was certainly helping to sweeten it.

Just as the thought of her entered his mind, his phone buzzed in his pocket. Still reeling from another encounter with his ex-fiancée, he smiled when he saw the text from Natalie. After the rollercoaster of life with Amba over the past couple of weeks, Natalie was like balm for his soul, and he found himself looking forward more and more to their clandestine meetings. *Got an hour off. You free?*

In more ways than one, thought Edward to himself. In the text, he replied, *Yes. Usual place in ten?*

The 'usual place' was the folly, way up on the hill behind Broughton Hall. And, lucky though they were to have it, thought Edward, huffing as he hurried across the fields, he couldn't help but wonder what it would be like making love to Natalie somewhere a little more – well – warm and comfortable.

Natalie was already there, sitting on the bench that overlooked the Broughton Hall estate, cheeks flushed from the walk, wrapped in a red Driza-Bone coat, jeans and boots. Her hair showed some hurried attention from a hairbrush, and she'd applied a slick of lip gloss, but otherwise she was just – *real*. And all the more beautiful for it.

'Hi,' she said shyly, standing up and shoving her hands in her pockets.

'Hi,' he said, smiling and drawing her in to him, kissing her softly. She smelt of hay, and scented soap, and toothpaste – but seemed oddly distracted.

Edward pulled away. 'What's the matter?'

She looked confused. 'Darren's been arrested.'

'Wha-at?' Edward stared at her in shock.

She nodded. 'Just now. For tax evasion, just like Roger.

But everyone at the yard reckons there's something else going on as well. Something even more underhand. Like, they reckon Roger wouldn't be refused bail simply on the basis of some unpaid tax on whatever scale. The police must have something on him.'

'So what would that be, then?' wondered Edward almost to himself.

'God knows. Just whatever it is, thank goodness it doesn't involve you!'

'I'd have never got involved in something dodgy,' said Edward with more conviction than he felt. After all, there had been a time back there when his friendship with Darren promised to set his life on a very different track, before he'd fallen hook, line and sinker for Amba. Maybe there were some things to thank her for, after all.

'So are the girls all right?' he asked, suddenly concerned. First their father, then their brother. Assuming Angie, Cheryl and Kimberley weren't involved – which, given the dynamics of that family, was the most likely scenario – they would probably be scared out of their wits.

Natalie frowned. 'Well, that's the weird thing. I expected them to be troubled by it – but they all seem fine. In fact I even saw Angie crack a smile yesterday! That was before Darren got arrested, of course,' she added quickly. 'Anyway, enough of them. I have the Skanktons morning, noon and night when I'm at work. I don't want to spend my precious time with you talking about them!'

Later, after they'd made passionate love, they sat

entwined in a corner of the folly, well out of sight and out of the biting November wind. In companionable silence they looked out over the estate, the beautiful house and the wintry gardens.

'You seem preoccupied,' Natalie said finally. 'Is everything OK?'

'Well, if you discount a house in mourning, a miserable sister, a murder investigation and a mad ex-fiancée refusing to leave my bedroom, yes, everything's fine,' said Edward. His tone was lighthearted, but it held an underlying seriousness. When he was with Natalie, Amba seemed like she came from another lifetime – truthfully, at this moment she was the last thing he was worried about.

'Sorry, I was miles away,' he said, remembering that he only had snatched moments with Natalie and he should be making the most of them.

'Where else could you ever want to be but here?' she replied. 'It's one of the most beautiful views I could imagine.'

'That's what I was thinking,' said Edward. 'I know I haven't lived here long, but it's part of my soul already. And I was just wondering how my father could ever have wanted to take that away from me.'

'Well, he didn't, did he?' reasoned Natalie. 'Whatever happens, it's still going to stay in the family. He just wanted what was best for the family as a whole, I reckon.'

'Maybe,' said Edward, unconvinced, feeling the familiar stab of bitterness towards George.

'And I'm sure that's what he'll get,' she continued, hugging his arm tightly and trying to get eye contact with him.

'Well, he will if I have my way,' muttered Edward, immediately regretting it. Natalie pulled away from him with a searching look.

'What do you mean?'

'Oh, nothing.'

She sat up and turned to face him. 'No, tell me. What do you mean, if you have your way?'

Edward shrugged. 'I'm contesting the will,' he said. Even as the words left his lips, they sounded mean-minded. 'It's my birthright.'

Natalie sat back, stunned. 'OK,' she said doubtfully.

Edward frowned. 'Honestly, Nat, if you were in my shoes, you'd do the same.'

She looked at him, aghast. 'I very much doubt it. You've got a loving family, a beautiful home – what more do you want? It's not as if your mother – or Lyric, for that matter – would see you out on the street, even if Lyric does have the first heir. Why go against your father's dying wish?'

Edward shrugged. 'Maybe if I understood his dying wish I might feel more magnanimous about it,' he grumbled. 'But I don't. And until someone can explain it to me in words I understand, I'm going to fight until Broughton Hall is mine.'

~

'Miss Lyric, I have the detective for you.' Jeffries gave his customary bow, and disappeared backwards out of the drawing-room.

'Oh!' said Lyric in surprise and raised her eyebrows at Laura. Her friend had arrived on a cheer-up mission earlier that morning, and they were currently ensconced in the window seat with a coffee while Max and Kitty played hide and seek among the huge velvet curtains.

'We'll, erm, go and have a run around outside for a little while,' said Laura. 'Give you some privacy.' She stood up and ushered the children out of the door, smiling at the inspector as she passed him. He nodded back respectfully, his moustache twitching slightly as Max and Kitty gave him cheeky grins as they ran through.

'Can I get you some coffee?' asked Lyric pleasantly, indicating her own cup.

'No, no, Miss Charlton, thank you, but I shan't keep you long. I have some updates on the murder investigation, and also Mr Skankton's case that I thought—'

'Yoo-hoo! Is that that lovely inspector man?' The door was flung open and Constance floated in on a wave of Fracas, her tailored trousers and twin set adorned with a Moroccan shawl. Some habits, thought Lyric, really did die hard . . .

'Now, you really must have some tea,' said Constance, picking up the bell and calling for Jeffries. 'And I know Mrs Gunners has just made a cherry cake.' She put her hand up to quell his protests. 'We won't hear a word, Inspector. Us girls love nothing better than watching a man enjoy his food – especially when we don't indulge so often.' She smoothed her clothes carefully, drawing attention to her still svelte figure – a testament to a lifetime on shakes and pills – and smiled coquettishly. Lyric's eyes nearly popped out of her head. When her mother had stopped flirting with younger men, she hadn't expected her to immediately turn her attentions to men her *own* age . . .

The detective cleared his throat and pulled some papers from the inside pocket of his raincoat. 'I, erm, have some developments in the death of your racehorse, Miss Charlton,' he began, nodding unenthusiastically at the arrival of a pot of tea and a huge slab of cake. He attempted to juggle the papers, the plate and a cup of tea Constance was thrusting at him, and failed. Admitting defeat, he sat down and allowed her to add two cubes of sugar and stir before he continued.

'Why have you brought them?' prompted Lyric. 'I mean, aren't you investigating Daddy's death? What on earth could Thumper's have to do with it all?'

The detective cleared his throat again. 'Well, Miss Charlton, I knew you had asked for a more detailed autopsy on your horse, and as a matter of interest I asked to be kept up to speed on this. And it seems it was worth my while.'

He stopped for a bite of cake and a sip of tea and Lyric felt like she might burst with impatience.

'Why? What happened to Thumper?'

The detective shook his head. 'I'm not sure what happened to your horse, Miss Charlton. But what I am sure of, finally, is one of the contributing factors in how he died.'

There was a silence. Lyric swallowed hard.

'Go on.'

'Viagra.'

There was another silence, followed by a hoot from Constance. 'Now, come on – I know it might just seem like a silly old nag to you, but Lyric was very fond of that horse. So be serious and tell us what you've really found.'

'Lady Charlton, I can assure you I'm not joking. The second post-mortem discovered high levels of Viagra in the horse's bloodstream. It appeared he must have been digesting the drug for many months before his death.'

Another silence. When Lyric spoke, her voice was nothing more than a whisper.

'But why?'

The detective shrugged. 'Apparently now common practice in the United States. If you'll allow me, I'll read direct from the report – horses aren't really my, erm, bag.' He rustled with his papers, cleared his throat again and began to read out loud. 'Viagra, whilst undetectable by the current doping tests, can improve a horse's performance. The key to a horse's performance is the ability to breathe well, and rather than making them run faster, Viagra improves the blood-flow into their lungs.' He looked up. 'This would, apparently, explain the sudden success that the horse enjoyed before it, erm, died. Now, while we cannot as yet ascertain whether the administration of this drug actually led directly to the horse's death, I'm told that any heart defect or weakness could have been exacerbated by huge amounts of the drug in the system.'

'Thumper was *murdered*?' Lyric felt the world spinning around her.

'Well, not as such,' said the detective carefully.

'It was horse slaughter!' shrieked Constance. 'Oh my God. Jeffries! Get me my salts!' With that, she swooned onto the nearest chair.

Lyric rushed to her side then, having made sure her mother was OK, turned back to the detective.

'But who would want to do that? Who would have anything to gain from . . .' She trailed off. 'Roger Skankton.'

'We are leaving no stone unturned,' said the detective efficiently, neatly bypassing the question. 'And we are pursuing matters through our existing investigations into Mr Skankton's other, erm, business operations.'

There was yet another pause.

'We are also looking into possible links with the death of your horse and the death of your father.'

Lyric stared at him, stunned.

'So you're saying, whoever killed Thumper, killed Daddy?'

~

Quentin strolled around the formal gardens for the seventh time that hour. Ever since his spell in India, he found exercise was good not only for the body, but also for the soul. And right now, he had a lot on his mind.

Broughton Hall was giving him sleepless nights, and the horseshoe was causing him grief, too. So near, yet so far . . . Not for the first time in his life, Quentin felt the frustration of a huge pot of wealth just inches out of reach. But he was determined to get it. He was only a degree of separation away from that girl, after all. With Skankton out of the way – for now, at any rate – he could get a good run at it, but he had to strike fast. There had to be a way of finding it without harming her. Well, without harming her *much*.

He stopped suddenly and slapped both hands on his head in agony. He knew there was a solution to this – so why wouldn't his brain deliver it? He sat down on the bench overlooking the ornamental fish pond and gazed into it irritably.

'Mummy! Mummy! There's the pond with the fishes in it!'

As if in a dream, Quentin looked up and saw two little children running towards him. A boy, whom he vaguely remembered from family events in the past. It was Lyric's friend Laura's little boy, Max. And behind him, Laura herself – along with Kitty, Gatekeeper of The Shoe. He chuckled quietly, then more loudly. It was meant to be! At last, Lady Luck was on his side. The solution had been handed to him on a bloody plate!

'Mummy, why is that old man laughing like that?'

Laura smiled apologetically at Quentin. 'He's not an old

man, Max. That's Aunt Lyric's Uncle Quentin. He's probably laughing at the fishes, just like you will.' She turned back to Quentin again. 'How are you, Quentin?'

He shrugged. 'Oh, you know. Can't complain. Still reeling from all that business with George. Doesn't seem real, somehow.'

'No, I know. I'm so sorry,' Laura said simply. She sat down on the bench next to him and touched his knee lightly, and Quentin stared at her in surprise at the unexpected kindness. No one else around here treated him like that!

He shook himself. He had a mission to accomplish here. No point getting all sentimental.

'Lyric's taken it hard, of course,' he said craftily. 'And after all that business with her horse, too. Can't be easy for her.'

Laura looked at him in shock. 'I know Lyric was very fond of Thumper, but I'm not sure she would put losing him into the same bracket as losing her father,' she said sharply.

Quentin laughed. 'Oh, my dear, you misunderstand me,' he said smoothly. 'I mean, she hadn't yet recovered from losing the horse when this came along like a body blow. Poor kid.'

'Mmmm,' said Laura. 'I wish I knew how to make her feel better. Especially now she and Philippe have fallen out.'

Quentin made out he was thinking for a moment. 'Well, I did hear her say the other day that she would love a memento of Thumper,' he said slowly, as though inspiration had just struck. 'You know, like some of his mane, to make into a keepsake – or even a shoe! They were always falling off, his shoes, and I heard her say she wished she'd kept one!'

Laura stared at him, her face lighting up with joy. 'But we have a shoe of Thumper's! Don't we, Kitty?'

Kitty turned from where she was trying to fish with a stick.

'Yes, Mummy. It was Thumper's, but it's mine now.'

'Well, darling, wouldn't you like to give it to your Aunt Lyric to cheer her up a little?'

'Mu-um! Help!' There was a shout from down by the herb garden, to where Max had run off and evidently got into some kind of minor scrape.

'Coming, darling!' called Laura. She scooped Kitty up and started to run down the path after Max.

'I'll sort it!' she called back to Quentin.

'Send it to me!' he called back, trying not to sound too keen. 'I can give it to her as a surprise!'

His smile didn't last long. 'I'm not going to give it to Aunt Lyric, Mummy,' Quentin overheard Kitty lisp to Laura as they walked away. 'I'm going to give it to Uncle Crispin at his wedding. For good luck!'

Are you, Kitty, dear, he thought to himself. *Are you, indeed.*

∽

'Now, now, Queenie, just you take a good long sip of this sweet tea and tell me all about it again.' Mrs Gunners, for once not scowling at her charge, looked over her shoulder and nodded furiously at Jeffries to leave them alone. He looked at her over the top of his paper and then, ignoring her completely, resumed reading it.

Sighing, she turned back to Queenie. 'Now, Mr Gunners always says there's nothing for shock like good sweet tea,' she continued. 'You take your time, my girl.'

'Oh, Mrs Gunners. It's a rum old do. To think she's had us all fooled, all this time.'

'She's never had me fooled,' said Mrs Gunners grimly. 'I've suspected her all along of being up to summat. But this! Well, I never. Married! What say you, Mr Jeffries?'

A rustle of the paper indicated Jeffries was not participating in this particular conversation.

'So tell me again what you found, Queenie.'

'It was a ring, Mrs Gunners. I wasn't snooping, like, honest – but it was there! Beside her bed! In the drawer, like, not even hidden away!'

Mrs Gunners opened her mouth to say something but then clearly thought better of it.

'Go on.'

'It was a ring, like a wedding ring. Just gold, you know, nothing special – that's how I know it was a wedding one.'

Again, Mrs Gunners seemed to think twice about saying something.

'And I might never have taken notice of it, but for something it was resting on.'

She stopped for effect, clearly enjoying herself now.

'Well, go on, girl – what was it?' urged Mrs Gunners impatiently. Even Jeffries folded down the top of his newspaper in interest.

'A photograph. Of Amba herself, in some far-off country, with a family. Kids! *Her* kids, by the looks of it.'

'Come on now, Queenie, how would we know that they were her children from a mere photograph?' said Mrs Gunners. 'They could be anyone's!'

'They looked like her,' said Queenie authoritatively. 'And there was someone a bit out of shot, like, kissing her on the head. If she's not already married with kids, I'm a Dutchman.'

'Sounds to me like there's a lot of that going around,' said Jeffries drily and resumed reading his newspaper.

'Married,' said Mrs Gunners, shaking her head sadly. 'Taking poor Master Edward for a total fool. I don't know what the world is coming to.'

'But, lor, Mrs Gunners, that's not the only thing I found today.' Again, Queenie stopped for effect, but a little more panicky now. 'I was clearing out the master's effects, like Lady C told me, and see here. It's a letter. In the master's hand.' She held aloft a handwritten envelope. 'I found a whole bunch of other notes in the master's handwriting with it, too.'

'Why didn't you give this to Lady C immediately, Queenie?' asked Mrs Gunners.

'Because it clearly says here, "For Scotland Yard",' said Queenie, tripping over the words a little.

They both looked at the thick cream watermarked envelope and then back at each other. Both were uncharacteristically speechless.

Eventually, Mrs Gunners broke the silence.

'I thinks this is one for the detective, Queenie.'

~

Whistling softly to himself, Edward strolled back across the fields to Broughton Hall. Well, that was a turn up . . . He smiled softly at the memory of the previous few hours. Sex with Natalie was nothing like with Amba. There was none of the raw passion, insatiable desire or gymnastics that he and Amba experienced. Instead, it was warm, loving and satisfying on more than a physical level. It was better.

This really had set the cat amongst the pigeons. On the one hand he was heir to a huge estate, and expected to make a good marriage. He was also ostensibly engaged, to one of the most beautiful women in society.

But was he in *love*?

Edward mulled over the question that had been at the back of his mind for weeks. Sure, Amba aroused in him feelings like he'd never before experienced, but the more time he spent with her, the more it seemed to be just that – lust. For a start, he still knew very little about her – how could he be sure that he really did want to spend the rest of his life with her?

And on the other hand, he had found what felt like a real, deep-rooted affinity with a stable girl. Someone who more than likely had no money, no standing and would hardly cement his new position in society. It didn't take a rocket scientist to work out that this was, at the very least, social suicide.

Not that he cared. His position in society had hardly been a consideration until these past few months since finding his family, and from the behaviour Amba had displayed recently, he might not have any kind of dilemma left anyway.

He turned up the drive and tempered his pace a little, not wishing to draw attention to his later-than-late return with the sound of his footsteps striding up the drive. On a whim, he decided the back entrance would be the safest one to use and turned up the path that led around the side of the house.

As he wandered past the drawing room, his eye was caught by the flash of what looked, through the sheer Moroccan curtains, like a torch. Edward's brow furrowed. By rights, the rest of the family should long be in bed by now. And even if someone was having a sleepless night, why wouldn't they simply turn on the light, rather than sneaking around by flashlight? Senses suddenly on red alert, Edward crouched down, crept up towards the nearest window and peered over the sill. Behind him, dawn was beginning to break and, together with the brightly coloured muslin covering the huge sash windows, it gave a curiously dreamlike appearance to the darkened room behind the glass. Suddenly, another flash of light circled the room, throwing eerie shadows. Briefly, Edward was sure he saw the silhouette of a person and the flash of something else – what, he couldn't tell – silver? He silently thanked his mother for having removed the heavy curtains that had hung there since time immemorial – he would have had no chance of seeing anything with those still in place – and he clambered onto a narrow ledge to get a better view inside the room. The light was improving by the second, and now, with his head well above the sill, Edward could clearly see the outline of a person carrying a small torch and what looked like a dustbin bag. His mind raced as his heartbeat went into overdrive. Clearly, Broughton Hall was being burgled. But what was he to do? He made a quick assessment of his situation. There was no telling whether the burglar was alone, or armed. Indeed, he had no way of knowing if his family were safe in their beds or had been attacked in some way. Edward's mouth went dry with fear at the thought. The only thing he potentially had in his favour was the psychological advantage of surprise, and his phone. He fingered his mobile in his pocket. Calling the police now could potentially alert the burglar to his presence and risk his life. Not calling them could leave him without back-up – also risking his life.

Suddenly, the torchlight flashed in his direction and

Edward ducked out of sight. He heard the pitter-patter of light footsteps hurrying over to the window and he pressed himself against the wall under the sill, heart beating wildly. There was a scraping as the wood frame of the window was pushed open, and then a leg appeared over the sill, dangling next to Edward's nose. He barely dared breathe. Another leg followed, and then there was a clanking noise as something – the bag? – was dragged over the sill.

He was right. A huge dustbin bag was dropped onto the ground in front of him, and the burglar followed suit, landing softly on the flower bed. He was tall, slightly built, and seemed fit and agile. He was dressed in a black tracksuit and a balaclava and trainers. The good news was, he didn't seem to be carrying a weapon.

But Edward had no time to investigate further. As the thief paused to steady himself, Edward felt a surge of white-hot anger, and an unfamiliar force overwhelmed him. He lunged forward, knocking the burglar to the floor face first. Stunned, he lay still for an instant and Edward snatched the advantage, locking the intruder's arms behind him in a half nelson. As the man began to struggle, desperately trying to free himself, Edward straddled him, using his whole body weight to pin him to the ground while he delved in his pocket for his mobile. He prayed the police would come quickly. The intruder was strong, and there was no telling how long he could hold him down.

'Police, please,' he hissed into the phone, still uncertain as to whether there might be any accomplices. 'I need urgent assistance at Broughton Hall. I've apprehended a burglar.'

Edward struggled with the man as he relayed more information to the emergency services. Suddenly, he noticed a lock of jet-black hair escaping from the balaclava. He stopped dead in shock, and the intruder turned round under him and lashed out with his free arm. Fired up with outrage, Edward blocked the blows with one hand and pulled off the intruder's balaclava with the other.

He gasped in shock.

'Amba!'

~

The blue light of dawn was intensified by the intermittent flash of lights from the police cars as they sped up the drive to Broughton Hall. Edward breathed a sigh of relief. Amba had struggled hard against her capture, displaying hidden strengths as she tried to bite, scratch and hit Edward, and he had begun to tire of keeping her captive.

As the cars pulled up around them, a crack team of armed officers leapt out of the back of a van and spread out around the house, presumably checking Broughton Hall for other intruders. Edward was certain they wouldn't find any. The only culprit they were looking for was here, between his legs – his former fiancée.

The same plain-clothes detective who had investigated George's death opened the door of one of the cars and ran across to Edward, followed closely by two uniformed officers. The men grabbed Amba from Edward and he relinquished his hold with relief. Spitting and scratching like an alley cat, Amba tried to resist their attempts to handcuff her. She freed her left arm and swung round to catch one of the policemen square on the jaw. Edward stared in shock. He never realized she had that kind of strength. No wonder he had only just managed to hold her down.

'Mr Charlton. Are you injured?' asked the detective urgently.

'No, no,' said Edward, looking first at Amba and then at the bag she'd been carrying. It was spilling over with silver and antiquities that he recognized from the Hall. There must be thousands, maybe hundreds of thousand of pounds' worth of valuables in there. Had she planned this all along?

He took a deep breath as the full weight of the shock hit him. Somewhere from within the house, through the open window, he could hear Constance shrieking at the men searching her home.

The detective turned to Amba. 'Babur Amba, I am arresting you for burglary and assault. You have the right to remain silent . . .'

Edward stared, stunned, as the detective finished reading Amba her rights. Finally, he spoke directly to her.

'Babur Amba? That's your real name?'

Amba shook her head defiantly. 'Yes. And what of it?'

The detective cleared his throat delicately.

'Amba's real name is not the only thing that you don't

know.' He looked Edward directly in the eye, and Edward was sure he detected pity in his gaze. He bristled.

'Interpol has been following Babur Amba for some time now as a known criminal, wanted for several serious crimes internationally.'

He paused.

'And not only that. Babur Amba is a man.'

There was a silence, and Edward stared in disbelief. Behind the policemen, Constance and Lyric, standing together in their dressing gowns, gasped in shock.

'A man?' Edward's voice was flat and emotionless.

'Indeed,' continued the detective. 'With a wife and four-teen children in Uzbekistan.'

Edward looked at Amba. 'A man?' he repeated. He felt numb with shock. Expensive cosmetic surgery had trans-formed every bit of her into the beautiful preying mantis she had become – every bit of her, that is, apart from her big man's hands.

Amba shook his/her head again proudly. 'I am no man. I am a woman in all but birth certificate. I am a transsexual, and proud of it. Women – they have all the opportunity in life, if only they knew how to use it. But I know it – and I have used it – and I make no apologies for this. I make a fine husband, a loving father and a beautiful woman – with the help of some excellent surgeons.' She tossed her black hair defiantly.

Edward started. Those hands – those big hands. So often in gloves. Snatched away from him. Man's hands. Something even the most expensive cosmetic surgery couldn't hide . . .

Amba pulled a photograph from her pocket and held it up proudly. It showed Amba – as a woman – surrounded by a group of children and another woman. All were as good-looking as Amba was beautiful. All were finely dressed. All were smiling. 'It is the rest of you who are fools.'

Edward looked at her miserably. That was putting it mildly.

Twenty-nine

Lyric placed her teacup back on the saucer and stretched. She couldn't quite believe she was here – this really was the epitome of luxury. As eccentric as her mother could still be, she absolutely knew how to treat her daughter; when she had suggested Claridge's, Lyric had at first baulked at the extravagance, and then, after her mother had insisted, she'd accepted. It had always been her father's favourite hotel, and when the detective had dropped his bombshell about Thumper, after her father's death and following Amba's arrest, Lyric had felt the need to escape, to be anywhere but Broughton or her mews house in London.

In the chic but comfortable caramel, beige and wood luxury of the penthouse suite, she felt totally cosseted and reassuringly distanced from the maelstrom that her life had become. Broughton Hall seemed to be home to a new and unwelcome development every day. In her London house, she'd be surrounded by memories of happier times with Philippe. Here, curled up on the sumptuous sofa, next to a roaring log fire, it felt like she'd found a temporary haven away from the chaos.

Her phone rang – Edward. She picked it up with a twang of guilt. Had she mentioned to him where she was going before she left Broughton Hall?

'Lyric, where the hell are you?'

No, clearly she hadn't.

'Edward! I'm so sorry – I'm sure Mummy's told you about the new development in the case? It all just got a bit too much, I needed to get away . . .'

'So where are you?' he repeated, though his voice was less harsh now.

'I'm at Claridge's,' she said in a small voice, suddenly ashamed of her mother's extravagance. 'In the penthouse.'

There was a silence and then Edward burst out laughing.

'Oh my God, Lyric, that is so spoilt,' he said. 'You can take the girl out of the It . . .'

Lyric giggled. 'I got upgraded! Mummy suggested I get away. I think she wanted me out from under her feet, to be honest. And the mews house is too much about me and Philippe – for all I know, he could be there . . .' her voice trailed off.

Edward was suddenly serious again.

'So you haven't seen him since he left Broughton Hall?'

'Nope,' said Lyric lightly, trying to ignore the lurch of her stomach as she said it.

Edward tutted. 'It's not right. Haven't you at least tried calling him? Don't you want to hear his side of the story?'

'No,' said Lyric stubbornly. 'What's he going to say?

I've seen the evidence for myself, and anyway, if there had been a viable explanation, he would have given it to me when I first asked him to. No, Edward. I'm not calling him. I'm over it.'

'Maybe he was too pissed off about the PI?' suggested Edward.

'I don't care,' snapped Lyric. 'Whether or not I was justified in hiring a PI, I did what I did. And right now I deserve some answers. He clearly doesn't feel the same. So, finito. We're doing pretty well in our family, aren't we – everyone's dropping like flies.'

'Hmmm,' said Edward distractedly. He seemed reluctant, awkward, about whatever he was going to say next. Lyric could almost imagine him, hopping from one foot to the next in discomfort. 'Look, Lyric, I've got some news. It's the last thing I should be telling you over the phone, but I want you to hear it from me.'

Lyric's heart suddenly starting beating loudly in her chest. She sat upright. What now?

'We had a visit from the police today. It's about Amba.'

'Don't tell me, they're letting her out so she can marry Quentin,' quipped Lyric, then kicked herself for her thoughtlessness. 'I'm sorry, Edward, I didn't mean . . .'

'I don't give a monkey's,' he said roughly. 'She screwed me up good and proper, but I'm over it now. At least, I'm getting there,' he admitted. 'And you never know, I might have met someone else . . .'

'Yeah, right,' laughed Lyric. 'I'm sure even you couldn't work that quickly, Edward. Anyway, what about Amba?'

He hesitated. 'She's been charged with Father's death.'

There was a silence, and then a whooshing sound. It was a few moments before Lyric realized it was the blood rushing to her head. She sat down abruptly on the sofa.

'What?'

'What, I say,' said Edward hesitantly. 'I'm not sure I understand fully myself, to be honest, but I'll try and explain. It seems Father knew the police were tailing Amba. They contacted him that day at the races when I first introduced them.' His voice broke at this. Not just his pride, but his whole sense of self-worth had taken a huge knock at the discovery that his girlfriend had actually been a man, and it was taking a lot of time – and a lot of therapy – to get over it. Not to mention the fact he blamed himself for bringing Amba into the family. 'He was keeping an eye on her for them – helping them with surveillance, I guess. It seems that my dear ex-fiancée is actually a sociopath suspected of murdering a string of her exes and pocketing huge inheritances. They just never had the evidence to convict him.'

'But why . . . ?' started Lyric.

'In the notes Queenie found, Father documented the whole sorry affair, and they almost became a diary of events,' interrupted Edward, pre-empting her question. 'He battled with what the right path was. It seems he decided not to tell me outright because he didn't want to crush my self-confidence. He was scared of it coming between me and him – of damaging our relationship before it had even really begun,' said Edward miserably. 'I guess he was hoping it would resolve itself some other way. How, I don't know. But he had my best interests at heart, it seems.

'Daddy . . .' breathed Lyric. 'Oh, Daddy.' How her father would have loved the excitement of being involved in a police case. And how he would have hated that Amba was trying to dupe his only son, to hurt his family. How he would have wanted to expose her.

'Yes,' said Edward, sensing her thoughts with a twin's intuition. 'Unfortunately, it backfired on him not Amba. It seems he was poisoned. The notes documented how she used the massage session to try to get at Broughton Hall through Father. At first, she tried to seduce him.'

Lyric gasped in disgust.

'Yes. And then, when that didn't work, she continued to work her wiles on him throughout their massage sessions, telling him how much she loved me and urging him to change his will in my – and, ultimately, her – favour. Of course, Father knew her little secret and so as a precaution altered the will so that only a grandchild would inherit. From the notes, it appears he thought himself rather clever over this – I'm sure he never dreamed it would actually uncover her.'

'So how—' interrupted Lyric.

'How did she poison him?' finished Edward. 'Well, again, Father seemed to think he was on top of the situation and documented occasions when he thought Amba was trying to "do away with him". I think he began to look on it as a game – like some real-life Poirot. What he didn't realize was that the massage cream she was administering was actually Thallium.'

'Thallium?' repeated Lyric. 'What's that?'

'It's poison. Remember the gloves Amba always wore for massage? Well, they weren't just hiding her man hands. They were protecting her from the poisonous effects of the cream,' spat Edward angrily. 'Slowly, but surely, Father was falling foul of them. His bouts of vomiting, diarrhoea and nausea were direct results of the poison – as was his hair loss and apparently wandering mind.'

Edward stopped for breath, carried away on a wave of grief and anger.

'But I don't understand why the initial post-mortem didn't pick it up?' said Lyric in a small voice, her mind reeling. Daddy, poisoned – by Amba?

'They weren't looking for it,' said Edward wearily. 'Like the Viagra that led to Thumper's death – unless you are specifically looking for it, it is almost impossible to detect. More so than other poisons. It was a highly sophisticated choice.'

'I don't know what to say,' said Lyric. She felt empty. A hollow shell.

'No,' said Edward uncertainly. 'Are you OK? Do you want me to come into town, or . . .'

'No,' said Lyric decisively. 'No, I'll come home. In fact, I'll come home now.'

What was she doing here in London when her family were at home and needed her support?

'I'll be back before you know it. Give my love to Mummy.'

Lyric placed the phone beside her on the sofa and drew her knees up to her chest. She almost didn't know where to start.

Before she had a chance to, her phone rang again. She looked at it absently, her thoughts still on Edward's call. Seeing who was calling, her heart skipped a beat. The PI? What on earth could he want now . . .

She picked it up with some trepidation. Surely there could be nothing to add to the way Philippe had already betrayed her? Surely, not more bad news?

'Lyric?'

'Yes, yes it's me. Is everything all right?'

There was a pause. 'Well, I have some news for you. Since we last spoke, I have continued my surveillance of your fiancé. As you know, I felt there was more to the pictures than met the eye. Something wasn't quite ringing true for me. And I have a confirmed sighting of him right now, in a restaurant, with The Girl.'

Lyric felt like she'd been punched in the stomach. No wonder Philippe hadn't tried to contact her. He was too busy with his new life. With his new girl.

'OK. And why should I care about that? We're not together any more.'

Another pause. 'Well, Lyric, in fulfilling my brief, it's

my job to try and bring every case to a satisfactory conclusion, where possible. This one felt unfinished. And it seems I was right. Today, your fiancé and The Girl are not alone. There is another man – well, boy – with them.'

Another pause.

'And the boy seems very close to the girl,' continued the PI. 'In, erm, a romantic sense. The romantic sense we had at first thought was the case with her and your fiancé.'

Lyric sat, stunned, her head spinning. So – Philippe hadn't been unfaithful after all? But the pictures . . .

'It seems there is more to this than meets the eye,' said the PI gently. 'So I suggest I continue my investigations into the girl. We have so far uncovered nothing about her, which is in itself most odd. But there must be something—'

'No, thank you,' said Lyric, jumping up from the sofa and looking around for her handbag. 'That won't be necessary. I'm going to deal with this myself.'

'I'm not sure I understand?'

'What's the name of the restaurant?'

~

Lyric leaned forward in the taxi, willing it to move faster through the midweek London traffic. She cursed the impetuousness that had prompted her to hail a taxi at all – it would have been much quicker to run.

She glanced at her watch: two p.m., half an hour since the PI called, which meant that it was probably about an hour since Philippe had first been spotted. Would he still be there? She couldn't bear to think that she might have missed him.

The cab nudged a little further down Piccadilly, and Lyric let out a sigh of frustration.

'Excuse me – can you just drop me here?' she called through the partition.

Thrusting a tenner at the driver, she leapt out and started to sprint down Piccadilly, past the Ritz and right into Arlington Street. She barely noticed the surprised glances as she sped past – running in heels had never posed any problems for her, and right now her YSL Tributes were serving her as well as if they'd been Nike trainers.

She slowed a little as she approached Le Caprice, her run becoming more of a jog at the familiar sight of the neon sign. She slowed further into a fast walk, brushing the hair from her eyes and dabbing gently at the slight sweat around her hairline.

She entered through the revolving doors to the surprised face of Jesus, the maître d'hôtel she knew so well.

'Lyric! How wonderful to see you! I didn't realize you would be joining Mr Chappeau?'

She nodded. 'So he's still here, then?'

'Why yes, yes, of course, they have only just finished their main course,' he said, leading her through the bustling restaurant. She nodded at a couple of people she knew, but their faces were a blur. All she could focus on was the back of Philippe's head, sitting at their favourite table tucked away in the corner.

There were two people facing him, chatting intimately between themselves as Philippe discussed something with a waiter.

She approached with trepidation and stood behind his chair, hand hovering over his shoulder.

'Monsieur Chappeau, Miss Charlton has arrived to join you.'

It seemed to Lyric that you could have heard a pin drop. Philippe stopped speaking to the waiter and paused for a nanosecond before slowly turning to face Lyric. Seeing her, delight crossed his face before the shadow of separation closed it up again.

He stood up.

'Lyric! *Chérie!*'

His words were familiar, but beneath the casual greeting was a waver of uncertainty. 'What are you doing here?'

Lyric's heart pounded in her chest. She looked around, as if surprised no one else could hear it.

'I came to find you. To say I was wrong. And to find out the truth and why . . .' Her voice cracked with emotion. 'To find out why you couldn't tell me in the first place.'

He gazed at her and, as their eyes met, the shadow seemed to lift from his face, to be replaced with a look that said what a thousand words never could.

The spell lasted for a few seconds, when Lyric suddenly realized she was still standing gormlessly at the side of the table. A waiter was discreetly laying a place for her next to Philippe, and she looked at it doubtfully, then at the young girl and the young man staring at Lyric wide-eyed with admiration, and then back to Philippe. The girl was pretty, kind of ethereal-looking, with the same honey-blonde hair and dark eyes from the photographs. But young. Very young. Much younger than the pictures had made out. She couldn't be more than seventeen. And the boy next to her – maybe a couple of years older – was dark, broodingly handsome and muscular. Like a young Philippe.

A look of deep shame overcame Philippe's face. He bowed his head and ran his fingers nervously through his hair. Eventually he looked up, first at Lyric, then at the young girl at the table, then back at Lyric again.

'*Chérie*, sit down, please. I am a fool. And I have underestimated you. But at the time . . . at the time, it seemed to me that I had no choice.' He took a deep breath. '*Chérie*, this is Amira. She is my protégée. I saved her as a little girl from Afghanistan. Her home had been bombed – her family –' His voice caught and Lyric saw the girl lower her eyes as if at a painful memory. 'She was orphaned, penniless. I smuggled her back with me,' continued Philippe in a low voice. 'But she had to leave France, and we lost touch. She found me again several months ago. I've been fighting for her political asylum ever since. But we had to keep it completely secret. I wanted to tell you, and I nearly did many times, but I had given my word. I felt it was important to keep it.'

'And this?' interrupted Lyric, pointing at the boy, heart in her mouth.

Philippe swallowed. 'This, I'm proud to say, is Amira's fiancé, Zak.'

Lyric stared from one to the other. She couldn't absorb the magnitude of what Philippe was telling her, but what she *did* know for certain was that everything was very different to how it had seemed. Very different indeed. Philippe hadn't been entirely honest with her, that was for sure. But he hadn't been unfaithful. And this – this story – could it be the key to the elusive part of Philippe she'd never quite understood? She had her faults and her secrets, too, after all . . .

She touched his arm lightly. 'I'm sorry. I'm just so sorry.'

There was a pause, and then his face broke into a crinkly-eyed smile – that smile she'd so missed over the past weeks and months.

'No, *chérie*, it is I who am sorry.'

There was another pause, and then Lyric turned around in search of a waiter. What a morning. She almost couldn't digest the series of revelations she'd been party to. One was almost too much – never mind two . . .

'So, what does a girl have to do to get a martini in here?'

Thirty

Lyric watched the crocodile file of headlights wending their way along the mountain road to their destination – the cable car, where she and Crispin were waiting out of sight. Gabe was already at the top of the mountain, waiting for Crispin, in his designated role as groom after having lost the argument over who got to do the bridal 'reveal'.

'Wow. Pretty impressive, huh, sweedie?' Crispin snuggled further inside his white mink coat – Lyric's one concession to OTT camp – and almost purred with satisfaction. 'All those fabulous people coming to Klosters, to our little old wedding!'

Lyric laughed. 'Crispin, there's nothing little or old about this event . . . starting with the "wedding cars".' She glanced at the twinkling fairy lights hanging from the cabins as they took the guests up to the wedding ceremony. They had been decorated to reflect the 'Doctor Zhivago' theme, and she had to admit they looked remarkably like aerial equivalents of horse-drawn sleighs. Whatever they might look like . . .

She felt a surge of excitement as she turned back to the

approaching cars. The guests themselves must be in a hyper state of anticipation, having already been flown out by private jet from Heathrow. Or, make that *jets* . . . to accommodate the huge guest list, Lyric had been forced to call in favours from everyone she knew, to the tune of one converted 757, two Learjets and a G6. They had flown not, as anticipated, to the decoy wedding venue in Courchevel, where the paparazzi thought they were heading, but to St Gallen en route to Klosters. After a forty-minute drive up the winding roads, through the scented pine forests and picturesque villages perched precariously on the steep slopes, they had checked in to their wonderful chalets, changed and headed off once again for the cable car.

Lyric breathed the cold mountain air in deeply. This had been the obvious venue for Crispin's wedding. It was so dear to her and to the people she loved best. Klosters and its people had seen her grow up; they'd accepted her for who she was and, in her high-profile years, given her private space when she'd needed it – from her first shaky ski steps as a three-year-old, to her first walk of shame as an eighteen-year-old after a long New Year's Eve (not, she had vehemently protested to Mummy and Daddy, a one-night stand), when she'd had to trip-trip her way through the snow, past all the early morning skiers, wearing a silver chainmail Versace dress and high heels. While *le tout de* Klosters was heading towards the ski lift, she'd been walking back from the nightclub – one of the most embarrassing things that she could remember. It had been Crispin she'd called for support, wailing, for him to come and minimize the shame for her. Now this was her turn to say thank you to him, and also to Klosters – indeed, the whole town was already giddy with the sense of celebration.

The lights drew nearer, and Lyric hugged herself in excitement. Somewhere in amongst the huge cortège of people were Philippe, Edward, Mummy and all their friends. She felt a pang that her father wouldn't be here. The only thing she hadn't managed to arrange was snow, she thought, with a pang of disappointment. Still, as Crispin said in consolation, at least the guests wouldn't ruin their Louboutin soles in it . . . nor would Crispin, for that matter. She stole a glance at the silver stilettos poking out from the bottom of his Tom Ford tuxedo, and smiled to herself. They'd compromised on their differing views about wedding attire by agreeing to her wearing her hair up in a loose bun and white Adidas trainers, and Crispin – as the other groom – had been allowed high heels and women's underwear. Well, as he'd pointed out, it was less controversial than a pink meringue.

As the guests started to emerge from the cars, Lyric's heart leapt when she saw Philippe. Dressed in his Russian *ushanka* hat, with a Burberry greatcoat, grey slacks and fur boots, he looked as if he was ten feet tall. And very handsome. They had now resolved their differences – she regaining her trust, and he admitting his part in their problems. Lyric hadn't realized until then how she had neglected their relationship since Edward had reappeared in her life, and Philippe had admitted his error in hiding Amira from Lyric after having given his word to those working for her asylum. The guilt he'd felt about the secret he was keeping from her had made him defensive and chippy. Amira had brought back long-buried memories of Afghanistan, and, while he was struggling to come to terms with them, he was also having serious misgivings about Edward. Combined with their miscarriage, he had felt isolated and alone. Now, not only were he and Lyric back to their passionate best, but he was finally seeking treatment for post-traumatic stress from his time in the army in order to ensure a similar episode never happened again. She hugged herself happily. It was as though the past few months of turmoil between them had been no more than a hideous nightmare. During the past few weeks, they had returned to their former closeness, and it was hard to believe now that they'd ever let anything come between them.

'I love you, *chéri*,' Lyric whispered under her breath.

She watched as her family and closest friends gathered by the cable cars, marvelling at how different they all were. Edward, with his new flame Natalie on his arm, looked like the cool ski bum he'd once been – and still was, at heart – despite his fur hat and military-style coat. Next to him Natalie had scrubbed up pretty well – but even her wholesome prettiness paled next to Treeva's glow-in-the-dark tan and head-to-toe Chanel ski wear, which – even down to her matching Ugg boots – was ostentatiously logoed. Constance, on the other hand, was wearing so much fur she looked as though she'd escaped from the zoo. If Lyric hadn't recognized her full-length silver fox-fur coat and matching hat, she might never have known her own mother. It was hard to ascertain whether she was a person or an animal. Still, Constance always loved a theme – and it was so like her to embrace it fully.

Further back was a heavily pregnant Laura, with the children and Robert. Still putting on a brave face, then. Lyric felt her heart go out to her friend. It wasn't so long since she'd thought she needed to salvage her own relationship – she knew how hard the choices were, and was determined not to judge Laura for her decisions. Close behind them, looking flustered in his ratty get-up, a scarf trailing down his back and his old ski coat showing signs of ash and tobacco, was Uncle Quentin, puffing and complaining about slopes and panting like a wounded stag. There were very few physical signs of the new-look Quentin these days. He was certainly drinking and smoking again – in fact, Lyric had learned that when he'd arrived at his chalet this morning he'd sent the staff spinning by barking for 'something to give it a kick, old chap' at the offer of a cup of coffee. But Crispin and he had found an unexpected bond since the newly enlightened Quentin had returned from India, embracing his son's homosexuality; and, after George's death, Crispin had insisted Quentin should be invited as a continuation of the rehabilitation started by George. Jacob, too, was here, with Johann, that

fit 'manny' of Treeva's on his arm. Hadn't Treeva once had
her eye on him? Mind you, was there anyone Treeva hadn't
had her eye on at one time or another . . .

Lyric looked back to where Treeva was obsessively
checking her phone. Lyric frowned. She hoped Treeva
wasn't going to cause a fuss and turn all the attention on to
herself, as usual.

After all, this was Crispin's day. And nothing was going
to ruin it for him.

~

As the cable car reached the top of the Gotschnagrat, it
rumbled over the last pylon and then swung around into
the stop. Lyric opened the door for the groom, and giggled
as Crispin wobbled in his heels when he stepped out onto
the pink carpet.

'Remind me what we do now, sweedie?' hissed Crispin
nervously.

'Well, I would have thought it was fairly obvious,
wouldn't you?' replied Lyric airily. 'You go and get yourself married!'

She kissed him on the cheek fondly. It was so unlike
Crispin to admit he was anything other than uber-confident.

'Personally, I'm not sure what to do with my hands,'
mused Lyric, looking at his rear view with amusement.
Crispin's full-length mink spread in a white pool around
his legs, bridal style. 'We didn't discuss this bit. We've got
no bridesmaids to carry your train, or Gabe's, and I'm

never going to manage to carry one of them on my own, let alone both!'

'Don't worry, sweedie, we'll be taking them off straight after the ceremony,' said Crispin. 'Otherwise no one will see the suits. Let's go!' Pirouetting as best he could in his heels, he made his way down a beautiful pine walkway.

'Wow!' he breathed. 'Oh, sweedie, this is just beyond.' Lyric smiled widely and took his arm. This was only the beginning.

As they walked along, little children in white lederhosen walked out of the forest and threw white rose petals in their path. After a hundred yards or so, the carpet led to a clearing. It was lit by tall fires placed at intervals around the circle, and a huge ice rink had been set up, surrounded by chairs for the guests. Half-naked Cirque du Soleil-style acrobatic skaters skimmed the perimeter, like little ice-dancing sprites and fairies flying through the air, and in the middle, on an elegant candlelit dais, Gabe – resplendent in a billowing white cape and Swarovski aviators – awaited his groom with the wedding registrar.

'Oh wow,' breathed Crispin.

'It's amazing, isn't it?' said Lyric, taking in the spectacular setting.

'Sweedie, Gabe's been trying to get those sunglasses like, forever,' marvelled Crispin, standing stock still in admiration.

Trying to keep a straight face, Lyric nudged her friend forward.

As Crispin arrived at the 'altar', the air was filled with a feeling of excited anticipation. The guests sat in breathless silence at the beauty of the surroundings, as Crispin and Gabe exchanged their personal vows. Gabe promised always to Sky+ *Melrose Place*, and Crispin vowed never to mess with the recipe of Gabe's favourite banana smoothie. Only Crispin repeatedly fluffing his lines threatened to break the spell, and the friendly laughs it raised only added to the proceedings.

'And now, before I pronounce this couple married, I must at first ask if anyone knows of any reason why Crispin and Gabe should not be joined in matrimony?'

There was a silence, and everyone looked to the minister to conclude the ceremony.

'Well, I'd say the only person likely to object would be Jacob, but he's now attached to that other rather luscious young man of Treeva's, isn't he?' Constance's voice rang around the clearing as if she was hooked up to a microphone, and there was a momentary horrified silence.

Then, suddenly, the guests exploded with laughter.

'I now pronounce you married,' grinned the registrar.

'Wow,' said Gabe, turning to kiss Crispin. They embraced, and the guests applauded. Crispin turned to them, smiling widely.

'Fabulous. Now, LET'S PARTY!'

~

From the clearing, the guests were transported by horse-drawn sleighs to a huge chalet, from which twinkly lights shone through every window. Crispin and Gabe stood welcoming their guests at the head of the world's most glamorous receiving line. Lyric watched from the warmth inside the chalet, Philippe's arms wrapped around her.

'That was so romantic, wasn't it?' She snuggled further into Philippe's embrace.

'*Oui, chérie*. But I'm sure ours will be even more so. *Complètement* unforgettable.'

~

The banquet and the speeches over, the master of ceremonies invited the guests to move outside.

'Oooh goody, more surprises!' exclaimed Crispin as they stepped onto the terrace and were handed warming glasses of glühwein and a foil blanket to keep out the sub-zero chill. 'I notice the surprise isn't snow, though.'

Lyric smiled, though her heart was suddenly heavy. *God*, she thought to herself as she looked out at the velvety night sky, *how I wish Daddy were here*. If George had been here, she thought, there would definitely have been snow. It was a Charlton family joke that whenever George went to Klosters the resort would have fresh snow.

Philippe came alongside her and brushed her cheek softly with the back of his forefinger. 'He is here, *non*? George, I mean. I can feel him all around us.'

Lyric's eyes welled up – not just at the memory of her father, but at Philippe's instinctive understanding of how she was feeling. She looked up into the sky. 'Hope you're happy, Daddy, wherever you are,' she whispered into the air.

Just then, she felt something cold on her nose. And again. She turned round to Philippe, mouth wide open in shock. It was snowing!

'You see,' whispered Philippe in her ear. 'He is here, *chérie* – in spirit, at the very least.'

'Woo-hoo!' shouted Crispin. '*Il neige!*'

The snow came down faster by the second, covering the ground in a soft white blanket, and Lyric drew the wrap closer around her.

The strains of 'Nessun Dorma' suddenly boomed out of invisible speakers, accompanied by a huge bang that signified the start of the fireworks, and an 'oooh' from the crowd. Lyric looked out expectantly. The fireworks were meant to be the *pièce de résistance*, the grand finale and the 'going away' moment for Crispin and Gabe, who would then be spirited off the mountain in a helicopter and into married life together. She'd spent huge amounts of time and money making sure this moment was nothing short of spectacular – a display to beat all displays, set against a view that looked over all of Switzerland. There was another loud bang, and every guest looked expectantly into the sky: nothing but more and more falling flakes of snow. Lyric stared in dismay as 'Nessun Dorma' boomed on.

Her display had been foiled by the one thing they had been looking forward to most – the snow!

She looked around for Crispin, who was kneeling down chatting to Laura's son Max. He didn't seem to have noticed – but he would. Lyric wandered over, ready to break the news to him. At that moment, Kitty ran past her holding something with a big bow on it.

'Crispin! Crispin! I have a present for you!' she lisped. 'It's good luck for you and Gay!'

He looked up, smiling, still kneeling, and held his arms out for the gift. Just then, as the music reached its first crescendo, Lyric saw Uncle Quentin dive for the gift, then run away into the darkness. As he sped past her, Lyric was sure it looked like a horseshoe.

She turned, open-mouthed, first to Crispin and then to Laura. But there was no time to ask what was going on. Next to speed past her was a man in a raincoat, speaking rapidly into a radio. 'Roger, roger! Assistance required!' he fired into it. 'Suspect exiting north-east.' With what appeared to be a sudden awareness of the number of people standing staring at him, the man pulled a badge from inside his coat. 'Police!' he shouted unnecessarily.

There was a collective shriek of horror, and then silence, punctuated only by the steady crescendo of the music and the crack of an invisible firework. Somewhere in the distance, the whir of a helicopter came into earshot, but no one took any notice. All anyone wanted to know about was Quentin, the horseshoe and the police chase.

It must only have been a moment before the policemen reappeared up the slope of the chalet grounds, red-faced and panting, the collar of Quentin's coat in one hand and the horseshoe in another.

'Sorry for the intrusion, everyone,' he said cheerfully. 'But I am arresting Mr Quentin Charlton on suspicion of gold smuggling. We have been following a gang we know he is involved with on a professional level for major gold trafficking. The arrest of Roger Skankton confirmed him as the leader, and we are now in the process of mopping up his lieutenants. We have reason to believe that Mr Charlton here was not only involved, but that he coerced a young child to smuggle the gold across the border here to Switzer-land.'

Somewhere in the crowd, there was a swooning sigh as Constance fainted onto someone.

'But – Uncle Quentin's never had any gold,' said Lyric, voicing everyone's confusion. 'And what makes you think he's smuggled any of it over this weekend?'

'This,' said the policeman, triumphantly holding the horseshoe aloft. There was another collective 'Oooh'. 'Mr Skankton has been using his horses as gold mules, with hundreds of thousands of pounds' worth of the precious metal packed into their horseshoes. When one of his horses died—'

'Oh God – Thumper,' stammered Lyric.

The policemen nodded his affirmation. 'When one of the horses died, a shoe went missing. We knew whoever was aware of the shoe's value would follow it until they had it for themselves. It was the perfect trap – and Mr Charlton here has proved himself to be the perfect villain. Now, if you'll excuse us . . .' Roughly pushing Quentin, he nodded at two of the closest security guards to help move him away from the party.

'It wasn't me. Honestly! This is all a terrible mistake,' pleaded Quentin to anyone who would listen as he walked past his fellow guests.

His protests were drowned out by the diminishing notes of 'Nessun Dorma', as the fireworks continued to pop and the guests looked at each other in mute shock.

Philippe put both his arms around Lyric and drew her to him. '*Chérie*,' he whispered in her ear. 'Maybe our wedding doesn't need to be quite this unforgettable . . .'

Epilogue

Lyric snuggled further into the crook of Philippe's arm in the corner of the threadbare sofa, grabbed a cushion to hug and looked around the Christmassy scene in the drawing room. With the seven-foot tree in the bay window, covered in the familiar ancient decorations and tatty tinsel, cards on the mantelpiece and a sprinkling of snow outside, one would be forgiven for thinking that Morocco-gate had never happened here.

But Morocco-gate *had* happened, along with all of the year's other monumental events, and this was a more subdued Christmas Eve than Lyric could ever remember.

Across the room, Edward and Natalie sat, heads together, studying the *Radio Times* for the next day's big films. Lyric found it hard to believe there had ever been a time when they weren't together; they just seemed to fit, and in the past few weeks Natalie had become as much a part of the family as Edward.

In an armchair, nursing a small glass of dry sherry and staring into the fire, was her mother – a calmer, quieter mother than she had ever known – who tonight, at the beginning of her first Christmas without her husband, was clearly lost in her own reflections and memories.

Outside, Angus – invited as always but here for the first time in some twenty years – was taking a call from a TV production company. Lyric smiled. After sixty-odd years of living his life through a racecourse, with no official employment or occupation, Angus was fast becoming a celebrity since the press had got wind of the story of George's murder. His role – built up by them to that of the stoic British underdog, who, despite being outfoxed by the villain not once but three times, stuck to his guns – had caught the public's imagination and there was talk of him being offered his own game show, *Under Starter's Orders.*

With both Roger and Darren Skankton locked up in prison for tax fraud, horse doping and now, it transpired, gold smuggling (evidence against Prince Abu Rhuba was also apparently mounting, with his private jets allegedly being used to transport the contraband precious metals. He even, according to Edward, had a ring engraved with 'GM' – which, her brother had now deduced, rather than the 'General Manager' Rhuba and Darren had alluded to on the private jet, stood for Gold Mule), Constance had invited Angie and the girls over to spend the festive season with them, but they had gracefully declined. According to Mrs Gunner's sources, this was because they were getting on very nicely without that bully of a husband and father and oaf of a brother. Angie was, by all accounts, flourishing – she had not only started spending Roger's money lavishly, she had even installed a man twenty years her junior in the house.

Crispin and Gabe, of course, were still on extended honeymoon. 'Well, sweedie, we considered coming back for Christmas and just thought, "What the hell,"' Crispin had confided during a Skype conversation with Lyric from a luxury Caribbean yacht they were staying on. 'I mean, nothing really gets going again until at least February, does it?'

Jacob was en route from London – with Johann – where they had been looking into adopting a 'rainbow family'. Lyric had to hand it to her cousin, he certainly moved fast.

Mind you, she thought, the same could be said for all of them. Edward and Natalie, her and Philippe, Jacob and Johann . . .

She glanced up at Philippe happily. There was only one thing that could make them any more content together . . .

Lyric looked around the room again and wondered if she should go over to the piano and start the customary carol singing they'd had every Christmas since she could remember, and then almost immediately decided against it. It wasn't the right moment. Tonight didn't seem so much about the people who were here, as those who weren't.

She wondered how Jacob would feel about his father not being there for the first time ever. Quentin had been deported back to the UK from Switzerland and remained in custody. Oddly, his initial and predictable protests about a miscarriage of justice and being in the wrong place at the wrong time had quietened over the past couple of weeks. Apparently, aristocrats were treated like lords by their fellow lags, and Quentin – with his notorious past – was no exception. According to a text she'd received from Jacob earlier this week, his father had decided he actually quite liked it in there and was now plotting how to ensure a lengthy incarceration.

But the person leaving the greatest hole tonight was, of course, her father. She was getting used to him not being around – she'd stopped listening for his slippered shuffle down the hallway, or expecting to see him around every corner. Although Constance had always hosted Christmas, her father had somehow 'been' Christmas, and she was feeling his absence as keenly tonight as she had at the funeral – especially since Amba's arrest had confirmed he hadn't, after all, died of natural causes.

She sighed. What the notes George had left couldn't do was reverse his final wishes, and so the will and its strange covenant still stood. How would this affect the way that the rest of the family took their news when they announced it tomorrow? wondered Lyric.

Edward suddenly cleared his throat, and they all looked up in surprise.

'Look, I – erm – we've got something to tell you. We were going to wait until Christmas lunch, but I think it's more appropriate in front of present company first,' he said haltingly. Beside him, Natalie squeezed his hand encouragingly.

'We're pregnant!' he said, clearly chuffed to bits.

There was an audible gasp from Constance, and Lyric sat up, eyes shining. She looked at Philippe and he winked back at her, then prised himself away from her and walked over to shake Edward's hand.

'Well, *félicitations*!' he said. 'So are we!'

Suddenly, the room erupted in laughter. Angus came rushing in, still halfway through his phone conversation. Jacob and Johann walked through the door, cheeks glowing from the cold air outside. Constance was ringing for champagne and everyone seemed to be hugging or laughing or crying or all three.

'So, what's it to be now?' joked Edward to Lyric as he picked her up and swung her around. 'Two more sets of twins?'

He set her down, and Lyric laughed. 'I'll settle for one healthy, happy baby,' she said. *A boy*, she silently added to herself. And, as she looked back at Edward's eyes, shining with joy, she had a twin's intuition that he was wishing for exactly the same . . .

Acknowledgements

I would like to thank Pan Macmillan, as a company and as a team of talented individuals, for their continued encouragement and inspiration. It's such an honour to be included with your great and good.

Enormous thanks also to my Team of Girls On Tour: Becca Barr and Carly Lorenz (aka Wolf and Snowy) from Becca Barr Management, and my lawyer Rhian Williams (aka Shark) for unstinting support and friendship. I would not say I'm the easiest representation . . .

My Gordon, who proves over and over again that it IS all about being Wise (not thighs or size). He's a man for all seasons and without him I would not have written this book at all. A girl like me dreams of an agent like him, and I would not have anyone else for all the tea in China.

Claire Irvin, I am so hugely indebted to you. You are the genius who tidies up all my characters, stories and fantasies and turns them into a book. Thank you, Claire, for 'getting the point'. You are one in a million!

Jeremy Trevathan, I am now a million moon miles from that first Cosmopolitan I made for you to celebrate my new

London penthouse. And now we're using cassis instead of Ribena. We've come a long way. Wayne Brookes, it's a pleasure to be edited by you.

I would like to thank my mother, who edited the manuscript with the skill of a ruthless editor, the finesse of a true lady and the love of a mother. Mummy, thank you for everything – and more.

And Uncle Micko Phillips, who came to my rescue when he made me realize that the racing world was not about *my* shiny coat, but actually about horses, trainers, owners and riders, and shared his limitless knowledge of them all. Micko, thank you for backing me, and more importantly, believing in me – still not half as much as I believe in you.

Joe Simon, you once saved me from a firework rocket ricochet. You're a girl's best friend and the ideal person to share a boxed set with.

Julian Fellowes, I've loved *Downton Abbey* and it was, and continues to be, a huge inspiration.

My thanks to my family. But, last but not least, writing a book keeps you up at night, and I want to thank William Shawcross for always picking up when I called.

extracts reading groups
competitions books new
discounts extracts
competitions extracts discounts
books new extracts
events books
extracts new titles reading groups
interviews
reading groups events extracts
discounts
new books events
events new
discounts extracts discounts

www.panmacmillan.com

extracts events reading groups
competitions books extracts new